Twenty-four hours ago Jeff Blanchard had been sitting before the television set in his comfortable apartment, a whiskey-and-soda in his hand—a man with a good job, a settled routine, an ordinary past, and a predictable future. And a son, who had embarked on what Blanchard had called a year to goof off. Mike had insisted it was a time to find himself.

Now Jeff was suddenly alone in a foreign country, tired and wet and bewildered, with none of those security blankets.

And his son and Mike's young bride were both missing...

The LAIR

a novel by

Louis Charbonneau

FAWCETT GOLD MEDAL • NEW YORK

THE LAIR

© 1979 Louis Charbonneau
All rights reserved

Published by Fawcett Gold Medal Books, a unit of CBS Publications, the Consumer Publishing Division of CBS Inc.

All the characters in this book are fictitious, and any resemblance to actual persons living or dead is purely coincidental.

ISBN: 0-449-14311-2

Printed in the United States of America

First Fawcett Gold Medal printing: January 1980

10 9 8 7 6 5 4 3 2 1

1   Los Angeles

1972

1

The phone call came first, then the letter. Or at any rate he didn't see the letter until the next day. The sequence would later remind Jeff Blanchard of one of those tragic incidents involving wives or parents of soldiers killed in action, who, after enduring the harsh economy of the telegram, the bleakly official notice of condolence, later faced the shock of a letter that seemed to come from beyond the grave, written days or weeks earlier by that dead husband or son. Blanchard had often thought that such letters must be almost unbearable to read. Better, once the tears had dried, to hear nothing more.

He didn't know what he would have done if he had ever discovered a posthumous letter from Elaine. He doubted that he could have read it. Not for a long time anyway.

But there was no hint of tragedy to come when his phone rang that Sunday afternoon in September, interrupting his vigil before the television screen. He was alone in the studio apartment he had recently moved into on the west side of Los Angeles, enjoying his Sunday saturation diet of professional football. It was a good way to kill half of an idle day. Like a few million other American males he had long ago become a pro football fanatic, and if some of the zest seemed to have gone out of this vicarious violence, as it had out of so many things, his appreciation for the astonishing degree of professionalism in the sport remained. And a few of the cells devoted to pumping up adrenaline still functioned.

The call was long distance. The local operator and the one at the other end of the crackling line were having trouble communicating. The more distant voice, which faded away at times but came back clearly at others, was speaking Spanish, or an English that was hardly distinguishable from Spanish.

The Los Angeles operator said, "I have a collect call from Guadalajara, Mexico, person to person for Mr. Jeff Blanchard."

"This is Jeff Blanchard."

"Will you accept the charges?"

"Yes." He figured that it was his son Mike, and there was a slight testiness in his tone.

"Mr. Blanchard?" A fourth voice, young and feminine, came on the line. Blanchard did not recognize it but he felt a tug of apprehension.

"Go ahead, Guadalajara," said the American operator.

"This is Angie." She came through with sudden clarity, as if she were calling from next door or the next room. "I'm sorry I had to call collect."

"That's all right. I figured it had to be you or Mike." Jeff Blanchard had never before spoken to his daughter-in-law. All he really knew about her was that her name had been Wylie and was now Blanchard, and that his son thought she was "outa sight." Mike had not thought it important to bring her home to meet his father before or after their sudden marriage. "It's nice to hear from you. How's Mike?"

"That's just it, Mr. Blanchard." There was something wrong with her voice, as if she was struggling to keep from breaking down. "He's gone!"

"Gone? I don't understand, Angie."

"Oh, I know it's crazy calling you like this, but I didn't know what else to do. I don't speak any Spanish, just a few words, and no one will tell me anything."

"What happened? Did you have a fight?"

"No, no, it's nothing like that..." A few words faded out of hearing. "...don't understand. He's disappeared!"

"Disappeared," Blanchard repeated doubtfully. His son had married this girl, this stranger, less than two months before. As nearly as he had been able to learn, they had known each other for about three weeks before that. The Mexican trip was part of a continuous honeymoon. A first quarrel was hardly any more surprising than her denial of it. My God, they were strangers to each other! How could they help discovering areas of conflict, unwelcome truths about each other which they had never suspected?

"You don't believe me."

"Suppose you just tell me what's happened."

"I guess Michael was right. He said you wouldn't care."

"That's hardly fair, Angie," Blanchard said gently. "You haven't told me what I should care about yet."

"About *us*! About our getting married so suddenly, without even letting you know. Michael said you wouldn't approve, but you were too wrapped up in your work to care."

"I don't know what that's supposed to mean exactly, but it's not true. I did care that I wasn't told. And if you're in some kind of trouble now, I want to help."

"Oh, my God, what am I going to do?"

"You could tell me what's happened as a start."

"But I told you—Michael's gone. He's been kidnapped!"

In spite of the very real panic he heard in Angie's voice, Blanchard still felt a reluctance to take her fears seriously. That panic would be just as real if Mike had gone off by himself. He had done that often enough, Blanchard thought, without giving any warning or explanation. It might be new to Angie; it was not to him.

"Why would anyone do that, Angie? I don't have that kind of money." He paused, speculating. "Is Mike involved in something I don't know about?"

"It's that friend of yours—he's been following us. That's what Michael said. I didn't see him, but..."

"Friend of mine?" Blanchard was genuinely puzzled. "I don't know anyone in Mexico, no one that I can think of. Who? Did Mike say who it was?"

"But he *wrote* you!"

"I haven't had any letter."

"He sent it to your office. You know how Michael is, he didn't have your new address written down, only this phone number, so he mailed it there."

"How long ago?"

"A week ago! You should have had it by now."

"The Mexican mails can be slow. It's probably on my desk. Did Mike say who this friend of mine was?"

"An army friend—oh, I don't remember." Her voice caught in a sudden, involuntary sob. "I shouldn't have called you like this but I didn't know what else to do. I found your phone number in Mike's notebook and I...I'm sorry I bothered you, Mr. Blanchard." Something had gone out of her voice now. Hope, Blanchard thought, frowning.

"Don't talk like a damned fool," he said roughly. "How long has Mike been gone?"

"Since yesterday. He—"

"That's not very long," Blanchard said gently.

"We've never been separated more than two hours since we...since it happened with us." The offended dignity in her quiet rebuff had the effect of pulling Jeff Blanchard up short. He had been being negative, he realized, discounting everything she said. What if he admitted to himself that walking away from a father was a far different thing from deserting a young bride of two months? What if he really started to listen to Angie—to assume not that she was simply being hysterical but that she knew perfectly well what she was saying?

What if she was right?

Blanchard felt the first chill of real alarm.

"Mike left no word? No note or anything?"

"No, nothing."

"Have you told the police?"

"No. Michael said that...we shouldn't have anything to do with the police down here."

"They can't be as bad as all that," Blanchard said drily. "Unless you've broken one of their laws." He was thinking quickly now, taking Angie at her word. He had to. This was his son they were talking about as well as her husband. If there was the remotest possibility that something had happened to him— even leaving out the melodramatic suggestion of a kidnapping—he couldn't ignore or discount it. "The first thing to do is notify the American consul. There's a consular office in Guadalajara, isn't there?"

"I...I think so."

"Call them. Or better yet, go in to see them. Tell them who you are and exactly what's happened, as far as you know." He hesitated. "No surmises, Angie, no guesses. Just tell them Mike has disappeared and explain the circumstances. Is that clear?"

"Yes."

"I'll catch the first flight I can make out of here tomorrow."

"You will?" She sounded surprised, a reaction that caused Blanchard to check a feeling of irritation—or discomfort.

"Yes. I'll have to check in briefly at the *News* in the morning, but I should be able to make an afternoon or evening flight."

"I see."

Her response was definitely cooler, and Blanchard realized that his answer had apparently confirmed her previous judgment. He wondered what kind of a portrait his son had painted of him. A man who was all wrapped up in his job at the newspaper, who didn't care what happened to his son, who was indifferent to the notion of meeting his daughter-in-law. It wasn't a true image and he could remember a time when Mike would never have believed that it was. But they had both had Elaine then, a bridge over troubled waters. Without that bridge they had become stranded on opposite sides of a widening chasm. Too often the only way they had found to communicate was by shouting.

"No, you don't see," he said a little sharply. "To understand, you'd have to have spent twenty years of your life at a job you thought was important—" He broke off. She wasn't going to be made to understand by a few words over the telephone, especially when all she could think about was the fact that her young husband had suddenly vanished. Somewhat defensively he added, "Besides, I have to see if that letter's there. It might tell us something important."

He found out where Angie was staying in Guadalajara—at the Campo Bello, an old and modest motel out on López Mateos in the Juárez sector, popular with American tourists, the kind of place that could be found listed in the *Mexico on $5 & $10 a Day* guidebooks, where two could stay in a clean room for about sixty pesos or so—still under five dollars. Blanchard had stayed there with Elaine one night on their Mexican holiday nearly ten years ago. He could still remember every place they had stayed, mostly because he had been sick nearly every day for two weeks. Mostly he remembered the bathrooms.

He hoped that he would have a little better luck this time.

Not that it mattered. Mike's safety was what mattered.

"Do you have a car?" he asked Angie.

"Yes, Michael's bug. That's another reason I know something has happened. He wouldn't have gone off anywhere without it."

Unless he wanted you to have it, Blanchard thought. But he said, "All right, Angie, I believe you. I don't want to, but I do. Stay at the Campo Bello so I can find you. I'll let you know when I'll be arriving. It's not going to help if *you* disappear."

She promised. Then she said, "Mr. Blanchard?"

"Yes?"

"Thanks."

"There's nothing to thank me for, Angie. He's my son."

2

On the Aeromexico flight south Jeff Blanchard kept thinking about what Angie had said, particularly the cryptic reference to an old army friend who had been following them. That friend's identity had been confirmed by Mike's letter, written nearly a week before and sent airmail from San Miguel de Allende. The letter was on Blanchard's desk when he arrived at the *News* early Monday morning. He didn't find it at all unusual that Mike had carelessly failed to write down the address of his new apartment; if anything it was surprising that he had made a note of the phone number.

Blanchard had skimmed through the letter hastily—long enough to verify Angie's story and to sharpen the feeling of apprehension which had grown during a restless night. He stuck the letter in his pocket and went directly to Wes Marrick's office.

That was when his very important job, with which he had been briefly tempted to put Angie down, blew up in his face.

Blanchard did not have an appointment and

Marrick was busy. He gave Blanchard a glad hand, which he would do even when he was angry, and suggested that he come back later. Couldn't it wait?

Blanchard explained that it couldn't. His son was in trouble, down in Mexico. He was catching the first Aeromexico flight south.

Marrick studied him as if he couldn't believe what he had heard. With a jerk of his head he dismissed his assistant, Ted Andrews, from the big mahogany-paneled office. "Jesus, Jeff, you sound serious."

"I am. At least, it could be serious," Blanchard said honestly.

"Hell, I wish... this is a rough time, boy."

"I know that and I'm sorry to run out on you. I'll get back as soon as I can. Collins can take over for me."

Marrick was shaking his head. "I've got Collins tied up on something else—that department-store presentation."

Blanchard began to sense that something was wrong. You're a little slow this morning, he thought. He had slept little, and his mind was already airborne on its way to Mexico. He brought it back to earth and told it to pay attention.

"I hate like hell to play the ogre, Jeff, but I can't let you go."

Blanchard stared at him in disbelief. As anger stirred it came to Blanchard that what Wes Marrick liked best—and did best—was play the ogre.

Blanchard and Marrick had come to the *News* at about the same time, some twenty years ago. They had both gone to work for the display-advertising department as space salesmen. While no one wrote plays or made hit movies about how the display-ad department of a modern metropolitan daily functioned, the fact was that most newspapers existed on their advertising. Actual newspaper sales kept few presses running. Blanchard had liked to think that his twenty years had played a part in the development of the *News* into a major newspaper. Wes

Marrick was always a step or two ahead of him. He had been a salesman of a different breed—tall, good-looking, deep-voiced, aggressive, the right image for an ambitious and expanding newspaper. The fact that he had never bothered to learn a great deal about advertising hardly mattered; he knew how to sell it. Moreover, as the two men worked their way up the management ladder, it turned out that, where Blanchard had a talent for paperwork and planning, Wes Marrick had a more valuable commodity: the ability to inspire fear in those who worked under him. Fear, Marrick had often said, was what made that special animal, the space salesman, function at his best, toward the common goal of selling more linage and showing a greater profit each year. Now, when both men were in their mid-forties, Blanchard was an administrative assistant to one of the sales managers; Wes Marrick was his boss: the display-advertising director.

"We've got the budget thing coming up for next year," Marrick was explaining—he usually didn't bother to explain. "You know I can't postpone that. No way."

"It's pretty well set already—"

"The hell it is! Now goddamn it, Jeff, don't make me put the boots to you. You know I can't spare anybody right now."

"I don't think you understand, Wes. My son Mike has disappeared."

"Jesus Christ, what's so different about that? That's what kids do best these days. He'll turn up, just wait and see. He's probably down there balling one of those Mexican chicks."

Wes Marrick wasn't really listening and it would have made little difference if he was. Blanchard stood up. He was a little sorry to see that his hands were shaking. Marrick was good at his job.

"Maybe he *will* turn up," Blanchard said tightly. "I hope you're right. But if he does, I'll be there to make sure."

Marrick stared at him in amazement. Blanchard wondered how long it had been since anyone under him had bucked Wes Marrick in anything.

"Sit down, Blanchard."

"I don't have much time. If Collins isn't available, I'll have to brief someone else on my part of the budget estimate."

"You don't have to brief anybody. You're not going anywhere."

Blanchard smiled. "What are you going to do, tear up my plane ticket?"

"If I have to. Look, Blanchard, I don't like to see you do this to yourself. You can't just walk out of here whenever you feel like it."

"I don't and you know it. This time I have to."

"The hell you do—not if you like your job, you don't."

He cracked out the threat like a whiplash. It was meant to frighten and intimidate by its force and fury as much as by the words themselves. The whole scene had got completely out of hand, Jeff Blanchard thought. He wondered suddenly if Marrick was using his request as an excuse to get rid of him, but almost instantly he rejected the notion. No matter what happened now, he had done a good job for the *News* for a long time. He knew it and Marrick knew it.

"I've been here twenty years—"

"You're not going to make twenty-one. Not this way. Shit, you won't make twenty years and a *day* if you walk out of here now."

Blanchard took a deep breath, surprised to discover that he felt quite calm. Maybe nothing mattered as much anymore, he thought, football games or dining out or empty apartments or a job that he had been comfortable with, even happy with, working for a newspaper that he had become proud of.

But Mike still mattered.

And so, perhaps, did pride.

He gave Wes Marrick a tight smile. "Well, I won't say it hasn't been fun..."

"You stupid son of a bitch, you think it makes any difference to me if you throw your job out the window? You think it will really make any difference to this department—or the *News*?"

"I thought you said I couldn't be spared."

"You want to know how much we'll miss you?" Marrick's dark eyes were cold, without a trace of the jovial good-fellowship with which he had greeted Blanchard that morning and a few thousand other mornings. He snapped his fingers. "We won't miss a beat."

Jeff Blanchard thought fleetingly of those twenty years. There was a feeling of surprise and regret, but there was also something else: an odd relief. Everyone was probably a little schizophrenic about his job, he thought; he simply hadn't realized that he was.

"Not even a heartbeat?" he asked.

"Not even that."

Blanchard nodded slowly. "In that case," he said, "I wouldn't want to work here anyway."

It had been a good enough exit line, he thought, staring out the window—the Aeromexico jet was half empty and he had a seat by the window—at the arid, mountainous desert that was the northern half of Mexico. Only along the coastline was there a belt of greenery visible, a thick, lush, incredibly green tropical jungle, Blanchard knew from ground-level travels. But exit lines were for plays and daydreams. They had little purpose in real life. Even the sense of self-satisfaction he had felt had been short-lived.

He fished Mike's airmail letter from his pocket and opened it again, smoothing out the wrinkled paper absently. He and Mike had both been poor correspondents, but in a contest Mike would have come in second, he thought. There was a strange reserve in most of his letters, a coolness, an impression almost of indifference.

Blanchard sat with the letter in his hand, not looking at it but knowing what it said, and contemplated with mild astonishment how completely his life had turned around in only twenty-four hours. Walking out on his job, for instance, wasn't in character for steady Jeff Blanchard. He had a hunch that that was what had stampeded Wes Marrick; he simply hadn't expected that degree of defiance. The fact was that large companies—and the *News* was a big one—didn't like to fire people. They seldom did it, for the obvious reason that it promised a great deal of trouble and expense, and it created a bad image. Image was everything, as Marrick certainly knew better than most. And you didn't fire a man for being concerned about his family; that wouldn't go over well at all before a labor-relations board.

No, Blanchard thought. He was out of a job because he had pushed the confrontation that far himself. This perception was new, and it puzzled him.

A few years ago he would have reacted far differently to the threat of being fired. Then he had had a wife and a teenage son: responsibilities. A man would take a lot when those were the preliminary conditions of battle. But when he was a man alone—his wife taken from him prematurely by a sudden, unexpected explosion of cells into runaway, anarchic life in her lungs; and his son, out of pain or anger or the plain need to assert his own readiness for living, a rebellious runaway of another kind—under those circumstances that same man might find an odd streak of independence asserting itself.

The fact was, Blanchard thought, that he had walked out on a lifetime job because it didn't mean very much to him anymore. Because he had nothing to lose. Because, in a way never before articulated, he was admitting to himself that his race had been run, that what he did no longer mattered to anyone, least of all to himself. All those corporate ties that bind—the free life and health insurance, the profit-sharing plan, the retirement plan, the job security—had been cut with surprising ease because they were no longer important.

And there was something else.

It was in Mike's letter, and Blanchard had not fully come to grips with it yet. He wondered if Darrell Kinney's name in that letter had nearly as much to do with his presence on this Mexican jet as the possible predicament in which his son had become entangled. Thoughtfully he read the letter again.

Hi Pops—

Buenas noches, as we say down here in old Mexico. If it's night, that is. They're funny about that. I mean, it's *buenos días* in the morning but as soon as it hits twelve noon on the dot then it becomes *buenas tardes*, not *días*. And after six in the evening it's *noches*, which is what it is right now. End of lesson. This trip has been wild, mainly because of Angie. Like I told you before, she's something else. I don't know how I got so lucky all of a sudden. Maybe it's the law of averages.

We've both been doing battle with Montezuma's revenge, but it's nothing serious.

I guess you know this town, San Miguel. It has this crazy church and a way-out school, the Instituto Allende, I guess they call it. I've been thinking of enrolling for some art classes and Angie says it's okay, she'll take macrame or something.

But what I wanted to tell you about is this crazy thing that happened in San Miguel. I bumped into this guy I recognized—that is, I thought I did. I'd seen him a couple of places around town but it took me a while to figure out who he was because he's different from what I remembered, older.

To make a long story short, I'll swear it's Sergeant Kinney (do I have the name right?), that guy you knew in the old air corps, the one you were always talking about. You know, "my buddy" and all that. I know he's supposed to be dead, you told me he was killed in France, but I seem to remember you saying he was never found, I mean he just turned up missing in action. And I swear to God this guy I saw in San Miguel is the one in those snapshots you used to have, the two of you standing there in your fatigues or whatever, with your arms around each other's shoulders, grinning like a couple of drunks, and one where you're the Old Sarge and Kinney has his Warrant Officer's bars or whatever they were. I guess this guy noticed me staring at him, so, just on a hunch, I says, "It's Sergeant Kinney, isn't it?" Because that's what you used to call him, maybe because you knew him as a sergeant longer than he was a warrant officer. Well, he just about jumps out of his skin. Then he covers up quick and gives me this fishy-eyed stare, real cool, and says I must be mistaken. But I wasn't. It was him all right. I'd swear it. I know the name shook him up. Besides, he didn't let go of it the way he would have if he wasn't Kinney. He warmed up too quick, and when Angie showed up he gave her the glad eye and wanted to know who we were and where we were from. When I told him the name was Blanchard I know that hit him, even though he tried to do the cover act again. Well, how's that for a mystery? That's all there is, because we ditched him and went off to do our own thing, but I thought you'd like to know your old buddy is alive and well in San Miguel. Voice from the grave and all that. Oh, and there's another thing. This guy had webbed fingers. Didn't your Sergeant Kinney have webbed fingers?

I gotta split. The *mariachis* are banging it out, and Angie says the Entero-Vioformo has done the job and she feels like trying the *chilis rellenos* again. Take care.

Mike

There were many things in the letter that claimed Jeff Blanchard's attention. Like the breezy salutation and the cool "take care." Mike hadn't been able to write "Dear Dad" at the beginning any more than he could say "love" at the end. Blanchard understood that those words embarrassed his son right now, but he couldn't help wondering if it was more than self-consciousness, a deeper estrangement.

And the line about the "law of averages" disturbed him. There was something just a little self-pitying about it. Understandable, maybe, but nevertheless jarring.

And Mike had apparently been wrong about ditching the stranger in San Miguel. Angie had said that the man followed them. From San Miguel? All the way to Guadalajara?

Frowning, Blanchard opened his card case and removed a small wartime snapshot, the only one of Darrell Kinney and himself that he had been able to find the night before in his haste to pack and make travel arrangements. This was the photo Mike had mentioned in which he wore his sergeant's stripes and Kinney his W.O. bars. Arms across the shoulders. Yes, and grinning into the camera like a couple of drunks.

Blanchard remembered exactly where and when that snapshot had been taken. Southport, England, summer of 1944. He and Kinney had gone there on several overnight or weekend passes. A seaside resort with a couple of good hotels. They would start drinking at eleven in the morning when the pubs opened. These shut down at three, and they'd have two or three hours to kill before the liquor would flow again, so they would stagger out onto the broad lawn behind this big hotel where they were staying and flop in the sun, if there was any sun, while the world reeled around them. By five o'clock or so they'd be sober enough for the evening's drinking to begin. Blanchard was a bare twenty years old, Kinney four or five years older, although he seemed more than that, the older brother Blanchard hadn't had. Unless you'd found a couple of girls, drinking was what two soldiers did on leave, that incredible lifetime ago.

On this particular afternoon one of them had had a camera along, and they had talked some Limey into taking a picture of them while they propped each other up and grinned into the camera.

Darrell Kinney was dead. The cargo plane in which he had been flying had gone down in France more than twenty-five years ago. But Mike's claim that he had recognized the stranger in San Miguel de Allende as Kinney had hit Blanchard hard.

His mind kept coming back to several pieces of fact—or intuition so strong that it could be taken as fact.

One was the conviction, long submerged, that Darrell Kinney was not the kind of man who got himself killed just when the war was moving swiftly toward its end and the real celebrating could begin.

Jeff Blanchard and Darrell Kinney had met in England. Both men were with the 8th Air Force, in supply. Blanchard had fallen into that classification by pure chance, Kinney by choice. He always had a knack for looking out for himself, for being in the right place at the right time. He was an expert at ingratiating himself with the right people, which in those days could mean an assignment clerk or almost any officer. Kinney could get hold of things nobody else could—a bottle of whisky, a jeep, a girl—and he wasn't reluctant to do a favor for some officer who could return it in another way. Kinney had made certain that he had a nice, safe niche for himself that would last out the war. That he would have strayed into the path of German antiaircraft fire, or died in a meaningless air crash, had always seemed incredible to Jeff Blanchard.

Their particular assignment, working out of base air depots in England, and later out of forward supply dumps, involved running down vital aircraft parts, engines, or other supplies that were urgently needed and in short supply. Often that assignment gave them unusual license to get around, either in a commandeered jeep or truck or in a cargo plane—which Kinney could and did fly himself at times, without authorization. He had a civilian pilot's license. Sometimes Kinney would travel with an officer, but after he'd made W.O. himself he was usually on his own and he'd take a noncom or two along—more often than not including Jeff Blanchard.

After they moved over to France, following safely behind the advancing Allied lines, Kinney became friendly with a man transferred to the outfit, Carl Creasey. Sergeant Creasey was in his thirties, a tough, hard-drinking, reckless Georgian who didn't seem to give a damn about anything, his wild streak matching the one in Darrell Kinney. Blanchard knew that he was a lot tamer in those days than either Kinney or Creasey—he had always had what was once called on a psychological test a "mature attitude toward authority figures," meaning parents and superior officers and, he supposed, God and government, the kind of attitude common enough in his generation but hardly as typical today. (Certainly not typical of Mike, he thought.) Creasey's reckless spirit amused Darrell Kinney and he started taking the Georgian along more and more on his supply hunts. At that stage of the war events were moving very fast, and in all that confused shuffling of men and hardware Kinney managed to maneuver with a great deal of freedom. He and Creasey reached Paris not long after the Allies took the city. He brought back photos of himself and Creasey drunkenly involved in an orgy with four French women, all of them tangled naked on one bed. Blanchard felt left out.

Kinney and Creasey were together when their cargo plane crashed in terrain overrun by the Germans in one of the abortive strikes—the dangerous convulsions of the dying beast—late in the last winter of the war. The two men were listed as missing in action, later presumed dead.

Missing, Jeff Blanchard thought.

It was not at all beyond imagination that Darrell Kinney had simply chosen—and somehow managed—to disappear, getting out of a war that was nearly over anyway. Blanchard could easily picture him holed up with Creasey and those four French whores in Paris during the last months of the fighting.

There was only one catch. Why hadn't Kinney turned up later? Because he was AWOL? Because he was afraid of a court-martial? Surely he could have talked his way out of that.

Frowning, Blanchard stared again at the old snapshot.

Fact two, he thought: The man in San Miguel had reacted to the name Kinney. Mike could have been mistaken, of course, looking for confirmation of an opinion already formed. But Mike had seen many snapshots of Kinney. He could have recognized him, even after all these years, even though he had never seen Kinney in the flesh. Between twenty-five and fifty, give or take a couple of years, a man didn't change all that much. He matured, his hair thinned out or turned gray, the lines in his face deepened, the waistline thickened. But he was an older version of the same man.

Fact three, and a crucial one: The stranger in San Miguel had webbed fingers. Darrell Kinney had webbed fingers and toes. Periodically he had the finger webs cut because they tended to restrict the movement of the fingers when they grew out. This physical phenomenon was probably not all that rare, Blanchard thought, but it was unusual enough to carry a lot of conviction when it was coupled with other resemblances close enough for Mike to remember some old snapshots he hadn't seen in years.

Fact four: The man from San Miguel had continued to follow Mike and Angie across Mexico.

Why, if he was not Kinney, would he follow them?

And why, if he was? Would Kinney be afraid, even after all these years, of being recognized and identified? Surely he would know that he had nothing to fear from Blanchard—or his son.

There remained one other fact—Blanchard was beginning to accept it as fact, and the realization brought an unmistakable chill: Mike had been kidnapped.

Less than a week after recognizing the man in San Miguel as Darrell Kinney.

Interlude One: Morelia

1.

The morning was sunny, and for a change he was able to enjoy his early workout out-of-doors, sliding quickly and pleasurably into the routine he observed through the long dry winters, when there was no rain for more than six months at a stretch, when he could jog each morning along the garden paths, perform his crab-walk on all fours across the lawns, or follow the set ritual of limbering-up exercises George Robbins had designed for him, relishing the feel of the sun on his bronzed skin as he worked, the soothing oil of sweat bathing his body, the brilliant blue of the Mexican sky overhead, the lacework of clouds veiling the peaks of the rim of mountains to the north, and, perhaps most of all, the sense of openness and freedom.

He ran up a low flight of flagstone steps and paused at the top, breathing easily. Wulf, the huge German-shepherd watchdog, trotted after him, pausing when he did. Off to their right, the old gardener crouched on his haunches, patiently weeding. He too was an early riser. Men of our age do not sleep as long, Ernst von Schoenwald thought with conscious irony.

The gardener was a small, gnarled *viejo* whose face and hands had the texture and color of a discarded alligator wallet. Every one of his seventy years was revealed in his face and body, which was stooped of shoulder and crabbed of movement. Yet in his own way he was as tough, as unbreakable, as the taller man who watched him idly, seeing the big-knuckled hands gently probe and work the damp soil of a garden bed. In the past dozen years Enrique García Morales had missed no more than three days at his work, those being occasions during recent months when he had had to have several teeth removed. Even then he had seldom stayed away the full day. His bent back under the flat-brimmed straw hat he always wore was as familiar to Ernst von Schoenwald as the orchids growing in their pots or plugs along the stone walls, as natural as the curve of a palm frond or the blaze of color from trailing hibiscus or spiky bougainvillea. And of the same level of importance to the German, observed and appreciated but only in passing. Enrique and von Schoenwald seldom spoke. When the German passed him, the old Mexican generally kept his head down, as if they shared a tacit understanding of his silence.

Followed patiently by Wulf, von Schoenwald moved along one of the neatly laid stone paths threading the gardens of what had once been an abandoned monastery, until he came to a point where he could look out over the lower garden wall toward the city far below. At no point were the outer walls, formidable barriers of stone topped by a frosting of broken glass, less than ten feet high, but the gardens were terraced, and from the place where von Schoenwald stopped he had a clear view over the north wall. There were new storm clouds gathering above the mountains to the north and west, piling high and black, but the broad green valley in which the city of Morelia lay, like a pink jewel set on green velvet, was drenched in morning sunlight. The twin towers of the cathedral glowed pink. The entire city looked pink in the sun, clean and pretty and toylike, as remote from von Schoenwald as the Alpine village in one of the paintings hanging in his study. His glance roved, taking in the ring of mountains that surrounded the valley as completely as his high garden walls enclosed his monastic seclusion.

In twenty years Ernst von Schoenwald had not stepped outside those walls.

For a fleeting instant a frown touched the German's strong, handsome face, a face that seemed surprisingly unlined, its integrity protected by strong bones. Who would have believed that he was sixty years old this past spring—that he and Enrique García Morales, that shriveled gardener, were more or less of the same generation?

And who would not envy him this sanctuary in the Santa María hills, overlooking the ancient city of Morelia in the Mexican highlands, the land of Eternal Spring? Assuredly he had come a long way, in time and distance, from his beloved green Rhineland, from the glitter of the opera house in Berlin or the pomp of the Reichschancellery or the peaceful beauty of his family home at Schwanenwerder on the Wannsee.

For the first time in—was it years?—he thought of Ingeblücke clearly, distinctly. Tall, blonde, statuesque, devoted, all that a German officer, a proud follower of the Führer, could ask in his wife. How excited she had been that last time in Berlin when they had attended the traditional SS festival at the Philharmonic Hall! Almost everyone of importance in the Party was there, and the Reichsführer-SS,

Heinrich Himmler, had addressed von Schoenwald by name, remembering him, and had flattered Inge extravagantly.

Inge. And Dieter. Ernst Dietrich von Schoenwald, his son.

He had had her move out of the Berlin flat with the boy when the air raids became so frequent, so unbelievably frequent and devastating, against all logic, all belief. Inge had moved to the house at Wannsee on the island, just across the little bridge from the mainland, where she and Dieter would be safe with von Schoenwald's parents in the big, comfortable house whose lawns ran down to the water's edge.

The house had taken a direct hit. Goebbels' country house, which was also on the island, an even more handsome place, was demolished also by the torrent of fire that fell from the sky that night, out of the open bellies of the American bombers.

A long way away. It was as unreal as, yes, as any of those idealized scenes of the past the young Jew painted for him, so quick to understand what he wanted, so clever with his hands. An idealized German woman and a straight-bodied, blue-eyed boy with hair so pale it burned white in the summer sun...

They had meant everything to him. Yet he had survived them by more than a quarter-century. What then did love mean? He had fought to save himself, fought and killed and bargained—he would have struck any bargain in order to survive.

In the end this isolated retreat near a poor Mexican village in the hills above Morelia was his bargain. It would serve. It *had* served, because it was necessary that it should. That was simply a matter of discipline, perhaps the most important kind.

Discipline! The word whipcracked in Ernst von Schoenwald's mind like a parade-ground command. Discipline of the mind—to read, to question, to think, always to learn. Discipline of the senses, training them so that every sensual experience was distinct and wholly realized. Discipline of the body, enforced in his daily punishment of exercise, erratically in the early years when he was still a young man, more consistently as the years passed and the need became more obvious that he must force activity upon himself in his confinement, like a tiger prowling his cage. And with a precisely ordered repetition since George Robbins had become his aide nearly ten years ago.

Aide. The old concepts persisted when loving memories dimmed.

Von Schoenwald smiled. He had been fifty when he first met George Robbins. He had become conscious of threatened slackness—of mind as well as body. Robbins had been an American expatriate, compelled to flee his corrupt homeland because of some incident in California in which a neo-Nazi group to which he belonged had attacked some student civil-rights demonstrators with excessive enthusiasm and broken some heads.

It was still amusing to recall Robbins' astonishment when he was brought into Ernst von Schoenwald's presence. That had been Rafael Sánchez's doing—something he had to thank the good doctor for. Von Schoenwald had wanted a physical therapist. Robbins, passing through Morelia, had somehow come to Sánchez's attention. Von Schoenwald sometimes wondered if Sánchez, for all his way with the ladies, had an equal interest in young men that he kept well hidden. Not that Robbins had been as young then as he appeared; his lean body was deceptive, and his features had been boyish. In recent years he had aged suddenly, the childish face, with its long simian upper lip and small, deep-set eyes, taking on the appearance of an aging monkey's.

In the beginning Robbins had not known von Schoenwald's real identity, of course. That had come much later, when the German was sure of him. But Robbins had sensed something of the truth that first day. It had been in his eyes, a look of stunned surprise that yielded slowly to the light of unaffected admiration.

What had begun as an experiment had become almost an essential relationship for Ernst von Schoenwald—as essential as any he would allow. Robbins was an athlete, trained in various lethal arts of self-defense, judo and karate and American military tactics of hand-to-hand combat. Although he was a slender, wiry man, much smaller than von Schoenwald, in a fight he was as deadly as a ticking bomb. He was devoted to his own body and its care, and he had quickly extended that devotion to von Schoenwald's physical conditioning with an organized efficiency that the German could not but admire.

In time he had proved himself invaluable in other ways. Von Schoenwald trusted no one completely, but George Robbins more than any man. "Like you, Wulf," he murmured aloud. The big dog pricked up his ears on hearing his name. "You would die for me, eh?"

Certainly Robbins was more to be trusted than Darrell Kinney. Von Schoenwald's hold over Kinney was one of greed—and perhaps, after so many years, of habit. What held Robbins in bondage and insured his loyalty was something far more intense, far more reliable.

Once again a small frown briefly creased von Schoenwald's smooth brow. He was remembering the incident which had interrupted his late supper the night before, the second of two recent and urgent phone calls from Darrell Kinney.

2

Ernst von Schoenwald's daily conditioning program included, three or four times a week without fail, except on those rare occasions when George Robbins was sent on extensive errands, a personal duel between the German and his red-haired mentor on the wrestling mat in the room he had had fitted out as a complete gymnasium, where on rainy days he did all of his exercises.

They wrestled naked, speaking little, the match punctuated only by grunts of effort, by ritual explosions of sound when the day's choice was judo or karate, by the slap of flesh on flesh. Rather than merely going through the motions, the two men fought realistically, although specifically crippling blows were forbidden. Von Schoenwald had never contested against another man in anything without a compulsive desire to win, and Robbins had learned early that it was a mistake to throw a match or to make it easy for the German to defeat him. Robbins was admittedly a more skilled combatant, and von Schoenwald could tolerate a fall or pinning by the smaller man more equably than he could accept the demeaning pretense of a false victory handed to him.

This morning the German had chosen the traditional form of European wrestling that could be traced back to ancient Grecian games. He knew that the choice always pleased Robbins; it involved more direct physical contact.

To any onlooker the physical appearance of the two men would have suggested an unequal combat. Von Schoenwald, his white hair cropped close as it had always been, was six feet tall with wide shoulders and a deep chest. At this stage of his life he weighed a hundred and ninety-five pounds, a figure that had not varied by more than ten pounds in his entire adult life. Except for the white band around his buttocks, ordinarily covered by his shorts when he worked outdoors, his muscular body was deeply bronzed. A confessed sun worshipper, he lay under a sun lamp when the weather kept him indoors. His sculptured pads of pectoral and belly muscles, the heavy biceps, even his white buttocks were remarkably firm and solid for a man of his age. By contrast

George Robbins was three inches shorter and nearly forty pounds lighter. His hair had thinned to a cleric's halo, and he covered his baldness, even now, with a strikingly bright red wig. His skin had the typical redhead's freckled whiteness; it turned pink or burned from exposure to the sun, never acquiring the golden tan in which von Schoenwald took such pride. Slender and wiry, his muscles hard cords rather than heavy pads, Robbins had to rely on his quickness and superior skills against the German's advantages of weight and strength. Usually they were enough. Even after years of such duels, when each man knew virtually every one of the other's moves, Robbins managed to win nearly two falls out of three.

Five minutes after this day's match began, he had von Schoenwald on his back in an armlock, his shoulders close to the mat. The German flipped out of the hold before he could be pinned. They rose and began again in a formal posture, braced against each other at arms' length, legs back and planted firmly, strength pitted against strength. Feeling his leg muscles begin to quiver under increasing strain, Robbins went down voluntarily, turning von Schoenwald's aggressive pressure against him and flipping him over his head to a hard fall. Breath exploded from the German's lungs. Robbins twisted quickly to clamp on another armlock, sensing that the German's right arm had been weakened by the earlier hold, but again von Schoenwald squirmed free.

The silent contest continued for some minutes. The end came with surprising suddenness. The two men were down on the mat, searching for telling holds while fending off or breaking others, their bodies now slick with sweat in the humid warmth of the morning. They became locked in opposing holds that immobilized them in a near-embrace. Von Schoenwald refused to let the impasse be broken. Using his greater weight he applied a steady, unrelenting pressure that slowly forced Robbins' shoulders toward the mat. He could feel the heat in Robbins' loins pressed against him. Staring into the red-haired man's eyes, which were as pale and colorless as his hair was bright, von Schoenwald permitted a faint smile to touch his lips.

Suddenly he released his pressure. Robbins, intent on slipping clear, suddenly felt his arm caught and twisted high behind his back. At the same instant von Schoenwald used all his weight to drive the lighter man against the mat.

Robbins was pinned face down, his left arm pulled back and upward, von Schoenwald's knee pressed against the back of the shoulder socket. The German's superior strength was brought fully to bear, holding Robbins helpless. Slowly von Schoenwald began to increase the strain upon the twisted arm he held. A white line of pain appeared around Robbins' mouth. "Enough," he whispered.

"You are certain?"

"Yes, yes, enough!"

Von Schoenwald smiled more broadly. He gave a sudden, brief wrench that extended the tortured muscles of Robbins' taut arm another inch. He saw Robbins' eyes roll upward and heard a gasp of pain. Then he released his hold.

Von Schoenwald sprang to his feet. Sweat dripped from his brow and ran down his glistening chest and belly. George Robbins was much slower to rise. His left arm hung limp, the shoulder crumpled inward. When he was standing, his pale eyes sought the German's face. The look in Robbins' eyes was one of pure adoration.

3

Rafael Sánchez, who had timed his arrival as close to one o'clock as possible, knowing Señor Brugmann's precise habits, was blocked by a long procession of schoolchildren marching in formation across the Avenida Juárez just below the traffic circle. He fretted through a delay of more than five minutes. Then a bus stalled in front of him on the rain-pitted foothill road. A second bus pulled up alongside the first, blocking the way effectively. The two drivers chatted amiably over the problem. Sánchez looked at his watch. Three minutes to one—he would be late! Angrily he honked his horn. After another delay for shouting back at him and obscene gesturing, the bus drivers made room for him to swing around them. He turned sharply right and raced up the hill.

Baldur Brugmann's midday *comida*, the main meal of the day, was served at one o'clock exactly, neither a minute before nor a minute after. The food set out on his table was superior to that in any of Morelia's restaurants and inns, even Ray Cote's famed cuisine at his Villa Montana. It was the equal, in Rafael Sánchez's opinion, of anything to be found in Mexico City itself. On those rare occasions when Sánchez had been invited to share the German's repast, the event had always been a memorable treat to one who placed culinary pleasures high on his list.

He glanced at the young girl riding beside him in the little Volkswagen. The girl, whose name was María Teresa Calderón y Flores, and who was the reason for his visit to the monastery in the Santa María hills, smiled back at him tentatively.

Dr. Rafael Sánchez had a way with women. He was a short, compact man with regular features in a very square face, a neat black moustache, and thick, wavy black hair. His smile was a brilliant display of even white teeth. He dressed well—often, as now, in white—and he was the kind of man who might once have been called dapper. The white suit today was in respect to the German on the hill and the anticipated invitation to dine with him. Sánchez had little trouble charming young girls like María Teresa, whose whole soul seemed to be in her huge, anxious brown eyes. He had little trouble charming virtually any woman, young or old, when he chose to make the effort. His wife Consuela, for instance. Rafael Sánchez had a tendency to be impatient, and from the first day of his medical practice he had yearned to have a clinic of his own, perhaps one catering to foreign residents who had the money to pay for truly first-class care and could seldom find it in Mexico outside of Mexico City and Guadalajara. Unfortunately he had neither the money for such an enterprise nor the powerful friends in influential places. (One, assuredly, often went with the other.) Of the many, many women he might have married, Consuela had been an ambitious rather than a passionate choice. Plump and placid, she was pleasing enough to look at but hardly a beauty. But her father, Antonio Ruiz, scion of one of Morelia's old families, had money, property, extensive investments. Surely, Rafael Sánchez had reasoned, it would not take long for him to be persuaded—out of joy for his daughter's happy marriage, if for no other reason—to finance his son-in-law's clinic, which would be good for everyone concerned—even good business. Unfortunately it had turned out that Antonio Ruiz had no intention of releasing a single peso that he had not squeezed dry. He cherished his daughter but he merely tolerated Rafael Sánchez. The couple and their children, who now numbered four, lived in the large home of her parents, an arrangement that provided many luxuries of life but left Sánchez resentful, trapped in the kind of bondage he had always sworn to avoid. The luxuries he enjoyed were not *his*; there was always the feeling of being a guest in the house—a poor guest in a very rich house.

Soon, he thought, all that would be changed.

He drove over the uneven bed of rocks that formed the private road leading to the gates of Baldur Brugmann's walled estate. As always when he came here, Sánchez recalled his first visit, the first time he was summoned to attend to the old German. That was a dozen years ago, and he had approached the old monastery without much interest. He knew of Brugmann, of course; everyone in Morelia did. Brugmann had been living in the city since shortly after the first World War, and he had been a recluse since the second. Sánchez expected to find an old man of modest means. It was said that Brugmann had lived for many years in a single room of the two-hundred-year-old monastery, surrounded by crumbling ruins, and although there had been rumors in recent years of extensive work behind those high walls, of laborers and artisans being brought in from various parts of Mexico, of truckloads of tiles shipped in from Puebla, Rafael Sánchez, like most people, discounted the stories as exaggerated or uninformed gossip.

He was completely unprepared for what he found inside the gates of the monastery.

The gardens themselves, including the stone paths and terrace walls and patios, had been completely renovated. The lawns were carefully groomed. Flowers bloomed everywhere in profusion. On the outside the massive structure seemed little changed, except that there were no broken half-walls, windows without glass or roofs open to the sky. Sánchez's real astonishment came when he was ushered inside.

What had once been a neglected ruin was now an ornate and elegantly detailed palace. There were polished tile floors accented by handwoven rugs in which the arts of Mexico and Persia lived happily together. The whitewashed walls soared upward to ceilings supported by heavy carved beams. The furnishings, tastefully spare rather than overcrowded, allowing full appreciation of the sense of space and fine detailing of individual pieces, were Colonial and European antiques of excellent craftsmanship and design. Although the German's taste in paintings seemed undistinguished—once, through an open door, Sánchez had glimpsed a half-dozen of the most ordinary oil paintings of stereotyped German scenes hanging on the walls of the study, a concession, he reasoned, to sentiment rather than beauty—in other respects Señor Brugmann was revealed as a man of discriminating taste and perception. Everywhere were examples of the finest pottery and exquisite crafts in gold and silver, wood and metal and clay, including what was already a superb and costly collection of pre-Columbian figures, some of the smaller ones presented in glass cases, others displayed on tables or in niches set into the white walls.

Soon a tall, distinguished man appeared. He had light blond hair cut to a bristle, in which traces of white were just beginning to appear. In his attitude as in his body he exuded an air of power and authority. He might have been anywhere from forty to fifty—only close medical examination suggested that the latter was a more accurate guess—surely not as old as Baldur Brugmann had to be. His manner was polite, aristocratic, and thoroughly intimidating. Sánchez found himself stammering answers to the German's questions, ill-at-ease when those cold blue eyes were fixed upon him, absurdly anxious to please.

Of course the man was not Baldur Brugmann, although he claimed that name. In fact, Rafael Sánchez had never dared to ask where the real Brugmann was or what had become of him. To the world beyond the monastery's walls *this* man was Brugmann, and on that day Sánchez had found himself irrevocably committed never to reveal otherwise.

He did not know that he had been thoroughly investigated before being summoned—his situation, his character, his weaknesses known—and that he had been chosen not because he could be trusted implicitly but because he could be bought. The German—to this day Sánchez addressed him always as Señor Brugmann, knowing no other name—paid handsomely for the doctor's occasional services, both medical and, as it turned out, social. Rewarded with payment far beyond his customary fees, Rafael Sánchez found himself gaining a small independence from his father-in-law's domination. That and his fear of Brugmann, a fear that he did not allow himself to face directly, had purchased his silence and encouraged him to perform such other services as the one in which he was now engaged. The German had a strong appetite for the pleasures of female companionship in his isolated castle on the hill. Rafael Sánchez, drawing upon his country's inexhaustible supply of impoverished people, for whom morality and even love had to come second to survival, had readily been able to appease that appetite.

Outwardly Sánchez's relationship with the German had altered little since that first visit, when he was able to diagnose and treat successfully a case of gonorrhea. In fact, however, although he continued to treat Brugmann's minor ills as necessary and to supply him with ever-younger girls as well as other trustworthy servants, Sánchez had come to hate the man who pretended to be Baldur Brugmann even more passionately than he resented his father-in-law. Slowly he had been drawn into another kind of trap, like his domestic prison, in which he was a person to be treated with polite disdain, his "services" rewarded with fees he could not reject but which succeeded only in binding him to a permanently inferior and contemptible role.

Nothing of this reaction showed as Rafael Sánchez stood at the outer gates of the monastery with María Teresa Calderón and pulled the cord that rang a small bell overhead. A servant, whom Sánchez recognized as Jesús Hernández, came to the gates, recognized the doctor, and, head down, admitted them. Jesús's glance briefly touched María Teresa and Sánchez before he lowered his head once more.

Sánchez thought he saw something chilling in that glance. It left him frowning as he was shown into the house.

It was then two minutes past one o'clock, but neither Brugmann nor George Robbins, his omnipresent aide and a man almost as frightening as the German, appeared. Sánchez and María Teresa were shown into one of the comfortable sitting rooms. Jesús disappeared for a few minutes. When he returned he offered Rafael Sánchez some wine, which he accepted. Surely this was preliminary to an invitation to dinner.

It was not.

As the minutes passed, Rafael Sánchez began to realize that Brugmann was already dining—there was activity in that part of the house where he took his meals, occasional tinklings of glass or china and murmurs of conversation—and that he was to be kept waiting. Brugmann was taking advantage of his well-known insistence upon a rigid timetable in his daily habits to insult Sánchez!

The doctor sat in silence with María Teresa Calderón, a very quiet girl of fourteen who continued to watch him anxiously, uncertain of what was in store for her in this strangely beautiful place. Sánchez had been deliberately vague with her mother and curt with her drunken father, although both parents had understood what Sánchez did not openly express. Vagueness made acceptance easier, as if evil were made less when it was not discussed.

At the end of an hour Rafael Sánchez was extremely hungry, his empty stomach growling. He was also extremely angry, and he had begun to contemplate with pleasure certain events that had already been set in motion, events in which Sánchez was to play an important part.

María Teresa Calderón was not the only one for whom the near future held unexpected and painful surprises.

In the dining room Ernst von Schoenwald and George Robbins were discussing an isolated incident that was part of the pattern occupying Rafael Sánchez's speculations as an antidote to his anger over the German's deliberate slight. Von Schoenwald and Robbins spoke casually, for the German was not seriously disturbed or even concerned over a potentially minor annoyance. His attention was more preoccupied with a delicious meal whose centerpiece was the *cabrito*, whole baby goat which was at its most succulent when it was no more than six weeks old.

"Kinney has been recognized," von Schoenwald had said calmly. Robbins had not been present the night before when Kinney phoned, nor had he been informed of Kinney's earlier call from San Miguel de Allende.

"How is that possible?"

Von Schoenwald shrugged. "It was an accident, but such things are always possible." It was the reason he himself had never left the monastery in over twenty years, a decision that had tested even *his* iron self-discipline. "There are always many tourists in San Miguel, many of them Americans, as there are in Patzcuaro and other places Kinney must go on business. Perhaps it was inevitable that he would one day encounter someone who once knew him. Although after so many years..."

"It was someone who knew him a long time ago?"

"The son of such a man. The son of someone Kinney knew in the war, one who had pictures of him, Kinney says. The boy must have seen these snapshots, I suppose, and remembered them."

Robbins scowled, his simian face wrinkling. "There's no mistake?"

"He is quite certain."

There was a brief silence while the two men ate and Robbins digested the information. He knew that von Schoenwald had almost certainly made any necessary decision about what should be done. The chance of a known connection between his real identity and Kinney was impossibly remote. Nevertheless, a small danger existed, perhaps more threatening to Kinney than to von Schoenwald.

"What does it mean?" Robbins asked finally.

"Kinney followed the boy to Guadalajara," von Schoenwald said, smacking his lips over the roast kid with obvious pleasure. "He has taken steps to insure that... there will be no talk."

"Was that a good idea?"

"It was necessary. The danger, perhaps, was minimal"—he paused to sip the delicate wine, an imported rosé he favored with the tender meat of the *cabrito*—"but it had to be removed."

"Is there anything you want me to do?"

"You will go to Guadalajara yourself... immediately. Our friend Mr. Kinney has caused this problem, and up to now I have allowed him to attend to it. But if there are any difficulties..." He shrugged.

"You trust Kinney in this?"

Von Schoenwald smiled. "My dear George, I trust Kinney to do whatever is necessary to protect himself. It so happens that in this instance his interests will also serve mine. Even a devious man can be trusted when his interests coincide with yours."

"Yes." Robbins remained thoughtful. "There could be complications."

"That is why I wish you to meet Kinney in Guadalajara and give him whatever assistance is required."

"I was just thinking that Americans tend to make a fuss when one of them gets into trouble."

Von Schoenwald regarded him coolly, his blue eyes like milk glass. "In these days of American young men dropping out, as they say, going into hiding when they are afraid to fight for their country, vanishing into the so-called drug culture—you see, George, I keep up with the news—who will pay attention if one more young man has disappeared in Mexico? But enough," he concluded, dismissing the subject. "Shall we meet our guests now? Before you leave, you must see what choice morsel Dr. Sánchez has brought with him."

5

She was a slender girl in her early teens, von Schoenwald guessed, her eyes two huge dark pools of panic in a bony face of startling innocence.

"You are called María Teresa?"

The girl nodded, speechless. Von Schoenwald glanced at Rafael Sánchez with a smile. "Charming," he said. "My congratulations, Doctor. You have outdone yourself. Yours is a poor country, but it is rich in the beauty of its children."

Sánchez, who had taken great pains to hide his rage over being kept waiting, increasingly hungry, well past the time of his normal midday *comida*, seemed gratified by the German's words of praise.

Von Schoenwald asked the girl if she was pleased to join his household. She nodded dumbly once more. *"Ven acá, niña,"* he murmured. His Spanish was excellent, although he remained isolated from the people in whose country he had chosen to live. Learning the language had been an intellectual discipline, part of the regimen by which he continued to discipline mind and body. "Come closer so that I may look at you."

María Teresa Calderón approached him, trembling. That she was frightened by this big, tanned, white-haired stranger in his fine house was obvious, but there was also awe in her dark eyes, an expression not unlike that which filled them when she knelt in church and stared at the altar and the bloodstained figure on the cross above it, aching with the hopes and hungers of childhood.

"You are trembling, my child. There is no need to be frightened." She was thin to the point of boniness; her small breasts under the paper-thin dress she wore were hardly developed. "Utterly charming," he said again, taking her hand in his, where it quivered like a small, captive bird. "*Ya comiste?* Have you had *la comida*?" When she shook her head von Schoenwald smiled. He rose, ignoring the effect of his words on Rafael Sánchez's grumbling stomach. "Then you must have it now. One pleasure before another, eh? Come."

In the archway he glanced back at Sánchez. "Excellent, my good doctor. You will be rewarded, of course. But you must come again in time to dine with us. Soon, soon."

He left, holding María Teresa's small hand in his huge one. The sight of his broad, powerful figure next to the girl's sticklike, undernourished form gave Rafael Sánchez a moment of guilty dismay approaching anguish. So small, so frail a creature! What had he done?

Then George Robbins was escorting him to the outer gates, smilingly closing and locking them behind him, leaving the white-suited doctor standing outside under gathering clouds. Distant heavenly rumbles of thunder echoed his inner complaints, and suddenly María Teresa was forgotten in the return of Sánchez's righteous anger.

He would have his revenge—soon.

2   Guadalajara

1

The plane's wing dipped and Blanchard caught a glimpse of Mazatlán below, the next Acapulco, already sprouting a mushroom patch of luxury hotels along the north shore of the bay. Mexico without the poverty and pain, he thought. Strictly for *gringos*.

There was a huge bank of black clouds visible to the south as the jet swooped in for a landing at Mazatlán, the only stop on the flight to Guadalajara. It was still the hurricane season, Blanchard remembered, and that season brought heavy rains to the southerly coastlines and the high plains of Mexico from May through October.

The stop at Mazatlán was brief, for which Blanchard was grateful after feeling the thick, humid layer of tropical heat. An hour later the Aeromexico flight ended at Guadalajara, the jet descending through a dense curtain of rain, confirming Blanchard's hunch about those clouds. In his haste he had left Los Angeles with neither raincoat nor umbrella.

He had wired his time of arrival to Angie at the Campo Bello, but there was no lanky young American girl hanging around the terminal looking for a middle-aged man. Blanchard didn't know if Angie would be able to recognize him—there were always similarities between fathers and sons, although Mike, with his brown eyes and dark hair, more closely resembled his mother—and he had never set eyes on the girl. All he knew was that in Mike's view she was a raving beauty.

After the flurry of activity involved in getting through customs, Jeff Blanchard found himself standing outside the terminal watching the eager taxicabs peel away, while heavy rain wove patterns in the widening puddles that framed the pavement. Still no young American beauty lingering—a few had come in on his flight as tourists, others were waiting in the terminal for other flights. No green Volkswagen waiting in the puddled parking area.

A boy tried to sell him something in a shoebox with holes punched into the sides—a lizard or a snake, Blanchard guessed. Another boy, hardly ten years old, wanted to shine his shoes. There didn't seem to be much point in a shoeshine before walking out into that rain, but Blanchard accepted one anyway. It was a fast and expert spit shine, well worth the peso it cost. The boy went away grinning, as if he had outwitted the *norteamericano*.

Angie wasn't there.

On the drive into town in the cab he tried not to let her failure to appear worry him. Mexican telegraph service, like the telephone or mail service, was not always reliable. Angie could have gone out—she could have gone to the U.S. Consulate, for instance— or she might simply have failed to receive his message.

The taxi took the bypass road, avoiding the city's congestion, over to Highway 15, the Mexico City—Morelia road, then drove in on López Mateos. Blanchard noticed a handsome Holiday Inn along the way, looking exactly like one of its cousins in the States, sleek and modern, comfortable and air conditioned. He made a resolve to return there if he spent much time in Guadalajara. He wasn't going to do Mike any good by staying at budget motels and eating at questionable restaurants, battling fatigue and the *turista*. He seemed a long way past the time when staying at picturesque little inns where the plumbing didn't work and the bedroom was shared with mosquitoes, the bathroom with roaches, was his idea of a lark.

Or was that because he was alone?

He passed the Plaza del Sol, new since his last visit to Guadalajara, and for a moment he might have been transported back to Southern California, driving past a suburban shopping mall in Downey or the San Fernando Valley. There was even a Denny's Coffee Shop. He wondered if Guadalajarans were proud of their bright new mall. He suspected that they were, and found himself wishing that there was some way for Mexico to modernize its cities without making them over into imitation U.S. suburbs.

It was still raining heavily when Blanchard reached the Campo Bello—in fact, the traffic circle at Las Rosas was flooded and impassable. There was a myth about rain in Mexico, Blanchard thought as his taxi detoured along back streets, searching for a way around the flooded area. It said that the rain started in the afternoon, fell for an hour or so, then departed while the sun came out again and the day was so dry and beautiful that you'd never know it had rained. The myth was fostered by romantic guidebooks and the come-ons penned by Americans living in Mexico for a while; it had little to do with reality. During the long rainy season, which lasted nearly half the year, coincident with the hurricane season in the Caribbean and the Pacific Ocean, torrential downpours struck repeatedly at Mazatlán and Vera Cruz on opposite coasts, at the high plateau cities from Guadalajara to Mexico City, as likely to last eight hours as one or two. Flooded streets and leaking roofs were a commonplace of Mexican life, like the potholes dug out of the streets and highways each year by the incessant pounding of the rains. Guadalajara had three times the annual rainfall of Los Angeles. The pretty little tourist town of Taxco saw five times as much—around sixty inches a year. If you broke that down—statistical breakdowns were a large part of Blanchard's work at the *News*—it came to about three inches a week, every week, for five months. Blanchard and Elaine had once spent a week of their Mexican holiday at Lake Patzcuaro, in August, without ever seeing a dry cobblestone.

The Motel Campo Bello seemed cold and cheerless in the rainy darkness when Jeff Blanchard climbed out of the taxi, stepping into six inches of water at the curbside. No lovely young American dream waited to fling herself into his arms with a sob of relief and joy. In fact, few people seemed to be there at all. This was late September, well past the summer tourist season and too early for the winter visitors. The restaurant adjoining the reception desk was a large, bare room filled with empty tables and chairs.

A young, buxom Mexican girl appeared in response to Blanchard's tap on the bell at the desk. She spoke a limited English—most of the Campo Bello's trade was American tourist. The sample restaurant menu on the counter said that the dinner special that night had been pot roast.

"Señora Blanchard. Can you tell me what room she's staying in?" When the black-haired girl behind the counter hesitated, he added, "She's my daughter-in-law."

The desk clerk was sorry, but the señora had left the motel early that afternoon. There was no message.

Blanchard stood there stupidly, staring at her.

He had actually made no plans beyond this moment, preferring to wait until he had talked again and in greater detail with Angie. Everything depended on her. She had been with Mike up until the time he had disappeared. She knew where they had been, whom they had seen, what they had done or said. Without her he could do little. He didn't even know where to begin.

San Miguel de Allende, he thought. That was where Mike had recognized the man he believed to be Darrell Kinney. Had Angie gone there? Had she heard from Mike? Had something come up so suddenly that it caused her to leave the motel without even taking time to leave a message for him?

Or had she too disappeared?

Blanchard asked the desk clerk to phone the U.S. Consulate for him. It was the only thing he could think of to do. The consulate was closed. He thought of trying to obtain the name and number of the emergency duty officer but decided against it. He might have to ask for extraordinary help later; he wanted to be more sure of the facts before he did.

The truth was that Angie's unexpected absence had left him momentarily demoralized. Twenty-four hours ago he had been sitting before the television screen in his comfortable apartment, a whiskey-and-soda in his hand, a man with a good job, a settled routine, an ordinary past, and a predictable future. And a son, even if he was a college dropout, embarked on what Blanchard had called a year to goof off and Mike had insisted was a time to "find out where it's at." Now he found himself alone in a foreign country, tired and wet and bewildered, with none of those security blankets.

And his son and his young bride were both missing.

2

Charmian Stewart's pessimism over the budget accommodations at the Campo Bello had been misplaced. More power to Messrs. Wilcock and Foreman for their traveling-teacher's bible. The room was large and clean and comfortable, if relatively spartan. The shower was passable. There was a pitcher full of purified water, and she had remembered to brush her teeth and rinse her mouth with it.

She had been hoping for another sunny morning, but low rain clouds hung over the city in the wake of the night's severe storm. The air was heavy and humid. She had anticipated driving over to the *panadería* she had discovered on her first morning in Guadalajara, on Avenida Vallarta just east of the Minerva fountain. There she had sat out in the morning sun at one of the sidewalk tables, enjoying a tall glass of *naranja* (squeezed from fresh oranges, not frozen pulp), strong black coffee, and a delicious variety of *pan dulce*. Along with a table full of American medical students she had watched the young office girls of Guadalajara boarding the bus on their way to work. They all wore slacks or miniskirts, the new thick-soled platform shoes, long straight hair parted in the middle. Except for the almost universal blackness of the hair (the beautiful jet black she envied, her own dark tresses being far from that depth of color) she might have been watching her own students back at Santa Monica City College.

But that was yesterday. Now the threatening rain decided her to have breakfast in the rather cheerless restaurant at the Campo Bello, enlivened this morning by the presence of several Americans. The Mexican bacon, as she had discovered anew on the drive down along the coast through Guaymas and Mazatlán, was marvelous, the eggs and toast and jam as good as you could find anywhere. What had to be avoided at all costs were pancakes, staple of the American traveler. Apparently the secret of good pancakes continued to elude Mexicans in general, like the secrets of good plumbing.

The red-haired teacher from Columbus, Ohio, came over to her table, delighted as before over the good fortune of bumping into another American teacher. He and his wife were exploring the possibilities of Guadalajara for their retirement, which seemed to be just around the corner. Their name was Robbins, George and Betty. Betty said little and smiled a great deal. Charmian guessed that she had been doing that, and listening, for so long that she was not conscious of the habit any more. George Robbins was a man close to fifty, but he wore his hair in a youthful cut, combed forward and dyed bright red. It made his lined face older, not younger, almost a caricature.

Robbins' enthusiasm had not flagged. "Have you visited the *barrancas* north of the city? Those are the big canyons."

"Yes, I know," she said with a smile.

"That's right, you speak Spanish—I keep forgetting. Some friends drove us out there yesterday. Truly spectacular. You shouldn't miss them. Everything we see here just bowls us over, both me and Betty. There are some beautiful new homes out that way, a whole development of them. This one place we looked at was right on the edge of the canyon, with a view you just wouldn't believe."

"I hope you didn't get caught in the rain."

"Oh, we didn't mind that, it just added to the spectacle. That's another thing, we can't get over the weather. Even the rain—we love it! And they say this is the worst season. The really beautiful time is winter, when it's sunshine and blue skies every day, with no rain for six or seven months, temperatures always in the seventies. The land of eternal spring, that's what the Spanish called it, you know."

Charmian resisted the temptation to say "I know" again.

"It's humid this morning," she said. She was perspiring over the hot coffee.

"Oh, this is nothing—you should be in Columbus when it's humid. That's real humidity. No, Betty and I were saying to each other, we keep looking for something *wrong*, you know? Something to complain about. It's a big step, moving all the way down here, leaving all our friends and family. We have a son lives in New York, up near Albany. We don't want to close our eyes to anything, but really, we can't find a thing that isn't just *perfect!*"

George Robbins' enthusiasm was a little overwhelming, especially early in the morning, and Charmian was guiltily relieved when he returned to his table.

The older couple from Oregon, the Waldecks, were also there for breakfast. She was originally from New Zealand, Charmian had discovered with interest, her curiosity about faraway places as lively as it had been when she was a child. Peter Waldeck had a bad case of arthritis in one arm from an accident, and they were also looking for a place to retire. The cost of living is driving us out of our own country, Charmian thought; where will we go when all the charming little villages in Mexico are full of Americans, all overpaying their maids and eagerly driving the prices upward? The med students at the *panadería* had been complaining about rising rents in Guadalajara. One was living in a small apartment at $150 a month, another with a wife and child was paying $200 for a modest house. And a house in Mexico City's fashionable Chapultepec district, Charmian had heard, now rented at a rate comparable to a similar place in Brentwood or Beverly Hills.

She smiled and waved as the Waldecks greeted her. We're all so much friendlier with each other when we meet in a foreign country, she mused. Her glance drifted toward the quiet, middle-aged man at a table in the corner near the front windows. Except for him. He was worrying about something, and he didn't know anyone else was in the room.

Middle-aged was slightly unfair, she thought. He was probably about forty-five, but his face had the good strong lines that were pleasing to artists and photographers, bone structure that kept a face young. He had not let himself give up on the battle of the bulge either, as Tom Redman had begun to do, she thought with a trace of satisfaction. Altogether the man in the corner had a nice face and a nice body to go with it. His eyes, deep-set and gray, had been thoughtful when they touched her briefly with a curious glance, thoughtful without that cool calculation that she found infuriating.

Oh, stop it, Charmian Stewart, she admonished herself. That schoolteacher-on-a-holiday story has been written, remember? You're not Katharine Hepburn, he's certainly not Rossano Brazzi, and summer is over. And let's forget about the symbolism in *that*.

But she could not help wondering what was worrying him.

The promised showers proved scattered and light. When, later that morning, patches of blue sky appeared—that brilliant blue for which Mexico was justly famous, a color hardly more than a memory in Los Angeles—she decided to drive over to Tlaquepaque.

She was a good driver, and her Vega wagon was small and nimble enough to hold its own against the antics of Mexican drivers, even when whirling around one of the many *glorietas*. In its design and atmosphere Guadalajara was a European city, with its wide parkways, its many trees and sparkling fountains, its busy traffic circles overlooked by massive statues to the *Niños Heroes* or other revolutionary heroes. Its beauty and climate lent themselves to the many outdoor restaurants Charmian found so delightful, and she spent part of the drive trying to decide where she would enjoy her midday *comida*.

This trip she had only one near-accident, when a young Mexican in an old car used the left-turn lane at a traffic light as a passing lane, timing his move so that he raced through as the light turned green and darted in front of her, so close that she thought she heard their bumpers ticking. She drove after him, furious, but in a moment she was laughing. She had had an image of her father's outrage if he had ever been exposed to such innocently reckless drivers.

At one glassware factory in Tlaquepaque she chose six more of the amber drinking glasses she had decided on. Then she spent an hour at her favorite pottery shop, which featured wares from nearby Tonala, carefully going over the "seconds" for enough plates and mugs to round out her set. On her teacher's salary she had learned how to hunt for bargains, and the fact that she had a year's sabbatical before her (a year for which she had paid in full, she thought ruefully) hardly changed the need to count her pesos.

She was caught in the open patio among the chipped and burned and discolored pieces of Tonala pottery when a sudden shower drenched her.

Waiting inside the shop for the rain to pass, she thought suddenly of a line of Vonnegut's in *Slaughterhouse-Five* about lonely women seeking meaning for their lives among the gift and novelty shops of Sante Fe. Was she one of those women? Was this her Santa Fe?

Returning to her car after the shower had passed, she caught the melancholy blare of trumpets from the plaza, evoking sudden nostalgia for her first visit to Mexico, her first delight in its color and warmth and simple joys. Jalisco was the birthplace and home of *mariachi* music, and its sounds drew her now to the great square at the center of Tlaquepaque. The plaza was enclosed on all four sides by a roofed arcade. Inside and under roof were row upon row of tables, surrounding a square so large that three or four different *mariachi* groups were playing in different sections, vying with each other in spirit and enthusiasm if not in musical harmony.

Charmian sat at one of the tables and ordered a Carta Blanca. (She hardly ever drank beer back home; here both the beer and the atmosphere were different.) Little girls came by in a steady parade, selling chiclets or tortillas or cheap souvenirs. Through a nearby passageway a *mariachi* group straggled into the square, taking up its place a few tables from her. Their once-proud costumes were in a worn and faded state, the players hardly less bedraggled. They were fat and thin, tall and short, but all alike in one thing: each man appeared to be sixty years old or more. A weed-thin trumpeter whose body seemed too frail for the enormous traditional sombrero he wore led the *mariachis* into ragged renditions of the popular and lively "Guadalajara!" and "La Raspa." As they paused the wispy leader flashed wide-spaced yellow teeth at Charmian. Even his drooping gray moustache was thin and stained. He brought the small band closer to her table and led them into "Jarabe Tapatío," the familiar "Mexican Hat Dance." Feeling obligated, Charmian asked the group to play "Esta Tristeza Mía" and "La Cama de Piedra," two of the mournful lovers' laments that were part of the folk-music tradition of the *mariachis*. The old trumpeter was delighted. Bowing to her, he swept off his great sombrero, put down his trumpet, and sang to her, his cracked voice only occasionally equal to the higher notes he must once have sung with passionate vigor. Now there was only the deep emotion left. (And why do you want to hear sad songs about beds of stone, she asked herself; the soft guitars, the mournful trumpets answered her.)

She tipped the little band generously. As they moved away, Charmian looked around her at the huge square with a sense of shock, seeing it crumbling and littered and dirty, as worn and shabby as her *mariachi* players. She wondered where all of the younger musicians had gone. To the Guadalajara Hilton, she supposed, to Mexico City, or north to El Paso and on to Ventura and Los Angeles, where the money was.

Saddened, she drove slowly back into the city and, partly as an antidote to Tlaquepaque's plaza, she decided to have lunch at La Copa de Leche in downtown Guadalajara. On her previous visits to the city it had always been her favorite dining place, a terraced restaurant on three levels. Her favorite was the outdoor patio on the balcony level, overlooking the activity of the busy Avenida Juárez.

After a short wait she was given a small table in the sun. As always the setting was delightful, the flowers and the decor adding to the charm of a day that had turned bright and warm and sparkling in the aftermath of the morning rain. Charmian decided, in spite of the beer at Tlaquepaque, to have a margarita before lunch. The place was astonishingly crowded and busy, and service was slow. More than slow, she soon realized; indifferent.

Gradually she took in the changing mood of the popular restaurant. It had become too aware of itself as a tourist attraction, explaining the indifferent service. The balcony was crowded with young people—American girls excited by the expectation of experiencing the real Mexico, and shrewd-eyed, elegantly dressed Mexican youths cruising, flashing their dark eyes and gleaming white teeth at their targets, which seemed as often to be young men as young girls.

The prices on the menu had soared too, Charmian discovered. She would not be able to eat here often.

With regret she realized that she would not want to.

A second, almost determined margarita, and the day's luncheon special, *enchiladas rancheras*, a dollop of sour cream and another of *guacamole* flavoring the cheese-filled tortillas in a green chili sauce, combined with several openly admiring glances to restore her spirits. For some reason the Mexican male's habit of staring openly at a woman he found attractive was not offensive. She had decided that this was because he was truly admiring, not simply calculating (excepting those knowing-eyed youths drifting in and out, studying the occupants of the tables quickly, moving on). Not that the Mexican male was without his northern brother's ego; on the contrary, male ego seemed to be his dominant characteristic, as it was in the Italian man. But his attention was cheerfully direct and honest. Perhaps the difference was that he didn't feel or show any guilt over his wordless but eloquent flattery; he accepted the beauty and appeal of a woman as natural. He wasn't a puritan.

And you are certainly qualified as an expert judge of men, Miss Hepburn, she thought wryly. If you resemble dear Katharine in any way at all, it's the prim but stalwart Hepburn of *The African Queen*.

But the stares continued, the admiration seemed genuine, the drinks had quickened her blood, and she allowed herself to go on enjoying the attention, the color, and the sun, while the busy city moved around her until the midday mealtime was over and the tempo of life slowed. Even the traffic began to thin out during the early afternoon. Around four o'clock or so it would again be brisk as the city reawakened from its siesta.

Would she have an awakening? Surely there was still time at thirty-seven. Was that what she hoped for from this year of recovery?

Tom Redman had suggested that she take her sabbatical now. Oh, she was entitled to it—she had already postponed it for one year, as she had postponed so many things—but he had his own reasons. It would make things easier for both of them, he said.

Charmian Stewart had never married. The fact managed to surprise her as much as it did her friends, who never ceased to ask how a woman as attractive, intelligent and all-around *talented* had never been besieged with offers. (There had been a few, none compelling enough.) When she was in her early twenties she was an eager student, discovering in herself a special talent for languages. At UCLA she went happily on to graduate studies in Spanish. She spent two summers studying in Saltillo, and one full year at the *Instituto* in Mexico City before she started teaching. The result was, as Tom Redman had told her more than once, that she spoke more fluent

Spanish than any other teacher on the staff, some of whom couldn't even order from a menu in a Mexican restaurant. But a corollary was the discovery in her late twenties that she had few close friends—and no lovers worthy of the name. Her friends had married and moved on; she had been too busy to make many new ones.

Oh, there had been a brief, lighthearted affair or two, including one with that tour guide in Mexico City that year, but nothing serious. After a while she came to understand that her brains scared most men off. Not that she thought of herself as an intellectual—her father had been the genuine article, so she knew what *they* were like—but most intelligent men seemed to take a special pride in choosing women who were supposed to be less smart, as if they were afraid of competition. She didn't mind *being* less intelligent than some particular man, but she could not bring herself to pretend to be something that she wasn't.

Then, her first teaching position was in a high school in Rialto; that hadn't helped. Rialto was a town about ninety miles inland from Los Angeles, too sleepy and too small to have its own Colonel Sanders chicken stand. There was absolutely no chance of meeting anyone in Rialto. Anyone interesting had already left.

When she moved to Santa Monica she was a month short of turning thirty. Tom Redman joined the department as its new chairman three years later, and for a while they were no more than friendly colleagues. Then one summer Charmian returned from vacation with an unexpected eagerness—not for students or work or classes, but for the chance to see Tom Redman again, to be around him almost every day, to enjoy morning coffee and an occasional lunch with him.

And suddenly, one night in the empty office, an explosion of passion that left her shaken, cut off from any moorings, lost.

And, wonder of wonders, Tom felt the same. He

had loved her in silence, he said, for over a year.

There was only one problem: Tom was already married. And he had two children.

For two years her dreams and hopes triumphed over logic and doubts. At last she began to see what she had been ignoring or refusing to recognize for some time: the small evasions, the apologies, the lies that were meant to appease her, the vagueness about the future.

In June of this year she had forced herself to the confrontation she hated. She asked Tom Redman to decide what he really wanted, for his own and his family's sake as well as hers. She saw the truth in the answer he could not give her, heard it in his mumbled concern about "the kids."

It had taken her another three months, and this long slow drive into Mexico, shedding memories and self-pity along the way, to realize that she was glad.

When Charmian returned to the Campo Bello around three o'clock in the afternoon, the man with the thoughtful gray eyes was still sitting alone in a corner of the restaurant. They'll think he is truly one crazy *gringo*, she thought with a smile, sitting there with his Carta Blanca beer when any sane man would be enjoying his siesta.

After parking in front of her unit she hesitated, unable to deny the impulse to find out what was on yon stranger's mind. He didn't look like the brooding drinker, she thought. Whatever was troubling him was more serious.

She walked back to the office, telling herself that she was only going to get a copy of *The News*, the English-language newspaper published daily in Mexico City and distributed all over the country. She read the Mexican papers for practice, but for news about the States she, like almost every American staying in Mexico, turned to *The News*. It even had the baseball and football scores, not to mention Li'l Abner and Alley Oop.

At the counter next to the restaurant, having paid for the paper, Charmian stood irresolute, debating whether she had the nerve to walk over to the man in the corner and ask if there was anything she could do to help.

She found that she didn't.

As she was about to leave, the desk phone rang. There followed a scene of confusion. The girl on duty during this quiet hour was a substitute who spoke almost no English. The call was for a Señor Blanchard, who turned out to be the worried man in the restaurant. He came quickly to the counter and spoke into the phone. Or rather he listened. There was a rapid outpouring from the other end of the line. Blanchard looked up helplessly, and his worried gray eyes met the curious brown of Charmian Stewart's.

"I speak a little Spanish," she said. "Perhaps I can help."

3

"I don't know what I would have done if you hadn't been there," Jeff Blanchard said.

"You'd have taken a taxi and got to Ajijic faster," she replied with a laugh.

"I mean on the phone. I couldn't make heads or tails of what that man was saying, even though part of it was supposedly in English."

She laughed again—a pleasant sound, Blanchard thought. In spite of his impatience to reach Ajijic he found himself enjoying her company, glad that he had accepted the offer of a ride instead of having to sit in the back seat of a taxi alone with nothing to do but worry.

Charmian Stewart had handled the telephone call easily, switching the caller from his mixture of Spanish and broken English to fluent Spanish. The message itself did nothing to answer all the questions puzzling Blanchard. It simply said that Angie would be at the Posada del Lago in Ajijic that evening and that he should meet her there. No, that wasn't quite accurate; she would contact *him* there.

"You're sure he said I'm not supposed to try to identify her?"

"Yes, that's what he said. She'll be in touch with you when it's safe." Charmian Stewart was silent for a moment, but he caught a sidelong glance, curious and concerned. "Do you really think there's any danger?"

"I don't know. But my son is missing." That was all Blanchard had told her, without going into the details.

"What an awful thing to be hit with out of the blue—especially at long distance like that, without knowing anything for sure." She frowned. "I don't understand why your daughter-in-law didn't wait for you at the Campo Bello."

"She must have had a message from Mike. Or..." Blanchard found himself reluctant to say the word. "Or the kidnappers."

"You don't have any real reason to believe he's been kidnapped."

"No. No, damn it, I don't have anything solid to go on. I hope to God Angie hasn't got herself into anything she can't handle."

"Most of the girls her age these days can handle themselves a lot better than we could." There was a dry note in the comment, the tone of someone taking an objective and unsparing look at herself when she was Angie's age.

"You're putting yourself in my generation. I doubt that you qualify."

"Close enough, Mr. Blanchard."

"Jeff."

"Then you're stuck with calling me Charmian."

"It's a pretty name. Unusual, too."

"My father was a Shakespearean scholar, so he's to blame. Charmian was one of Cleopatra's handmaidens in *Antony and Cleopatra*."

"Who was the other handmaiden? Wait—Iras, wasn't it?"

"That's right. And Iras is my middle name," she said with amusement. "Dad didn't want to leave anything out."

"He has nothing to apologize for, Charmian."

"You didn't have to go through school trying to explain that name."

They were climbing now, and as they rose higher the city of Guadalajara took shape behind them, sprawled out across the flat plain in the gathering darkness, its features fading as a pattern of lights caught fire and spread rapidly. Charmian Stewart, who seemed to know Guadalajara well, had taken the bypass south of the city that went by the airport, turning south along Highway 35 toward Chapala. She drove with relaxed competence, sure of herself and her car. She was dressed casually in an embroidered Mexican wedding shirt and a blue skirt, her dark hair pulled back from her forehead and ears, held by a blue band. She was not making a pointed display of breasts or thighs, and she didn't seem conscious of his appraisal. Mike probably would not have classified her as out of sight, Blanchard thought, or anything sensational. An attractive schoolteacher, brushing up on her Spanish, the kind of unassertive woman who could easily be overlooked in a crowd of noisier ones, a woman no longer able to compete with the leggy sexpots in their miniskirts.

Blanchard brought himself up short, conscious in that moment of how he had become conditioned to seeing and judging women in artificial terms. *He* no longer skipped down the stairs, if he ever had. His waist wasn't as narrow or his belly as hard as it once was, in spite of handball and tennis and bicycling. His legs had never been noted for their shapeliness or straightness, and his feet had always had a tendency to toe out. The face that regarded him from any mirror was a long way down the road from wide-eyed youth, although he had to admit he liked it somewhat better than that of the apple-cheeked kid in the snapshot with Darrell Kinney. Faces that young were necessarily empty.

Correction: American white middle-class faces. He had seen quite a few Mexican children with faces as old as his.

Charmian's was a younger face but it wasn't empty. She was somewhere in her mid-thirties, he guessed, and she had the look of a woman who was still searching for something, which was a lot better than looking as if you'd been everywhere and seen everything and didn't much like any of it. She had undoubtedly been pretty enough at twenty, but, perhaps fortunately, not the startling beauty who was elected Homecoming Queen or first-string Miss Ohio—the kind of premature success that always seemed to mean arrested development. Right now, at thirty-five or thirty-six, hers was a truly lovely woman's face. And no matter how hard the Friedans and Steinems tried to erase the differences, that was a very special kind of loveliness, softer than a man's face should be without being weaker, humorously understanding, gentler around the mouth, cool in the current sense of the term but without being insolent or smug or arrogant, characteristics that Blanchard seemed to find too often in the faces of the young.

It was a face that was alive, he thought.

What business did he have with the living?

Charmian Stewart said, "Do I pass muster?"

"You certainly do, whatever that is."

She smiled. "I'm glad you're able to think of something besides Mike—" She stopped, uncharacteristically flustered, as if she had said the wrong thing.

"I ought to feel guilty about that, I suppose. But there really isn't much a man can do about his reaction to a good night's sleep or a beautiful sunset or being with a pretty woman. It just happens."

She took refuge in silence, and it was Blanchard's turn to smile. He decided to get things back on a lighter plane. "You drive very well," he said, "like an old Mexico hand."

"I feel a lot surer of myself back home," she admitted, "but I've been coming down here for a long time on vacations, and I've learned something about driving in Mexico."

"Such as?"

"Oh, like never driving at night away from the big cities. This road is an exception because it's so built up all along the way, but even here you have to look out for stray horses and cattle. But the main thing is, I never argue with the other driver. I mean, it isn't a *macho* thing with me the way it is with them. For a Mexican—sometimes the women are worse than the men, although not many of them drive—a car is a way to prove yourself. Besides, I think they believe in fate more than I want to. A Mexican will just toot his horn and trust to luck or his great skill with his machine, even if the skill and the machine are both questionable. Like at a blind intersection in a town—there are a lot of those, with the narrow streets and the houses built right to the sidewalks, if there are any sidewalks—it's accepted practice that the one who toots his horn first goes through first. So any Mexican driver will just beep-beep and sail on through without even slowing down. I won't. I've come too close to being hit too often. I peer around the corner and scuttle across. You also have to remember that it's different for an American driving down here. Anyone who has an accident is guilty until proven otherwise, and the law says you can spend the first night in jail, or as long as they want until someone gets around to deciding who's to blame. And since all Americans are rich, it's only fair that they accept some of the blame, whatever happened."

Blanchard grinned at this account. "Why do you come down so often? Do you like it here that much?"

"Yes. I love the people, their politeness and gentleness and joy in what looks to us like a pretty meager life. And their fiestas and their churches and their funny processions that no one else believes in anymore. Mostly, of course, I come to improve my Spanish, but that's just how it got started. That's my job, my... life, I guess you could say. But I don't come here just to brush up on my vocabulary, although I do get to know new ways of saying and thinking things in Spanish every time I come. You never learn it the way any five-year-old American has learned English or any five-year-old Mexican his Spanish. But I try to get closer to that, to what it's like to *be* Mexican. When you know more about how a person thinks and feels, you know more about how he uses his language, how he shapes it to say what he wants to say. To say what he *is*. And then you find out that the Mexican isn't just a simple peasant at all but a very complex human being, with a culture as mixed and divided as our own."

"I wish you'd been my Spanish teacher."

She flashed a smile and fell silent once more. Blanchard wondered if she had been talking to take his mind off Mike and Angie after blundering onto the subject. If so, he liked that impulse in her.

There were quite a few things he was beginning to like about Charmian Stewart.

They swept over a high crest and came into view of Lake Chapala, blue in the pale light of evening under an early evening quarter-moon that had just appeared over the mountains as if on cue. The small village of Chapala, now a retirement paradise for retired American admirals and colonels, with American-style golf-and-country-club developments to the east and west, grew away from the lake shore and climbed the foothills. The Vega swept down the curving road toward the lake and its sprinkling of lights, descending into full darkness.

At the bottom of the hill they turned right and drove along the lakeshore road, past an elegant new resort hotel that proudly proclaimed its private membership and, facing the water, sprawling new homes, expensive and often startling in their imaginative architectural use of concrete and stone, all of them impressively luxurious. There were supposed to be many Mexicos, Charmian Stewart commented, but this one didn't seem to belong to Mexicans any more. All they had left was the Chapala pier for Sunday family promenading, and even there the music that sounded in the cafés and clubs for young people to dance to was hard rock, not soft guitar. Their chaperoning *abuelas* must be bewildered by it all, Charmian mused, anxiously watching their grandchildren turn into something they could not understand.

They drove past the Chula Vista Country Club development and the huge Camino Real. The latter, a blaze of lights, was at the edge of Ajijic. The town itself was another of those picturesque Indian villages whose climate and setting on the shore of the lake, with narrow cobbled or dirt streets and tiny adobe houses behind high walls, had led to its being taken over by the horde of *norteamericanos* looking for a place to live on their pensions without having to scrimp—and with the luxury of a maid and a gardener. Most of the houses had been or were being modernized with U.S.-style bathrooms and kitchens.

The Vega wagon bounced along an uneven, narrow road through the village, whose Americanization did not include filling the chuckholes. Unlike Chapala, which had been quiet as Blanchard and Charmian Stewart drove through, the streets of Ajijic seemed crowded with Americans out for a stroll or Mexicans standing in open doorways. The tiny plaza at the center of the village was busy. There was a movie theater featuring Sean Connery in a James Bond rerun. On the corner opposite was a small, brightly lit and very modern *supermercado*, its shelves lined with American canned goods, cigarettes and magazines.

"You've been here before?" Blanchard asked, as Charmian Stewart turned along a dark, one-way street leading away from the plaza.

"I bought this skirt at one of the gift shops here. It's a pretty little town. You should see it in daylight."

"Do any Mexicans still live here?"

She laughed. "Of course. Who do you suppose the servants are?"

Many of the gift and curio shops were still open, ranging from small native shops featuring serapes or ponchos to smart, sophisticated, American-run boutiques. Charmian parked her compact car along a side street and they walked back to the Posada del Lago.

The inn was built around a lushly overgrown tropical garden. From the small tiled lobby, winding paths led through the gardens, whose thick green fronds and flowering bushes arched overhead to form closed tunnels feebly brightened here and there by what looked like tiki torches in wrought-iron holders. It occurred to Blanchard that the dense growth offered perfect concealment for anyone watching the footpaths. The notion that he might be being watched caused his scalp to prickle.

The crooked path brought them to the restaurant on one side and a large cocktail lounge on the right, both almost at the edge of the lake. Blanchard and Charmian Stewart paused at the entrance to the lounge, struck by the beauty of the scene outside. At the water's edge, just a few feet away, a group of young men and women, most of them with the look and air of affluent Americans, were arranging themselves on horses for an evening ride along the beach, calling out to each other or breaking into sudden laughter. A handsome, slender Mexican youth with the flashing smile of the Indian signaled and turned his horse along the shore of the lake, leading the riders in single file. The water lapped into their tracks in the wet sand.

"I don't suppose Angie could be one of them," Charmian wondered aloud.

It had not occurred to Blanchard that she might be going for a joyride, but he could make little sense of anything that was happening here so far. "Surely not," he said.

They sat at one of the leather-covered tables near

the windows facing the water, settling into the surprisingly comfortable leather basket chairs called *equipales*. A small but noisy *mariachi* trio erupted into song. Two or three couples moved onto a tiny dance floor. Blanchard waited for the waiter to bring margaritas. He smiled feebly at Charmian as he raised his glass.

"Do you think it would be better if I weren't here?" she asked suddenly, leaning across the table to be heard over the music.

"It probably looks more natural this way," he said, wondering as he spoke why it should seem important to be "natural."

He sipped the salt-rimmed tequila cocktail and made an attempt at glancing casually around the room.

For a Tuesday night it was a lively place. The *posada* was the social center of the town, Charmian told Blanchard, particularly for swingers, or what passed for swingers in this part of the world. At one table a sixty-year-old red-faced American with a bull neck and a stiff back looked exactly like a retired Marine general, which he might well have been. The younger man, who acted as if he wanted to light the general's cigar and settled for lighting their wives' cigarettes, was his aide, Blanchard decided. And the two women, dyed blonde and dyed jet-black, respectively fifty and sixty, had the brittle, weathered smartness of career-officers' wives.

"Golf and bridge," Charmian murmured. "Those are the big things around here. And good tequila or Jamaican rum at two dollars a quart. They say the party starts about ten in the morning every day. And as often as not, this is a good place to wind it up at night."

Most of the dancing couples were young, a mix of tanned Americans and Mexicans barely old enough to drink, or to get by with the claim. Conspicuous were several older American women, in their indeterminate thirties, striving to look and dress and act with the carefree, loose-haired style of the twenty-year-olds but achieving instead a note of desperation. One, thick-waisted and homely in a very expensive little dress that only reached the top of her heavy thighs, seemed to be in the special charge of a full-bellied young Mexican with enormous white teeth that were in constant display. He seemed to know everyone—the waiters and musicians, the young girls and older women. He wore black pants as tight-fitting as a matador's, high-heeled black boots that gave him an inch or two of needed height, and a bell-sleeved white shirt that was open almost to his waist, exposing an ample expanse of smooth brown chest and stomach. His name was Pepe—one of the musicians called out to him with a grin—and he put on a vii Joso performance. For his size and weight he danced with surprising lightness and skill, separating from a partner and going into a mincing solo, teeth flashing and fingers snapping as his eyes closed soulfully in response to the rhythm, returning to swing her around, pressing her against his swelling belly, his lips nuzzling her ear while he whispered something that caused her to shriek with delighted laughter. His black eyes were always busy, missing nothing, seeing everyone—they seemed to rivet on Charmian with special attention for a moment; Blanchard suspected that women old enough to be lonely or insecure were his bag—and while he danced with one partner he was often looking over her shoulder to wink and smile at another.

By the time the second round of margaritas had been reduced to empty, salt-rimmed glasses and their waiter was hovering expectantly nearby, Jeff Blanchard was becoming increasingly restless. Where was Angie? Which one of the young girls in the lounge—if any—was she? Why hadn't she identified herself? And what had brought her so hastily to Ajijic?

"Do you have any idea which one she is?"

Charmian asked, reading his thoughts.

Blanchard shook his head. One of the young American girls who had danced with Pepe had seemed to glance toward their table with more than passing interest, but he might have imagined it. She was blue-eyed, with honey-colored skin and straight, sun-bleached hair to match. She wore a dusty beige miniskirt in brushed suede that allowed a pair of remarkable long legs to win attention, and a crinkle-crepe blouse under which her small breasts stirred freely. Yes, Mike would have said that she was out of sight, Blanchard thought. But a number of others in the room might qualify.

"It seems funny," Charmian said. "Funny-strange. Having a daughter-in-law you can't recognize."

"It wasn't my idea," Blanchard said, a little defensively.

"How did it happen, if I'm not being too nosy?"

The *mariachis* switched into a very fast Latin dance rhythm, a signal for fat Pepe to go into a rather startling imitation of early George Raft, blended with Valentino and Elvis Presley, eyes and teeth flashing, cries of delight escaping, his nimble booted feet twisting and moving the heavy body with eye-catching grace. He was now dancing with a slender redheaded girl whose excited responses suggested a Texas drawl not far in the background. Mike and Angie had been in Texas when they decided to get married. Did that mean that she was a Texan?

"Mike and I haven't got along all that well since his mother died," Blanchard said after a moment. "Communications broke down, as they say nowadays. Then he decided to drop out of college for a year and we disagreed on that. I'm not sure I was right, now. I think I just didn't want him to go off on his own." He paused, not wanting to inflict family problems on someone who was, after all, a stranger. "Anyway, he went to Miami for the conventions, mainly to protest the war, and maybe just because it was the thing to do. He met Angie there. I'm not sure now, because Mike was a little vague, but I have the idea that Angie was an alternate delegate at the Democratic convention, but I can't remember what state she's from." He shook his head with a rueful smile. "I don't even know that much. I do know they left Miami together sometime in July, I guess they were finding out about each other, rapping together, and by the time they got to Texas they decided they wanted to get married. Not just live together, mind you, but actually get married. They headed down across the border, were married, and just kept going."

"They've been all over Mexico in the past two months?"

"Yes. Oaxaca, Mexico City, Vera Cruz, San Miguel, down to the coast at Manzanillo, Guadalajara, Puerto Vallarta to wave at Liz and Dick, as Mike put it, back to San Miguel for some fiesta, Guadalajara again... and that's where he vanished. They haven't missed much. All I've had were a couple of postcards listing the itinerary and hinting that Mike was very, very happy, until that letter came on Monday that he sent from San Miguel."

"Any number of things could have happened that would make him disappear for a few days," Charmian said thoughtfully. "It doesn't have to be anything serious."

"No, but Angie thinks it is. And she's been with him."

They both looked around the cocktail lounge again, wondering which of the twenty-year-olds was Angie, and Blanchard knew that they were both thinking the same thing: that Angie must have regarded the situation as very serious indeed to call him for help and then to arrange this cloak-and-dagger meeting. Even allowing for youthful tendency toward melodrama, Blanchard had to take it seriously.

Over Charmian's protest he signaled the waiter for another round of drinks. "At this rate we'll end up on the dance floor ourselves," he said. "And I don't mean that it wouldn't be a pleasure."

She smiled. "I suspect everyone here thinks we're past that stage."

"I think you're right." They probably did look as if they belonged together, Blanchard thought. A mature couple, the wife a little younger but not too much so, comfortable with each other, content to sip their cocktails and watch the children take over the dance floor. "Or they may think I'm an aging rake who's found himself another pretty young thing."

Charmian laughed outright.

That was the moment the waiter arrived with their two margaritas on a tray. At exactly the same moment Pepe was swinging past the table with the thick-waisted and anxiously merry American woman who was the object of most of his most ardent attentions. The waiter and Pepe collided. The drinks went flying. Blanchard saw liquid spill across the front of Charmian's shirt as she tried to duck. He felt surprise as well as dismay—Pepe was not that clumsy. The fat man fell against the table, reaching out to grab the back of Charmian's chair to keep from falling. Blanchard could barely hear his hissed whisper: "*La playa—a la media noche.*"

Then Pepe was stumbling back, red-faced, bowing and apologizing profusely. "*Discúlpenme, discúlpenme, señores,*" he exclaimed. His heavy shoulders shrugged helplessly. "*Lo siento.*"

"*De nada,*" Charmian murmured. She was standing, dabbing at her shirt front with a napkin.

"I'm sorry," Blanchard said. "It was an accident—"

"Yes, I know. It doesn't matter." She sponged some liquid from the arm of her basket chair and sat down with a rueful smile, having picked up her cue instantly. She was very quick and a good actress, Blanchard thought. "But I will have that other drink now."

The general and his aide were staring at them, Blanchard noticed, along with most of the other people in the room. Had anyone else heard Pepe's whisper? He doubted it. With the music and the talk and the crash of falling glasses, he had hardly made out the words.

He forced himself to wait until the embarrassed waiter had brought them another round of cocktails and a small consolation bowl of salted peanuts. Then he leaned forward across the table. "I heard him but I don't understand. Do you know what he said?"

Charmian smiled brightly, as if she were reassuring him over his concern about the accident. "He said 'The beach—at midnight.'" Instinctively they both glanced out the window at the narrow strip of sand. "I guess you're supposed to meet him there."

"Or Angie," Blanchard said thoughtfully.

He surveyed the room once more. Pepe and his eager date were leaving. His attention was completely devoted to her. He acted the gigolo beautifully, Blanchard thought, but he might also be a very clever man.

4

Blanchard took a room at the *posada* and urged Charmian Stewart to do the same. She demurred. She really had to get back to the city, and anyway she had a room at the Campo Bello. A teacher on holiday couldn't afford two separate rooms for the same night.

"It's my doing," he urged her. "Let me pay for it. You said yourself it's not a good idea to drive at night."

"I also said that the Chapala road is better than most. I'll be all right."

"I may need my translator."

"I have an idea our friend Pepe can communicate

in English if he wants to. I had dinner here a week ago, on a Saturday night, and I'm sure Pepe was here that evening too, with a different giggling American lady friend. If he's that busy an escort, he must have learned a few words.

"I've an idea Pepe doesn't need words to communicate," Blanchard said with a grin.

There was a moment of awkward, self-conscious intimacy between them. Blanchard was absurdly conscious of the proximity of the room he had booked, and the good practical sense of Charmian staying overnight instead of driving back to Guadalajara in darkness alone. She was aware of what was in his mind, he knew, and he was sure that she felt the same sudden closeness, the same tension of mutual attraction. They were not youngsters, he thought, and they were both unattached. There was no good reason why she shouldn't stay.

Except that he had something else that claimed his first allegiance.

"Thanks for a very interesting evening, Jeff," she said. "I wish I knew how it was going to turn out."

"You can. Are you going to be at the Campo Bello for a while?"

She hesitated only an instant. "Not for long. I'm going to be traveling." She smiled, too brightly, as if she were once more trying to fool someone watching her. "Maybe we'll run into each other again. If not here in Mexico, there's always Santa Monica."

"I won't forget that."

"I hope you find Mike." Her brown eyes sobered. "I'm sure he'll turn up safe. Kids will do anything these days." She spoke the cliché hopefully, but with no more conviction than Blanchard felt.

He walked her to her car. She seemed almost anxious to get away, and she had her car door open and was starting the engine before Blanchard had time to thank her properly for all her help.

And for just being there.

As the small car pulled away, bounced through a

puddle, and turned sharply left at the first corner, he felt a strong disappointment, an emotional letdown. For a long minute he stood there in the empty street, staring toward the corner past the long sightless wall with the broken pieces of glass crowning it, and the huge block letters that spelled out the name of Mexico's president, ECHEVERRÍA, while he listened for the hard rap of the Vega's engine until it had faded into the night.

He walked back through the *posada*'s garden to his small room. He had left his suitcase at the Campo Bello, not knowing what lay ahead in Ajijic, but he had an idea that he would have other things on his mind besides sleeping this night or worrying about how he was going to shave in the morning.

He lay on the bed in the darkened room. More than an hour till midnight. On impulse, fearing that he might doze off, he walked back to the lobby and borrowed a small alarm clock. On the way back he was struck once more by the darkness of the garden and its narrow paths. Yet the inn seemed peaceful, buffered from the lounge's activity by the miniature jungle. There was a pool off to one side, almost hidden by a thick screen of plantings, and Blanchard thought he heard movement from that direction. He paused, listening. There was nothing. Only the thin call of the *mariachis* crying the lonely dove's lament: *"Cucurucucú... cucurucucú... paloma...!"*

He opened the door to his room and stepped inside, fumbling for the light switch.

There was a subliminal warning, a whisper of sound unheard, as of displaced air, a smell of unfamiliar sweat and bay rum. Then something crashed against the back of his skull and the dark room lit up with an explosion of Mexican fireworks. He was falling through a velvet sky among the fiery Roman candles, falling, whirling past silent bursts of color, until the last lights diminished and winked out, leaving only blackness.

5

The ticking of the alarm clock woke him, a jackhammer working much too close by. When he moved, pain pierced the area behind his left ear, and the tile floor lurched beneath him like a small boat caught in a side swell. Jeff Blanchard probed a sensitive lump, finding broken skin. There had been a small amount of bleeding, but it had apparently stopped. There was also a gritty substance trapped in the blood-matted hair that he identified as sand. He thought of the leather saps he had seen for sale once in a Mexican leather shop, the end weighted with sand.

He could have hit me directly on the temple, Blanchard thought. He hadn't wanted to crush the skull.

Who?

He sat up too quickly. The small boat dropped sideways down the long trough of the wave. Nausea welled threateningly from his stomach. With shaking fingers he picked up the alarm clock and held it close enough to make out the two luminescent hands, glowing faintly in the darkness. 11:35. He had been unconscious for more than a half-hour.

He remembered reading somewhere that a blow on the head hard enough to knock you out was considerably more dangerous and incapacitating than private-eye novels and movies led you to believe. He realized that he was not going to scramble up and chase anyone. Not right away.

Moving slowly and cautiously, he climbed to his feet and checked the door. His assailant had closed it behind him. Blanchard sucked in a breath and closed his eyes and flicked on the light switch next to the door.

After the ache behind his eyes began to ease he

shuffled over to the room's only chair and sat in it, letting himself down gingerly.

His wallet was lying open on a corner of the bed.

There was a strange swimming sensation in his head that made him think uneasily of a concussion, but he could have felt worse. After a moment he was able to drag himself over to the bed and retrieve the wallet.

Someone had gone through it thoroughly. The money he had carried was gone, a mixture of dollars and pesos. He was relieved to find that all of his identification and credit cards were still there. But the thief had checked everything. When he had stuffed the I.D. and the bank book and the cellophane case with Blanchard's driver's license and a few photographs and some other cards back he hadn't got them arranged the way Blanchard always did, not by any special plan but from lifetime habit.

He hadn't been your ordinary thief. He had lifted the cash only because it was too easily available, or to make it look like a robbery. He hadn't taken any of the credit cards.

But he had taken the snapshot of Blanchard with Darrell Kinney.

Someone had wanted to make sure of his identity.

Kinney would not have found that necessary, Blanchard reasoned. But someone working for him would have had to make sure.

The missing snapshot was clear proof, both ways. For the thief and for Blanchard.

The incredible notion that Kinney was alive and somehow involved in Mike's disappearance had suddenly become far more plausible. The possibility of real danger to Mike was no longer in doubt. No one went around sapping strangers in order to take a peek at their identification cards without good reason.

And might that danger not be just as real for Angie?

Blanchard checked the alarm clock again—it was

easier to read than his watch, for his eyes were not focusing clearly yet—and saw that he still had almost fifteen minutes.

He had a headache that could have won an Emmy award and he was generally shaky, but he would keep that appointment on the beach at midnight, one way or another.

After swallowing some *purificada* from the pitcher provided, Blanchard splashed water on his face, dried himself, and looked around the room for some kind of a weapon. There was none, unless he wanted to count an alarm clock small enough to carry in his hand. And noisy. He rejected it.

He decided that he wouldn't need a weapon anyway. He didn't know Angie but he was willing to gamble on one conviction: she would not knowingly lead him into a trap. And nothing would be gained by attacking him a second time, now that they were certain who he was... whoever *they* were.

As Blanchard let himself out of his room into the tunneled darkness of the garden he heard church bells in the village begin to chime the hour of midnight. He felt quick concern. Was the alarm clock a few minutes slow?

Once he was moving he discovered that he had good control of his limbs, and the pain in his head was no worse than when he was sitting or standing still. The faint blurring of vision seemed also to have cleared, although he could see little in the feeble light of the tiki torches.

He could no longer hear the *mariachis*, but the cocktail lounge was still open and doing light business. He slipped quickly past the entrance, his passing glance noting that more than half of the early evening crowd had departed, leaving only the older ones, the hard drinkers.

The beach was empty. Blanchard walked slowly away from the lighted windows of the *posada*'s lounge, guessing that anyone who wanted to make his presence known in this surreptitious fashion would prefer deep shadows. The three-quarters moon had disappeared behind a thick cloud cover that promised more rain. He could smell rain in the air again, and a light wind had risen to ruffle the placid surface of the lake, a black-glass mirror reaching almost to his feet.

Along the open stretch of beach to his right he could see no one. He turned left, walking slowly away from the inn toward some large old trees leaning against a high wall, creating impenetrable shadows.

The church bells were silent now. There was no sound at all from the village or from the Posada del Lago. Blanchard was able to hear the lapping of each small wave clearly against the shoreline, under the shriller din of crickets and the occasional tuba croak of a frog. He had a sense of isolation, a feeling of being far away from the crowded, jostling civilization he knew, thrust closer to a world more primitive and free.

And more dangerous?

Perhaps. Los Angeles had its share of kidnappings and burglaries and muggings. This lonely beach might be safer at night.

A thick shadow separated from the trunk of a large tree whose branches thrust over the high wall in one direction and spread beyond the shoreline in the other. Blanchard stumbled over a projecting root.

"Señor Blanchard?"

"Yes."

"Sígame, por favor."

"You'll have to speak English."

"You will follow me, señor."

"Where's Angie?"

"I will take you to her."

Pepe's English was heavily accented but clear enough, at least for the few simple phrases he had spoken.

The fat man started along the beach, his footsteps totally silent on the sand. Blanchard wondered if he could move as quickly and silently in a dark room.

"Did you visit my room tonight?"

"No, señor." Pepe chuckled. *"Estaba ocupado con una amigita."*

"No comprendo," Blanchard managed. "You're saying you didn't? You were with someone?"

"Sí, that is right."

"What about my son? Do you know where he is?"

"Mejor no hablar más. It is better not to talk more."

Pepe presented his broad back, effectively cutting off any more conversation. He might act the fool on the dance floor, Blanchard judged, but it was just that: a very good performance.

Blanchard wavered along the beach behind Pepe, walking none too steadily, as if he had had too many margaritas instead of a blow on the head. However, the fresh damp air had the effect of clearing his brain slightly, enough so that he began to wonder what Pepe's exact role was—emissary, messenger, strong-arm man, tipster? A professional gigolo would be in a very good position to single out likely targets for any kind of shakedown, including kidnapping.

The only flaw in that reasoning was that Mike didn't seem a likely target for anything like that. Surely it would have seemed more logical to kidnap Angie, if money was what this was all about.

Every turn of argument led Blanchard back to the fact that his son was missing because of who he was. Mike Blanchard.

And that brought him back to Darrell Kinney.

They came to the end of a long wall and to a cobblestoned road that ended at the edge of the lake. Beyond the road was another wall, newer and whiter, behind which could be seen the red-tiled roofs of newer homes. Pepe stopped at the corner, peering along the road. Then he started forward, hugging the wall as he slipped away from the lake, beckoning Blanchard to follow.

Close behind the fat man Blanchard said, "Did Kinney send you?"

He thought that there was a break in Pepe's

movement, a barely perceptible reaction, but he might have imagined it.

"Qué quiere decir eso?"

"The American named Kinney. Did he put you up to this?"

"I do not know such a man," Pepe said curtly. *"Cállese, por favor."*

Blanchard gave it up for the time being. It was obvious that Pepe wasn't going to tell him anything that he wasn't supposed to hear. And in any event Kinney could be going under another name—almost certainly would be, when you thought about it. Blanchard could only hope that Angie knew more of what was going on.

At the first break in the wall a pair of gates stood open. Near them was a small, weather-streaked sign: VISTA SANTA INEZ. Beyond were spacious grounds, shadowed by trees and flowering shrubs, almost as dark as the inner garden at the Posada del Lago. Blanchard was able to make out the low, huddled mass of various buildings. There was a light in the rear of the nearest, which he guessed must be the owner's unit or office. Everything else was dark.

A few light drops of rain fell.

Blanchard followed Pepe along a gravel road that led into the grounds of the Vista Santa Inez. They passed several cottage units with plastered adobe walls and red tile roofs, fronted by wide porches. The spacious landscaped grounds and the style of the buildings suggested an older resort, and as Blanchard's eyes made out more details he saw that the place had fallen into a state of neglect. The lawns were overgrown, the shrubbery untrimmed, doors and woodwork on the units unpainted and peeling. He saw only two cars parked beside darkened cottages.

Pepe paused outside the last unit in the row, which stood well apart from the others. For the first time Blanchard saw light inside, concealed behind heavy draperies.

"La señora está por dentro."

He pointed, and Blanchard understood his gesture rather than the words. Angie was inside.

"Where will you be?" he asked.

Pepe's heavy shoulders moved in what might have been a shrug, but he did not reply.

"I want to talk to you," Blanchard said sharply. "Damn it, what the hell *is* all this? You can tell Kinney I don't like playing games—"

He broke off. Pepe had melted away into the darkness, disappearing almost instantly. Blanchard listened intently but he heard no footstep along the gravel path.

He went up two steps onto a long porch. Before he reached the door it jerked open. A tall, slender girl faced him, her eyes anxious, the lids swollen as if she had been crying. She had been laughing when Pepe danced with her in the lounge of the Posada del Lago three hours ago, one of several girls he rewarded with his attentions, even as he reserved his special nuzzlings and rolling eyes and whispered intimacies for the homely woman who left the lounge with him. The *amigita* who had provided him with an alibi, Blanchard thought.

"Angie?"

"Mr. Blanchard?"

Then very suddenly she was in his arms, sobbing, her head buried against his shoulder so that he couldn't see her face, the young lean length of her trembling against him. Awkwardly Blanchard patted a bare arm and a fall of blonde hair.

"Hey, it can't be that bad. Take it easy." The words sounded banal. He could only hope they were not empty as well.

After a moment Angie pulled away, still not letting him see her tears. She walked jerkily over to a table between twin beds and snatched a Kleenex from a box to dab at her eyes and cheeks.

"I'm sorry, I... I've been so scared."

"Don't apologize."

She faced him then. "I had to come here, Mr. Blanchard. He said if I didn't, I'd...never see Michael again!"

6

They sat and talked for two hours. By then Angie was exhausted and Blanchard was no longer capable of thinking clearly. He suggested that she lie down. They couldn't do anything before morning.

For a little while Blanchard watched her. She was all legs and silken hair, with just a hint of a Southern accent or something close to it. "South Maryland," she had said. Outa sight. Mike might be blind about some things, Blanchard thought, but his eyes and instincts had been working well this time.

They had had a little debate about what she should call him, settling on "Jeff." He had never liked hearing children call their parents David or Jill or whatever; it sounded cold. It seemed to deny a relationship. In the last year or so, he told Angie, Mike hadn't known what to call him. "Dad" seemed too juvenile to him in his new maturity. He had settled for light or faintly mocking variations such as "Poppa" or "Old Man," as in "Hey, Old Man, how about some bread?"

"I don't think I like that."

"Mike has his own ways of arriving at things."

"I know, it sounds just like him. But he's not always right."

Blanchard smiled. "I guess we can agree on that."

Angie told him about the frantic phone calls and the personal visit she had made to the U.S. Consulate. Nothing had exactly lit a fire under the officials she had talked to. "I don't think they took me seriously," she said bitterly. "They seemed to think we'd had a fight or something and Michael just split. You don't believe that, do you?"

"No." Blanchard had not told her about being

cracked over the head. She had been worried enough when he arrived, her fears and imaginings fed by the feeling of being alone and helpless.

"I started shouting at the man in the consulate and I think I finally got to him. But I think he was more worried about this girl who was on some crazy trip than about the possibility that something had really happened to Michael. My God, he's an American citizen. Don't they even care? Isn't that what they're supposed to be here for?"

"Obviously he didn't believe you." Blanchard refrained from suggesting that she might have sounded overexcited or even hysterical, nor did he mention his own initial skepticism. "I suppose they run into all kinds of funny situations with American couples or families down here. When a young woman on her honeymoon claims that her husband's disappeared..."

"You're defending them," she accused.

"I'm on your side, Angie," Blanchard said gently. "Go on. When did Pepe get in touch with you?"

"Monday afternoon. That's why I couldn't be at the airport to meet you. He told me I had to come to Ajijic and to meet him at the *posada*. He told me that he knew about Michael and where he was and that I had to do what he told me or..." She bit her full lower lip. "He also knew that you were coming."

"How did he know that?"

Angie looked startled. "I never thought... I mean, I just assumed that..." Her face went blank. "I don't know."

"Where did you call me from?"

"The desk at the Campo Bello. I had the woman put the call through for me—sometimes it's hard to make the operators understand when your Spanish isn't very good." She continued to worry her lip—a very pretty lip, Blanchard thought, part of a soft and gentle mouth that had not learned to stay bitter or disillusioned. For some reason he found himself wondering what Charmian Stewart would think of her. "I suppose anyone could have heard me."

Blanchard nodded. "Someone did." Someone who was waiting for her to make that call, he thought.

There was a sudden rush of wind and rain against the windows of the adobe cottage. Angie glanced toward the ceiling. Following her glance, Blanchard saw drops beginning to form between the cracks of the inner layer of flat tiles.

"The roof leaks," Angie said unnecessarily. "That bed is all wet up near the head. I was going to tell the manager but I wasn't sure if he had any part in this thing with Mike. Pepe told me to come here. I didn't want to talk to him without knowing."

"What's the manager like?"

"He's an American. The first night I was here—last night," she added, as if it seemed a long time ago, "he seemed to want to tell me all about himself, about his rich society wife and how they weren't right for each other, because he's a hunting and fishing type and she's all society and operas. Then he told me how he was the sales representative for some big American company operating in Mexico and South America, and he personally went on duck-hunting trips with Echeverría before he became president and they met the president of Guatemala and he knew all the bigwigs in the revolution there and so on. I don't think any of it's true. I think what happened is his mother owned this place and she died, so he inherited it. It's been going downhill ever since."

"How old is he? About my age?"

"No, he's younger." Angie managed a smile. "Sorry about that. Blond hair, kind of chubby-cheeked. He looks like an owl."

Blanchard relaxed. Darrell Kinney might have worn well, but he was in his fifties, and he would be neither blond nor chubby.

"Let's get back to Pepe. Where does he fit in? Is he one of the kidnappers?"

"I don't know. He says he isn't, but that doesn't mean anything. Supposedly he knows where Michael is and he can arrange a meeting with the people who..." Her voice threatened to unravel. "Who have Michael."

"Did he mention ransom?" Blanchard asked grimly. He wished that he had been a little rougher with Pepe on the beach, although it was obvious that he had been in no shape to throw his weight around. Pepe also had the advantage in weight.

"No, but..." She pressed her lips flat in a disgusted grimace. "He wants money for himself."

"Well, that figures."

Someone had already helped himself to an advance payment from his wallet, Blanchard thought. However, he still had the bulk of what he had brought to Mexico in traveler's checks, safely in his locked suitcase at the Campo Bello. And he had made arrangements with his bank before leaving Los Angeles on Monday to have an additional sum transferred if it proved necessary.

It was beginning to look as if it would be. That part didn't bother Blanchard. When you got down to asking yourself what the life of someone very close to you was worth, the answer was very simple: Everything.

"Pepe also said that we shouldn't go to the Mexican police... that it would be dangerous for Michael."

"He makes a lot of threats."

But the warning was to be expected. In fact, the revelation that they were apparently dealing with kidnappers had actually brought some relief to Blanchard. It eliminated some of the mystery. Kidnapping was a conventional if horrible crime, something that could be dealt with. He had a hunch that Mexican kidnappers might be more reluctant to harm or kill an American captive than kidnappers in the United States would be. Making a deal for money was the Mexican way in just about everything. *La mordida*, the payoff, was a way of life. It was also the American way, you could argue, as so many of Mike and Angie's generation did, but the Mexicans were more candid about it. They would also know that neither Blanchard nor the FBI could touch them once they had their money; they would have less reason to silence their victim.

Blanchard didn't know if this let Darrell Kinney out or put him smack in the middle of the plot. He could worry about that later, after Mike was safe.

"All right," Blanchard said, "he gets whatever he wants."

"I've already paid him. Everything I could. I just kept a few pesos for phone calls and gasoline."

Blanchard looked at her gratefully, thinking that his son had found himself more than a girl with a pretty face and a gentle mouth and beautiful legs.

"What happens next?"

"We're supposed to follow Pepe to Guanajuato. I mean, we're supposed to meet him there."

"Guanajuato!"

"Yes. It's...oh, five or six hours' drive northeast."

"I know, I...stayed there once. With Mike's mother."

They had stayed at the Castillo de Santa Cecilia, a huge old stone hotel that was large and gloomy enough to legitimately claim to be a castle. Elaine had been delighted with the place and with the Old World character of the town. Guanajuato had been her favorite place in all of Mexico. Jeff Blanchard had been less enthusiastic. The city had been built along the floor of a deep gorge, filling the canyon bottom and trying to climb the walls that rose steeply on both sides and seemed to loom over the town. For him the place had had an almost claustrophobic atmosphere that was not lessened by the story he was told about the last great flood back in 1905, when a forty-foot wall of water had roared down upon the town by way of the Guanajuato River channel that led through its center, inundating and smashing buildings, sweeping away thousands of Guanajuato's citizens. The river's course had since been diverted, but the local citizens seemed almost proud of their city's history of flood disasters. Many of the old buildings in the heart of the town had markers showing the height of the flood waters during the worst of the floods that had visited Guanajuato periodically ever since the gold-and-silver-hungry Spaniards had discovered a rich mother lode there more than four hundred years ago. Walking through the canyon city, Blanchard had too often been vividly reminded of that torrent of water plunging down the mountain....

And there were also the catacombs, he remembered. Elaine had shuddered over the tombs.

"I don't get it," he said. "Why do we have to chase around Mexico? Why can't arrangements be made right here?"

"I... I don't know." Angie looked anxious, as if she was afraid that he was going to balk at the arrangements Pepe had made with her.

"There really isn't much we can do but go along," he admitted reluctantly. "We don't have any physical evidence, no written threat or demand for a ransom, nothing we can take to the consul-general or the Mexican police. I guess whoever is behind this thought of that—planned it that way." What he was doing was thinking out loud, and when he got that far he found himself nodding agreement. "All right, when do we go?"

"In the morning. If you agreed to come, I was supposed to leave a message with the manager, that's all. When we leave."

"Then you'd better get some sleep."

"What about you? You can stay here if you don't mind that wet bed."

Blanchard walked slowly toward the door, thinking how close he had come to inviting another woman to share his room at the *posada* that night. Turning to smile at Angie, he said, "I'm an old man, Angie, but not that old. And you're much too attractive. Besides, I've registered at the *posada*, and I'll sleep better in my own room." That part of it was true, he thought, as it was true that she would sleep better without him there.

He checked the door lock and glanced out at the dark grounds of the Santa Inez, listening to the pounding of the rain. The situation now seemed clearer, but he didn't feel any easier about stepping out into that foreign and threatening darkness.

"You're going to get soaked," Angie said suddenly. "Don't you have a raincoat?"

"I forgot to bring it."

"Then take mine."

She retrieved a raincoat from a closet hook. It was too short and too small, its fitted belt hitting Blanchard around the lower rib cage instead of his waist, but he could wear it over his shoulders.

At the door, helping him to wrap the coat around his shoulders, Angie leaned forward and kissed him impulsively.

"What's that for?"

"Because I felt like it. That's what you're supposed to do—reach out and touch. That's what you and Michael weren't doing."

He thought about that. "Sometimes it isn't easy. I guess Elaine—Mike's mother—did it for both of us."

"I think Michael was wrong about you."

"How's that?"

"You *are* on our side."

Blanchard felt as if he had just won a gold medal. He looked through the open doorway, feeling the chill of the rain, not meeting her eyes and thus hiding the vulnerability in his own, because he couldn't be like her, he couldn't let it all hang out. He hadn't learned how.

He remembered what Charmian Stewart had said about learning Spanish. If you started when you were young enough, it became part of you. Otherwise it would never be. All you could do was work at it.

"Lock the door after me," he said. "Don't open it until you hear my voice."

This time there was no one waiting for him in his room at the Posada del Lago. He lay on the bed, closed his eyes, and tried to sleep. He was physically exhausted, his whole body as well as his head feeling as if it had been battered—a feeling unknown to nubile twenty-year-olds, he thought—but his mind roved restlessly over the events of the past two days, denying sleep. It kept coming back to an old sore: Darrell Kinney.

Blanchard had met Kinney at Burtonwood in 1943. That was Base Air Depot (BAD) No. 1, located near Warrington, England, which was about halfway between the port of Liverpool and the industrial city of Manchester. When Blanchard arrived there he had just won his corporal's stripes; Kinney was already a master sergeant. Blanchard was nineteen years old and he had just crossed the Atlantic in a convoy that lost two ships. He was green and patriotic and eager. Looking back, he could suppose that he amused Darrell Kinney, but for some reason Kinney chose to adopt him. Sometimes Blanchard wondered if they became friends because Kinney liked to use people and he was the perfect flunky.

Kinney had come from Detroit, Michigan, or, more specifically, from a well-to-do suburb, Grosse Pointe Park. When he talked about Detroit it wasn't about factories and goon squads and the Tigers, it was about the yacht club and how he starred as a halfback at Cranbrook, a posh school whose buildings had been designed by Saarinen, about iceboating on Lake St. Clair in the winter and sailing in the summer on the lake off the family's summer home near Petoskey. After the war Blanchard once took delivery on a new car at Dearborn, and he and Elaine drove it back across country to California. While they were in Detroit he looked up Kinney's name in the phone book, wondering if he ought to call his family and identify himself as someone who had once served with their son overseas in the Air Corps. He couldn't find any Kinneys listed for the address he had in Grosse Pointe. He decided it was just as well. Why stir up old grief?

Kinney was an expert poker player and a hard drinker, as popular with the men who served under him as with his superior officers. No one either noticed or cared that Sergeant Kinney never did any detail work and couldn't have been less concerned about such things as showing up for roll call. He used to drink Captain Callaway under the table, and somewhere he found a steady supply of the Cuban cigars the captain liked. Lieutenant Sands liked Kinney as well as anyone and in fact seemed a little in awe of him, for that Grosse Pointe background as much as Kinney's army expertise. Sands was a washed-out bombardier who was anxious to make good under Callaway, and Kinney made sure that everything ran smoothly and Sands looked good. Kinney might have been indifferent to routine himself, but he found people who were eager to do the work for him. Jeff Blanchard was one of them.

Kinney was about five feet ten, well built, handsome in a sleek, tanned, well-curried way like the actor Robert Stack, with that same ready grin that showed even, flawless teeth, and wavy black hair. Kinney was nearsighted and wore rimless gold glasses, tinted a pale blue because his eyes were sensitive to light. He would no more have anything to do with Army-issue spectacles than with regulation clothing. Even before he made warrant officer Kinney habitually wore custom-made officer's slacks he had had tailored before leaving the States, and he almost always wore a brown leather flight jacket, which wasn't issue for ground troops. And a crushed officer's cap.

He had a way with women—he treated them with a kind of humorous contempt that you would have thought would have made them angry but had the opposite effect. But all Kinney ever did was whore around, in his own words. He not only wasn't going to get tied up with any one woman, he didn't even keep one around long enough to start clinging. Kinney liked it best, Blanchard thought, when they went to France. There, when he and Creasey went into a town and enjoyed a free-for-all and an all-night drunk, it was easy to walk away. Kinney wouldn't even remember the names of the French girls he was with. He called them all Fifi.

Sometimes when they were still in England Kinney would even go on a twenty-four-hour pass with Jack Prescott, a test pilot permanently attached to BAD No. 1, a good-looking guy who was rumored to be "a queer." Sergeant Kinney was the only man in the outfit who could have gotten away with that without having elbows nudge and whispers start. Everyone knew that Kinney was only doing Prescott a favor, letting him look good, in exchange for a leather flight jacket or two.

The truth was that there probably wasn't anyone on the base who knew Kinney who wouldn't have been glad to be his drinking buddy—including Jeff Blanchard. When they were together in a bar drinking and talking Kinney never pulled rank and he was a good talker and listener. He was always asking Blanchard about California, and he'd talk about how he wasn't going back to Grosse Pointe because when he was being shipped to a base down in Tucson, Arizona, he'd gone through a little town in lower Nevada called Las Vegas, and he knew that big things were going to happen there and he wanted to be in on the action from the beginning, because there was a lot of money going into Las Vegas. Kinney didn't want to live a conventional life on his father's money, everything predictable and safe and getting dull by the time you were forty.

That streak of wildness was always there, Blanchard thought. It was always in Kinney's eyes, a kind of mocking recklessness. Blanchard had always believed that it got Kinney killed, that, grounded by the Air Corps because of his eyes, Kinney had probably been flying the cargo plane when it went down behind the German lines.

But he hadn't died, Blanchard thought. He had come out of that disaster smiling, as always.

Now he was in Mexico.

And now, deliberately, he had kidnapped Blanchard's son, or had him kidnapped, knowing that the action would bring Blanchard to Mexico.

Blanchard lay in the darkness, unable to sleep, trying to figure out why.

And trying to understand the mixture of anger and hatred and grief that threatened to tear him apart.

Interlude Two: Morelia

1

Of the half-dozen paintings hanging in Ernst von Schoenwald's study, only one was what it seemed to be—a sentimental scene of a village in the Bavarian Alps, dwarfed by towering, snow-clad mountains under an impossibly blue sky that was, in fact, precisely the way von Schoenwald remembered those shimmering skies from his youthful skiing expeditions. This painting had been the topmost one in the roll of canvases the German had brought with him across the Guatemalan border into Mexico. In the event that, in spite of his heavy bribe, a customs official might have become curious about the paintings and sought to inspect them, he would have found nothing of interest in the painting of the Alpine village. And the remaining paintings were of a similar nature, without value to anyone but a German nostalgic for his homeland.

As it happened, the paintings had aroused no curiosity. The canvases had not even been unrolled.

They hung now, in their hand-carved Mexican frames, in the same condition of innocence which had protected them during von Schoenwald's long odyssey to reach this final, unlikely destination. Only one was unmasked, an exquisite study of a boy with violin by Pissarro. He had often considered having the others restored for his personal pleasure, but always he had pulled up short of that risk, however slight. Looking at them, as he did now, he took an ironic pleasure in the knowledge that they remained a hidden treasure, concealed even when they were revealed. Even that was a rare occasion, for no one entered his study, not even George Robbins, without his invitation.

Like Browning's Duke, the German thought, glancing at María Teresa Calderón. *"None puts by the curtain I have drawn for you, but I."*

It had amused him to draw the curtain for her, escorting her for the first time into his study. It amused him even more to note that the single restored painting, priceless now, was the one the girl had passed over most quickly, disinterested. It was the others that had caused her to exclaim in delight.

"You like them?" the German asked.

"Oh, *sí*! Yes, yes, I like them very much. They are very...pretty. Is it not so?"

"Yes, very pretty."

"It must be such a pretty country to live in." María stared in appreciative wonder at a scene of a castle on the Rhine. Von Schoenwald wondered if it reminded her, as it did him, of the Disneyland castle over which she had exclaimed in amazement when she had seen it the night before on the television screen.

"It is ... very beautiful."

She turned to him, huge dark eyes curious. "Why did you leave?"

The question was absurdly innocent, and it caused von Schoenwald to laugh. "Mexico is also beautiful," he answered. "And in Mexico there is María Teresa."

The girl smiled, delighted as always with his amused compliments. She half turned her head in order to look up at him from the corners of her eyes, coquettishly.

Von Schoenwald, who was not ready to be diverted at the moment, looked away from her at the paintings on the mahogany paneled walls. She really thought they were pretty pictures, he thought. In a way, he supposed, they were like those Mexican paintings on velvet so popular with tourists and Mexicans alike, vivid colors on black backgrounds, portraits of dancing ladies, of bullfighters swirling their gaudy capes in the *verónica*, of the Last Supper or Christ's Bleeding Heart. Cheap sentiment and atrocious art.

Mexico and its people seemed suddenly young and naïve and innocent, as foolishly happy as María Teresa in her new-found life, and von Schoenwald felt a sense of displacement, of being lost, impossibly remote from the real world, his world of culture and sophistication and power.

Incredible that he had come here, hidden himself away here, lived more than a third of his life here, the best middle years when he should have been in that other world, exercising his brain and his ability to command, his capacity for inspiring loyalty and obedience. Incredible....

Suddenly he was impatient, almost angry. "Come. It is almost time for supper."

"But it is early." María, thinking that it must have been expected of her when she was ushered into this fine, private room, shrugged her shoulders, which were bare over the embroidered blouse the German had given her, in a provocative gesture. "There is time, no?"

"No," von Schoenwald said, with a harshness that caused the girl to feel a sudden panic, unsure what mistake she had made. "I will tell you when there is time."

At the study door he paused to look back. Incredible, he thought again. His gaze returned to the posterlike picture of the castle overlooking the Rhine, triggering memory of another castle, more somber and gray, hazy in the dimness of events more than a quarter of a century old.

As he slowly drew the door closed and followed María Teresa toward the dining room, he was thinking not of a girl's bare shoulders or a waiting feast, but of Darrell Kinney.

2

Ernst von Schoenwald had met Kinney in an abandoned castle near Strasbourg on the Rhine, in eastern France—only two miles from the German border. The time was the first week of March in 1945. He had been Colonel von Schoenwald then, an SS-Standartenführer and an expert in what Hitler called *schrecklichkeit*—methods of torture and terror. Kinney had been a warrant officer in the United States Army Air Corps, and he was in the company of an American sergeant named Carl Creasey.

All three men had dropped out of the war.

Von Schoenwald had begun making plans against impending disaster more than six months before, after it became certain that the invading Allied armies had broken out of their Normandy pocket. The interrogations in which he participated had made it clear to the SS officer that Germany could not survive the combined pressures of the forces on eastern and western fronts and the erratic leadership in Berlin. Even then there were organizations that hedged against the possibility of defeat, but von Schoenwald had felt the necessity to provide for himself in a potentially hostile and dangerous postwar world.

He had "liberated" a cache of priceless French Impressionist paintings from a bank vault in the Östmark, as Austria was then called. The paintings were part of the collection of a wealthy Jewish baron. Von Schoenwald, who had a good knowledge of art, had hit upon the idea of carrying his treasure with him openly. He had prevailed upon a young, unknown, but talented Jewish artist—promising relief from imprisonment in a concentration camp and certain death—to create for him a series of sentimental, conventionally German paintings, scenes of the Rhine and its castles, of the Black Forest, of an Alpine village and hunting lodge, of an open-air café in Heidelberg. As his canvases the artist had used the Impressionist masterpieces themselves, which included works by Manet and Pissarro, taking pains, of course, not to damage the originals. After all, von Schoenwald had reasoned, many great works of art had been painted over during the centuries, some of them later discovered and restored only by chance. With modern techniques and materials, surely the same could be done here without harm. The young Jewish artist had been both proud of his finished work and horrified by it, but he had carried out his assignment well.

Then von Schoenwald had had him killed.

When he was reassigned in the fall of 1944 to the Army Group of the Upper Rhine, where Himmler himself was in command from early December until mid-January, von Schoenwald, to the amusement of more than one less-sentimental fellow officer, transported the small collection of eleven paintings with him. He had them in his possession during his winter occupation of the castle on the French side of the Rhine near Strasbourg, the castle having been taken over by the SS. In January, when the Allied armies reached and crossed the Rhine, the castle was hastily abandoned. Von Schoenwald was forced to leave his innocent-looking collection behind, stored in a cellar of the castle.

There had been six weeks of anxiety and danger before he was able to return secretly—and at considerable personal risk, moving behind the advancing enemy lines—to the deserted headquarters. He had been lucky, aided by the confusion of the swiftly-moving events of those last weeks of the war. He had reached the castle safely and found it empty, his collection of sentimental German scenes untouched.

Four days after he hid out in the castle, Darrell Kinney and Carl Creasey had descended a flight of steps to the lower levels in search of a wine cellar. Von Schoenwald, trapped, unaware that they were not alone, had not dared to fire on them. Instead he had put down his pistol and stepped out into the open as Kinney and Creasey stared at him in astonishment.

"I'll be goddamned!" Kinney had exclaimed with a grin. "Take a look, Carl. Look what we've found."

Accepting the necessity of surrender, von Schoenwald had been prepared to gamble that his stolen treasure might go undetected. Seemingly there had been no choice. Then, to his chagrin, he had discovered too late that Kinney and Creasey were alone, not part of the larger search mission he had expected to appear behind them. In fact, they had no more desire for wasting their lives in combat than he had.

During the days that followed in the castle, still cursing himself for failing to kill the two Americans when he had had the chance, Ernst von Schoenwald conceived and discarded a dozen plans to escape or to attack his captors. For all their reckless good humor, however, they gave him no opportunity. They seemed amused by their catch, spending long hours joking in von Schoenwald's presence over what kind of medals they might be awarded when they turned up with an SS colonel as their prisoner.

Meanwhile von Schoenwald had shown them a well-stocked wine cellar and food stores. The two Americans were in no hurry to leave.

Von Schoenwald's command of English, though stilted and heavily accented when he spoke it, was precise and fluent, and he spent those days learning to understand his captors. Slowly he began to consider the possibility of another way out of his predicament. He recognized something of himself in Darrell Kinney, an opportunist with a predilection for indulging his own needs and desires over those of others, a completely amoral man who cared nothing for abstract concepts of patriotism or duty—and therefore, von Schoenwald guessed, a vulnerable man.

Creasey was less predictable, in his way more dangerous, but Kinney was the leader of the two. He was the one von Schoenwald had to win over.

He bided his time. One night, while they were drinking amiably together, Creasey having passed out in an adjoining room, von Schoenwald broached the possibility of being allowed to escape, in return for a share of his still unrevealed treasure. Kinney's skepticism was gradually replaced by a bright-eyed eagerness. Behind his tinted glasses von Schoenwald read greed and duplicity. Kinney could not be trusted—but he could be tempted and used. And von Schoenwald believed that he himself was far more ruthless and treacherous than the American.

They talked through most of the night. In the end their discussion became a simple bargaining session. Kinney wanted more than a small share of von Schoenwald's hidden fortune, whatever it was. He wanted a full partnership. In return he would do more than help von Schoenwald to escape to Switzerland. Kinney would go with him.

The next day they talked it over with Carl Creasey. The stocky sergeant was in a surly mood. He didn't trust the SS officer, and he remained suspicious of his claim of a hidden treasure. Where was it? They had combed the castle thoroughly.

"Use your head, Sarge," Kinney argued. "What's he doing here anyway if he's not telling the truth? Why would he stick his neck out coming back here alone if he didn't have a real stake in it?"

"Okay, let him trot out his treasure."

Kinney turned to the German with an easy smile. "Maybe old Carl's got a point there. You could be lying. Why not show us a sample? That's not too much to ask."

Von Schoenwald shook his head. "You'll have to take my word for it."

"The hell you say!" Creasey retorted. "Listen, I don't trust this Nazi son of a bitch, not for a minute. And I'm not gambling on his word as an officer and a fucking gentleman. We go along with this and get caught, we'll have our asses in a sling."

"But if he's telling the truth," Kinney said softly, staring at the German, that oddly magnified stare produced by his glasses, "we're set for life. Think about it, Carl. We never have to take any shit from anybody for as long as we live. We've got it made."

"No!" Creasey exploded. "I don't buy it. He's tryin' to pull something. Once we got him out of here, we'd never be able to turn our backs on him."

"How about that, Ernie?" Kinney asked.

At that moment he was holding von Schoenwald's Luger, which the German had surrendered when they met. He pointed it idly across the room at the SS officer. "Maybe we should try pulling out a few toenails or some of that other stuff you know all about. That's what you SS boys do, isn't it? Toenails and lighted cigarettes against the nipples and a few kicks in the balls. Hell, we've seen enough movies to know what to do. Right, Carl?"

"Yeah," Creasey said, relaxing as his point was won. "Give me a couple hours with him and I'll find out if there's any goddamn treasure and where it is. But I'm bettin' it's a stall."

Kinney nodded. "But if it's not, Carl. That's the thing I keep coming back to."

"You'll learn nothing from me," von Schoenwald said coldly, sensing that he had lost his gamble. He was disappointed, as much in his poor judgment of Kinney as in the failure; the risk was one that he had had to take, sooner or later.

"We'll see about that." Creasey took a step toward von Schoenwald.

The movement brought him in front of the window in the library where they were talking, and a step beyond Darrell Kinney. Kinney turned toward him casually, still balancing the Luger lightly in his hand. Its muzzle tipped toward Creasey.

Without warning he fired at Creasey's head from a distance of less than three feet. Blood and bits of skull bone and flesh sprayed against the panes of the leaded glass window and began to drip down the glass in a grisly trickle. Ernst von Schoenwald froze in a half-crouch, heart pounding, his ears clotted from the gun's explosion in that confined space, his sudden frantic movement out of his chair stopped when he realized what Kinney had done.

Smiling, Darrell Kinney faced him. "Now how about it, Ernie? What the hell is this hidden treasure you've been talking about?"

Both men understood that they needed each other. It was only after Kinney had accepted this and agreed to let von Schoenwald carry his own gun that the German learned about the C-47 Kinney had force-landed on an abandoned airstrip nearby.

They ran the damaged plane off the field into a

wooded canyon, where one of the wings was ripped off as the craft trundled down the slope and crashed among the trees. It came to rest at an ungainly tilt. They placed Carl Creasey's body inside and blew up the plane.

Two weeks later, on foot, two men in American army uniforms crossed the Swiss border and disappeared.

3

For supper there was *huachinango,* freshly caught in the Gulf of Mexico and flown to Morelia that morning, as the German explained to María Teresa Calderón in his stilted but grammatically precise Spanish, a style of language that reminded the girl of her grandfather, the father of her mother. The girl wolfed down her portion, scraping her plate with the fork until she saw him watching her with a smile. Then she ate more slowly and carefully, glancing up at von Schoenwald anxiously now and then to see if he was watching.

Lupe came around again with the platter of fish, and von Schoenwald said, *"Es magnífico, Lupe."*

"Gracias, Señor."

"Qué te parece, María?"

"Pues sí... muy rico. Is very good!" she stammered in English.

He smiled again. She believed that he was pleased with her today, although his moods were not predictable and she had already experienced the terror of his anger as well as the pleasures of his tolerant indulgence.

"Más champaña, querida?"

She held out her glass eagerly, for she had quickly discovered a delight in the sparkling wine von Schoenwald preferred with his meals.

"Gracias. Es muy buena."

Lupe had turned toward the kitchen, and María spoke suddenly, sharply, her tone unconsciously mimicking von Schoenwald's imperious manner in addressing his staff of servants. "I would like more fish." Lupe had not offered the platter to her.

Lupe turned to stare at her. She seemed to hesitate. María read disapproval in that brief pause, but she stared back defiantly. Then Lupe came in silence to her side and María triumphantly scraped another serving of the delicious red snapper onto her plate. Only when Lupe had gone and she had sampled another bite of fish did she admit to herself that she didn't really want it. She was not hungry.

She regarded the fact with some surprise. There had been few times in her life when she had not been hungry. In the first days of her coming to the big house in the hills of Santa María she would not have believed it possible that she would ever have enough of the wonders opened out to her.

Not all had been pleasure. From the beginning she had regarded von Schoenwald with a mixture of terror and stunned admiration. Although he seemed older than her father—at times much older—he had the body and vigor of a young man, muscular and handsome and very powerful. At first he had caused her unbelievable pain, he was so large and strong and ruthless in his passion, but in the end he had aroused in her piercing sensations of pleasure. In spite of her childish wisdom of the streets, she had found the whole experience quite astonishing.

In her confusion of emotions she had cried herself to sleep that first night, alone in the huge bedroom to which the German had banished her when he was satiated. She felt lost and afraid. She longed for the closeness of other bodies in her bed—she had always slept in the same room with her three brothers and two sisters, a tiny room almost filled by two mattresses wedged together at right angles—for the sounds of movement and breathing, of snores and whispers and giggles.

Those feelings had quickly dimmed. The succeeding days had brought new wonders, and fewer moments of pain and terror. The German, she realized vaguely, had been patient and at times even gentle with her—and always generous. She had been given new clothes and perfumes, jewelry and trinkets—it seemed that all she had to do was wish for anything and it was hers. She had come to enjoy the sanctuary of her own huge bedroom, where she spent hours before the mirrors, trying on her new clothes over and over. She dined daily on foods both strange and familiar, all superbly prepared and served in the elegance of the dining room, with María facing the German across the table as she did now, as mistress of the household. She was even beginning to accept the daily bath, taken in a huge tub with flowers floating on the surface of the water, while von Schoenwald sat nearby, watching her.

In recent days, María realized, she had hardly thought of her family at all. Already they seemed far away, in another world. How she would have loved to describe her new life to all of them, to see the envy in the eyes of Dolores, her older sister, and the skeptical wonder in her brothers' faces!

A sudden feeling of longing swept over her, a sense of being lost in a strange dream, unable to escape from the dream back to reality. Then the champagne tickled her nose as she sipped at it, and she giggled.

She had no desire to go back. The dream was real. She would make the German happy—already she was finding new ways to please him in his bed. There would be no morning wakening to the cold, grubby house where she had spent most of her fourteen years, to the dirt floors and the leaking tile roof and the pangs of hunger.

A new vision had begun to take shape, in which she saw herself assuming a permanent role as mistress of the German's great house. Jesús and Lupe—she did not regret taking the extra fish even if she wasn't hungry—would learn to regard her as special and important, someone to be attended eagerly and obsequiously. She would show them how to treat her!

María Teresa Calderón drew herself up in her chair, holding her glass of champagne in a tiny hand, and smiled brightly across the table at Ernst von Schoenwald. "You will love me always?" she asked. There was no anxiety in the question. She knew that it must be true.

The German smiled, but his manner did not reveal his reaction to the incredible naïvete of the question. "*Siempre, querida,*" he murmured. "Like the dove of your song."

4

The call from Robbins came shortly after supper. The connection was poor, with intermittent static, and Robbins' voice came and went. Von Schoenwald listened with rising impatience.

"Do you wish me to come back when I have taken care of *el gordo*, the fat one?"

"No, you must follow the other. I want to know what this man Blanchard does."

"What about Kinney?"

"He must stay out of it now. Blanchard would recognize him even more quickly than his son did."

"I can..." The suggestion was lost in a burst of static. "It would be quick and easy."

"No," von Schoenwald said. He was not worried, not personally threatened, and he guessed the lethal character of Robbins' proposal without hearing it clearly. "Blanchard works for a Los Angeles newspaper, is that not so?"

"...what Kinney says."

"There would be too much of a furor. No one will pay attention to the son's disappearance, but the father would be different. No, he must be discouraged, even frightened, but that is all. For now."

"Whatever you say." There was a pause. "You are well? How is your little María?"

Von Schoenwald smiled at the phone, hearing the anxiety that Robbins did not dare express. "She is a child. But I am well enough." Deliberately he hesitated before he added, "I will be better when you return, my dear George. Let us get this other business over quickly, eh?"

Robbins' reply was lost in another burst of static.

3   Guanajuato

1

In the morning Jeff Blanchard discovered that Angie, having given most of her money to Pepe—nearly two thousand pesos, or a hundred and sixty dollars American—had had nothing to eat the previous day except for the free peanuts and taco chips in the lounge of the Posada del Lago. They had a delicious breakfast in the restaurant overlooking the lake, whose calm surface was like smoked glass under an overcast sky. Blanchard took pleasure in watching Angie eat with the uncomplicated enthusiasm of the young.

"It's clear you're not a vegetarian," he said at one point.

"I've thought about it. I mean, it's something you have to think about. Sometimes I go on diets like that, you know, like into organic foods, but I'm weak. I like to eat too much."

"It doesn't show." Middle-aged comment, he thought.

They drove into Guadalajara in the battered green Volkswagen Mike had bought before leaving California. It seemed to thrive better than most U.S. cars at the high altitudes and on the dirty gasolines of Mexico.

Blanchard picked up his luggage at the Campo Bello and inquired about the Señorita Stewart, telling himself that he only wished to thank her for her help. He was told that she had checked out earlier that morning. He didn't try to hide his disappointment from himself.

Maybe you'll run into her in Santa Monica sometime, he told himself, coming out of a shoe store on the mall. But he doubted it.

It was noon when they left Guadalajara behind. In spite of one long stretch of badly pitted highway, through which Angie drove with the nimble ease of a test driver on an obstacle course—like most VW drivers, Blanchard thought, wherever they were driving—the trip to Guanajuato was pleasant and easy. All afternoon Blanchard was aware of black storm clouds piling high above the mountains to the south and east, but they seemed to run away from most of the rain, enjoying spectacular bursts of sunshine and dazzling blue skies.

East of Silao on the Guanajuato road they ran into brief showers. They drove out of them into bright sunshine once more. The road dipped through a small gorge and rose among rocky hills dotted with occasional houses and abandoned ruins and churches. In the distance, crowning a rugged peak, a white statue glowed in the sun as if it were on fire. The Sanborn's guide in the car identified it as *El Cristo Rey*, a seventy-five-foot statue of Christ the King, standing on top of a peak considered to be the geographical center of Mexico. From that lofty prominence the statue overlooked the largest of the seven great valley basins that form the great Mexican central plateau. At the heart of this, the Bahio country, was Guanajuato.

They came upon the city suddenly, glittering in the rain-washed sunlight under a sky as blue as a

Madonna's cape. A toy city, almost unbelievably picturesque at the bottom of its deep gorge. To the east the mountains rose steeply. Blanchard had a glimpse of the road leading up toward the old hotel where he had stayed with Elaine, high above the city and opposite La Valenciana, the greatest of the silver mines that had made Guanajuato a famous name in the capitals of Europe long before any of the great cities of the United States had become nameless settlements.

Then, abruptly, they were swept into the subterranean expressway that races through Guanajuato along the sunken bed of what was once the Guanajuato River channel. Stone walls rose on either side of the winding one-way passage—the same ancient walls that had once contained the river. Blanchard had taken his turn at the wheel of the little car, and now he sped under the old stone arches and bridges, transported magically into a medieval village invaded by twentieth-century motor cars. So medieval European is Guanajuato in its atmosphere that the famous spring pageant of sixteenth-century plays and sketches is presented out-of-doors in the tiny plazas and on the steps of buildings, making the city itself an appropriate medieval setting for the dramas.

Blanchard looked up as he drove under one of the ancient bridges and saw Darrell Kinney leaning over the parapet, staring down at him.

He almost lost control of the car. It was moving too fast, carried along in the stream of traffic entering the city, and he was unable to move over to the right in time to catch the next off ramp. Then he reached an open stretch from which there was no exit. He drove along in increasing frustration, cursing softly under his breath, for nearly a mile.

As suddenly as it had begun the sunken freeway ended. The VW swooped out of a tunnel onto a surface road.

At a well-groomed park Blanchard managed to swing around and start back. Angie was watching him, puzzled. "What's wrong?"

"I'm not sure. I thought I saw..."

He didn't name Kinney. He could have been mistaken, conjuring up an illusion from his imagined fears and expectations. It hardly seemed plausible that Kinney could have been waiting for them to arrive. Were they being that closely watched?

The subterranean thoroughfare carried only the traffic entering the city. Surface streets took Blanchard and Angie back through downtown Guanajuato. He was quickly lost in the twists and turns of the crowded center of the town. It soon became obvious that he had no chance of finding his way back to the particular stone bridge over which a man who looked like Darrell Kinney had been leaning, observing the flow of traffic into the town.

Blanchard found a place to park in a narrow side street. They made their way through a cramped warren of streets and steps and passageways that opened unexpectedly to pretty little parks and striking buildings, most of them old, most of them in the Spanish Colonial style. Guanajuato proved to be a town small enough for visitors to rediscover the pleasures of walking, but so crowded and winding that it was easy to get turned around.

"It's fantastic!" Angie cried in delight as they stood at the edge of the Jardín de la Unión, a tiny gem of a plaza. "It really is! Michael and I—" She broke off, guilt-stricken over her momentary pleasure.

"You'll come here again," Blanchard promised.

Just up the street was the famous Teatro Juárez, one of the most elaborately designed opera houses in Mexico. Looming over the city above the theater was an enormous statue, a monument more massive than beautiful to Pípila, the miner who became a hero during the battle for this city in Mexico's War of Independence. Staring up at it, Blanchard was conscious of the canyon walls pressing down upon him, reminding him of the claustrophobic feeling he had had on his last visit there.

He spent an hour familiarizing himself with the town, giving particular attention to the busy market where they were supposed to wait to be contacted the next day. Then he walked Angie back to the car.

He booked two rooms at a small motel opposite one of the pretty parks south of the downtown area. It had comfortable units built around an inviting patio where they had dinner and the delicious Carta Blanca beer.

Blanchard asked Angie if she wanted to walk back through the town in the evening, but she declined. Her mood had changed, the temporary pleasure and curiosity of the tourist giving way to depression as the awareness bore upon her that she should have been walking the romantic, lantern-lit streets of this old city with her Michael, not with his father.

After Angie retired to her room, Blanchard sat outside in the patio alone, smoking, trying out some of the two-peso pipe tobacco he had picked up while wandering through downtown Guanajuato. The canyon widened out slightly at this part of the city, but he was aware of the presence further up this end of the gorge of the two dams that, some sixty-seven years ago, had burst without warning, releasing a murderous avalanche of water. Even though a great tunnel had since been dug to carry away the overflow from the rebuilt dams, it struck Blanchard that he would never be able to rest easy in their shadow.

Or maybe it was the other threat hanging over him that caused the thicker darkness of the canyon to seem oppressive. He knew so little. He was fumbling blindly toward something he could not yet see or fully comprehend, and somewhere in that murky puzzle his son was a helpless pawn.

Or so he had been led to believe. There was really no solid proof of what had happened to Mike—or that he was still alive.

And there was something naggingly wrong about

the summons that had brought Blanchard here with Angie. He had the irrational conviction that his search had only begun, that someone—Darrell Kinney or someone else he didn't know at all—was manipulating him, leading him toward an unknown goal, a dangerous confrontation he could not yet even imagine.

2

Guanajuato has only one main street, paralleled by a few twisting, tortuous tributaries. The connecting roads and corridors are sometimes paths no more than shoulder-width across, and some are not streets at all but a series of steps leading to another level. So steeply do these steps rise at some places that the balcony of one home may overlook the tiled roof of its immediate neighbor. And so narrow are some of the streets that it is said that a lover, leaning out from his balcony toward his beloved in hers, may sometimes find her close enough for their lips to meet.

The crowded market where Pepe's brief instructions to Angie had directed them to go shared the stepped character of the city. It spilled up and down steps to different levels that carried the market from one street to another. Lively and colorful, like most Mexican markets, it was a confusing melange of tiny stalls and tables and sidewalk displays, featuring fruits and beans, fish and fried pork, leather goods, lacquerware, native crafts, and some familiar tourist souvenirs. Some were less familiar. The fame of its catacombs has made Guanajuato a city so devoted to death that candy and iced cookies in the form of white human skulls are among its most popular wares. The same death's heads are featured in everything from key rings to pottery ashtrays.

Paradoxically its fine university makes Guanajuato also a city of youth. The streets and the market seemed overrun with the hordes of students offering their services as guides to the museum or the tombs or the pink *plateresco* church on the hill. The young men crowded grinning around Angie and followed her through the noisy confusion of the market. Whether from the brightness of the morning or a night's rest or the infectious enthusiasm of the admiring students, Angie's depression of the night before had lifted somewhat. Once Blanchard was pleased to hear her laugh outright at a particularly outrageous pantomime of devotion on the part of a slender, dark-eyed young man.

The morning passed. Blanchard and Angie lingered, looked around, drifted on. A woman knelt before her spread-out blanket, carefully arranging on it her small limes in neat little piles of six or seven, offered for a peso but available for less with polite bargaining. Another woman set out a half-dozen different kinds of beans in separate bins. An old man shuffled toward them, bearing his day's offering of huge, colorful paper flowers. Another held out his hand-made serapes, smiling eagerly, lowering his price as they moved on.

No sign of Pepe.

Nor of Darrell Kinney.

Blanchard's senses began to ache, overwhelmed by the noise, the jostling, the vivid colors of the market. His nerves were stretched taut by the tension of waiting, looking, wondering.

They had coffee at a tiny counter. A small, dark boy wanted to shine Blanchard's shoes. He shook his head. Another boy thrust a box toward him. "No," Blanchard said firmly. "*Gracias*, but no."

The boy pushed it at him again, looking up with huge black eyes and grinning broadly. Mexico's wealth was her children, Blanchard thought.

"*Sí*," the boy insisted. "It is for you, señor."

There was something familiar about it, but Mexico is full of old beggars and young children, offering trained birds that do not fly away because they have been filled with buckshot or live crickets in tiny cages or nameless treasures in shoeboxes with airholes punched into the sides.

"No," Blanchard said again.

Angie was smiling gently down at the ragged boy. "What is it?" she asked.

"I don't know. He seems to think I ought to have it. You see them standing along the roads all through the desert to the north with boxes like that or homemade cages. It's probably a lizard."

"As long as it's not a snake."

Suddenly the boy thrust the cardboard box at Blanchard. Instinctively he seized it to keep it from dropping to the cobblestones. "Hey, I told you—!"

The boy was gone, racing away through the crowded lines of stalls, leaping up some steps, disappearing almost at once. You'll never be able to pick him out, Blanchard thought with a grimace. There were a hundred boys exactly like him within shouting distance, all as poor and thin and dark.

"He didn't even ask for his peso," Blanchard said, caught between amusement and annoyance. He had no need for a pet lizard right now.

"Maybe you'd better look inside."

The box was light, but heavier than an empty shoebox would be. There was something in it, but there was no sound or feel of anything scurrying or squirming around inside.

Blanchard moved out of the stream of tourists and shoppers and beggars, finding breathing space between two stalls against a whitewashed wall that bore the familiar name of the president painted across its length. Blanchard didn't know how much else Echeverría had done for the economy of Mexico, but he had certainly provided work for its sign painters.

The shoebox was tied with ordinary string. Unable to break it easily, Blanchard slipped the string off one end and slid the center knot downward until it came free.

112

While Angie peered past his shoulder, he lifted the lid.

She gave a whimpering gasp that turned into a stifled scream.

Lying inside the box was a desert lizard about ten inches long, normally more fierce in appearance than in fact. This one would never harm anything.

Its head had been severed cleanly. On the protruding stump of its neck had been jammed a ring, engraved gold with a ruby set into it, the stone bearing an old-fashioned crest.

It was Mike's high-school graduation ring.

3

The second "message," like the first, was delivered so innocently and naturally that Jeff Blanchard was slow to grasp its meaning.

Angie had been physically and emotionally sickened by the sight of Mike's ring on the headless lizard. When she was unable to return to the market, Blanchard left her in her room and drove back through the city alone. After his initial shock he was more angered than shaken by the incident. The bizarre proof that Mike was indeed a captive had been pointlessly grotesque—or was that demonstration merely the first salvo in a psychological war of nerves?

It had given him hard evidence that he could take to the U.S. Consul or to the Mexican police. He had debated that move with Angie after returning to the motel. She had argued emotionally against it. The message of the ring had done its work with her; she was afraid of what might happen to Mike if they went to the authorities. Pepe had specifically warned her against any such move.

"They always say that, but they can hardly expect us to do nothing."

In the end Blanchard agreed to wait, more because he was convinced that the authorities would be unable to do anything than through any fear of a reprisal. The Mexican police were at best unpredictable, and U.S. officials in Mexico were severely limited by the lack of any real power or influence over foreign nationals.

He reached the market around four in the afternoon, when activity normally returned after the lull of the siesta. There were few tourists this afternoon because the weather had abruptly changed once more, the blue sky overrun by low clouds tumbling swiftly before strong winds, the lower level torn into ragged streamers, the higher clouds swollen and black with rain. Blanchard wandered back and forth through the market, pretending to inspect different wares. After a while the sellers in the stalls began to ignore him.

Except for the old woman in the *panedería* on the upper level. Each time he came near she stepped out to show him her display of *pan dulce*. Late in the day Blanchard finally stopped and bought an assortment of the sweet breads, thinking that Angie might at least eat one or two of them with coffee after refusing lunch. The assorted rolls were handed to him in a paper sack which he carried around with him.

The rain arrived around six o'clock, a violent cloudburst.

Blanchard stood under an awning while the stream of tourists thinned to a trickle and the more disheartened of the artisans and farmers and merchants rolled up their blankets or closed their stalls and left. Blanchard felt very conspicuous standing there on a deserted landing in the gathering gloom, a crazy *gringo* who was not even wearing a raincoat (he ought to buy a poncho, he thought), holding his little paper sack of *pan dulce*.

He was as conspicuous as he wanted to be, but no one approached him, not even a shoeshine boy or a student guide.

At last he gave up. He had to run the best part of a normal city block to the parked Volkswagen. By the time he reached it in heavy rain he was no longer hurrying. Wet clothes and shoes were beginning to feel natural, he thought glumly.

Angie was waiting anxiously at the motel, looking pale, self-critical over her weakness. Blanchard shook his head in response to her unspoken question. No news.

He offered her a sweet roll. She nodded. "I don't think I want any dinner."

"Should I have a couple of beers sent over?"

"No, you have one. Do you suppose they have any of that manzanilla tea? It's supposed to settle your stomach."

"If they don't, I'll go find some."

He opened the paper sack, which had been soaked during his run, and displayed the *pan dulce* as a kind of offering to tempt her appetite.

On top were two cookies with white icing. The eyes of each death's head and the grinning mouth were black. Blanchard stared at them, frowning.

"I guess they're a bonus," he said after a pause.

"You didn't ask for them?"

"No."

Angie came over to him and picked up one of the grinning masks. "You bought the others at the market?"

"That's right."

"Did you notice anything about...whoever sold them to you?"

Blanchard began to see what was in her mind. "She kept trying to get me to buy," he said slowly. "All afternoon."

"Maybe this is a message too...like the ring."

"What kind of a message? My God, Angie, you're not saying that you think Mike is—"

"No, no!" she said quickly. "Don't you see? They're telling us where to go!"

"I don't..." But the meaning was suddenly clear.

115

"All those skulls refer to the same thing," Angie said. "You know, we've seen them everywhere in all the shops, skulls of one kind or another. They all have to do with the mummies in the old cemetery."

4

Jesús José María Ramírez y González paused at the top of the steep, narrow spiral staircase at the center of the *panteón*. The stairs led to the catacombs some thirty feet below; they were illuminated by pale, ghostly lights set into the wall in niches once used for candles. Pepe, for this was the familiar name by which he was called, glanced once more around the old cemetery, surrounded by its high wall of crypts. Even as he scoffed at his unease he made the sign of the cross swiftly, a flick of his fingers from his forehead to his ample chest to his shoulders in turn.

He was not a religious man, nor ordinarily superstitious, but the gesture at that moment was fervent and almost devout. So it was with his brother Ángel, who aspired to be a professional baseball player skilled enough to one day go north to *los Estados Unidos* where he would win fame and fortune, perhaps as a shortstop for Los Angeles Dodgers. Ángel, who currently played that position for his team from Hermosillo, always stopped for a moment, head down and eyes earnestly closed, when he prepared to step into the batter's box to face the opposing pitcher. In that moment his flying fingers would trace the same traditional diamond pattern, ending with a kiss of the thumb. Ángel had been a lifelong thief, he had fathered countless children whose plump mothers he couldn't remember, he hadn't been in church since his first and only communion as a boy, but at such times of crisis his gesture was sincere, his prayer an act of faith. When one stepped up to hit, it was well to have any possible help one could find.

Thus Pepe glanced skyward, seeing the morning sun touch the eastern slopes of El Cerro del Cubilete with gold, before he descended into the chill, sunless depths of the catacombs. His mother's wisdom in choosing how he would be called was now apparent, for he was able to ask for the intercession of the entire Holy Family to protect him from evil.

The caretaker was not in sight. That old one had no desire to descend into the corridors of the dead any more than was necessary—which meant infrequently. After all, he would joke, no one in his care was going to run away.

The *norteamericano* must have known that when he arranged this strange meeting place, Pepe thought, and when he chose a time early in the morning before the first visitation of tourists. That one with his duck's hands and his eyes like stones under water had been very careful not to be seen with Pepe.

Pepe's steps seemed loud on the stone stairway. His pace was not eager but suitably funereal.

The vaulted corridors below were silent, dusty, empty. Empty, that is, if one did not count the mummies lining the walls. Pepe did not look at them. He had no wish to inspect the well-preserved bodies of the dead, the shoes they had worn in life, the hairs still clinging miraculously to their scalps.

Why had the *gringo* chosen such a place? Pepe shrugged off a feeling of restlessness, almost of anger. There must be a good reason, which he would soon be told. Like the reason for the sending of the dead lizard with the young *norteamericano*'s ring. The young man's father, the one called Jeff Blanchard, had to be frightened first, made to know fear; then he would be more ready to pay.

He must be very rich, Pepe had decided, even though the man Blanchard had not looked or acted like Pepe's idea of a rich man. One could not always tell such things about the Americans from the north. The *gringo* who had hired Pepe, who hid his strange hands and spoke Spanish well, must know.

Footsteps. He was coming. Pepe moved along a dusty hall toward the foot of the steps, chilled, glad to end his lonely vigil among the dead.

But he was disappointed. The man descending the steps, pausing at their foot, was not the one Pepe waited for but evidently a tourist, a wiry little man with a monkey's face and peculiar red hair the color of an orange.

"*Buenos días!*" he said cheerfully with a quick smile. Trying out his terrible Spanish, Pepe thought with impatience, turning away.

Pepe's brain registered a vague warning but in his nervousness he paid no heed. The brain was truly a remarkable instrument; it missed nothing if one only paid attention. It told him now that he had seen this monkey-faced man before, but as quickly it also knew that this was not unusual. Suspicions were lulled by the familiar. The *turistas* from the north were always turning up in the same places, making the same rounds. You would see them in the glass and pottery factories in Tlaquepaque, buying souvenirs at Las Artesanías in Agua Azul Park or at the Mercado Libertad, staring at the murals by Orozco in the nearby Orphanage, eating at Focolare or La Copa de Leche or Cazadores Américas, staying at the Campo Bello or the Holiday Inn or the Posada del Lago in Ajijic. And when they left Guadalajara it was of course to visit the markets in Patzcuaro or Toluca or the tombs of Guanajuato. Always the same places, so that it was not at all unusual to see the same eager faces wherever you went, to hear the same nasal voices struggling badly with the same Spanish phrases.

The red-haired man was speaking to him now in English. "Are you the guide? Perhaps you can tell me about..."

But Pepe shook his head, turning away impatiently from this nuisance of a stranger. Perhaps the one he waited for had not come down into the tombs because he knew that Pepe was not alone. Pepe wished that the redheaded one would complete his sightseeing and leave soon.

And in his impatience Pepe ignored the second warning his brain tried to give him. It was too early in the day for any of the regular tours, very early for anyone to be visiting the *panteón*.

But here too the *norteamericanos* were unpredictable. They wandered everywhere, poking their noses wherever they wished without apology. This one was a teacher, he was saying now, insisting on following Pepe and speaking to him. Professors were naturally curious men; they liked to explore whatever they found interesting or unusual; they always asked a great many questions, as this man wanted to.

He could have entered the tombs as Pepe did. There was no one around to stop him. Or if the old caretaker had appeared, the *gringo* would have had only to put his hand to his wallet, as he had when asking Pepe if he was a guide.

The redheaded man was a great admirer of Mexico, he said. He thought that it was a wonderful country filled with simple people who were always happy, always laughing. It was a land of sunshine and laughter, he said. He did not know anything, Pepe thought. For a professor he talked like a fool.

The teacher said that he was soon going to retire and that he planned to return to live in Mexico. Pepe could not understand everything the man said, he missed many words, but the sense of it was clear. Pepe's command of English, especially his understanding of the spoken language, was far better than he generally let on. The redheaded man had a fine house in Ohio, he said, which he would sell. He would also have his pension. There would be enough for him to live well in Mexico, to enjoy the fruits of his work during his last years.

This Pepe understood very well. The man was

talking about money, about dollars. Yankee dollars. That's what it was all about, Pepe thought, using the phrase he had picked up from the young American girls in Ajijic. Yankee dollars had brought Pepe here to these dusty catacombs, among the dead where he had no desire to be, waiting for the other *norteamericano* to come with money to pay Pepe for his clever work in Ajijic and to give him new instructions.

Yankee dollars had become the story of Pepe's life. It was for this that he danced and laughed and made love to the skinny and frightened ladies from the north, with their pale skin and paler passions, the older ones girdled by their fears and inhibitions, the younger ones pretending to be old and wise and daring.

The adventure in which Pepe now found himself would end all that. The man Blanchard would pay handsomely to have his son returned to him safely. Pepe would have more dollars than he had ever seen before, enough to forget about the bony ladies at the Posada del Lago. It had been promised. Even the advance payment had been generous.

He and Chelita would be able to go away together. She was another kind of armful, brown as a berry, plump and passionate and laughing-eyed. Chelita was married, of course, to that fool Hernández, who was only half a man and could never make such a woman happy. Until now Pepe and Chelita had always had to meet in secret, and that was often difficult when Pepe was so busy making a living. But when Blanchard had paid to see his son alive, and Pepe had received his share of the money, there would be dollars enough for him to take Chelita far away, perhaps enough to buy a small café or other business of their own somewhere in the north, where there were many *gringo* tourists and where Hernández would never find them.

The smiling, talkative redheaded professor had completed his inspection of the main hall where the standing mummies looked down from their niches in the walls. His casual tour had brought him unexpectedly close to where Pepe was standing, waiting, glancing frequently toward the stairway and listening for footsteps.

The professor smiled at him. He was such a skinny little man that Pepe had found no reason to be concerned about him, certainly no reason to fear him, but now he felt a clear unease. The earlier, unheeded warnings sounded again, sharpened into alarm. What was the redheaded man doing here in the tombs at this hour? Where had Pepe seen him before? Why was he talking so much?

"You should have been paying more attention," the stranger said lightly.

His right hand shot out like the strike of a snake, the fingers splayed out and rigid. Twin hammer blows exploded against Pepe's eyes. The fat man bellowed in agony. He lunged at the smaller man in blind rage. His powerful arms clutched only air.

To his right, close by, the redheaded man chuckled softly.

Pepe charged at the sound, groping frantically. Missing, he blundered into the stone wall. His eyes were on fire, red with blood.

In that moment of pain and terror Pepe Ramírez knew that he had been duped. He did not understand. He had done all that was asked of him, everything, he had done it well—there was no reason to punish him!

But there was one. In that last moment, turning, sightless, to face his tormentor, Pepe saw the reason clearly, terribly, the reason of the headless lizard, and he cried out once more: "*Jesucristo!*"

Then the gun crushed the dusty silence of the tombs, so close that it deafened him, so close that his last sensation of life was the searing sting of the gunpowder against his cheek.

5

"You don't have to go down there," Jeff Blanchard told Angie.

"I'm not a baby. Yesterday was...it just happened. It won't happen again."

"You sure?"

The girl nodded emphatically. Blanchard remained dubious. After the grisly message in the shoebox, a tour of Guanajuato's ancient cemetery with its underground catacombs seemed hardly the right prescription for settling the nerves.

Blanchard had never been able to comprehend the appeal of ghoulish sideshows or *memento mori*. The fascination of catching a glimpse into an ancient civilization was something quite different, but part of the supposed appeal of Guanajuato's tombs was the fact that many of the mummies were recently deceased. The old cemetery had long been full. Every time someone in the city died and was buried there, another body had to be dug up to make room for the new one. Space in the ground or in the wall of crypts surrounding the cemetery was purchased for five years—only the wealthy could afford to renew the interval. When the bodies were dug up or removed from the crypts at the end of their term, the bones were removed to a common grave in the mountains—except for those that were especially well preserved, earning a place of display among the mummies in the catacombs below the old graveyard.

Kinney, or whoever was leading him on this chase, had a macabre sense of humor, Blanchard thought that morning enroute to the *panteón* with Angie. Or he was elaborating a deliberate, well-orchestrated plan to work on Blanchard's nerves, softening him up for the demands to come.

There had to be demands, he thought.

This was a Friday morning, the end of September, an off season for tourists. There were no guides hanging around outside the walls or within the cemetery when Angie parked the Volkswagen nearby and they walked slowly toward the entrance. A caretaker appeared out of nowhere, like a very physical ghost materializing. He was a bent old man with rheumy eyes, the dirt of ages hardened in the leathery seams of his neck, and an arthritic hobble. He pointed out the crypts in the fifteen-foot-high walls around the *panteón*, remindful of the Roman catacombs, but he showed no inclination to descend into the chill of the underground tombs. Blanchard tipped him and he limped away.

Just then a tour bus pulled up outside, backfiring noisily. A brisk little man in spectacles motherhenned his charges, a dozen or so American tourists, with furious little pecks of sound through the entrance and along the path toward the top of the spiral staircase where Blanchard and Angie had paused. "No, no, no, this way, yes, yes, all together, we do not wish to lose anyone down there, ha, ha!" He seemed surprised to find Blanchard and Angie by the stairs, acting as if he might have mislaid them.

Blanchard thought the tour group a little too animated by the thrill of descending into the gloomy caverns below; nevertheless, he was glad to have them along, for Angie's sake if not his own.

It occurred to him that the bearded professor's arrival had been lucky. If someone was supposed to contact him in the catacombs, a tour group offered perfect cover. He could watch Blanchard and Angie unobserved, waiting for the right moment.

Right for what?

Blanchard had no answer for that.

The professor, familiar with the catacombs, led the way down the steep spiral of steps. The voices and giggling laughter of the tourists echoed hollowly along the staircase and through the stone corridors below. As she passed under a light Blanchard saw gooseflesh on Angie's arms. She hugged herself, shivering.

While the little tour guide's charges whispered and tittered as he delivered a short lecture in comic English, Blanchard edged past them into the vaulted chamber. It seemed to extend for a couple of hundred feet, Blanchard saw with surprise. And along the walls were the standing mummies that had made these tombs a special tourist attraction. He heard the professor behind him explaining that the very dry air of the region accounted for the phenomenon of the *momias*. Remembering how he had been drenched in the late afternoon storm the previous day, Blanchard concluded that he had run into another spell of "unusual weather this year."

But the air in the chamber was dry. Dust glinted like drifting gold around the lights, which revealed the rows of mummified bodies standing in niches cut into the walls. He walked slowly along the corridor, pretending to view the ghoulish display, listening to the tour guide's anxious pecking and the murmurs of the tourists, who were unconsciously whispering in the presence of the dead bodies.

Nothing happened. Blanchard found himself wishing he had questioned the clue of the iced cookies more critically. They might simply have been a gift with his purchase of the *pan dulce*, a souvenir and nothing else.

"Oh, my God!"

Blanchard heard Angie's whisper of horror as her fingers clutched his sleeve. She was staring at one of the bodies set into the section of wall toward which they were moving. He followed her stare.

The dead man glared back at them with eyes of blood. He was neither old nor thin nor shrunken.

"Look!" a man cried. "Jesus God, look at that!"

Nearby a woman screamed. The shrill terror of that cry sliced along Blanchard's nerves like screeching chalk. It seemed to gather strength and volume as it shivered through the dusty chamber. Suddenly there was a babble of shouts and cries all around as shock slid quickly into anger or panic. The anger turned against the bearded professor, as if he were personally responsible for this outrage. It wasn't on the tour's itinerary at all.

Angie had gone rigid, her whole body taut with the struggle for self-control. Blanchard held her arm tightly as he took a few steps closer to the niche in which the dead man had been propped up. Then he stopped abruptly, repressing a shudder. He did not need to move any nearer to recognize Pepe's full belly and tight pants, the round face no longer smiling, the black eyes now pools of red, open in an awful, sightless stare.

The head was turned slightly inward, as if Pepe were avoiding the accusation of the hysterical woman whose husband was trying to break through her screams. There was a small black hole in Pepe's temple about two inches behind his left eye.

Blanchard knew that the exit hole on the opposite side of his skull would not be as neat and small.

6

Charmian Stewart was staying at a small motel on spacious, attractive grounds a few miles from the center of Patzcuaro. Her smile and command of Spanish had obtained her a single unit for seventy-five pesos, or six dollars American. It was the right half of a duplex but the thick adobe walls provided ample privacy. The unit also had a fireplace and a supply of damp, green wood. After being caught in the rain while exploring the islands of Lake Patzcuaro on her first afternoon there, she had spent more than an hour in an exasperating struggle before she finally got a fire going in that fireplace. It had been more than welcome. Even without the rain, the nights could be sharply cold above seven thousand feet at this time of year. Add the chill from wet clothes and damp walls and some kind of heat was essential to the survival of a pampered *norteamericana*, used to her central heating and her mild seaside climate.

She spent Thursday morning puttering through the many gift and craft shops in the area. Near the larger park in the center of the village she discovered the House of the Eleven Patios, a network of small shops under one sprawling roof, each of them featuring a different craft native to the state of Michoacán and to the Indians of the district. Many of the artisans were at work in the little shops creating the elegantly lacquered trays and tables, the green pottery, the hemp and wool rugs, the serapes and embroidered dresses, and the beautifully hand-carved Tarascán tables and chairs. Charmian had looked at far more than she could afford to buy or had room to carry—remembering that she would be accumulating things as she went, for as long as she elected to stay in Mexico during this year of freedom. She was unable to resist one small round Tarascán table, a lacquered tray that was one of the special crafts of this area and therefore an ideal memento of her visit, and a small green-and-black pottery vase that she regarded as a prize (it had cost a little over a dollar after some bargaining).

You ought to go into business, she thought without conviction. You could stain and finish that ten-dollar table with its hand-carved fish and filigree border design, and sell it for four times what you paid.

But she knew that she never would. She wouldn't want to part with such a table after she had found it, picked it out, carried it all the way home and worked on it. She had a way of making objects her own, of possessing them in a very personal way.

She wondered if she had been too much like that with Tom Redman.

No, she thought.

All she had been with Tom Redman was blind and foolish.

Charmian had decided that Thursday would be her last night in Patzcuaro, even though the village's Friday market was considered to be one of the most interesting in all of Mexico. She would have plenty of time to come back to Patzcuaro, perhaps later in the year when it was drier. It was so damp now, near the end of the long rainy season, that you had to walk carefully up the cobblestoned steps and inclines, for they were everywhere covered with slippery green moss or mold that made the footing treacherous. Meanwhile, she wanted to drive to San Miguel de Allende for the weekend. On her previous visits to that popular little town she had always managed to miss the Sunday house tour, for which selected local American residents opened their houses to visitors. All the guidebooks, even David Dodge's rather cynical one, said that this was a highlight that shouldn't be missed. Somehow she had always come to San Miguel at midweek and in the middle of a time crunch. This trip she had her schedule all worked out. She would spend no more than an hour at the market in the morning, then leave in time to reach San Miguel late in the day. That would leave her Saturday for browsing through the shops, and she would be there for the house tour, first in line, on Sunday.

This visit would also be a good time to check out the schedules and costs of the winter courses offered at the Instituto Allende.

So it was settled. Charmian was aware that she seemed to be keeping herself excessively occupied, on the move and busy with shopping and plans.

That way she didn't have the time to think about or worry about Jeff Blanchard and his missing son.

For her last night in Patzcuaro she had been looking forward to a very special treat, the *pescado blanco* caught only in this lake, a delicacy deservedly renowned through all Mexico.

There was supposed to be a running rivalry between the fishermen of Lake Chapala and those of

Lake Patzcuaro (and gourmet champions of the two lakes) over the relative excellence of the whitefish caught in each lake. Charmian had sampled both many times, and she would eagerly have volunteered as a judge in any contest. Except that she was totally biased. There was no question in her mind that the *pescado blanco* of Lake Patzcuaro was the best she had ever tasted anywhere. Thin, as light as powdered sugar, delicately flavored whether done in an egg batter or simply grilled, it was always a dining experience to remember.

And to anticipate.

It was dark when she drove into the village and turned along an unpaved, rain-pitted road toward the lake. Near the lakefront she found the modest little restaurant she had remembered.

There were checkered cloths on the tables, candles set in wine bottles, waiters made more friendly by the absence of many customers. Alas, no *mariachi* musicians, but a jukebox in one corner had several recordings of the Trio Los Panchos and one featuring the late Javier Solís. She selected a half-dozen records and went happily back to her table.

A moment later, while the seductively romantic voice of Solís filled the restaurant, Charmian glanced up from her musings to find a stranger standing by the table, smiling down at her.

"Your taste in music is impeccable," he said. "I was afraid we were going to get the Rolling Stones."

"They can be good listening too," she said with a smile, wishing that he would leave her alone.

"But noisier," he said. "And less romantic."

He showed no inclination to move away. Why did every American man believe that every single American woman on a holiday was just dying to be picked up? Probably because most of us are, she answered herself wryly.

"Are you alone?"

"Yes, but—"

"If you'll allow me to join you, I promise to let you

listen to Javier Solís without interruption."

After a moment's hesitation she relented. Anyone who liked Solís couldn't be all bad. Besides, it was time to put to rest the ghost of Mr. Blanchard of Guadalajara and Ajijic and Los Angeles.

He noted that she was drinking beer and ordered another for her, along with a rum-on-the-rocks-with-twist-of-lime for himself.

He introduced himself as Alan Slater.

"Charmian Stewart," she said, amused at the idea that she was just possibly allowing herself to be picked up.

"Your first visit, Miss Stewart?"

"No, I've been here before."

"Then you know about our famous *pescado blanco*."

"Yes, that's what I planned to have." On my special quiet evening alone, she thought.

And then she told herself that this reluctance to open up to new experiences was probably the very reason why, at thirty-seven years of age, she *was* alone. So she sat back in her chair and relaxed determinedly, looking more closely at her uninvited companion.

Our whitefish.

At first she had mistaken him for another tourist. Now, interested, she sensed that he wasn't. He was too much at ease in his pale blue *guayabera* shirt and his *huaraches*, the popular open-weave leather moccasins. Too quick also with his rough Spanish in ordering her *cerveza* and him rum-and-lime. A great many tourists knew their few necessary phrases, which could include ordering drinks, but they didn't throw out the words with that careless fluency. They were always too proud of themselves for remembering.

Alan Slater appeared to be a man in his early fifties, but an alert and vigorous middle age (she had almost thought virile). His black hair was a distinguished silver at the temples, where it had been allowed to grow thick and was brushed back. He was of medium height, solid without being heavy, as carelessly relaxed sitting in his scarred leather *equipales* chair as he would have been, she guessed, in a drawing room. She could not have said why this latter conviction surfaced; something in the smoothness of his approach, the cool confidence in his pale eyes.

Violet eyes. She had heard that Elizabeth Taylor had eyes of that striking hue. Now she realized that the lenses of Slater's modishly oversized goggle-type glasses were tinted in that violet shade. Behind their huge lenses Slater's eyes were probably a very pale gray-blue.

The waiter came. The *pescado blanco* was available prepared in two ways: *empanizado*, fried in a batter, or *moje de ajo*, marinated in a garlic sauce. Charmian decided on the latter, but Alan Slater interrupted, addressing the waiter brusquely.

"*Oye!*" he snapped. Then, to her, "Those are good ways to ruin an excellent fish. May I?" In rapid and surprisingly idiomatic, if sometimes ungrammatical, Spanish he directed the waiter to have the *pescado blanco* simply grilled with the lightest of seasonings.

Initially irritated by his intrusion and his curt treatment of the waiter, Charmian then, womanlike, found herself enjoying the knowledgeable and authoritative way Slater took over. He knew what he was doing and he did not hesitate to show it or to act upon it. That authority could be a welcome discovery in a world increasingly peopled with diffident, unassertive men.

But Jeff Blanchard would not have treated the waiter with such an open air of superiority. Was she approving of that?

Oh, don't be ridiculous! she scolded herself. Blanchard was nice without being timid, but he was also someone she had simply met in passing, a stranger who had his own problems and worries, who had moved on in their pursuit and was certainly not looking back.

"Never look back," she remembered. Wasn't that Satchel Paige's famous line? "—Something might be gaining on you."

Look across the table then, and find out who this rather handsome, confident man is, watching you so attentively. Why was he bothering with dowdy Miss Hepburn?

They talked of Patzcuaro and of the fishermen with their unique butterfly nets. Slater told her that these were now used only for the delight of tourists, the real fishing being done with large commercial nets, using techniques practiced in most parts of the world. "And if the nets keep getting bigger, the techniques more efficient, maybe they'll do the same thing they're doing everywhere, fish out the lake. End of *pescado blanco* at prices for the multitude."

Slater obviously did not include himself in the multitude, and the way in which he spoke the word, with the barest trace of contempt, reminded her of his manner with the waiter—an officiousness which had, ironically, resulted in remarkably attentive service. This attitude chilled her, enabling her to observe Slater's charm and strength of personality more objectively than she might have otherwise.

The fish, Charmian was compelled to admit, was superb, even better than she remembered it. She complimented Slater for his expertise.

"The Mexican palate has been burned so often that it isn't used to preserving delicate flavors," he said. "Mind you, some of their sauces are superb—you can't compare good old Southern-fried chicken with a good *mole*—but they'll ruin a fish like this if you let them. It used to be that you couldn't buy a good steak outside of Mexico City, they always cremated beef, but the truth was that their beef has always been inferior. You had to overcook it and beat it in order to chew it. That's begun to change in recent years. There are a few places now, even out in the provinces. There's a little motel east of Morelia on Highway 15 to Mexico City, owned by Americans who raise their own Angus cattle and serve their own beef. You ought to stop there if you're going that way."

Bypassing the implied question, she said, "You sound as if you've lived here quite a long time."

His hesitation was barely perceptible. "Half my life," he said with a smile. "I won't tell you exactly how long that is, but I'd guess you must have been in about the seventh grade when I first came to Mexico to stay. If that."

"Then you must love Mexico." She wondered why he gave her the opposite impression.

"I've made a good life here."

"What do you do?" She had been trying to decide if he was a writer or an artist or simply a man who had inherited money and had chosen this way to enjoy it. In which case he would be well known to all the waiters and bell captains and socially conscious American residents in Acapulco and Cuernavaca and Mexico City.

Slater surprised her. "I own a gift shop here in Patzcuaro, and another over in Morelia, where I live most of the time. You see, I have an ulterior motive in joining you tonight. Now you'll have to visit my shops." He smiled easily and often, but the smile didn't always reach the pale eyes, slightly magnified behind their wide thick lenses.

Charmian had the sudden, inexplicable impression that he was amused by her, that he really did have a particular motive for introducing himself to her and, in telling her so, he was gently mocking her.

Rubbish!

Aloud she said, "I'd love to. Visiting gift shops is what we traveling schoolteachers do best."

"You're a schoolteacher?"

"Yes. Hadn't you guessed?"

"No, and that's a compliment. What do you teach? And where, if you don't mind telling me?"

"I teach Spanish at Santa Monica City College. That's next to Los Angeles on the coast."

"Yes, I know. I...once knew someone who came from that area, back when there were farms and open spaces between Los Angeles and the beach cities. A long time ago."

"It was a different world then."

"Yes." Slater looked past her speculatively, as if he were contemplating that distant world, and there was in his face and his strange eyes something chilling, as of a deep and carefully controlled rage momentarily rising close to the surface like a sea monster native to the darkest, coldest depths. His smile denied the insight. "Hasn't the school year started? We don't get many teachers this time of year."

"I'm on leave this year. A whole year to myself, to do whatever I want."

"So you're down here practicing your Spanish for the future benefit of your students?"

"Well, I don't need to practice ordering from the menu, but...yes, in a way that's true."

"You'd probably find mine a rough-and-ready use of the language."

"But you communicate well."

Slater shrugged. "I've made my life here. I sell to tourists, mostly American or Canadian, some French. But I buy from the Indians and my help is mostly Mexican. I wouldn't have lasted if I couldn't tell them what I wanted and bargain with them on even terms. And if I didn't know what they were saying behind my back."

"You don't sound as if you like them much."

His eyebrows lifted. They were grayer than his well-groomed hair, and she wondered if those silvery-blue temples came out of a bottle. "Have I given you that impression? I would hardly have stayed here all this time if I didn't have some empathy for this country and its people."

The statement was an obvious one, irrefutable under the circumstances, yet Charmian Stewart felt that it lacked conviction. It was a lukewarm, perfunctory protest. But what else would explain his presence here, a man of evident style and background and intelligence? A crime? A scandal? Something so terrible that he could never return to the United States?

"How long have you been down, this trip?"

"Less than two weeks. It was warm along the coast or I would have taken longer. I'll go back to Mazatlán when it's cooler. And out of the bug season."

"Where are you bound for now? On to Mexico City? The ruins at Oaxaca?"

"Eventually. I thought first..." She paused, struck by the impression that Slater's questions had ceased to be idle. He was probing, seeking information.

"Yes?"

"I may try one of the courses at the institute in San Miguel if it works out."

"Perhaps I'll see you there if you do. I get over to San Miguel quite often. Some of my Indians do good work and I'm able to place some of their things in the better shops there, like the Casa Maxwell."

"And you live in Morelia?"

"I have a house there in the Santa María Hills. Where you will also find La Cosecha de la Miel. You know what that means, of course."

"The honey-harvest."

"Very good. My shops are known familiarly as La Cosecha. Anyway, I really divide my time between there and here, where I keep an apartment, except when I'm in the field, looking for things I can sell or for artifacts."

"Artifacts? Don't tell me you're one of those who's involved in smuggling pre-Columbian treasures out of the country."

Slater was amused. "You make it sound very naughty."

"Isn't it?"

Slater's shrug this time was contemptuous. "Where do you think those treasures end up when they're confiscated by the Mexican authorities, Miss Stewart? In the hands of American and European collectors, generally. The only question is, who will get paid for them?"

"That's cynical."

"I've lived here for more than twenty years," Slater said curtly. "It's not cynical at all, simply a fact of life."

The *pescado blanco* had been delicious, and the strong black coffee was a welcome conclusion to the meal. Charmian would have enjoyed another cup but she didn't ask for one. Mexican restaurants had still not learned about Americans and their second cups of coffee. Seldom did you receive an automatic refill, and if you asked for one you usually received a new cup and a separate charge. More coffee on this occasion would have meant lingering longer, more conversation, more careful questions, and she found that she wanted this visit with Alan Slater to end. And she wanted it to be the last one.

Perhaps you really prefer quieter, less forceful men, she thought. And perhaps the pale-eyed Mr. Slater frightens you.

He too was looking around, snapping his fingers at the waiter in summons. He did that like a Mexican. Slater had lost interest in her, Charmian realized. At what point? When he learned that she was an innocent schoolteacher? That she was traveling alone? That she was full of conventional attitudes about smuggling and the equality of dark-skinned *indios* and the place of *mordida*, the bribe, in the Mexican character and economy?

Something else had caught her attention, something hidden from her all during the meal. While Slater paid the bill, brushing aside her protest, she found herself staring.

He had webbed fingers. The web grew up between the fingers to the middle knuckles. She had never seen the curious phenomenon before.

Slater saw that she was staring at him. "I wish you'd let me pay for my own dinner," she said.

135

"Nonsense," Alan Slater replied. "The pleasure was mine. And I hope I'll see you in one of my shops before you leave the area."

"Yes, of course," she said. But she wouldn't visit his shops, she thought. She didn't want those violet eyes pinning her down, as if she were a specimen on a glass plate, studying her with the clinical indifference of a scientist for the minimal form of life he observed, analyzing reactions to stimuli, to pleasure and pain.

Slater rose and Charmian had the clear impression that he was dismissing her.

"Good night then, Miss Stewart. I trust you'll enjoy your stay in Mexico."

He strode across the restaurant and exited into the darkness of the chilly night, leaving her at her table.

You struck out again, she told herself wryly.

But she could hardly have been more relieved.

7

Jeff Blanchard was detained for twenty-four hours in Guanajuato by the Mexican police. He was not arrested, but the officer in charge of investigating the death of Pepe Ramírez seemed determined to find some flaw in Blanchard's story about his son's disappearance and his tenuous connection with Pepe. Late Friday afternoon an official from the U.S. Consulate in Guadalajara arrived to intervene in his behalf. His name was John Wilcox. While he didn't seem to credit Blanchard's story any more than the local police did, he managed to divert some of the pressure. The Guanajuato authorities, conscious of the importance of tourism to the local economy, seemed more susceptible than many in the country to the consul's influence. "Besides," Wilcox confided, "they're not overly concerned about this fellow Pepe anyway. Just sit tight, and for God's sake don't get into any more trouble."

Blanchard wondered what kind of trouble Wilcox thought he might get into.

To divert his own and Angie's thoughts from the grim revelations they had found in this City of the Dead, Blanchard tried to get Angie to talk about herself and Mike. At first she was reluctant, but then she began to realize what he was trying to do and she found relief in forcing herself to talk about normal things. She spoke of Miami and the exciting sense of involvement in what she saw as a genuine crusade, an attempt to bring the real people of the country into political action, an opening up of what had become a closed and privileged structure.

"Oh, I guess we didn't do everything right, and we were naïve about a lot of things—the way things actually work at a convention, the pulling and the tugging. And the compromising." The last word brought a grimace. "Still, there was a feeling of things really happening. We believed we were really turning things around. Just the idea that that *could* happen was exciting."

As an alternate delegate Angie had never actually had the opportunity to vote, but she had been allowed inside the convention hall, she had been part of the scene, she had got inside the structure and that was important to her.

She had bumped into Mike two or three times at rallies, and after the first convention ended they had met again at a victory party. It was then that she realized that Mike was searching her out. She became aware of him as a person for the first time.

"After that we just... we zinged. Oh, wow, did we ever! You'd think we just discovered about boys and girls, and about two people feeling the same way about things."

Although their motel in Guanajuato seemed to have the best food in town, Blanchard thought that getting out was a good idea. He allowed Angie to discover one of the snack bars in which the city abounded, popular with students at the University of Guanajuato. They had lunch at the little Café Lulu at the foot of the university's formidable sweep of stairs. There Blanchard managed to get Angie to talk about herself.

She did not regard hers as a happy childhood, and she had left home when she was seventeen, largely to escape the quarrelsome atmosphere in which her parents seemed to thrive. She had so far worked her way through college, completing three years, getting by on the income from various part-time jobs. "Last year I had two jobs and seventeen credit hours. I was a Hertz counter girl four hours a day and I did library research for two of the doctors in the Department of Occupational Health. You know, looking into why people who breathe certain kinds of factory dust get sick and things like that."

Her parents had both been borderline alcoholics. "Or maybe they're over the line, I don't know. It's like they were always trying to drink each other under the table almost every day. They'd drink and then the shouting would start. I think they really enjoyed it. I used to think they hated each other and that was why they drank and fought all the time, but now I don't think that's it so much. They need each other, I guess, and that's the way they do their thing, that's all."

"Do you ever see them?"

"I went back last summer, but it was a mistake. Nothing was any different. After a couple of days we were all shouting at each other again."

Blanchard began to understand why Angie had not found it strange when Mike didn't believe it necessary to involve his father in his wedding plans.

On one subject Angie was—not unpredictably—touchy: drugs. "Sure, Michael and I smoke pot." Her blue eyes became instantly cooler, almost hostile. "Why not? That's our thing. We don't get belligerent and shout at each other and break the dishes and smash up the car." She had raised her voice, and a mixed group of students at the next table were staring at them, grinning. "You have your way and we have ours. *We* don't hurt anyone."

"That's a good yardstick," Blanchard murmured, skirting argument by refraining from mentioning that she was not comparing the mild use of pot to mild drinking, but to the alcoholic's rage. "I'm not judging you or Mike, Angie. But I know you can get into real trouble in Mexico over marijuana. Was Mike into anything like that? I'm just trying to find out if that could have anything at all to do with his disappearing." There was a great deal of money to be made from shipping drugs into the States—the kind of money, and the kind of nose-thumbing at the Establishment, that would have appealed to the old Darrell Kinney.

"No," she said coldly.

"And with Pepe's murder," he added.

The harsh word cut through Angie's defensive reaction. A flicker of worry crossed her face. Then she shook her head, long blonde hair rippling, spilling across one shoulder.

"No," she said again, firmly. "I would have known."

But the question disturbed her, not so much because it might be true, Blanchard guessed, as because it reminded her that there were many things about Mike that she didn't know, and that the mystery of his disappearance had shifted into an area of brutality and terror completely alien to her experience.

And you were going to take her mind off things, Blanchard kicked himself mentally.

Yet the question had been one he needed to ask.

The investigation into Pepe's death by the Guanajuato police, however, turned up a solution far more prosaic than Angie's or Blanchard's fears.

"Everything seems to be in order," John Wilcox informed Blanchard cheerfully over breakfast coffee on Saturday morning. "I believe the police in Guadalajara have a line on this fellow Ramírez. He's been fooling around with another man's wife over in Chapala, and the man is known to have threatened to kill him if he came near her again. The theory is that the jealous husband followed Ramírez and his wife to Guanajuato and caught them together. Both the man, whose name is Hernández, and his wife have disappeared. They'll undoubtedly turn up soon. I expect your son will turn up also, Mr. Blanchard. Ah, you realize, I'm sure, that a kidnapping seems farfetched."

"What about Mike's ring? I didn't imagine that gruesome business."

"Oh, yes, that. Well—ah..." Wilcox didn't want to consider this detail, which interrupted the smoothness of his explanation. "Your son isn't—ah—given to practical jokes, is he?"

"No. And he wouldn't do that to his wife."

"I see. Yes." Wilcox frowned. "Certainly we'll look into it, Mr. Blanchard, and it's as well that you've put the Mexican authorities on the alert. They're quite efficient, I assure you, in particular the *federales*— the Federal Police—even though it may not always seem that way. And I've been told that you're free to leave Guanajuato now if you wish. They're really quite convinced that Ramírez has simply paid for his sins." Wilcox produced a small chuckle. "You'd think the fellow would have been busy enough with the American ladies over in Ajijic, from what you've told me, without getting himself into trouble with a Mexican woman and a jealous husband. But it takes all kinds, doesn't it, Mr. Blanchard?"

Given the opportunity, Blanchard was anxious to leave Guanajuato, convinced that there would be no more "messages" there while U.S. and Mexican officials were interested in him. He informed Wilcox that he would be driving with Angie to San Miguel de Allende, where his son had last written him. Wilcox seemed relieved at the news.

If Angie was surprised over his sudden decision, she did not raise any objection. Pepe had told her nothing beyond the instruction to go to Guanajuato and wait to be contacted.

Blanchard knew that he was acting on a hunch. He was trusting his instinct, responding to a pattern of thought and action that took him back a quarter of a century, trying to find his way into the devious turnings of Darrell Kinney's mind.

That pattern had begun to emerge in San Miguel.

Blanchard drove, and for the first twenty miles or so, a tortuous climb up the mountain range east of Guanajuato on the way to Dolores Hidalgo, the numerous *curvas peligrosas* required all of his attention. When Angie finally broke the silence her words shocked him.

"Do you think Michael loves me, Mr. Blanchard?"

"Jeff, remember? And for God's sake what makes you ask a question like that?"

"The police... and that Mr. Wilcox... they don't believe he's in any trouble."

"They don't want to. But you and I know that Mike never sent that lizard to us with his ring. He just wouldn't do it. Maybe there are a lot of things about him that I don't know, but I believe that. Do you?"

"Yes..."

"And we both know Pepe wasn't killed by a jealous husband."

After a moment Angie's head began to nod. She pulled herself more erect in the bucket seat, staring out the windows at the green mesa they had reached after a long climb. The scenery was spectacular, but Blanchard had hardly noticed it.

"I believe that," Angie said. "I guess I just wanted to hear you say it like that, flat out." She turned her head to look at him directly. "Then what does it mean, Jeff? Why was Pepe killed?"

They had been avoiding probing too deeply into the meaning of the fat man's murder, like someone reluctant to find out just how bad an illness is, Blanchard thought. There was always hope when you didn't know the worst. Now it was time.

"I don't know," he said. "Maybe he got difficult, or tried a little blackmail. Pepe wasn't a savory type. He might have weighed the advantages of dealing directly with me against what he was promised as a go-between." He paused. "That's possible, but it isn't what I really think. Someone is leading me—us—by the nose, Angie. He's amusing himself with us, but murdering Pepe wasn't just for fun. Pepe didn't know that was going to be his role, but I think it was planned all along."

"What kind of a... a pig would do a thing like that? And why? Just to scare us?"

"There's more to it than that. It also tells us that this whole business—the danger to Mike—is deadly serious. In a way we're being conditioned."

"Why doesn't he just ask for his money?" Angie cried bitterly.

"We're being softened up, so we'll react in the proper way when the time comes. And..." Blanchard shook his head. Each time he thought he had caught a glimpse into the murky twistings of the mind he was trying to remember and understand, he found the way blocked. His first conclusion had been that for some reason Kinney couldn't have it known that he was alive and well in Mexico. That theory started to come unraveled when Mike's disappearance was followed by Pepe's murder. If all Kinney wanted to do was to silence Mike, why all the rest of it? Why make it appear that he was using Mike as bait to lure Jeff Blanchard into coming to him?

What did Kinney, after all these years, want with *him*?

Aloud, because Angie was waiting, he said, "There's a chance that money isn't all he wants. But if it is, he wants to make sure that we do exactly what he tells us to. And we will, Angie. Because now Pepe's murder tells us something about him that we couldn't have learned in any other way. We know that he holds other men's lives very cheaply."

Angie shivered visibly. Blanchard had not been trying to frighten her further—the rack was tight enough, he thought—but he was convinced that she had to face the worst possibilities of the situation, to accept the diagnosis even if it turned out to be something as painful and deadly as a runaway cancer.

"You really believe it *is* that man Michael saw...the one you knew in the war?"

"Yes. It's Kinney—it has to be."

"How can he be so...so obsessed that he doesn't care who else lives or dies or who gets hurt?" Angie cried in a sudden gust of anger.

Blanchard maneuvered the little car through a bad stretch of road, taking his time before answering. The paving had been gouged into a moonscape by the relentless rains—aided, almost certainly, by certain economies in the materials and construction, enabling the contractor to pocket a large portion of the money that should have gone into the road. "I'll tell you what I think, Angie. There are a million songs that say love makes the world go round, but I don't think it does, not as much as we like to pretend. Oh, it does for people like you and Mike right now, but you're in the minority. I think in some societies, at an early stage, maybe all societies, survival is what it's all about in the beginning, the primary thrust. Then that civilization moves past the stage of simple survival and love takes over—a higher motivation. Love and pride and faith in each other. But then that society becomes more sophisticated and complex and difficult, like ours, and it moves on to another level of ambition. I think in our society the primary fuel is greed. Greed for money, position, power, possessions. From simple avarice at a lower income level—the kind that keeps con men going on forever, using the same old dodges—to the big grain deals and land deals and oil-tax deals and political power plays at the top of the heap. We've made saving and having and owning and displaying and enjoying the whole point of our lives, not love and honest pride and compassion. It all adds up to one kind of greed or another."

"Oh, wow! Michael ought to hear you now. He wouldn't believe it."

"Mike and I didn't...care enough," Blanchard said with a bleak and bitter honesty. He dodged a deep pool in the middle of the road and frowned at some more heavy black clouds over the mountains to the south. Calm down, he thought; climb off the pulpit. "The only thing I don't see right now is how Kinney will benefit. I think he always had money, but he was still always looking for the soft berth and the easy payoff. Like, we'd check out some Air Corps supplies of photo equipment, for instance. There were always some good cameras in there, Leicas and what-have-you, that didn't really have anything to do with air reconnaissance. That's the way the military functions—as long as you're buying cameras, buy a little of everything. Kinney would manage to come away with a few of those cameras, and he would know where he could unload them. Easy money. You were a sucker not to take some of it when it was just lying there. That was Kinney, and the funny thing is that most of us admired him for his guts. But Angie, I don't have the kind of money that would justify all that's happened. That's where it breaks down. When Mike's mother was ill for so long, the hospital and medical bills chewed up everything we'd ever saved, and more. I'd give Kinney or any other kidnapper everything I have to get Mike back, but it isn't enough to keep that son of a bitch in style down here for a year."

"Maybe he doesn't know that."

"If I know anything about Darrell Kinney at all," Blanchard answered slowly, "it's that he wouldn't get himself involved in kidnapping and murder unless he knew exactly what he was going to get out of it."

"So we really don't know any more than we did before," Angie said helplessly. Blanchard had heard that note in her voice before when she called him long distance from Guadalajara an age ago, a sound of desperation and the crumbling of hope.

"We know a lot more," he said. "Including the fact that Mike is alive, Angie. Kinney wants something badly enough to murder for it, but somehow Mike is one of the keys. He *has* to keep him alive. Otherwise he has no leverage with either of us, and it's clear he wants that. I don't know yet why he needs that leverage, but he does."

In her desperation Angie seized on that, wanting to believe it. Blanchard hoped grimly that he wasn't building a fantasy structure for her—for both of them. If it collapsed...

"Do you think Kinney is in San Miguel?" Angie asked thoughtfully. "Is that why we have to go there now?"

"It's logical. I think it has to be someplace you and Mike were recently. The fact that he saw Darrell Kinney in San Miguel is the one solid fact we have to go on now. That's where we have to start, and Kinney knows it. Besides..." Blanchard was trying to read another detail in the murky picture. "If you're leading someone on a chase starting in Guadalajara and going from there to Guanajuato, unless you're heading north toward the States, which seems unlikely, you have to go on to the next part of the loop. That's San Miguel."

"What will we do? Just... wait?"

"We're going to do everything you and Mike did when you were there," Blanchard said. Then, smiling, he added, "Almost everything, that is. The rest is for you and Mike to make up, after we find him."

"Do you believe we'll find him, Jeff?"

For the first time she spoke to him like a child, like a daughter, he thought, in a small voice that carried an almost pathetic plea. She had begun to trust him, and that kind of responsibility was a little frightening.

"Yes," he said. "We'll find him."

Then he did something he hadn't done in a very long time. He thought of *El Cristo Rey*, standing high on a peak overlooking the known world, and he tried to find the words that formed a prayer.

Interlude Three: Morelia

1

The day had started badly, after a night which had brought to Ernst von Schoenwald, for one of the few times in his life, a cold-sweat moment of real fear.

It had rained heavily before dawn, saturating the grounds, and there was intermittent rain throughout the morning. The German had had to forgo his morning workout in the sun. With Robbins away, he had exercised alone in the gymnasium. His mood was gloomy, reflecting the weather and his worry, and he had felt an unaccustomed heaviness of limb. The dizziness of the night before was gone, but it had left behind a sharp headache. In the end he had uncharacteristically cut his workout short and, on impulse, sent for Rafael Sánchez.

It was foolish, he told himself, to be concerned about what were certainly perfectly ordinary symptoms, but at his age it was perhaps even more foolish to ignore them. The doctor could at least provide reassurance—and something for his headache other than *aspirina*.

It might also be useful to allow the good doctor to observe for himself how a life of ease and pampering had begun to affect his latest protégée, María Teresa Calderón.

Von Schoenwald's mood was exacerbated when he came to take his shower after his abbreviated workout. There was no hot water. An angry inquiry revealed that both propane-gas tanks were empty. The company which regularly provided gas was never reliable, and was now several days late on delivery; its truck had broken down.

The German fumed through a cold shower. In all of his years in Mexico he had never adapted to this aspect of the Mexican temperament. Inefficiency was bad enough. The smiling indifference to it of the *indio* was even more exasperating. Small wonder that, unlike Germany, Mexico remained a nation of peasants.

At breakfast María Teresa threw a temper tantrum, shouting at Lupe. The girl had arrived late and her eggs were cold.

"Are they so inedible?" von Schoenwald asked.

"They are cold," María insisted. "And I wanted sausages. I won't eat cold eggs."

"Then by all means you should not." The German was not amused. "Lupe, you will bring us some *pan dulce* and fresh coffee. Take the rest away."

"What about my sausages?" María demanded.

"They also are probably cold by now. I am sure you would not want to eat them either."

She tried being angry with him. When von Schoenwald ignored her while he drank his coffee in silence, she tried pouting. And when that failed to elicit a response, she came around the table to stand beside him, a narrow, bony hip pressing against his arm. One hand fingered the back of his neck until, in irritation, he pushed it away.

147

"Why are you angry with me?"

"I'm not angry."

"But you are angry. You did not wish me to be with you last night."

"That's not for you to question."

The girl stared at him. Some of her earlier petulance still showed in her eyes, but she dared not express it. She was wearing a short-skirted black dress with a lace bodice—an evening dress, totally inappropriate for the morning. At another time— even a few days ago—von Schoenwald would have been amused. He no longer found such ignorance charming. The truth was that, childlike, she had become spoiled in a remarkably short time.

And tiresome.

"I can make you feel good," María Teresa said softly.

She sank to her knees beside him. A finger began to trace slow circles over his thigh, creeping inward. She had learned such tricks quickly, too, he thought. "Does María Teresa not please you?"

For the second time he brushed her hand away. "María Teresa can have her morning sausage in the kitchen," he said, with a brutal humor that was lost on the girl.

In sudden impatience he scraped his chair back, causing her to jump away in alarm. Ignoring her, von Schoenwald strode from the room.

2

From the terrace Ernst von Schoenwald watched Rafael Sánchez's little white car race up the hill, dodging a small procession of mules trudging along the side of the road with their burdens of freshly cut wood. The sun had broken through the clouds as the morning's storm moved north over the mountains, and the green valley was bathed in freshly washed brilliance. From the distance of the German's hilltop sanctuary, the city and its surroundings presented a scene of tranquil beauty. He found it empty, unrewarding, forever alien.

He had once reacted differently, that summer of 1950 when he first discovered the city. It had seemed enchanting then. He had seen it as the end of his journey... his Shangri-La.

Ernst von Schoenwald and Darrell Kinney had come to the city separately, having traveled north by different routes, each changing his direction and method of passage several times. Von Schoenwald had crossed into Mexico over the Guatemalan border; Kinney had come by boat to Vera Cruz. The routes had been carefully planned, and von Schoenwald was convinced that neither he nor Kinney could have been tracked all the way by even the most diligent hunter. And even if they had been traced to Mexico, their trails would have vanished into the maze of Mexico City.

They had met by prearrangement in Morelia, at a hotel on Maderos whose roof von Schoenwald fancied he could see even now below him. Morelia was then a relatively sleepy city, albeit one of Mexico's colonial and cultural jewels. It had remained undiscovered by most tourists. It was remote from both Mexico City to the east and Guadalajara to the west, each an arduous journey away over twisting and poorly conditioned mountain roads.

It was not then certain that Morelia was to be the end of Ernst von Schoenwald's long flight from his Fatherland. But he was charmed by the old city with its sidewalk cafés that reminded him of Bonn, where he had gone to school in his youth, by the walled courtyards and the ancient viaduct, and most of all by the surrounding mountains that seemed to rise as a barrier to the relentless enemies from whom he had fled.

Chance intervened on his first morning in the city. A curious desk clerk happened to overhear a single phrase that enabled him to identify von Schoenwald's German accent, even though he had spoken in Spanish.

"You will wish to visit Señor Brugmann, perhaps?" Juan Valdez asked, displaying a wide expanse of flawless white teeth. "He is a countryman of yours."

Von Schoenwald stared at him coldly.

"An old gentleman," the clerk said, less certainly. "He lives in Santa María. We have seen few Germans in Morelia..."

Juan Valdez fell silent when the aristocratic visitor turned away without comment. Briefly the clerk wondered if he had been mistaken about the tall blond tourist's accent. Then he was forced to attend to other guests, and the incident was quickly forgotten. He never mentioned it to anyone.

That afternoon, his first in Morelia, von Schoenwald drove up into the hills south of the city with Darrell Kinney in a rented car, during the time Morelia dozed through its siesta. Discreet inquiries at an inn on the hill led them to Baldur Brugmann's isolated retreat.

They found an elderly German so little used to having his privacy intruded upon that he was visibly flustered. Yet Brugmann had an innate dignity and courtesy, and he made his unexpected visitors welcome. He was surprised to meet another German, and moved. He read habitually in his native language, but he had spoken German so little in thirty years—since he had come to Morelia shortly after World War I, he explained—that he felt compelled to apologize for his speech, as if certain that his command of his own tongue must have become rusty from disuse.

The abandoned monastery he had purchased many years ago was, behind the high perimeter walls that remained largely intact, little more than a ruin, a skeleton of half-walls and roofless rooms, like one of the bombed cities of von Schoenwald's own war.

Brugmann had repaired and enclosed a single room adjoining a large kitchen and a crude but functional bath. In this small section of the old monastery he lived, alone and at peace with his books.

He seemed to become aware that afternoon, as if for the first time, of the spartan simplicity of his dwelling, and he went out of his way to entertain his guests, even bringing forth a bottle of local red wine from a storage cellar, little more than a stone-walled hole behind the kitchen—although it actually led to a tunnel built by the monks who had first inhabited the monastery, providing a secret means of escape beyond the high walls.

Brugmann showed his guests through his gardens, which he had tended lovingly, including one large vegetable garden where he grew enough to supply most of his modest needs. The gardens were shaded by old oaks and even a few palm trees, and were sectioned by broken stone paths and low terrace walls. In one area were mounds of freshly turned earth where large rats scurried away as the men approached. Here Brugmann disposed of his garbage by the simple expedient of digging holes and filling them.

Ernst von Schoenwald inspected the peaceful and secluded gardens with growing excitement. He made note of the solid walls offering an impressive barrier to the curious world outside. The potential of the monastery itself for restoration did not escape him. Before the tour of the grounds was completed, he had made his decision.

He questioned Brugmann more closely. No, the old man seldom left his grounds. He had no need. He raised his own chickens, grew his own vegetables, occasionally purchased corn tortillas from a passing vendor or wood from the peasant cutters who daily journeyed up and down the hill, passing to and from the forests higher in the mountains. He lived simply, he desired no company, he required no servants. He had no relatives or close friends. His reclusive ways were well known in the district, and he was rarely disturbed.

Von Schoenwald needed to hear no more. He could hardly believe his good fortune. He was certain that his brief presence in Morelia would not have been noted. He saw clearly that, later that afternoon when the tourist who had called himself Schmidt checked out of the hotel on Maderos, continuing on his way to Guadalajara, Ernst von Schoenwald would vanish forever.

Returning to his bare kitchen, Baldur Brugmann began to pour a little more wine for his guests. He had enjoyed the opportunity of conversing in his mother tongue, and he had been saddened by the details of the terrible destruction visited upon his country. It surprised him that old feelings, long forgotten, could so readily be aroused by simple reminders of the scenes of his youth, by a few words spoken in German by a stranger. His hand, pouring the wine, shook plainly.

There was no warning. There was only the sensation of a massive weight crashing against his skull, a flash of crimson light and a brief explosion of pain. Then yawning blackness and oblivion.

On that summer afternoon in 1950 Baldur Brugmann died, and Ernst von Schoenwald took his place. The old German's body was buried beneath the garbage pits in a corner of the monastery gardens. No one beyond the high walls knew that any change had occurred within.

Three weeks later, returning to his home late from night duty at the hotel, Juan Valdez was struck and killed by a speeding car. No one witnessed the accident, nor was anyone ever apprehended.

For a long time afterward only Darrell Kinney knew that the man who lived in the old monastery on the hill was not the real Baldur Brugmann. Kinney remained useful to von Schoenwald as an outside liaison, his link with the world. But on the day von Schoenwald moved into the monastery, a subtle change in his relationship with the American took place. The partnership which Kinney had demanded, on which he had presumed, was dissolved.

While the monastery was slowly restored and converted into a luxurious dwelling for von Schoenwald and a growing retinue of servants—eventually including George Robbins—Darrell Kinney was set up in business under an assumed name outside the monastery walls. He entered only as a supplicant, forever dependent on von Schoenwald, held in thrall by his tenuous connection to the fortune in paintings that hung on the wall of the German's study.

There had been eleven paintings in the original collection the German had stolen from the West Austrian bank vault in 1944. One, a small portrait by the French Impressionist Manet, had been bartered in Switzerland, providing the price of passage for von Schoenwald and Kinney through Spain to South America. The dealer who had made arrangements for the sale had claimed some small damage to the lower left-hand corner of the painting during restoration—a claim the German did not believe but could not dispute. He had accepted a fraction of the painting's value—$25,000 in American dollars.

That sale, nevertheless, had confirmed von Schoenwald's estimate of the value of his stolen collection. Eventually, when he had been able to make connections through an arm of ODESSA in Argentina, he had sold four additional canvases, prudently claiming they were all he had. They had been sold on the black market through a European dealer to an American collector, and the many hands involved in the surreptitious transaction—and here too there were spurious claims of damage during restoration—had reduced von Schoenwald's ultimate share to a little over $150,000.

The Argentinean transactions had been a necessary risk at the time. Not long afterward Israeli agents had appeared, seeking to track down the source of the paintings. Long before the sale could be traced to him, von Schoenwald and Darrell Kinney had once more disappeared.

There had never been any need to sell more paintings. Von Schoenwald had given one small canvas to Kinney—a teasing promise of future sharing—but with the severe admonition that under no circumstances must it be sold. The others remained in his possession. In the years that followed their coming to Morelia, the money realized from the Argentinean sales had more than supplied the needs of von Schoenwald's luxurious way of life and Kinney's outside business interests—his visible excuse for settling in Morelia. Mexican investments had paid off far beyond the German's expectations, making possible the elaborate restoration of the monastery. Most of the time he had been able to live handsomely on the income from those investments, which had expanded and prospered as Mexico herself entered a prosperous era of expansion through the next two decades.

If, during the passing years, there were periods of restlessness and unaccountable depression, a sense of the emptiness of his life, Ernst von Schoenwald had found ways to surmount them. He was, after all, a man of discipline and self-sufficient strength, the true German of his Führer's dream.

And there were always new amusements to be found and pursued behind his protective walls.

Von Schoenwald turned away from his view of the rain-washed valley, thinking suddenly of María Teresa and the morning's outburst. She was exhibiting signs of becoming thoroughly spoiled by his indulgences. She had discovered the pleasures of power and place, and now she had taken to ordering the servants about capriciously. It was, perhaps, time to bring her back to her knees....

3

Rafael Sánchez displayed the sobriety of manner he felt was expected of him. Beneath that air of serious consideration, his heart beat rapidly as he sought to conceal his excitement.

"Well?" the German demanded.

"Para un viejo, se ve muy bien."

"Gracias a usted, Doctor."

"Hago lo que pueda. Pero a su edad, es joven, Señor."

It was not a lie, Sánchez thought. For his age, the German he knew only as Baldur Brugmann was a remarkable physical specimen. He looked twenty years younger than he surely was. But all of the German's physical discipline could only hide the appearance of age; it could not alter the fact.

And the fact was inescapable....

"What about this dizziness? What does it mean?"

"Probablamente nada."

"Probablamente?"

"It means nothing," Sánchez said more firmly. He knew better than to adopt the soothing tones that placated many of his patients. Brugmann would not be fooled by a bedside manner. He wanted reassurance, as they all did—for an instant, and for the first time in the years he had known the German, Rafael Sánchez felt superior—but it must be firm, definite, unequivocal. *"Está muy bien de salud."*

The German stared at him, and under the impact of those cold eyes Sánchez felt his heart skip. Did the German sense his excitement, his evasion?

"It is quite normal," the doctor added. He did not say that it was normal for an old man to begin to experience some hardening of the arteries. "A small blood clot in the inner ear, that is all. The dizziness has passed, no?"

"Yes."

"I will give you a prescription. And something also for your blood pressure, which is a little higher than it should be. But there is no reason for concern."

"It will not happen again?"

Sánchez shrugged. "With proper medication, there is no reason to expect that it will. You must understand that it is impossible to predict the future, but I assure you, Señor Brugmann, you have no reason to worry."

This, however, was clearly a lie. The German's attack was more serious than Sánchez had indicated. It might mean nothing—or everything. But in any event it would not matter. Baldur Brugmann had no future.

The German appeared to relax. For the first time since Sánchez had arrived at the monastery in response to Brugmann's call, the familiar ironic smile touched the German's lips. "Then, as the bearer of good tidings, you must do me the honor of dining with us, Doctor. I am sure María Teresa would be delighted. That is, if you have no other plans?"

"Me alegraría mucho!" Rafael Sánchez exclaimed with unfeigned enthusiasm. "The honor is mine, Señor Brugmann."

4

The ham was superb, and Rafael Sánchez had no intention, as he enjoyed it, of pointing out that pork filled much too great a part of the German's diet.

Ernst von Schoenwald, studying him, wondered if Sánchez had lied to him. He decided not. Sánchez had no reason to lie—in fact, it would have been to his advantage to play on any fears von Schoenwald's brief attack of dizziness the night before might have awakened. It was nothing, then. A small blood clot, that was all, in the inner ear, causing temporary dizziness. It could happen to anyone, as Sánchez had said. It had not been a stroke.

But if he was relieved, von Schoenwald's mood remained subdued, even uneasy. That momentary dizziness—he had fallen and only chance had kept him from injury—had frightened him. It had awakened more than his sense of mortality; it had also quickened a sense of danger.

Content to remain silent through most of the meal, von Schoenwald observed Sánchez's egregious flattery of María Teresa Calderón and the girl's foolish acceptance of it with some disgust. María had come pouting to the dinner table, but, soon responding to Sánchez's teasing and cajoling, she began to talk animatedly of her new life in this great house. After a while von Schoenwald stopped listening.

He had been too long immune to danger; that in itself was dangerous, for it dulled the senses, softened the instincts so necessary to survival. He had dismissed the incident with the Blanchard youth and Darrell Kinney in San Miguel as insignificant, posing no direct threat to him. Now, that threat was drawing closer. It had refused to go away. And the mere fact of proximity shifted some of the danger from Kinney to him.

Why had he allowed Kinney to live so long? Neither gratitude nor loyalty nor friendship existed between them. Perhaps it was only sentimentality; Kinney was a link with the past. Severing it would, in a sense, have cut von Schoenwald off more finally and inexorably from everything that he had been in that past. But there was more to it than that. Kinney had remained useful. There was always the possibility that an effort might have to be made to sell other paintings, and Kinney, in his role as a merchant, was in a position to travel freely without arousing interest in his activities either in Mexico or abroad. He was resourceful and opportunistic. And his business had also been a useful channel for von Schoenwald's investments.

The German was quite certain that Kinney hated him, but the fact had never worried him. There was nothing Kinney could do to him without jeopardizing his own situation—and any chance he had to inherit von Schoenwald's hidden treasure of art.

But this other American, Jeff Blanchard, was another quantity, an unknown one. He was stubborn and persistent. He had lost a son, and it was now clear that he would not abandon his search for the boy while he had any hope of finding him alive. There was no reason to believe that he would be able to follow the trail of his son beyond San Miguel, where he was apparently now heading, no reason at all to feel concern that the trail would lead him to Morelia. And yet...

Ernst von Schoenwald could feel himself quickening to the knowledge of danger. It angered him, but at the same time it made him feel more alive. He had something to react to. He faced the possible need for bold action to protect and defend himself. What was a man, after all, when he faced no threat, when he felt no need to test himself—was that what lay behind the intensity of his morning duels with George Robbins?—when there was nothing to be lost or gained?

The Führer had known this truth for their Fatherland. It had not been enough for Germany to be passive and safe. For Germany to come alive again, there had been a need for risk, danger, a reaching for power. He had risked all—and he had been right. Never had Germany been so alive, so great, as in those years of ever greater risk, ever greater power. Defeat did not alter the truth of those years. Hitler had been right.

In that moment Ernst von Schoenwald felt something almost like gratitude toward the American, Blanchard, and his hopeless search. Blanchard had given him back the sense of danger.

They were in the study. George Robbins had arrived shortly after the midday *comida*, and von Schoenwald had quickly dismissed Rafael Sánchez. Alert to his new realization that the American who had known Darrell Kinney during the war was not a pesky irritation to be casually brushed aside, the German studied Robbins closely, reading his fatigue and the worry behind it.

"Blanchard is a stubborn man," von Schoenwald commented.

"Yes," Robbins agreed. "But that's not what bothers me. There's something more...something about this whole situation I don't like."

"Is it so hard to understand? He has lost a son. I, too, once lost a son." He saw the shock registered in Robbins' eyes at the revelation. He had never before spoken to Robbins of his family.

"I...I didn't know."

Von Schoenwald dismissed the surprising disclosure with a deprecatory wave of his hand. "What matters is what Blanchard will do now. What *can* he do?"

"He's looking for Kinney, not just for his son. He won't give that up, not now."

"What of the Mexican police?"

Robbins shrugged. "They don't take him seriously. Why should they? It's like you said—he's just another American kid who's disappeared. They've got hundreds of 'em, and hundreds of frantic parents trying to find them. They'll make sympathetic noises, but there are just too many other stories like this one."

"Then what is it that bothers you, my dear George?"

Robbins regarded him shrewdly. "You're not worried?"

"Perhaps. But you haven't told me why you are."

"I don't know," Robbins admitted, his simian face wrinkling in a frown. "It's just...a feeling. Like there's more to this than shows. I don't trust Kinney."

"You don't *like* him, George. Has he done anything you haven't told me?"

Robbins slowly shook his head. "I can't put my finger on it. Except that he should never have used that fat one, Pepe, to get rid of the kid. That was stupid."

"Stupidity is never surprising, George. It is not even very unusual."

Robbins checked his reply. He didn't like Kinney, that was true, but he didn't believe Kinney was stupid. Yet there was nothing concrete he could point to to justify his suspicion, nothing that would explain his growing feeling of unease.

"Where is Kinney now?"

"He insisted on following Blanchard to San Miguel. I told him what you said—that he should stay out of sight. Hell, I guess he's smart enough to do that. But he's really uptight over Blanchard." Robbins paused. "Wouldn't the simplest thing be to see to it that Blanchard disappears, just like his kid?"

"No. In this Kinney is correct. At least... not yet."

Robbins hesitated. "There is something else."

"Well?" For the first time during the meeting Ernst von Schoenwald felt impatience with Robbins, and showed it.

"There's this girl...."

With transparent reluctance George Robbins removed a photograph from the side pocket of his white *guayabera* shirt and handed it to von Schoenwald. He watched the German as he stared at the Polaroid snapshot. It revealed a young American girl with long legs and honey blonde hair. Robbins correctly read the faint, sensual flaring of von Schoenwald's nostrils as he studied the picture.

"That's the kid's wife. The way Kinney tells it,

they were only married a couple of months. Blanchard—the father—didn't even know the girl before he came to Mexico, but they're traveling together now."

Von Schoenwald glanced up at him, but his gaze returned quickly to the girl in the snapshot. She was beautiful. He could envy the younger Blanchard his brief two months of marriage to such a woman.

Suddenly the idea of amusing himself that night with María Teresa Calderón lost much of its savor. He had had too long a procession of childish, darkskinned girls, none of whom had offered the challenge he read in the Blanchard girl's eyes, nor the fair-skinned, blue-eyed beauty that was an image of Inge's when they were both young.

"They are traveling together, you say? She is going with him to San Miguel?"

"Yeah. He likes her, that's obvious, even if he didn't know her before he came down here. And she is his daughter-in-law. Maybe all he figures he's got left of his kid."

Von Schoenwald nodded. There was a way to control Blanchard, after all, a way to force him to abandon his search if that proved necessary. A man who had lost so much could quickly be made to fear any further loss.

Abruptly von Schoenwald knew that his sense of danger was real, not a product of his moment of panic the night before over his attack of dizziness. Blanchard would not give up his search in San Miguel. Whatever had carried him this far would continue to drive him on... until he came to Morelia. Robbins felt this, too, and his instincts were almost always reliable.

And Kinney?

Were Robbins' instincts right about him?

Ernst von Schoenwald felt an abrupt chill, so sharp and distinct that he shivered. The feeling was old and deep, and his lips drew back over his teeth in a silent, reflex snarl. He remembered another time when Darrell Kinney had frightened him, that terrifying moment when Sergeant Creasey—Kinney's friend—stepped in front of the window and Kinney pulled the trigger of the Luger, and von Schoenwald lurched from his chair in panic, thinking the bullet was meant for him.

He had buried that fear, denying it, hating it. Why did it surface now?

"You will go to San Miguel," von Schoenwald said to Robbins.

"You mean...now?"

"If it is a game Kinney is playing, the game has already begun, and there is no time to waste. If it is not...well, this man Blanchard has tried my patience too far. He also is running out of time."

4 · San Miguel de Allende

1

On this Saturday afternoon San Miguel was unusually crowded. Blanchard had mistakenly got off the main road and then had trouble finding his way into the center of the town. Most of the streets seemed to be one-way, and the signs and arrows painted on the walls at the corners were often either missing or obscure. When he finally stumbled onto Avenida San Francisco, it carried him into the traffic jam around the pretty central plaza, facing the unique pink stone façade of the Parochial Church. Remembering it from long ago, Blanchard also remembered that the pink false front had been added in the nineteenth century by an unschooled Indian mason who had used picture postcards of great European cathedrals as his model, borrowing a bit from this, a spire from that. It reminded Blanchard of the quirky natural genius of Los Angeles's Watts Towers.

There was angle parking in front of the cathedral and he was lucky enough to catch a car just pulling out. As soon as he had parked, the VW was instantly surrounded by seven or eight young boys, averaging perhaps ten years of age, clamoring so loudly and insistently that he couldn't make out what they wanted.

"They want to watch our car," Angie explained, having been here just a fortnight before. "You're supposed to give one of them a peso an hour. Michael said it was a good idea. Either you pay to have the car watched or they steal your gas cap."

Blanchard picked out a grinning boy. "How are you called?"

"Me llamo Francisco, pero mis amigos me ponen Pancho."

"You've lost me. Does that mean we can call you Pancho?"

"Sí, señor."

As soon as agreement had been reached, Pancho raced off with his fellows, laughing and shouting among themselves. He was paying no attention at all to the car.

"How's he going to earn his peso if he just takes off?" Blanchard asked Angie as Pancho disappeared.

"Just try to get away without paying him."

Because the town seemed so crowded Blanchard suggested that they should try to find a place to stay for the night.

"Michael and I stayed right across the street." Angie pointed out a large colonial inn directly on the plaza. It adjoined the police station, which Blanchard didn't want to visit just then, having answered enough questions for the time being. However, the inn was full. And so, as it turned out, was every other hotel and motel and *pension* in town. They had arrived in the middle of a *fiesta*.

After a half-hour of fruitless asking and begging, plus several phone calls, Blanchard and Angie stood helplessly in the plaza, wondering what to try next.

"It's too late to drive anywhere else," Blanchard said. "Besides, I think we're expected to come here. And I want to follow yours and Mike's footsteps. You were here for the weekend, weren't you?"

"That's right."

"What did you do?"

"Mostly we just walked. We looked at the institute

and we went through all the shops."

"All right, as soon as we find rooms we'll go shopping." He spoke with more confidence than he was beginning to feel about the rooms. "What did you do on Sunday? Is everything open?"

"Some places are—oh, we went on the tour."

She explained about the Sunday tour of private homes thrown open by volunteer resident Americans. Blanchard's interest quickened. Could Mike and Angie actually have been in Darrell Kinney's house?

"We could try Sanborn's agent," Angie suggested suddenly. "He might find us rooms."

The local representative of the Texas-based insurance man from whom Mike had bought his Mexican auto coverage was delighted to help, sorrowful over the probability of failure. It was the Fiesta of San Miguel, he explained. People came from all over Mexico for this weekend, the last of September. There would be fireworks and much excitement.

He had an inspiration and leaped to the phone. A moment later, after an excited exchange, he turned to Blanchard beaming. "You are in luck very much. I have spoken to my good friend at the Casa Miguel who has one room only left. He has promised to hold it for you, but you must hurry, eh?"

He provided directions and a map of the town, fending off Blanchard's thanks.

They left the car where it was, in Pancho's care, for the address they had been given was within a few blocks of the central *jardín*. Casa Miguel turned out to be a very old inn whose blank façade concealed enormous gardens that seemed to be the size of a normal city block. There was also a menagerie of birds and animals. From the entry Blanchard saw two peacocks slowly strutting across a stretch of lawn. In a cage an animal whose parents might have been a raccoon and an opossum moved restlessly back and forth, back and forth. A choir of canaries was singing nearby, and a parrot complained in a raucous voice.

An old man padded around a corner to meet them. Smiling, he beckoned them into a spacious, high-ceilinged office that contained a huge old rolltop desk, some comfortable chairs, and, unexpectedly, a television set. Two elderly women were watching the flickering picture as Blanchard registered for himself and Angie. The old man appeared to speak not a word of English, but Blanchard was expected.

Also lucky, he thought. A hopeful family of American tourists arrived as he was leaving the office with an enormous room key. The old man shrugged his rounded shoulders and shook his head at the late arrivals. They were standing on the sidewalk, looking as helpless as Blanchard had felt a short time before, when he followed the old man along a wide, covered veranda to the room, Angie trailing, delighted by the peacocks.

A cat moved reluctantly away from the door to the room, which opened directly off the patio and faced the extensive gardens. In a dozen or more canary cages along the veranda bright yellow flashes of color accompanied sudden silence as Blanchard paused to wait for Angie. He took the key from the old man and pushed the door open and handed the key to Angie.

"This is for you. I can manage in the car for one night."

"No, that's silly. Really, I don't..."

She had entered the room and suddenly fell silent, gaping in astonishment that turned into an expression of rapture. Curious, Blanchard followed her inside.

The door itself was ten feet high and in proportion to the room, which was large enough for a game of volleyball. It held not one but three full-size beds, with at least six feet between the beds. The ceiling reached eighteen feet in height and featured a pair of enormous circular fans. Tall windows were set into the long wall facing the street, protected by folding shutters. The walls themselves were three feet thick.

"Wow!" Angie breathed. "We could hold our own convention."

Blanchard followed her into the bathroom. It was larger than a typical motel room, about twenty feet long, with floor and walls tiled to about the ten-foot level, the ceiling so high that it seemed lost overhead. But it was the shower at which Angie and Blanchard both stared, grinning spontaneously. That ancient apparatus had to be as old as he was, Blanchard thought, if not older. It was the grandfather of showers. The shower head was a huge disk over an open tiled space with a floor drain. It was about a foot in diameter. Beside it, at shoulder level, was a heavy iron lever about two feet long.

"How does it work?" Angie asked, awed.

"You stand underneath and pull down on the lever," he explained. "That big tank overhead holds the water. It's manual—you get water as long as you hold the lever down. Cold water," he added with a grin.

"Oh, Michael would..." She broke off, pleasure once more chilled by the reminder. Yet Blanchard found himself liking the way she always saw things not only from her own viewpoint but as they might be shared with Mike. Blanchard had become skeptical in recent years about the casual couplings and the scorn of long-range commitment in the young, but he would have bet in that moment that Angie and Mike would make it.

If they got the chance.

"There's plenty of room," Angie pointed out after they returned to the huge bedroom. "We could take in roomers."

"I know but... look, suppose I go and talk to that old man. Now that we're actually in and part of the family, maybe he can switch us around with someone else who needs more room."

"I don't think it'll work," Angie said dubiously. "Anyway, I'll tell Michael that we didn't want it to happen this way, the fates just conspired against us."

Blanchard laughed and went back to the office. The old man was off somewhere but he reappeared when Blanchard tapped the little bell on top of the rolltop desk. He tried to explain his problem. The young woman wasn't his wife or even his daughter, she was his daughter-in-law. Was there any way they could have separate rooms.

The old man smiled and nodded in a friendly way. He hadn't understood a word.

"Perhaps I can help," a voice said from behind Blanchard. "I speak a little Spanish."

He swung around quickly, knowing from the amused tone and the familiarity of those words that Charmian Stewart had come once more to his rescue.

2

Accommodations at the Casa Miguel included three meals a day in the eight-dollar daily rate. It was a kind of boardinghouse popular with students at the Instituto Allende, many of whom were staying there. Blanchard and Angie ate supper that evening with Charmian Stewart. He wondered how the two women would get along, since they were going to share the huge room while he had moved into Charmian's smaller unit. So far it seemed to be going well enough.

A late-afternoon shopping tour, after Blanchard had parked the Volkswagen in the Casa Miguel's locked garage, had proved uneventful. Angie had tried to retrace her casual wanderings with Mike. Every side street had its gift and souvenir shops. On this fiesta Saturday the shops were logjams of tourists from Los Angeles and Houston and Atlanta. In the better shops they could worry over the purchase of assorted sizes and shapes of glass-and-metal boxes, black pottery from Oaxaca, silk *rebozos* from Santa·María, hand-carved colonial furniture, leather belts and sandals and handwoven rugs. There was even a small but impressive gallery showing the oils and watercolors of local artists. But the authentic crafts and traditional wares of Mexico competed in other shops with a plethora of junk, cheap jewelry, and sombrero ashtrays and vivid paintings on velvet of huge-eyed waifs and gaudily resplendent bullfighters.

The *jardín*, core of the town, was crowded even more as evening neared, ringed with cars and the eager boys competing for their pesos. Blanchard recognized Pancho sitting on a bench at the edge of the plaza, aloof from the competition.

"Aren't you working?" he asked the boy.

"No, señor." The boy looked away. He had changed his shirt, Blanchard saw, and slicked back his black hair. "It is *sábado*."

Saturday night, Blanchard realized. He felt a sudden respect. At ten Pancho was a wage-earner, a working man, perhaps the chief wage-earner in his family. On Saturday night it was a matter of pride that he didn't work. He came to the plaza to sit and watch the girls, like other men.

A few old people also sat on benches, also observing the activity with the perplexed air of those who wonder how it could all change so fast, without their noticing what was happening. And among the throngs idling around the square were a large number of long-haired American girls in thin-ribbed pullovers that outlined their breasts and Indian belts draped over their narrow hips, scuffing along the cobblestones in their bare feet, trailed by long-haired young men in cut-off jeans and T-shirts, wearing necklaces and headbands. America's wandering youth culture had long ago discovered San Miguel.

Most of the town's Mexican visitors, attracted by the traditional fiesta, seemed to have gathered under the old arcade along the east side of the plaza, where there was a collection of *puestacitos*, small stands or booths or carts selling fruits and candies, toys and balloons, baskets and plastic novelties, *pan dulce*, *tamales*, *mole* and *carnitas*, assorted stews, *birria* or *menudo* rolled into soft tortillas, bottled colas and beers. This was part of the older San Miguel, clinging to a diminishing foothold; its ways were yielding to the dollars of the middle-aged American tourists or being trampled under by the spoiled *norteamericano* youths as indifferent to Mexican customs and traditions as they were to their own. Even the innocent laughter in the dark eyes of San Miguel's children was giving way to an older shrewdness, a more knowing merriment, as they swiftly learned the ways to milk the *gringos* of their pesos.

Blanchard had seen it all before under other guises, at every tourist attraction from New England's covered bridges to California's redwood country. San Miguel had become a tourist town. She was like a small-town girl who was too pretty by far, too aware of her charms, exploiting them until eventually they became imitations of themselves, false and exaggerated, and it was no longer easy to find the beauty beneath that had inspired so much admiration and affection.

Blanchard wondered if the resident Americans and Canadians, the retired doctors and the sprinkling of serious artists, ever left their remodeled homes on the hillsides to come down into the village any more.

Over supper, after he and Angie had returned to the Casa Miguel, Charmian Stewart asked him about his rendezvous with Pepe. After an exchange of glances with Angie, Blanchard decided to tell her something of what had occurred in Guanajuato, leaving out some of the more gruesome details, including the story of Mike's ring. Charmian was clearly shocked.

"Pepe was *murdered*?"

"Shot through the head."

"Have the police...do they know who did it?"

"They think they do," Blanchard said carefully. "A jealous husband."

Charmian's gaze was searching, as if she wanted to determine whether or not Blanchard agreed with the police. "That's awful," she said. "Did he tell you anything about your son?"

"I never got a chance to talk to him. Someone else got to him first."

"Then you're still looking for Mike?"

"Yes."

"Here? Is that why you're in San Miguel?"

"Mike was here with Angie two weeks ago. I have reason to believe that...something might have happened here then. It's a long shot, but..." He shrugged. He didn't like being evasive with her, remembering how readily she had volunteered to help him in Guadalajara, how much he had enjoyed being with her that afternoon and evening in Ajijic. At the same time he was reluctant to drag her more deeply into his problems than she already had.

After eating, the three of them walked over to the *jardín* and had a drink in one of the small cafés where they could watch the fireworks and listen to the strolling musicians. The sidewalks and streets were wall-to-wall crowds, festive and noisy, and after a while Blanchard noted signs of distress in Angie's face, pain in her eyes. She wasn't ready for this—not without Mike.

They left Charmian Stewart at the plaza and walked back to the Casa Miguel. Most of the way Angie was silent, thoughtful, but when they reached her room she stopped Blanchard as he turned away.

"How much do you know about Miss Stewart?"

"Only what she's told me. You know about as much as I do. Why? You don't mind sharing the room with her, do you, Angie?"

"It isn't that." She hesitated, an inner struggle mirrored in her worried eyes. "Doesn't it strike you as a little strange?"

"What is it, Angie?"

"That she would be at the Campo Bello when you were there, just when you needed help. And that she would be here, just when you needed a translator again."

Blanchard had been thinking it a particularly happy accident, one of life's rare serendipities, but at Angie's words he felt a distinct chill of warning.

His son was in the hands of a murderer. The feeling of being cleverly manipulated was sharpening. Could he really accept *anyone* at face value? The warmth he sensed in Charmian Stewart was, after all, the oldest lure in the world. How could he be sure that it had not been conveniently placed in his way?

"It's not so much of a coincidence," he said. "Seems like half of Mexico is here in San Miguel tonight. And Charmian couldn't have known we'd end up here at the Casa Miguel, could she? We didn't know it ourselves until we got here, and she arrived yesterday."

Angie's relief was transparent. Blanchard thought that she had been somewhat impressed by Charmian, although she wouldn't admit it openly. She hadn't dared to like anyone who might be involved in Mike's disappearance. While that suspicion hung over her Blanchard doubted that she would have been able to close her eyes with the older woman in the same room.

"I'm glad," Angie said. Then, with an amused cock of her head, "She likes you too, you know."

She closed the door on his surprise.

Nearby the bright-plumed parrot, green with a fiery red cap, also cocked its head as if in imitation of Angie. The bird was allowed its freedom on the veranda, and it was now clinging to the back of a chair. "Likes you," the parrot squawked. "Likes you, likes you."

"What the hell do you know about it Blanchard growled.

At which the parrot began to search diligently under its wing for parasites.

3

Around midnight Jeff Blanchard stepped outside his room and watched some of the brilliant pinwheels and Roman candles explode and cartwheel against a storm-black sky. The arrival of midnight brought a wild pealing of bells that seemed to go on interminably. There followed more fiery explosions of color to light up the darkness, distant strains of music, and, just as the midnight chimes at last came to an end, a fresh outburst of bell-ringing to signal the quarter-hour.

He went back inside and lay on the bed, listening to the thump of the rockets carrying their multicolored candles toward a fiery death. That blackness to the south over the mountains meant more rain; the fact had no significance, like a stone dropped into a bottomless pit, making no sound no matter how long you listened. Sun or rain, dry or wet, light or dark; he knew how Angie felt. There had been a time after Elaine's death when those differences had ceased to exist for him.

If anything happened to Mike, he thought, all that he had been in his adult life would end. Elaine and Mike had been the core, the thrust, the meaning of everything that he did, all that he deeply felt, all that he sought—and failed—to protect. If that purpose ended here, in an alien land, his whole life would drop into a void, awakening no echoes.

Not so, he thought.

There would be one sound: the cry of rage.

Wherever he was hiding, Darrell Kinney would hear it.

The house tour set off from the gates of the Instituto Allende at eleven o'clock Sunday morning. It was scheduled to end two hours later at the public library, which benefited from these invitational tours. The flyer on the bulletin board at the Casa Miguel had instructed those planning to take the tour not to plan to drive their own cars, since they were unfamiliar with the twisting hillside streets of the little town. As was the custom, residents of the foreign colony would provide volunteer transportation.

Angela Wylie Blanchard, standing apart from the crowd of sixty or more tourists who milled around the entrance to the grounds of the institute on this rain-dampened morning, waiting for the chauffeured cars to begin to arrive in the jovially hectic, catch-as-catch-can arrangements of the tour, wished herself anywhere else, away from all these people of another generation, another world, all looking secure and slightly addled with their cameras and their chatter, the women all wearing sandals or city shoes that would be a disaster on rough cobblestones. They would find out today. Angie wished herself far away. With Michael.

Three months, she thought. It was impossible to become so completely involved with another person in only three months that you went around with a great hollow emptiness inside when he wasn't there.

And now something was growing in that emptiness, a great fear growing in her every day in the way a child might have grown, except that it had grown from seed to embryo to this terrible *presence* in just two weeks.

She had not really learned to handle the reality of Michael Blanchard in those three months. How could she expect to handle this other mystery, the denial of him, the fear of a world in which there was no Michael?

She was liberated, independent, with-it. She had told herself that she would never let herself *need* anyone that much. Then along came California Golden Boy and *wham*!

In their first weeks she had enjoyed a familiar kind of boy-girl warfare. She had gotten a charge out of putting him down. Then all of a sudden it had ceased to be fun. Oh, the teasing remained wonderful, *pretending* to put him down, but not the real thing. Suddenly it was like putting herself down, as if she were part of him and he were part of her. They could still have fights, really monstrous fights, but not the kind that involved really cutting each other up.

It was too easy to hurt Michael, for one thing. In a funny way he was more vulnerable than she was.

Oh, stop it, stop it, *stop it*!

Angie looked away from the street toward the school grounds, blinking, as if afraid that someone would see the pain in her eyes. She was glad for the moment that Michael's father wasn't standing beside her. He was over talking to Charmian Stewart and another couple who were staying at the Casa Miguel. He would have seen the pain if he'd been standing there.

That was the thing that had surprised her about him. He *looked* at you. He really looked. It surprised her that Michael didn't know that about his own father.

Jeff Blanchard seemed to believe that it was important for them to do everything she had done with Michael here in San Miguel, to go to all the same places, to do all the same things. He seemed convinced that the man Kinney was watching them and would find some other way to...

Angie shivered. She thought that she would see those red eyes, Pepe's eyes, in her dreams as long as she lived.

Now Jeff Blanchard was edging through the

crowds toward her. The first cars were arriving and the waiting tourists were pushing and jostling in their surge toward the street. Angie found herself forced through the open gates to the edge of the road.

Blanchard reached her side. "Charmian will be right along. She'd met that couple before, the ones from Oregon. Nice people."

"I guess even people from Oregon can be nice," Angie said.

It was the kind of mock put-down she had come to enjoy with Michael. Now his father grinned at her in response, and Angie felt a jolt of recognition. He and Michael didn't resemble each other closely, but there were expressions of the eyes and mouth, inflections of their voices, *attitudes* that were exactly the same.

A small black car darted up to the gates. It stopped directly in front of them and the driver leaned across to open the rear door. "Two only," he called out cheerfully, his old man's face wrinkling in a smile. Only his gleaming bald head was smooth. He was looking directly at Angie and Blanchard. "Hop in, please."

Jeff Blanchard hesitated, looking back through the crowd. Looking for Charmian Stewart, Angie knew. She was not yet in sight, cut off by the movement toward the street of the other waiting tourists. Those close by were staring at Angie and Blanchard impatiently.

"Hurry along," the wrinkled little man in the black car called out. "Others're right behind me."

Jeff Blanchard glanced at Angie and shrugged. His disappointment was so evident that Angie almost smiled. Michael was equally transparent. She had known that he was in love with her long before he did.

A moment later they were in the back seat of the black car, a Renault. The front seat beside the driver was empty and Angie wondered idly why he had only wanted to accept two passengers. Then they were moving, turning abruptly along a back street and winding upward into the hills, bouncing over the cobblestone roads toward the handsome hillside homes of the resident colony. San Miguel was one of three cities in Mexico, Angie recalled, that had been designated a national monument by the government, which meant that anything built or restored had to conform to the Colonial style of the Spanish era. It was funny, Angie thought, they were so proud of their revolution, yet they wanted so many things to be Spanish. They even took pride in being light-skinned instead of dark like the true *indios*. Michael had said that that was why so many Mexican men grew mustaches, to prove that they had all this Spanish blood and were not just Indians.

"They really surprise you," she said suddenly, making an effort to shake off her depression. "The homes. They have these high blank walls and you can't see anything, you have no way of imagining what's inside. Then you walk into these intimate little patios or step out into a beautiful garden. It's really fantastic."

Their driver, a wiry little man of about fifty, Angie guessed, not as old as the first glimpse of his face had suggested, revealed that he was a retired surgeon from Cleveland. His name was Wilson. His bald crown was very white, as if he habitually wore a hat. He maneuvered his little car up the steep lanes of San Miguel with nimble self-assurance.

They drove by a small park where a stream tumbled down the hillside over a rocky bed toward its rendezvous with the river in the valley below. Along the edge of the stream a dozen or more women were washing clothes, scrubbing them on the rocks and then spreading the garments out on bushes to dry. The bushes were better for the task than clotheslines, Angie thought; the air would get at the clothes better. And clothes always smelled nice when they were dried in the sun, fresher somehow than when they came out of a dryer at the local laundromat. Not that there was much sun today. But the early morning clouds seemed to be breaking up here and there, showing patches of blue after the rain. The women probably knew, Angie thought, in the way farmers understood weather. Or else they had no choice but to hope. They certainly didn't have any gas dryers to depend on.

The Renault seemed to have left the other tour cars behind, or else the doctor had followed a different route. Just as Angie was noting this, noting also that Jeff Blanchard had been much more attentive than she, more alert, the little car swung sharply right onto a narrow street and skidded to a stop. A sign at the corner, painted on the wall of the corner house, read Avenida Ignacio.

"There it is," Wilson said, pointing across the way. "Number 124. House is open, so you can just walk right in. Enjoy yourselves, folks, and take as long as you like. You'll find the next homes listed on that mimeographed sheet you were given at the gates."

"Thanks a lot," Jeff Blanchard said. He appeared to have relaxed. "Where are the others?"

"Oh, they'll be right along," Wilson said with his cheerful bedside manner. "Be here now if they knew these streets as well as I do, and if they'd drive a sensible-sized car instead of those great big gas-eaters. Don't worry, I'll be parked down the line, near the last house, when you finish the tour."

As they walked across the newly cobblestoned road—its rough surface emulating the older streets—Angie saw Jeff Blanchard glancing hopefully over his shoulder. He was still wishing that Charmian hadn't become separated from them, Angie thought, and hoping that she would catch up.

The heavy, carved wooden door to Number 124 opened at a touch, ushering them into an open-ended, tiled passageway. Directly ahead was a short flight of steps and a path leading through a tiny garden to the main entrance. To the left of the steps was a small fountain and miniature waterfall. To the right of the entry was a single room and bath, separate from the main house. It was beautifully furnished in the Spanish Colonial style with what Angie was certain were genuine and expensive antiques. The colorfully tiled bathroom and the general decor could have come from the pages of *House Beautiful*.

"Fantastic," Angie murmured. "If you're gonna have a guest room, I mean, this is the only way to go."

There was irony in the comment, a quick perception of how much money had gone into this room, how far removed it was from the real Mexico it pretended to mimic. From those women in the park pounding their wash on the rocks, Angie thought, as they did almost every day of their lives.

She followed Jeff Blanchard up the steps of the little front garden patio and along a bricked path toward the house. "It's quiet," Blanchard said, sounding puzzled. "Don't the host and hostess hang around to greet their visitors?"

"They must be inside," Angie said.

She had really enjoyed the tour the first time she took it. That was because it was another new experience to share with Michael. Everything they had done was new to both of them, a world opening up as if for the first time, for them alone.

Blanchard glanced behind them. The street door had swung shut.

"The others will be along in a minute," Angie said with a faint smile. Including your Charmian Stewart.

And mine, she thought. They had talked a lot during the night, and Angie had found herself liking the other woman, not even thinking of her as belonging to that "older generation." Angie had surprised herself by the way in which she had opened up. Charmian had been around young people all her life; maybe that was why she related.

As Angie and Jeff Blanchard paused at the entrance to the house the silence around them seemed total. The high walls created complete privacy from the street, the hushed seclusion the owners of the house must cherish. Along the top of the wall fronting the street was the one jarring note Angie hated, inescapable wherever you went in Mexico: a layer of broken glass, meant to discourage anyone thinking of climbing over the wall.

The door leading into the tiled foyer was open in welcome. The house was cool and quiet. Although not large by American standards, it gained a sense of openness from the striking views through large windows at the rear. The design had been adapted to the hillside site, creating multiple levels inside and in the terraced gardens. In sharp contrast to the blank façade on the street side, the back walls of glass revealed a picturesque vista of walls and gardens and houses descending the hillside. Through the floor-to-ceiling windows of the living area, a few steps below the entry, Angie could see the spires of the Parochial Church and the twin domes of another cathedral, surrounded by the squatter walls and red roofs of the entire village of San Miguel.

Enchanted with the house in spite of her nagging depression, Angie wandered up a short flight of steps to an upstairs bedroom left of the entry. She peered over a balcony railing at Jeff Blanchard, who was thoughtfully standing in the sunken living room directly below her. As she turned into the bedroom behind her, she heard Jeff Blanchard's steps receding away from her toward another section of the house.

He was nervous, she thought; edgy. Waiting for something.

For some reason she found herself thinking of Dr. Wilson. She wondered if he lived in a house like this one, and if he drove his battered little Renault sedan not for economy but, as he had suggested, because it was adapted like a mountain goat to the steep and tortured streets of the village.

Angie was also wondering what it was about the house that disturbed her, when she heard a door slam.

Other tourists arriving, she thought, half listening for voices and footsteps. She had begun to wonder if Dr. Wilson had got the house number wrong. But that couldn't be; the house was obviously open for the tour.

The silence, she thought suddenly. And the coolness. The house was too quiet, and ever so slightly stale in smell. That was what had been bothering her. It had the smell of a house that has been empty for some time.

Well, there was nothing strange about that. Absentee owners probably allowed their homes to be opened for the tour. No mystery.

Angie sat pensively on a corner of the king-size bed in the upstairs bedroom. A lovely room, with its handwoven spread and colorful throw cushions, that hand-carved chest and the tin-framed mirror over it, the little private balcony outside, the string pictures on the whitewashed walls, a large oil painting of a Mexican street scene. San Miguel?

They had never had a room of their own, she and Michael. Angie had never really got around to thinking about it. They had known only motel and hotel rooms together, lots of those. It had never mattered, it had been fun, all those funny little rooms, all those squeaky beds...

She pushed off abruptly, turning to glare at the oversized bed with its beautiful spread almost angrily.

From somewhere in the house Jeff Blanchard called out. "Hey, where is everybody?"

Angie was starting toward the steps leading back to the entry when she passed the blue-tiled bathroom. It was so striking that she paused, stepping inside. The room was as elegant as the bedroom it served, rich with the color of its hand-made blue tiles from Puebla. The tiles covered the floor, the walls, and the counter top with its pink washbasin. There was also an old stone column that seemed to hold up one corner at the edge of a sunken tub. An antique column, Angie guessed, rescued from an old building, perhaps from the one that had stood on this site. How old would it be? Two hundred years? Three hundred?

"Angie?"

Another door opened and closed, its slam resounding.

I'm up here, she thought, waiting. If that had been Michael calling she would have run for the stairs. Flown. But it wasn't....

The image in the big mirror over the counter caught and held her eye. Who was that stranger, that girl with the haunted blue eyes and the hair that looked as if it had been dragged through a hedge? My God, was this what she was letting happen to her? What would Michael say if he thought she was giving up? She couldn't do that. His father was right. They had to keep looking, trying, hoping.

On impulse Angie dug into her purse for her comb. At least she could drag some of the hedge clippings out of her hair.

She attacked her long hair with something like ferocity, sensing that this was therapy, busy work, a woman's pretense at normality. She found a snag, jerked at it, felt the painful pull with something like pleasure. What had she thought she was doing, letting herself go like this, as if it didn't matter any more what she looked like, actually *quitting*! *I'm sorry, Michael. I'm scared. I'm afraid of being alone in the dark. I never was before. That's what you've done to me.*

She stopped, her arm arrested in mid-air, the teeth of the comb still holding a few strands of honey-colored hair. She stared at the face in the mirror, her eyes widening.

Not her face, but a new face behind her shoulder, a monkey face with bright-red hair crowning it. But the hair didn't belong there, she knew that face, it was—

Now there was another, dark-skinned and black-eyed and full of teeth, peering over her other shoulder, a brutal face with a hawk nose and prominent

182

cheekbones, the face of Geronimo or Cochise or Benito Juárez.

For an instant Angie stood paralyzed, staring at the two faces grinning over her shoulders like gargoyles. Then she whirled, her mouth opening to scream.

A hand clamped over her mouth, stifling the cry. Another hand grasped her arm and wrenched it painfully behind her back, twisting upward. There was something in the hand that pressed against her mouth and pushed upward. A sharp smell stung her nostrils.

She fought convulsively, kicking out. The pain in her arm bowed her back, driving her almost to her knees. Her staring, desperate eyes in the mirror saw the monkey face under the red wig, saw the white fold of cloth jammed against her nose and mouth, saw a length of cord in the powerful hands of the dark-skinned Mexican.

And suddenly she knew what the smell was. Chloroform.

The mirror misted over. Her knees melted and she sagged into his arms, not Michael's arms but the thin and corded and surprisingly strong arms of Dr. Wilson.

5

From the informal family room a half-level below the kitchen, Jeff Blanchard looked thoughtfully out at the terraced gardens. They descended in graceful steps all the way to the next street, the last step a sharp drop that placed the street at a considerably lower level on the hillside. Puzzled, Blanchard heard Angie moving around in the far bedroom wing.

"Hey, where is everybody?" he called out.

There was no answer. Something was wrong, he

thought. An empty house. Their chauffeur, Wilson, must have got the address wrong. Blanchard didn't have the mimeographed sheet. Angie had absently stuck it into her purse, not even bothering to look at it. But surely the others on the tour should have caught up by now. They hadn't come up the hill that fast.

He started up the half-flight of steps to the very modern kitchen, turned right and reached the entry. Here he was able to look across the sunken living area and the gardens to the street below. "Angie?" he said.

Then he saw Darrell Kinney.

He was standing motionless in the middle of the street, staring upward at the house. It seemed to Blanchard that Kinney was staring directly at him.

Blanchard ran across the living room and slammed through the door to the patio. He moved forward quickly to a low stone wall. He could feel his heart pumping strongly, the blood thick in his temples.

There was no mistake. Darrell Kinney, or a man who could have been his father, black hair silvered at the temples, was waiting below. His eyes were hidden behind dark glasses, but Blanchard saw him smile. The smile seemed to mock him.

"Kinney!" he shouted in sudden rage. "Damn you, where's my son?"

Kinney turned and began to trot easily along the street. Blanchard charged down the nearest flight of garden steps, found his way blocked, vaulted a wall, and landed on more steps. He stumbled, twisting an ankle. Limping, he plunged downward recklessly to the next level. He had lost sight of Kinney now. At the lower garden levels he could no longer see the street.

The last steps brought him close to the wall at the bottom of the garden. It was eight feet high. And the street beyond was still lower, Blanchard judged. A twelve-foot drop at least.

He had to try it. Looking around, baffled, he found no ladder, no bench, nothing movable that he could bring close to the high wall.

He jumped for it. He got one hand over the top of the wall. Sharp pain stabbed his fingers. He lost his hold, dropped back. The glass on top of the wall had opened a deep cut in the crease of his palm and across the bottom pads of two fingers.

Angry and frustrated, Blanchard pounded back up the staggered series of steps through the gardens to the upper patio. He ran toward the nearest door, the one he had used from the living room.

It would not open.

"Angie!" he yelled. "Hurry up—open this door!"

The room beyond the glass wall was empty of anything but the elegant furnishings. He could see a section of the bedroom balcony. She wasn't in sight.

Fear was beginning to slice through his angry excitement like a searching wind. He ran around the house to the door he had noticed in the family room. That entrance was also locked.

Quite suddenly Jeff Blanchard knew that all of the doors were locked. He had been trapped in the garden.

No. The fear cut deeper.

Angie had been trapped inside the house.

No one answered his shouts. There were no tourists inside, wandering through the rooms with delighted cries of admiration. Too late he realized that there would be none. This house had never been on the tour.

Kinney! He hadn't been there in the street by chance or blunder. He had deliberately lured Blanchard out of the house and through the gardens. Away from Angie.

Blanchard was looking around for a loose brick or a chair with which to smash a window when he realized that the side garden walls were no more than five feet high at the level of the upper patio. And between good neighbors there was no glass on top of the walls.

Vaulting over the side wall, Blanchard dropped onto a dining terrace. A man and a woman, white-haired and elderly, were sitting down to a late

Sunday breakfast. They stopped eating to gape at Blanchard. The man had a piece of scrambled egg clinging to one corner of his mouth.

He scraped back his chair. "I say, what does this mean?" His accent was British.

"I'm sorry—can't explain. How can I get through to the street?"

The Englishman glanced automatically toward the terrace doors. Blanchard swung around the table and ran through the house. A maid in a white dress stopped in the kitchen doorway as he bolted past her, her black eyes wide.

No one tried to stop him.

The street was quiet, empty. Its high blank walls concealed any hint of violence. There was no fleet of cars, no trail of happy tourists. How could he have been so easily tricked? He had been so ready for the unexpected that he had been readily fooled by the obvious.

He ran back to Number 124. The massive wooden door that faced the street was locked.

Blanchard stared helplessly at the high wall with its barrier of broken glass at the top. His hand was still bleeding freely. Angrily he jerked a handkerchief from his pocket and wrapped it savagely around the cuts.

Now Kinney had Angie as well as Mike.

Blanchard had to get back inside the house, to confirm the conviction that possessed him, seeping through his brain and his body like a transfusion of icy water.

But he knew already that he would not find Angie there.

6

Avenida Ignacio actually was on the list of houses thrown open for the Sunday tour, but the number was

101, and it was the last house on the list.

Jeff Blanchard found some of the volunteer tour guides with their charges on the next parallel street above Ignacio. He had trouble making himself understood, as if his wild story were something in another language.

"I don't understand," one of the volunteers repeated, perplexed. "Number 124 wasn't on the tour."

"But that's where he took us, damn it! That's what I'm trying to tell you."

"Who did you say was your driver?"

"His name is Wilson. Dr. Wilson. He has a black Renault."

A man with the swollen red-blotched complexion of the heavy drinker pushed into the center of the circle of curious onlookers. His name was Walsh, and he was well-known to the other volunteers. "We have no Wilson here," he said flatly, his hard nasal voice midwestern United States in origin.

"That was the name he gave us."

"I've lived in San Miguel for fifteen years. I know every American resident, that's for sure. There's no Dr. Wilson here."

The news did not surprise Blanchard.

He saw Charmian Stewart staring at him from the fringes of the crowd. She was not one of them, he thought. She couldn't be. There were some truths in life that asked to be taken on trust. This was one of them, that one's brain could be wrong but not one's heart.

But how many hearts had erred, in how many million conspiracies?

Someone came forward with the information that the owners of 124 Avenida Ignacio were the Randalls, a couple from Texas who spent their summers on their ranch and their winters in San Miguel. They were not expected to arrive from Texas before late October. They always timed their arrival for the departure of the tropical hurricane season and the rains it generated across the Mexican plateau. During their absence the house was not rented out but was looked after by a neighbor, year-round residents.

Blanchard knew the neighbors. They recognized him the moment their door was opened. The Englishman was identified as Richard Hartley, another doctor. Blanchard was vaguely surprised; he hadn't thought that doctors did as well under the English system of socialized medicine as American doctors did under the AMA.

"This is Mr. Blanchard, Dick. He claims his daughter-in-law got locked inside the Randall place." Walsh's tone was apologetic. An old-timer who liked his rum, he dropped his truculent manner where future invitations to stop by for a drink might be in order. "Don't you have the key?"

"Yes, but... I say, this fellow came right over our wall! Went right through the house without so much as a word!"

"I said I was sorry."

"Yes, well, look, Dick, would it be too much trouble to let us have the key so we could have a look round? Sort of check out the man's story?" Walsh smiled ingratiatingly. "Wouldn't want a young girl to be trapped in there until the Randalls roll up in their Caddie." When Hartley hesitated, Walsh added, "I'll stop by a bit later and fill you in. Sure it's all a mistake, but we can't afford to have anything that gives the tour a bad name."

"I've said all along we might consider dropping the whole thing," Hartley grumbled. "It served its purpose well enough, but that time's past."

In spite of his complaint, Hartley fetched a heavy iron ring with two sets of keys attached.

"Are those the only keys?" Blanchard asked.

Hartley regarded him indignantly. "I believe Randall keeps another set, but that's all. And I can assure you these haven't been out of my possession."

"The house looked dusted."

"Well, of course, the maid comes in once a week while they're away. But Lupe's been doing the Randalls for ten years!"

Blanchard nodded. It made little difference. If someone hadn't learned about Lupe's key, the garden walls were not impassable to a determined man with time and ingenuity. He would have required nothing more than the cover of darkness, a ladder or a rope, and something to throw across the glass on top to avoid cuts. All they had really wanted was an empty house and an improvised plan for separating Blanchard from Angie.

Darrell Kinney knew him better than he knew Kinney, Blanchard thought grimly. Kinney could predict his moves unerringly. His own, like his purpose, remained obscure.

The procession, which had grown as Blanchard's story was passed along, adding spice to the day's tour, trailed next door to the Randall house. Charmian Stewart appeared at Blanchard's side in unvoiced sympathy. They had trouble getting out of the way as the eagerly curious pushed ahead of them into the small front garden.

As Blanchard had expected, the house was empty.

There was no evidence of a struggle, nothing disturbed, no sign at all that anyone had been there.

7

That night, over a listless supper, Jeff Blanchard told Charmian everything that had happened since Angie's phone call on Sunday. If she was surprised to learn that he had not been completely frank with her before, she did not show it. Blanchard had the feeling that she understood.

The story left her subdued, picking at her food.

"It's not your problem," he said lamely. "I guess I had to unload it on someone."

"It *is* my problem," she retorted, stung. "That is, I...I liked Angie. I just can't believe it."

"It's not part of your everyday trip to Mexico."

"The police weren't very helpful?"

"They seemed to think I was confessing to a crime." He smiled humorlessly. "They all look like a film maker's idea of a bunch of Mexican *bandidos*, for what that's worth. That Walsh wasn't much help. He knew them all, he was kidding around with the sergeant. He talked quite a bit in Spanish, so I missed most of it, but I think he was ridiculing my story. It's my guess the police think it was all a joke on me, that Angie has run off to join Mike. They promised to check with the police in Guanajuato on what happened there. I don't know if that will help or not." Blanchard stared bleakly past her shoulder at the blank wall of the dining room in the Casa Miguel. "I have a feeling Kinney is a long way away from here by now. With Angie."

"You're sure the man in the street was him?"

Blanchard scowled. "This morning when I saw him I was dead positive. Now...I suppose I'm beginning to doubt my own story."

"Come off it," Charmian said bluntly. "You said your son recognized Kinney. The photograph was stolen in Ajijic. And now you've seen him. That's two witnesses, and both of you had reason to remember him. Especially you, Jeff. If you were close friends, drinking buddies, as you put it."

"Yeah. I wish I could have got closer to him, just to be more sure." He paused. In this innocent setting, amid the murmurs of other diners, while an old man shuffled along the veranda putting hoods over the cages of his canaries for the night, the very air around him seemed heavy with dread. "The trouble is, now I don't have the vaguest idea where to look next. Until now I've had something to go on, a next place to turn. Now..."

Charmian's hazel eyes were troubled; sympathetic. Blanchard felt their impact but could not respond.

Could he find a new center for his life, this late in the game? He doubted it. If, because of something in his past, because of Darrell Kinney, both Mike's and Angie's lives were in jeopardy, his own hung in the balance with them.

Kinney had to be counting on that. He knows *you*, Blanchard thought for the second time that day. He knows the conventional attitudes you accept, the traditional loyalties you hold important. That was something to remember.

"Is there anything about him," Charmian was saying, "that wouldn't have changed, anything that would make you sure..."

Blanchard jerked his attention back to her, trying to look interested.

"I'm sorry," she apologized. "I suppose I'm pushing." She started to rise.

"No, stay here. You're not pushing, you're doing exactly what I would want you to do...caring. And there is something about him that I couldn't forget and he couldn't change."

"What is it?"

"He has webbed fingers," Blanchard said.

He watched the blood drain slowly from her cheeks, leaving her white and drawn, as if she had been struck. "Oh my God," she whispered.

Interlude Four: Morelia

The savage barking of Wulf, the huge German shepherd who prowled the grounds at night, aroused

Jesús Gutiérrez, who in turn summoned Ernst von Schoenwald.

The German met George Robbins at the iron gate leading from the garage. The yellow light in the wrought-iron lantern over the gate gave Robbins' face a sallow cast, his cap of hair a strange orange hue.

"That damned dog," Robbins muttered.

"Be glad of him, my dear George. He guards us well." Von Schoenwald peered past Robbins toward the car. "You had no trouble?"

"No."

"Then I may assume you have the prize with you?"

"She's in the car."

Von Schoenwald nodded in satisfaction. "Is she as beautiful as her picture?"

"You can see for yourself," Robbins snapped. He was tired from the long night drive in poor visibility, and his temper was short.

"I can indeed," the German retorted coolly. "You will bring her inside. Who is that with you—Riki?"

"Yes. Where do you want her?"

"María's room will do. It has a good door, and the window is barred."

"What about María?"

Von Schoenwald was aware of Jesús Gutiérrez standing nearby, listening, his face as impassive as that of his brother Ricardo, who waited by the car. "I will take care of her." Jesús fancied the girl, he thought; now he could have her.

He went back through the house while Robbins did as he was ordered. María Teresa's door was closed but unlocked. He entered without knocking.

The girl sat up suddenly with a small cry when the light went on. She blinked at him, obsidian eyes anxious. *"Qué pasó? Qué tiene?"*

"Nothing is the matter, my dear María. However, I am in need of your room."

"I...I do not understand."

The girl, still sleepy, tried to summon up a coy

expression, misreading his hasty intrusion in the middle of the night. She knelt erect in the bed, letting the covers fall away. The pink satin nightgown she favored clung to her, molding her immature breasts. "I did not think you wished—"

"You were quite correct," von Schoenwald interrupted impatiently. "Now please get out of that bed, María."

Bewildered, the girl did not move. "You wish me to come to your room?"

"I wish you to do what I say!" Angrily von Schoenwald strode to the bed and dragged her from it. He jerked her arm painfully as he pulled her erect when she would have tumbled. "You will go to Lupe. She will find a place for you to sleep."

Consternation brought tears to the girl's huge dark eyes—the eyes of a waif in a sentimental portrait of Mexico, von Schoenwald thought with contempt. "But what is wrong? Why—?"

María broke off as George Robbins appeared in the doorway. Behind him loomed the dark, Indian face of Riki Gutiérrez. He was supporting the figure of a tall young woman, a *norteamericana*, whose head lolled loosely to one side as she sagged against the Mexican, as if she too had just awakened from a deep sleep. A spill of long blond hair fell partly across her face, which was very pale. Her mouth was slack.

"Quién es? Who is she? Why do you bring her here?" María felt a stab of jealousy and fear. "No!" she cried, as the swarthy Riki half carried the young woman into the room. *"No la va meter en mi lugar!"*

"It is no longer your place," Ernst von Schoenwald said sharply. "Now do what I say. Riki—" He nodded toward the bed. "Put her there. Then you will take María to Lupe."

"Why do you do this?" María demanded through her tears. *"No quiero irme! Por favor!"*

Von Schoenwald's anger exploded. His right hand, palm open, cracked across her cheek, rocking her head, stunning her with the force of the blow.

"You wish to know why? Because you are a vain and stupid child—that is reason enough. Now do as you are told!"

Riki Gutiérrez placed the tall American girl on the bed, where she slumped without resistance, boneless. He stepped quickly to María's side and took her arm, dragging her toward the door. Resisting, María wailed piteously. "What of my things? *Mi ropa! Mis joyas!*"

"You shall have them later," the German said with cold indifference, his attention already turning toward the young woman who had replaced María on the bed. "But you will have little need of fine clothes and jewels in the kitchen."

"No! No quiero!" María cried, struggling futilely in Riki's grip, suddenly realizing the full enormity of what was happening to her, remembering her haughty ways with Lupe in recent days. "I will go to *mi mamá!*"

"Riki!"

The harsh command was enough. Hastily Riki pulled the frightened, protesting girl from the room.

In the silence that followed, Ernst von Schoenwald glanced from the girl's limp figure on the bed toward George Robbins, who had waited in silence.

"She has not been harmed?"

Robbins shrugged. "We had to keep her quiet, that's all. You won't find any damage when she wakes up."

"No one saw you take her? You weren't followed?"

"No—no trouble."

"What of Kinney?"

"He was... cooperative. But after we took the girl, he disappeared. He was supposed to meet us, but he didn't show up. I don't know where the hell he is."

"Perhaps he simply didn't wish to risk being seen," von Schoenwald said thoughtfully.

"Blanchard saw him," Robbins answered shortly. "That's how we got him out of the way so we could take the girl. That was Kinney's idea. It worked well enough."

"I see." The German continued to look thoughtful, frowning slightly, but after a moment his glance went again to the bed. The girl wore a very short skirt. It was pushed even higher over her thighs as she lay sprawled in a drugged sleep. Her legs were long and slender and shapely....

"I still don't trust Kinney," George Robbins said.

"It does not matter," von Schoenwald replied. "If he is playing a game, we will soon know. With her we will control the American, Blanchard. As for Kinney, we must not be hasty, George. I will have to make some arrangements. But in the end you will have your way. Yes, George, I think it is time for us to end our relationship with Mr. Alan Slater."

For the first time since his arrival at the gate, George Robbins smiled.

5 Morelia

1

"Darrell Kinney wants me in Morelia," Blanchard said.

"How can you be sure?"

"I think that's what he must have had in mind from the beginning. For his own reasons he had to lead me along, step by step. He knew it when he forced himself on you there in Patzcuaro. He had to see where you might fit into his plans."

"Couldn't he simply have wanted to find out if there was any relationship...any connection between us?"

"Sure, that was the main reason, to learn how much you knew—what I might have said to you. But you told him you were going from there to San Miguel. I think he must have already worked things out to make sure I'd be in San Miguel with Angie. After Pepe was killed I *had* to go there."

"So he had to know there was a good chance we'd run into each other again."

"It's a small town," Blanchard said.

Charmian Stewart studied the narrow road ahead, squeezing over to the right as a truck passed them heading north. She was unable to avoid a deep chuckhole. The impact as the Vega's wheel slammed into the hole rattled dishes and packages and teeth. "Damn!" she said.

During the night someone with a hacksaw had cut through the heavy old padlock that secured the doors of the garage at the Casa Miguel. The garage faced a back street at the rear of the gardens, at least a hundred feet from the main buildings. The night watchman, who was also a daytime gardener and had to sleep sometime, had heard nothing. The only thing stolen from the garage was Mike and Angie's Volkswagen.

This time Blanchard had not bothered to go to the police. He was beginning to understand the Mexican's realistic attitude toward any such authority. If you get into trouble, the one thing you don't do is appeal to the police. Your chances of receiving a sympathetic hearing are not great, and the possibilities of getting into deeper trouble are.

He knew that Mike or Angie—Mike if the entry permit was in his name—would have trouble leaving Mexico without the car, but that was a worry for later. Now it didn't matter.

Stuck without transportation, and convinced that the web-fingered man Charmian had met in Patzcuaro, who called himself Alan Slater, was really Kinney, Blanchard's protests had been halfhearted when she offered to drive him to Morelia. If he could get there fast, he might for once catch Kinney unprepared.

Blanchard thought he understood Charmian's motives. She liked Angie; she seemed as worried about the girl as he was. He didn't ask himself if her offer had anything to do with him.

Now they were driving south on Highway 51 toward Celaya and the freeway in the Vega wagon. They passed a dead horse at the side of the road, bloated, rigid in rigor mortis, its legs sticking out like poles. Blanchard saw Charmian wince. Dead animals are a familiar sight along Mexico's highways— dogs, cows, burros, occasional horses. They are hit by indifferent Mexican truck drivers or by reckless tourists traveling at high speeds at night on those treacherous dark roads along which farm animals and strays roam freely, for there are few fences. Usually the animals are simply left along the road's apron or in a ditch at the side to rot or to be picked over by scavengers. Like the rabbits that litter the highways of northern Nevada, Blanchard thought. He was not sure why the killing of a horse seemed more terrible.

They passed a picturesque old mission on a hill, circled down a long grade and across some railroad tracks, and entered a small village. Charmian slowed, driving between high, blank white walls. Blank brown Indian faces watched them without expression; the Indians of North or South America have had little reason to trust light-skinned peoples. It was the kind of poor, shabby Mexican village that offered few of the amenities that attract American retirees. There were no *supermercados* or fine old Colonial houses easily remodeled into showplaces.

When they emerged at the south end of the village, Charmian broke a long silence. "Why did he kidnap Angie?" There was a controlled anger behind the question.

"Whatever it is he wants," Blanchard answered harshly, "he's willing to murder for it. He's made sure I know that. And now he has two lives to hold over my head."

"It seems so...so chancy, the way he's done things. I mean, gambling that we'd meet and that I'd tell you about him. Gambling that I would mention those webbed fingers. And then gambling that he could get you out of that house long enough for someone to grab Angie before you could get back."

"He took risks. Maybe that means he's desperate—and that could be an advantage if I only knew why. But if I had to choose one word to describe Kinney it would be that he's an opportunist. He was always quick to see any chance to score, with a woman or stolen supplies or an officer who didn't want to be bothered with how things got done as long as there

was no static, nothing to make him look bad."
Blanchard thought suddenly of Kinney's disappearance over France, the presumption of death by accident or encounter with the Germans during the war's last convulsions. What opportunity had he seen then and seized? Simply the chance to get out of the war before anyone else, to make his small black-market killings and to enjoy his French women and wines while the suckers went on fighting? Or had he stumbled onto something bigger, some larger score that made it vital no one should ever know he remained alive as Darrell Kinney? That would explain kidnapping Mike Blanchard, someone who had recognized him after all these years. But it still didn't explain the rest of it. Why not simply silence the boy?

Or did he know that Mike wrote a letter?

That might explain it. Kinney had to know how much Mike had told his father, how much Jeff Blanchard knew or guessed. So it was necessary to lure him into Mexico, to string him along until...

Blanchard scowled. It won't wash, he thought. He could have been silenced too, quickly and easily, that night at the Posada del Lago. Instead Kinney had authorized a sap-and-search mission, not search-and-destroy.

No, Darrell Kinney wanted him alive. And he wanted him in his home territory. Blanchard had checked the Mexican Tourist Bureau's *mapa* that Charmian carried in her glove compartment. Morelia and Patzcuaro, where Slater-Kinney had his two gift shops, were only about sixty-five kilometers apart, something like forty miles. An hour's drive. Somewhere in that circle Kinney was waiting for him.

And there, please God, he would find Mike and Angie safe, hostages for his coming.

Charmian was watching him with sidelong glances as she drove, curious, waiting. A nice patience in a woman, he thought.

He said, "He's still an opportunist. He knew what

he wanted to force me to do, but he kept his plans flexible, so he could adapt to any situation as it developed. Like you happening to be there at the Campo Bello and giving me a ride. He checked you out and kept you in mind."

"And used me to tell you where he was—where you could find him after Angie disappeared," Charmian said bitterly.

"That's what it looks like."

"What if I hadn't told you? He couldn't be sure."

"He would have found another way. It didn't really matter. You became a useful messenger, but he could have used another."

"He seems to have a great many people working for him. Willing to do anything for him. He couldn't have killed that man in Guanajuato himself. He was in Patzcuaro Thursday night."

"In any poor country life comes cheap," Blanchard answered. "So does a certain kind of loyalty. And muscle. You don't need much money to buy all of that you want."

"What about Dr. Wilson? He isn't Mexican."

Blanchard shrugged. "Maybe he works for Kinney. Kinney must have people working in his shops, and agents too, buyers. It's even possible that Wilson didn't know what it was all about. Or he knew enough to do what he was told."

The freeway appeared directly ahead of them. A ramp led onto the elevated *cuota*, one of the few freeways in Mexico. It was only a two-lane road, undivided, but the lanes were wide and the surface was smooth and well maintained. There was no cross traffic and there were fences along both sides of the road to keep out the stray animals. Here and there along the way an enterprising farmer disregarded the prohibition against grazing; the good grass on the highway side of the fencing was too tempting to ignore. But in general the freeway, though lacking the charm of a winding road that meandered along with the land's configuration, was safe and fast. There were no potholes and, because it was a toll road, most of the slower Mexican traffic followed the old Celaya road to the south.

They bypassed Celaya itself, taking advantage of as much freeway as possible. They finally left it at Salamanca, a booming industrial town whose belching smoke stacks, visible for twenty miles, modern suburban housing tracts, and excessive traffic made clear that it was plunging headlong into the modern world.

They stopped for lunch at a modern complex adjoining an American-style housing tract at the north edge of the city. The tract featured rows of separate small modern houses, flat-roofed, more or less identical except for a change in the color of the stucco, laid out in a formal grid. The restaurant was part of a private recreational compound that included a soccer field, children's playground, tennis courts, and swimming pool. The restaurant itself was huge, walled in with glass, nearly empty. It was on the second floor of a large building and its sweeping curve of glass overlooked the lawns and play areas and the huge swimming pool now crowded with children. The setting reminded Blanchard of the private country-club facilities now becoming part of so many housing developments in Southern California. They were looking at the children of Mexico's growing, newly affluent middle class, Blanchard thought, the kind who scorned Spanish Colonial and furnished their homes in French or Italian Provincial.

On the luncheon menu he found no *burritos*, *enchiladas*, or *chilis rellenos*. The featured special was a club sandwich. Perhaps more out of curiosity than desire, Blanchard and Charmian both ordered the special. She told him of a restaurant menu she had seen in San Miguel at the popular El Patio. The small steak came with french fries, not rice or beans, and with a kind of soft french roll, called a *bolillo*, not tortillas.

When the club sandwiches arrived they contained the right ingredients, pressed turkey and bacon and tomato and shredded lettuce in multiple layers, but, like so many attempts to imitate things American, the overall result was a disaster. The turkey tasted like rubber, the bacon was raw, the whole concoction was smothered in a thick layer of mayonnaise.

Charmian had been subdued since their talk in the car about Darrell Kinney. The crunch of what lay behind Blanchard, and what might lie ahead, pressed against them during that lunch. Blanchard tried to lighten the mood with conversation. They still had a long ride ahead and he was grateful to Charmian for what she was doing. She might be on a long sabbatical, but certainly she had better things to do than to chauffeur a worried father around Mexico.

"Sometimes I think the prophets are right and the whole world is in danger of becoming a spiritual suburb of Los Angeles," he said, looking through the curving expanse of glass toward the pool and the tennis courts. On the latter some brown young women in white shorts were playing, coiffed and dressed exactly like their cousins in the north. The lone waiter serving the restaurant watched the women idly from the vinyl-and-plastic-and-glass cocktail lounge adjoining. "The trouble is, the outsiders often don't get it quite right. Or they see and copy the superficial things. Which often means the worst things, so you end up with a copy of all our faults, the Hollywood dazzle. The worst of L.A. doesn't make the best of all possible worlds." He grimaced at the club sandwich, a soggy mess on his plate. "Clubhouses and club sandwiches in a country that needs housing and jobs and purified water."

Charmian managed a smile. "I thought it was only us tourists who needed *agua purificada*."

"I read an article in the Mexico City *News* the other day in Guadalajara when I was waiting to hear from Angie. It pointed out that forty percent of Mexico's population has endemic dysentery from birth. It's Mexico's worst baby killer, even more than hunger."

Something like pain flickered across Charmian's

face, but it was gone so quickly that Blanchard was momentarily unsure what he had seen. Then she said, quietly, "Are they going to be killed? Mike and Angie?"

"No. No, why... why would he kill them? It makes no sense. Whatever it is that Kinney wants, he knows he can't get it that way."

"You talk as if you're dealing with someone rational, reasonable, someone who thinks the same way you do."

"I don't know how sane Kinney is," Blanchard answered slowly. "I suppose that's a matter of definition. I think he has to be very clear in his own mind what he's after. And he's been shrewd enough and cunning enough to bring off two kidnappings and a murder, and to stay ahead of me at every step. That's frightening enough, Charmian, but it's neither crazy nor totally unpredictable."

She was abruptly contrite. "I know... I'm sorry, Jeff. I never should have said that. It just popped out. I've never met Mike, but he's your son and I know I'd like him. I care about him already. I do know Angie, we shared a beautiful big old room, and... I'm not coping very well with the idea that she's been kidnapped." She smiled wanly, a negative smile that Blanchard was beginning to recognize, the wry self-appraisal of an intelligent person who is overly self-critical. "I'm not much of a coper. All I can do is translate from the Spanish."

"Hey, cut that out."

"You're doing fine and I have to go and—"

"Stop knocking yourself."

Charmian stared at him as if she didn't understand.

"That's right. If you're going to keep up this anti-Charmian Stewart campaign, you'll have to sit still for a rebuttal."

"I wasn't—"

"Uh-huh. Yes you were. Want me to quote?"

"No, I don't think so."

"Because you know it's not true."

"I wasn't just saying something to trap you into defending me."

"I know that. You put yourself down often. It sounds like a habit."

"I hope you're not going to lecture me about the power of positive thinking and how other people take you at your own estimate of yourself."

"Not if you don't want me to."

For some reason they smiled at each other across the table, as if they had reached a new understanding. In a way they had, Blanchard thought. They were still strangers but they were oddly in tune, moving closer to a shorthand kind of communication, receiving more than the words they sent. That usually came with long acquaintance, he thought, as it had with Elaine over twenty years. Sometimes, if two people were lucky enough to meet, it happened very suddenly.

Blanchard thought of the sterile emptiness of his new apartment in Los Angeles since Mike went off on his own. He thought of the job he had walked out on so breezily after twenty years. He could probably get it back, he thought now with the perspective of time and distance; Wes Marrick had changed hasty or angry decisions before. The point was that it didn't matter.

He needed someone to help fill the emptiness, Jeff Blanchard thought, oddly without any feeling of disloyalty. Not a carbon of Elaine or of himself, but someone who responded to what he was thinking and feeling and saying without having everything spelled out. What was it the kids said now? Someone who felt the same vibes.

How close was he to wanting this woman with the warm hazel eyes, the generous mouth and instincts, there across the table whenever he looked up?

Well, Elaine, he thought, what now?

You'll do what you always do, she would have retorted. Life hadn't bowled her over, nor had it fooled her till the end, a fact that both he and Mike had leaned on too much, Blanchard thought. He could hear her adding with a smile, *You'll do what everyone does in the end. And that's just what you want to do.*

For another moment Blanchard studied Charmian, feeling the pull of attraction and need. Then he broke contact. "We'd better get moving. What's that word for the check?"

"La cuenta."

Blanchard looked around for the waiter, who was still watching the slender legs of the tennis players. He called out, *"La cuenta, por favor."*

He paid and they went back out into the bright Mexican sun, heading south toward Morelia.

2

Their troubles started before they were out of Salamanca. First they got lost in the town's confusing pattern of unmarked one-way streets. Eventually, by casting back and forth, they found an arrow pointing the way to Morelia, painted on a wall and hidden behind the pole of a traffic light.

At the south entry to the town there was a long narrow bridge that, like most Mexican bridges, having originally been constructed to carry horses and carts and burros, did not allow two cars to pass. Charmian, driving, waited for an opening in the steady line of traffic heading into Salamanca. When it came she hurried across the bridge. At the far end, where the road widened and northbound traffic waited for the way to clear, a block of wood had been placed in the road with huge nails sticking upward. Charmian saw it too late. She tried to swerve but had neither time nor room. The Vega hit the wooden block and rode over the protruding nails.

A half-mile past the bridge they heard and felt the thumping of a tire going flat.

While Blanchard changed the tire they both fumed a little at a group of children who had been waiting near the bridge, dark eyes sparkling, laughing gleefully as the car went over the nail-studded block of wood. Then they both calmed down and began to see the humor of the prank.

"I suppose when I was that age..." Blanchard said.

"With nothing to do."

"And no television."

"And your parents don't belong to the country club."

"And you've seen how upset *gringos* get over a flat tire."

"And they might even ask you to change it for a few pesos."

"I'd have done the same kind of thing."

"Aren't children doing it everywhere?" Charmian asked with a laugh. "Getting back at the adult world, one way or another?"

Finally they left Salamanca behind, leaving the flat plain crossed by the freeway and winding through a hilly terrain that turned green and wet and richer than any Blanchard had yet seen in Mexico, cultivated with fields of corn and beans and strawberries. The corn was high, the well-tilled fields puddled from recent heavy rains. Ahead of them now, over the mountains that ringed Morelia, loomed the familiar thunderheads of another storm. Although they still drove in sunlight, the air was heavy with the smell of rain.

They slowed to drive through a pretty village, highlighted by a handsome, colorful church and a busy plaza. A few miles south the road swung through a pass, and from its crest they looked out across a spectacular vista of green valleys and hills surrounding the lake of Yuriría. The peaks to the south were shrouded in mist, capped by black clouds.

It was shortly after that that the Vega's engine began to sputter and miss. It limped along, caught, and smoothed out for a while. They passed through another small village and came into view of another, larger lake. The village of Cuitzeo at the edge of the lake had been hit by a heavy downpour within the hour. The ditches along the road and the low-lying sections of the village were inundated by swiftly running muddy waters.

They reached a long causeway that sliced across a neck of the lake. A mile and a half long, its low crumbling stone walls attested to its age. Blanchard saw a few fishing boats out on the water, and the nets of others were visible in the marshy part of the lake to the west.

The Vega began to labor once more.

The causeway was too narrow to allow a car to move out of its lane to the side. Charmian drove anxiously, coaxing the car, her knuckles white on the steering wheel. For a while Blanchard feared that they wouldn't make it across. Then the engine smoothed out and the car shot forward, clearing the far shore of the lake. The road began to climb steeply toward Morelia, now only forty-five kilometers away.

"It could be the gasoline," Charmian said, worried yet relieved. "They say it's very dirty and it's easy for a fuel line to clog up." She flashed a brief smile. "Information courtesy of the Auto Club."

"We'll be there in a half-hour or so," Blanchard said. "Even if that rain hits."

He couldn't have been more wrong.

A few miles south of the *Lago de Cuitzeo*, on the curve of a long, climbing grade, the Vega quit.

After several futile attempts to start the engine Charmian Stewart looked at Blanchard helplessly. "Do you want to try it?"

"It knows you better than it does me," he said. "But I'll give it a whirl."

The gauge said they still had plenty of gasoline. It simply wasn't getting where it was supposed to. After five minutes of struggling, the battery began to grind down.

They were thoroughly stuck.

Blanchard climbed out of the car. There was no real apron on either side of the road. To the left a steep bank dropped sharply away; to the right was a muddy ditch about five feet deep, a bank climbing straight up on its far side. The time was late afternoon, the traffic suddenly heavier. Perhaps it only seemed that way because the Vega's situation was so precarious. Traffic from below had to go around them into the teeth of the cars, trucks and buses roaring down the grade from above. There was a curve about twenty yards or so above the Vega, another one below, cutting off vision in both directions.

"Maybe you'd better go up the hill until you can see around that curve and start directing traffic," Blanchard suggested to Charmian. "Wave your arms and point or whatever you have to do to warn them that there's trouble ahead."

Blanchard monitored the traffic approaching from the lake. Between times he lifted the hood and poked around the engine without much hope. He was no mechanic.

Between the flat tire and the stalled engine, this was taking on the appearance of a doomed trip, he thought; he hoped the run of luck wouldn't get worse.

By then black clouds were closing in on them, bringing a premature darkness. Blanchard stopped using the battery because it sounded feebler each time.

It began to rain.

When full darkness came Charmian was using a flashlight as a warning signal at the upper curve. Blanchard had set out flares below the Vega at the lower curve. There were only six of the flares and he lit two at a time. Even if he could manage to string them out for a couple of hours, he thought, they were going to be in trouble if they couldn't get the Vega off the highway. It was a long way down the hill to any place where there was room at the side of the road—a long way to coast backwards into a steady flow of traffic with no room to go around.

The old truck chugged around the curve around seven o'clock, when the last pair of flares were burning. Blanchard looked up ahead, saw that the way was clear, and waved the truck by. Instead it pulled up behind the Vega.

Two young men climbed down from the cab, smiling broadly. They spoke to Blanchard in rapid Spanish. He shrugged, pointing at the stalled car with its hood raised. He tried to see Charmian at the high curve, glimpsed the flicker of her flashlight. She might have to come down to communicate.

It is said that every Mexican truck driver is a mechanic by necessity. Often his truck is old. If it breaks down along an isolated road, as it usually does, there are probably no parts available. He must be a talented improviser with bits of wire or metal or cardboard—whatever he happens to have.

The two young Mexicans cheerfully inspected the Vega. One of them siphoned some gas from the tank, removed the filter, and fed some gas to the carburetor.

The engine started instantly.

Blanchard felt chagrin along with the leap of hope, but almost immediately the engine coughed and died.

A fire started around the carburetor on the second try. Laughing, one of the truck drivers smothered the fire with his jacket.

After several more unsuccessful attempts to start the engine, one more fire, and considerable debate, one of the men announced seriously that the problem was *la bomba*. He pointed to help Blanchard understand. *La bomba* was the fuel pump.

Blanchard decided to change places with Charmian; at least she would be able to communicate. Even the few words of Spanish that he knew seemed to have deserted him. He told Charmian to get inside the car out of the rain, which was now coming down heavily, but from above he saw that she was holding a flashlight for the two Mexicans. Blanchard wondered if he had ever run into drivers anywhere with as much good will.

Indifferent to the rain, the two young Mexicans worked for almost two hours in rain and darkness. They removed and cleaned spark plugs. They cleaned and adjusted the carburetor. They tried to blow out the fuel lines. Somehow, using pliers and a screwdriver, they removed, cleaned and replaced *la bomba*.

In the end they had to give up; the Vega failed to start.

They dug out a length of heavy rope at last and towed the Vega up the hill. Once the rope broke. The truck was a quarter-mile up the grade before it stopped. It backed down carefully and the rope was attached once more. Near the top of the hill Blanchard was able to steer the Vega off the road. Its wheels sank into a muddy pool, but it was safely clear of the traffic.

Cold and wet and exhausted, Blanchard and Charmian rode into Morelia in the crowded cab of the truck, the two young Mexican drivers laughing and chattering over the incident, delighted to discover that Charmian could talk Spanish and share their humor. She told Blanchard that they were continuing on to Zamora to the west, were now at least three hours behind schedule, and would be driving through most of the night.

When they dropped their passengers off at the big central plaza in Morelia, the truck drivers astounded Blanchard once more by refusing to accept anything for their help. After all, they had not fixed the car.

On a previous trip Charmian had stayed in a motel in the Santa María hills overlooking the city and its broad green valley. Blanchard found a taxi and they rode up the hill. He was too tired to notice much of the city, even if the rainy darkness had allowed much visibility. Later he would remember the jeep full of brown-clad soldiers that had cruised slowly past them when they were waving goodbye to the Mexican truck drivers.

In the Santa María hills there had been a power failure brought on by the storm. The entire hillside was in darkness. Candlelight in the windows of a restaurant and lounge of the Motel Vista del Parque drew them to its tall iron gates.

The gates were closed and locked. When Blanchard rattled them loudly, calling out, an old man appeared. He explained in Spanish, smiling, that they were too late. The motel closed its gates at ten o'clock. The office was closed, the desk clerk retired for the night. Nothing else on the hill was open.

The taxicab had disappeared down the hill. Blanchard and Charmian Stewart, standing in the rain at the muddy side of the road in the blackout, stared at each other and, simultaneously, began to laugh.

3

They heard the singing before the procession came into view around a corner of the motel. The voices were thin, lifted against the steady dripping of the rain, a sound both strange and enchanting in the total blackness of the night. A string of lights, flickering in a slender chain, moved up the road toward them. As the procession neared, Blanchard saw that it was made up of women and young children, all shielding their candles from wind and rain with their cupped hands. Each one in the chain wore a veil, and the girl at their head, her candlelit face as shining and serious as an angel's, was carrying a statue of the Virgin Mary.

The high, thin chant grew louder, taking form and rhythm as the procession went by. Blanchard noticed an American woman in the line. She glanced at him briefly before moving on.

"Adios, Virgen de Guadalupe," the wind-whipped voices sang. *"Adios, Madre del Salvador..."*

"It's part of a fiesta," Charmian said as they watched the procession turn along another narrow street and disappear, leaving behind a smoke trail of praise. "They're carrying the statue of Mary from one person's house to another. It stays in each house for one night during the celebration as a special honor."

Blanchard nodded, thinking that there had been no men in the group. The serious business of religion in Mexico, he suspected, was a matter best left to women and children.

There was another motel, the Vista Bella, and two large cottage-style inns, in the Santa María hills. The motel was full, its gates also locked. Of the two inns, one didn't answer its bell; at the other a night watchman, peering through the crack between its solid security gates, informed them that accommodations were available only by advance reservation.

Blanchard and Charmian returned to the main road, facing a long walk down the hill into the city in the now intermittent rain. Near the locked gates of the Motel Vista del Parque a woman was standing, watching them approach. Blanchard recognized the American woman from the procession.

Her name was Kate Rynders, and the first thing she said after identifying herself was, "You must be in trouble."

"We've had a day of it," Blanchard admitted.

"We hoped to get into the del Parque," Charmian explained, "but we were too late. Our taxi took off down the hill before we knew what was happening."

"They don't like to come up here late at night. You were lucky to find one at all, with all the student troubles we've been having."

"Oh?" Blanchard remembered the jeepload of soldiers.

"You both look soaked to the skin. You'll have to get out of this rain." Her own head was protected by the traditional gray *rebozo*. She wore it naturally and comfortably, like someone long accustomed to it. "I live just around the corner here."

"Could we phone for another taxi?" Charmian asked.

"I doubt that you'll get one up here now."

They followed Kate Rynders along a side street, its

surface broken and puddled, walking carefully but unable to avoid all of the mud and water. Blanchard noticed Charmian shivering in the chill night air.

Kate Rynders unlocked an iron gate and held it open while they ducked through and under the protection of a carport. A dog had barked at their approach, but Kate's appearance silenced the warning. Now Blanchard felt the cold muzzle touching his hand, sniffing, exploring, becoming familiar with the smells. A big dog, he noted.

He followed the two women into the house. The fire in the fireplace was a welcome sight. Its heat closed around him like warm water.

A young girl who had been reading a book at a dining table at the far end of the room rose to greet them, curious and polite. She was Kate Rynders' daughter Mary, a shy girl of fifteen who shared her mother's handsome combination of red hair, blue eyes, and freckles. Irish, Blanchard guessed, but at least a generation back; Kate's accent was pure American. Her daughter's by contrast was intriguingly Spanish, as if English was her second tongue.

After the introductions Kate Rynders said, "I was going to have some hot chocolate. Would you like some, or would you rather have tea or coffee?" She acted as if it was perfectly routine to open her house to two drenched strangers in the middle of a stormy night. Strangers in trouble, he thought. There had been a time when that kind of friendly hospitality *was* normal.

The comfort of an old rocking chair and the solid warmth of the fire made Blanchard conscious of an aching fatigue. He asked for coffee. He needed to stay alert. Charmian said she would love the hot chocolate.

While her daughter silently heated water and milk in the kitchen, Kate Rynders listened to Blanchard's account of their broken journey from San Miguel, a tale that probably did not seem as strange here as it would have sounded in the living room of a Los

Angeles suburban home. If Kate was surprised to hear that Blanchard and Charmian were not husband and wife, though they were traveling together, she gave no indication.

When Blanchard had finished talking, helped by Charmian's laughing interpretation of the two truck drivers who had given them a lift to Morelia, Kate Rynders said, "You can't leave your car there."

"Why not?"

She shook her head. "It just isn't a good idea." She looked at Blanchard in the direct, open manner that seemed characteristic. "We'll have to get Bud—he's my husband. He's... visiting someone up the hill. If I gave you directions, do you think you could find the place?"

Blanchard delayed long enough to swallow most of a large mug of hot black coffee, hoping that it would lift a little of the weight from his limbs and eyelids. Then he stumbled reluctantly into the chill darkness of the night once more, armed with a flashlight.

The rutted streets were so broken, a spill of rocks and gravel and mud, that he wondered how a car could travel a block without becoming mired or breaking an axle. On this night no one was trying. The streets were empty. Fortunately the rain was light, hardly more than spitting in his face. The flashlight's beam enabled him to pick his way up the hill, following Kate Rynders' careful directions, to the white-walled apartment building she had described.

Kate Rynders had even described the string pull for the bell outside the gate. A man called out from the darkness in response to Blanchard's ring. "*Quién es?* Who is it?"

"I'm looking for Bud Rynders. His wife said he might be up here."

There was an exchange of voices from within the house. A man came to the gate and invited Blanchard in.

The studio apartment startled him. Next to the

simplicity of the Rynders house, which was furnished with comfortable, well-chosen antiques, the apartment was opulent. Its high white walls were hung with colorful paintings of unmistakable quality, and modern weavings. A large sofa and two chairs, of elegant hardwoods and black leather, would not have been out of place in Beverely Hills, and there were other striking upholstered pieces, a beautifully handwoven Indian rug in bold colors, valuable Mexican and North American Indian artifacts on an assortment of shelves and tables, and well-filled bookshelves flanking a huge island fireplace whose blazing fire drew Blanchard almost hypnotically.

The man who had come to the gate was an American named Sedling. His cultivated accent suggested New England, his clothes, from the white-on-white embroidered silk shirt to the expensively tailored gray knit flannel slacks and leather sandals, the attire of the casual rich of the Riviera and the Costa del Sol and Acapulco. His eyes were cool and curious, neither openly hostile nor particularly friendly.

Bud Rynders rose from the thick black-leather cushions of the sofa, a highball glass in one hand. As he extended another broad hand in a powerful grip, he grinned at Blanchard as if they were old friends. "Kate sent you after me?"

"I think she thought I might need your help."

Sedling was openly curious, Rynders amiably relaxed. Jeff Blanchard briefly sketched the story he had told Kate Rynders. Listening to himself for the second time, he felt that the tale was beginning to sound bizarre. He suddenly found himself wondering what he was doing there in this lavishly appointed apartment, interrupting an evening of convivial drinking. "I'm sorry to break in on you like this," he finished lamely. "It was Mrs. Rynders' idea that we shouldn't leave our car out there overnight."

"Hell, no," Bud Rynders said. "Cal, this man needs a drink."

"Yes, of course. What would you like? Scotch? We're on rum, but there's plenty of Scotch and gin."

Blanchard hesitated, still questioning his ready acceptance of Kate Rynders' suggestion that he find her husband. That decision had come of fatigue. He said, "The rum will be fine."

While Sedling poured rum generously into a glass at a portable bar, adding the ice and splash of soda Blanchard asked for, he found himself studying Bud Rynders with interest. He was a man of Blanchard's age, powerfully built with wide shoulders and a narrow waist. His voice was deep and rich, his ruggedly handsome face the weathered tan of a man who enjoys the outdoors, his friendly eyes an even brighter blue than his wife's. His deep chest and muscular arms suggested that he worked at staying in shape. Close to exhaustion, Blanchard was skeptical of his reaction—his week in Mexico should have taught him not to trust appearances, he thought, especially now that he was close to Darrell Kinney—but he instinctively liked Bud Rynders. He'd be a good man to have at your side in a fight, he thought.

But those powerful hands and arms were deceptive, too. With interest Blanchard noted that at least two of the striking paintings on the walls of Sedling's apartment bore the same black scrawl in a corner: *Rynders*.

"Kate's right, you know," Cal Sedling said when he had brought Blanchard's drink and refilled his own and Rynders' glasses. "Can't leave that car out there in the mountains unguarded."

"That's what Mrs. Rynders said. Any special reason?"

Bud Rynders grinned. "It'll be stripped clean before morning. Tires, radio, anything that comes loose. Any luggage or other stuff in it?"

"Yes." They hadn't tried to carry anything with them in the truck except for Blanchard's traveler's checks and Charmian's smallest overnight case.

"You'll be lucky if it's still there."

"That's right," Sedling said. "They'll steal anything."

"It's a poor country," Bud Rynders said, agreeing, but without the trace of contempt in Sedling's remark. "Can't blame them if they see a rich American's car abandoned and they help themselves to whatever they can carry. But this isn't answering our friend's problem, Cal. What we need here is a council of war."

In the discussion that followed, which soon required another refill of the glasses all around, Blanchard became aware of how Bud Rynders' speech occasionally stumbled and how he would then choose his words cautiously, in the manner of a man who has had a great deal to drink. Cal Sedling had broken the stamp of a fresh bottle of rum to pour Blanchard's first drink, discarding an empty bottle. Blanchard wondered how long the two men had been sitting there drinking.

Bud Rynders carried his rum well, but Charmian's abandoned Vega seemed farther away than ever.

"He could hire a taxi," Sedling was arguing.

"Cost a fortune," Rynders grumbled in protest. "Besides, where's he gonna find a cab driver to take him all the way out there this time of night? In the rain too. Nope, I guess I'm just gonna have to take him myself."

"You? You're going to drive out there? In your condition?"

Rynders laughed. "Let's not speak delicately about my indelicate condition. Are you implying that I'm drunk?" He spoke to Sedling but winked at Blanchard.

"You're smashed," Sedling said. "You've killed more than half a quart since six o'clock."

Six o'clock, Blanchard thought. It was a wonder either man could stand up.

"I had some help."

"I meant by yourself."

Rynders grinned at Blanchard. "He pours a

helluva drink, but he's also a helluva liar. Come on, let's go see what's left of that car of yours."

"Hell, Bud, you can't drive that clunker of yours up into those mountains. Even if you were sober enough to see, which you aren't, you'd never make it!"

"Wanta come along?"

"You think I'm crazy?"

Sedling glanced at Blanchard with a shrug, as if to say that he had done his best. He assured Blanchard without much conviction that he hoped to see him again if he was staying around Morelia. Blanchard thanked him, volunteering nothing more. He was thinking that his best bet was to get back down the hill some way and look for a hotel that hadn't closed up tight for the night.

He reckoned without Bud Rynders' amiable determination.

"Kate, I'm heading for the mountains, me and Jeff here," he announced when they reached the Rynders house. "You know where those sleeping bags are? We'll need two of 'em."

"You're not driving anywhere."

"If I don't, who will? You think I'd let you go off into the hills with a good-looking *norteamericano* like this Blanchard? Where's my gun?"

"You're not taking that?"

"Now, look, Kate, chances are we can't do anything with that car before morning—what do you call it? Vega? It's black as a witch's teat out there."

"Bud!"

"Well, it is. So that means we're gonna camp out. We need those sleeping bags and that's all there is to it, right, Jeff?"

Bud Rynders was delighted with Charmian, showed it, and won a response from her that was immediate and warm. Blanchard felt something that might have been jealousy if he'd been ready to admit it.

"Do you really need that?" Charmian asked when Rynders took a big .45 revolver out of the drawer of a handsome old rolltop desk. She seemed caught between amusement and alarm.

"Well, I'll tell you, Miss Stewart," Rynders boomed at her, "I know those *indios* up in those mountains. Good people, most of 'em, but if I'm gonna spend the night out there I want any hungry *bandidos* who come around to know that it won't be easy, that's all. Hell, there's nothing to worry about." He grinned. "I'll see old Jeff gets back in one piece."

In spite of her objections, Kate Rynders and her daughter managed to find the pair of ragged-looking sleeping bags. Before he really knew how it happened Blanchard found himself climbing into a green 1955 Mercury sedan with loose windows and doors that didn't quite close. Standing in the carport to wave them off, Kate Rynders said, "Don't worry about Charmian, she'll sleep here. We've plenty of room."

"Take care of yourself, Jeff," Charmian said. She looked as if she wanted to say a lot more.

"Hang on," Bud Rynders said.

He took off down the hill as if it were broad daylight. Blanchard quickly learned that the ancient Mercury had more problems than loose fittings. The transmission whined fiercely at anything over twenty miles an hour, the power steering had gone out some time back and never been fixed, and the valves clattered like castanets.

"Listen," Bud Rynders said as they drove through the center of the city, quiet at the approach of midnight on a rainy night, "let me tell you something about this old car. She's like a woman who's been around a while. I mean, you can see all kinds of things wrong with her but she knows what she's supposed to do and she does it. It's that new little filly who leaves you stuck up there in the mountains when the going gets rough, you know what I mean?"

His reckless good humor was infectious. Blanchard grinned back at him, realizing that Rynders was enjoying himself hugely, relishing their mission as an adventure to enliven an otherwise quiet evening in a humdrum week.

He had to fight the heavy steering, and at one cramped intersection, when another car shot through without a warning blare of its horn, Rynders swerved the Mercury sharply, missing the other car by the thickness of a coat of nonexistent paint, slammed into the high curb, swore, and wobbled on.

They cleared the older, congested part of the town on the north side and accelerated onto the open highway. The rain was coming down harder, defeating the windshield wipers. Suddenly a bus loomed out of the blackness, bearing directly down on them. Bud Rynders rocked the Mercury hard to the right. They felt the hard buffeting of air as the big bus roared past them in a cloud of spray.

"Sweet Jesus!" Rynders said softly.

He slowed down.

For a while they drove in silence, Rynders sobered by the near-collision with the bus. A few minutes later he swung off the highway onto a bumpy road that took them into a village bypassed by the main road. It seemed dark, sleeping, but Rynders found a tiny shop open at the center of the village, with what looked like a lunch counter.

"I think maybe I need something to tone me down," he said. "How about you?"

Thinking he meant coffee, and remembering the bus, Blanchard agreed. But the counter turned out to be a small bar, hardly ten feet long, with a row of rickety wooden stools drawn up to it, backed by handmade shelves holding rows of rum and tequila. Bud Rynders cheerfully ordered beers for both of them.

Blanchard stared at the big artist. What the hell, he thought, he's as old as you are, someone must watch over him. He relaxed. Maybe some of Rynders' luck would rub off.

The beer came cold and delicious from an old

refrigerator behind the counter. Outside the rain dripped steadily and the wind rattled the battered shutter doors of the bar. Bud Rynders, overpowering his narrow stool, looked as if he was settling in for the night.

The artist spoke a rough but fluent Spanish. He talked freely with the gnarled old Mexican who owned the little bar, discussing their children, the changing times, the old days when the hunting was good down in the hot country, the venality of all governments, the relative quality of different weapons. Rynders filled Blanchard in with occasional asides. He pulled from a sheath a hunting knife made by Hank Bizet in Morelia, and the old Mexican admired it along with Blanchard. "You'll have to visit Hank's shop," Rynders told him. "It's up there on our hill. Hank makes the best knives and cutlery in all Mexico. Hell, he's been down here as long as I have—we met at the art school here after the war."

Blanchard learned that Rynders had come to Morelia's old and renowned art school after the second World War, figuring that his educational benefits under the G.I. Bill would go further at Mexican prices. He had stayed on. He was a painter and sculptor, working in a studio adjoining his house. He had seen Katherine Conroy dancing with a touring American company in Mexico City in 1950. He had followed the troupe across Mexico, and before it left Guadalajara to return to New York he had talked Kate into marrying him. They had lived in Mexico ever since, a good deal of the time in Morelia. He had been back to the States a few times for brief periods, working at what he called "survival jobs" that enabled him to return to Mexico and paint. He had never made a great deal of money, but you didn't need much money to live in Mexico. Besides, he and Kate had come to love it; he didn't think they could ever go back. Blanchard thought that Rynders was a man who was honest with himself and had done what he wanted to with his life, against all odds. He found himself liking the man even better.

By the time they left the tiny bar, the old Mexican behind the counter was treating them like old comrades; the parting was almost tearful—which might have had something to do with the rum and the beer, Blanchard thought. Then Rynders suggested that, if Blanchard had fifteen pesos to spare, perhaps they should take just a half-bottle of rum up into the mountains with them. "With this rain and all, it's gonna be cold, Jeff."

As an afterthought Rynders decided that they should also take a gallon of gasoline; he didn't quite believe Blanchard's insistence that the Vega had plenty of gas. There was a station across the street from the bar but it was closed. The old man came out from behind his counter and trotted across the way. After a few minutes he returned with a pail three-quarters full of gasoline. He apologized for the open pail; there was no gas can available.

Blanchard paid for the rum and fuel and they drove off. Gas fumes soon filled the interior of the old Mercury. Some of the liquid sloshed over the edges of the pail as the car jounced along the pitted road.

Blanchard tried to guess how far it was to the spot where they had abandoned the Vega, but the strangeness of the terrain, the darkness and the rain fooled him. When they came down the long grade to the edge of the Lago de Cuitzeo he knew that they missed the wagon.

On the second pass, creeping slowly in heavy rain, they found it. There was room for the old Mercury on the narrow turnoff near the top of the hill. The Vega was untouched. Nothing had been stolen.

"Got room in that thing for these sleeping bags?" Bud Rynders asked.

There was room with the back seat folded flat. They piled luggage and packages, souvenirs, and even a small table onto the two front seats, stacked high. Bud Rynders placed the pail with its gallon or so of gasoline under the Mercury to keep it out of the rain;

he didn't want to leave it in the car. Then he spread out the sleeping bags and settled in.

Rynders placed the loaded .45 revolver within easy reach, uncorked the half-bottle of rum, and handed it to Blanchard. "Might as well get warm, Jeff," he said. "Then you can start telling me what you're doing down here in darkest Mexico."

The remark was innocent enough, but Blanchard found himself wondering if there was a lay-it-on-the-line challenge in the artist's tone that hadn't been there before. He thought of the .45 at Rynders' side, of those powerfully muscled arms and broad hands. Hell, he wouldn't even need a gun.

Rejecting the suspicion angrily, Blanchard took a long pull at the bottle. Darrell Kinney couldn't have set this up. Even if he had engineered a breakdown for the Vega, by having sugar or ground glass or something dropped into the gas tank, he could hardly have plotted the rest. He couldn't have foreseen a couple of Good Samaritans on the road. He couldn't have known that Blanchard and Charmian would taxi up the hill instead of looking for a hotel in downtown Morelia. He couldn't have timed a procession for Our Lady of Guadalupe to coincide with their arrival.

You're becoming paranoid, Blanchard thought.

He thought again of the two Mexican truck drivers who had interrupted their long drive to spend more than two hours trying to get Charmian's Vega started, working in the rain, and had then cheerfully driven them into Morelia and refused even to accept payment for their time. He remembered Kate Rynders' quiet statement up there on the hill when they found her waiting for them near the Motel Vista del Parque: "You must be in trouble." So she had waited to see what she could do to help two strangers. And Bud Rynders had unhesitatingly left a warm house, a full bottle of rum, and a blazing fire to set off on a reckless, possibly dangerous ride through the rain to help someone he had never seen before tonight.

It was not all one-sided, Blanchard thought. There were the Kinneys and the Pepes and the Wilsons, but the human race still offered its pleasant surprises.

He passed the bottle to Bud Rynders, feeling sudden gratitude that he knew would only embarrass the artist to hear.

"I'll fill you in if you'll tell me one thing," Blanchard said.

"Name it, Jeff." He saw the bottle tilt high, heard the gurgle of the liquid, the deeply satisfied sigh.

"You've lived around here a long time. Do you know a man who goes by the name of Slater? Alan Slater?"

Rynders sat up slowly. His chest and shoulders were huge in the close darkness of the Vega wagon. "He a friend of yours?" Rynders asked. His voice was cold and hard, no longer friendly.

4

The rain lashed at the roof and windows of the Vega in noisy squalls, walling Blanchard into that dark enclosure with Bud Rynders, who was holding the bottle of rum, now more than half empty, like a raised weapon. Blanchard could not see his face clearly; he had to be guided by what he thought he heard in the artist's voice.

"No friend," he said. "You sound as if you don't much like him either."

The bottle was lowered slowly. "I don't."

"Mind telling me why?"

"Maybe. What do you have to do with Slater?"

Blanchard hesitated. "I'm trying to find him."

"That shouldn't be too hard. He owns a gift shop on the hill."

"Have you seen him around lately?"

"No. That doesn't mean much. He could be over in Patzcuaro—he has another shop there—or anywhere else for that matter. I don't have anything to do with him."

"You haven't said why."

"That's my business."

Bud Rynders still held the bottle, but he was no longer drinking. While he did not seem directly hostile, his earlier, open friendliness was now fenced off. He was suspicious, wondering, Blanchard guessed, who he was and why he had come seeking him out on this rainy night.

Suddenly Blanchard realized that he needed a friendly Rynders. He needed, if not Rynders' active cooperation, at least the kind of information he could provide if he were willing. He had lived in and around Morelia for over twenty years, surely as long as Kinney could have been there under the name of Alan Slater. Until now Kinney had had things all his own way because Blanchard had been feeling his way in the dark. Rynders might be able to help him to understand what Kinney was up to and why. Without that help all Blanchard could do was search for Kinney—or wait for him to make his next move.

And the longer he waited, the longer Mike and Angie were in danger, a danger that had to increase with the passage of time.

"I know Slater from way back," Jeff Blanchard said. "His real name is Darrell Kinney. And I think he's kidnapped my son and his wife."

5

They killed the rum long before first light. By that time Blanchard had told Bud Rynders the whole story of his journey through Mexico in search of his son, a quest that had led him finally, by chance, to Rynders' door.

At first puzzled and skeptical, Rynders had slowly come around to accepting the possibility that

Blanchard's accusation against Slater-Kinney was true. With belief came sympathetic concern along with a renewal of their friendly drinking. Blanchard continued to be in awe of Rynders' capacity. As for himself, unaccustomed to the high altitude and not having eaten anything since his half-finished club sandwich in the early afternoon, Blanchard found his head swimming, though he had drunk far less than Rynders.

"Where do you think Kinney is?" Blanchard asked. "Where do you think he could have Mike and Angie?"

"He could be anywhere. If he wants to hide in Morelia somewhere, behind a wall, you'll never find him. There's no way of getting over the walls down in the old town if he's there. Or he could be hiding out with old Brugmann. And you can't get in there either."

"Who's Brugmann?"

"An old German who lives up above us on the hill—up near the village of Santa María. His place used to be an old monastery. It's a couple of hundred years old. I was inside a couple of times, back when I came here and before the old bastard got so ornery. It was quite a place even then. They say a lot of work's been done on it since. From what I hear, it's like a palace now."

"Nobody goes there?"

Rynders was silent for a moment before replying. Then he said, "Only three, four people I know of. Brugmann never leaves the place—I don't think anybody's seen him outside in twenty years. Anything he needs outside his secretary takes care of. He's a scrawny little guy, but tough—I think he's a bodyguard more than he's a secretary, goes by the name of George Robbins. There's a doctor visits Brugmann—he's a friend of mine, Rafael Sánchez, that's how I know a little about Brugmann. And there's the local police captain, guy by the name of Ortiz, you wouldn't want to have anything to do with.

You want the truth, I think Brugmann buys his privacy and protection. If you have enough money, you can do that down here."

"Or anywhere else," Blanchard mumbled, shaking his head to clear it.

"The other one who goes there is Slater. Your pal Kinney."

Blanchard sat up. He tried to read Rynders' expression, dimly seen in the blackness of that night on the mountain. A remote suspicion tugged at him. "What does Kinney have to do with Brugmann?"

"They're partners," Bud Rynders said, taking the untouched bottle from Blanchard and holding it up, squinting to see if anything was left. He shook the bottle, tilted it, sighed and tossed it aside. It rolled against the wagon's side panel. "Brugmann set Slater up in business twenty years ago. And I was in on it too."

The reason for Bud Rynders' hostility toward the man he knew as Alan Slater emerged as he told Blanchard about their relationship back in the early 1950s. Slater had come to Rynders with the idea of opening a gift and crafts shop, catering to tourists. He was convinced that Mexico's postwar tourist business would boom, and that Morelia, located halfway between Mexico City and Guadalajara on the main connecting road, would inevitably be in the path of some of that business. Slater, new in the area, recognized that he needed someone with what he called "local knowledge" to get the shop started, someone who knew where and how to buy things, whose Spanish was good enough for bargaining purposes, who was familiar with Morelia and its surrounding villages in Michoacán. Rynders, recently married, a struggling artist not sure how he would make a living in Mexico, had jumped at the opportunity. He and Kate had both worked in the shop. For two years they had put everything of themselves into making it go, establishing contacts, finding sources for Michoacán's native arts and crafts as well as other crafts from all over Mexico, establishing the shop with tour guides, making it known to old Mexico hands, building good will. They had pulled it off; the shop was a success. Then one day, without warning, Slater-Kinney had walked in and said that he was taking over management of the shop himself. Bud Rynders and Kate were out in the cold. Since then the Slater gift shops, called La Cosecha—even the name had been Rynders' idea—had thrived. Rynders, after a long, rough fight, had slowly made it on his own, building a reputation for his paintings and sculpture.

"And Brugmann? Where did he come in?"

"It was his money," Rynders said with the harshness of bitter memory. "I thought it was Slater's, but Brugmann is the real owner of those shops. He always has been. Slater and I damn near had a fight when he took over that first shop. We exchanged some words, and he let it out that Brugmann was the real owner and Brugmann wanted me out."

"Did you go to Brugmann?"

"I tried to. He never would talk to me. He just stays up there behind those ten-foot walls of his, like a monk in the old days of the monastery, and counts his money, I guess." Suddenly Rynders chuckled, his momentary anger sliding away. "They say he's got quite a pile of it hidden away up there on the hill."

Blanchard's earlier suspicion was becoming clearer, seeming less fantastic. "Did Brugmann and Kinney come to Morelia together? Or about the same time?"

"Oh, hell no. Old Brugmann's been here since the first World War. 1919 or 1920, I guess it was, he came. He took out Mexican citizenship—that's why he's the real owner of those gift shops, besides putting up the money, though I guess Slater must be a citizen by now. You have to be to own a business here on your own. I don't know how Slater got to Brugmann, or conned him into putting up that money, but he did.

From what you say, I guess he was always good at conning people."

"Yes," Blanchard said, disappointed, his wild theory exploded. He lay back, folding his hands behind his head, staring up at the ceiling of the little wagon. The rain had ceased and a first faint haze of gray was filtering through the black walls enclosing them.

Kinney and Brugmann. Blanchard knew a lot more than he had before meeting Rynders, but none of it seemed to explain two kidnappings. None of it explained why Kinney had wanted to force Blanchard to come to him in Morelia—if, indeed, that guess was close to the truth. None of it told him where Mike and Angie might be being held.

Except that Brugmann's isolated monastery, the home of an old recluse who admitted only a few visitors, each with a close connection to him, was so ideal a place to hold two captives that it couldn't be ignored.

"I've got to get in there," Blanchard said after a while, thinking out loud.

"Huh? Where?"

"Brugmann's place."

"Are you kidding?" It was becoming light enough for Jeff Blanchard to see Rynders shake his head emphatically. "No way. Even if you could get over the wall, he's got a dog patrolling the grounds. And a couple of very *macho* bodyguards, including that Robbins, who's the kind of guy who'll go out of his way to run over a dog in the road—I saw him do it once, driving down the hill. That's not to mention the rest of his staff. Besides, you're an American, you don't belong here, and one thing you don't want to do, ever, is get into trouble with the Mexican police. And right now is the worst time you could possibly have picked. I don't know if you noticed them in town, but the place is crawling with *federales*, riot police. They've been having trouble all over Mexico with the students and radical groups. They've brought tanks into Mexico

230

City, according to the paper, and troops in a half-dozen cities, including Morelia. You start something now, like trying to break into Brugmann's place, and you'll either end up dead or buried so deep inside a Mexican jail that no one will ever find you. Or when you get out you'll be too old for it to make any difference. Don't mess with Brugmann."

"If my son is in there, and Angie..."

"Goddamn it, listen to what I'm telling you! There's no way for you to get in there. Besides, I don't buy it. Brugmann's lived here a helluva long time. He may be a recluse and an ornery old bastard, but I never heard of him doing anyone any wrong except me—and I think that was really Slater's doing. Brugmann's no kidnapper. Anyway, why would he? What for? Not for money. He's rich, and he must be damned near ninety years old. He doesn't need anything from you."

"Kinney does. That's the only thing that makes sense."

"Then go after Kinney. Forget Brugmann."

Blanchard nodded, only half-convinced. The huge walled estate on the hill was too obvious a place to hide a pair of victims. It was hard to shake the conviction that it—and Brugmann—were part of Darrell Kinney's scheme. Rynders was too ready to dismiss the fact that Kinney and Brugmann were partners.

"If you're right," he said, "there's one way to confirm it, aside from my trying to break in there. You could help me."

"Hell, I'll do what I can, but..." Rynders scowled. "How?"

"Your friend Rafael. You said he's Brugmann's doctor. He must go in and out, if Brugmann never leaves."

"Sure he does, but... damn it, Jeff, haven't you been listening to anything I've said?"

"My son might be in there! I have to know—I have to be sure!"

231

Bud Rynders stared at him in the first gray light of the new day. After a while his head began to nod. "I guess that would do it," he murmured. "If I thought anyone had Mary..."

"Then you'll talk to Rafael Sánchez? You can get me to him?"

Rynders frowned. "It'll have to be someplace where you won't be seen together. And we'll have to spring it on him—he probably wouldn't come if he knew." He shook his head and sighed. A big hand clapped over Blanchard's shoulder, squeezing hard enough to raise bruises. "I'm probably as much of a damned fool as you are, but... I'll see what I can do."

Interlude Five: Morelia

Waking, Angie felt a lurch of panic that set her heart pounding. Her eyes searched the darkness anxiously, found nothing. There was no one there.

She fell back against the pillow. Her head ached ferociously and her thoughts were scattered and confused. Fumbling among the tangle, she came upon the house tour. Then she remembered. She had been combing her hair. Michael's father had been calling to her from somewhere in the house, his voice echoing in the emptiness.

She sat up as the vivid image from the mirror leaped into her mind. And there had been another face in the glass, that of an Indian, a savage warrior from another time.

Where was she? Where had they taken her?

She thought of Michael. Longing hope stabbed deep at the possibility that she had been brought where he was, that he was close to her, a prisoner but—like her—alive.

She tried to sit up. The movement caused the pounding in her head to intensify. She remembered smelling chloroform, but they must have used drugs as well. Wondering how long she had been asleep, she recalled the reason for her panic.

She had awakened—it seemed a long time ago—in this same room. She recognized the big bed with its handwoven orange cover, the white curtains over a barred window, the bars sharply etched by an outdoor floodlight.

But that time she had not been alone.

He had been standing beside the bed, staring down at her. A tall, aristocratic figure in a white Mexican wedding shirt and white slacks, with a deeply bronzed face, white hair cropped close. He had not spoken, and she had stared at him without moving or speaking, afraid to open her mouth and let the scream escape. He had leaned toward her, and...

The memory slipped away, elusive as any dream.

Who was he? He was not the man Michael had recognized in San Miguel, his father's wartime friend. But she hadn't dreamed him up. No way. The image was too vivid. Even the cruel line of his mouth was starkly clear.

Swinging her feet to the floor, Angie tried to stand. Her legs were wobbly, and the pain skidded through her head to bang against her skull and ricochet. Oh wow, was this trip really necessary? She waited a moment for dizziness to pass. As she waited, she was aware of her stomach's rumblings. Hunger pangs. How long did that mean she had been out of it?

Her eyes, accustomed now to the darkness, probed details of the room. A carved wooden chest with a mirror over it, one of those elaborately detailed tin frames with scrolls and flowers worked into the thin metal. The dim light from the window reflected off another mirror across the room, this one smaller, a circle of glass in a sunburst frame. Beside the bed was a low, lacquered table, carrying a black pottery lamp. She reached for the lamp and clicked on the light.

The sudden brilliance hurt her eyes. She squeezed them shut and turned away. When she opened her eyes, the man was standing in the doorway.

Angie gasped aloud.

"So you are awake."

The tall, austere and frightening figure of her dream was real. He closed the door and advanced toward her. Angie fell back a step. Her knee bumped against the edge of the bed. "Who are you? Why did you bring me here?"

"You don't know?" His accent was heavy, distinctive. German, she thought. He looked the part, like the haughty, villainous German officer of a hundred movies. And she had not made up the theatrical cruelty of that strong mouth, or the cold shock of his bright blue eyes.

"Why should I know? How could I?" Defiance rose abruptly out of a well of anger. "What have you done with Michael?"

"Michael?"

"You know who I mean!"

"Are you so certain? Then surely you must know who I am."

"No, I... I don't. But you must—" She broke off, at a loss. She was not dreaming, but everything that was happening had a nightmarish quality. Even the presence of this remarkable man was a detail from a bad trip.

He had moved closer to her, and when she tried instinctively to retreat, shrinking from him, she lost her balance and sat awkwardly on the bed. Her breasts stirred under her gown, and she saw the direction of his gaze. The gown was strange to her, a flimsy piece of silk and lace, too small for her and almost transparent. She felt naked before the

German's probing gaze, and the thought that someone had undressed her while she was unconscious, and put this silly exotic gown on her, made her cheeks flame. She had never thought herself uptight about sex, but even the way the tall German stared at her made her feel violated, stripped of privacy and dignity.

"I can think of many reasons you should be here," he murmured. "You are very lovely, my dear."

She tried to recapture her courage and defiance. "You haven't answered me. Where is Michael?"

"Do you know where *you* are?"

"Well...no."

"This is my house, in Morelia."

"Morelia! But..." She was bewildered. She and Michael had not been to Morelia. They had taken other routes in their brief travels. She knew little about it beyond a rough notion of where it was, and the fact that it had been on Michael's list. "Supposed to be another Colonial jewel," Michael had said. "I think every other place is a Colonial jewel." The memory of Michael and their honeymoon journey was too much for her. Her eyes filled with unbidden tears. She said, "I don't understand. Why have you done this to us? What do we mean to you?"

"You have never heard of me?"

"No. Why should I?"

The German's eyes narrowed thoughtfully. "I am Baldur Brugmann." When she failed to react to the name, his gaze hardened with skepticism. "You are either ignorant or very clever. You were traveling with Jeff Blanchard. Surely he spoke of me."

"No. He didn't understand what was going on any more than I did."

"He didn't speak of Kinney? Darrell Kinney?" He shot the question at her.

"No, he..." She stumbled in confusion. "Yes! Of course he did! That was the man Michael saw in San Miguel. Michael said he followed us. But what does that have to do with you?" Her buried panic over

Michael surfaced, and her voice shook. "Why did he follow us? We didn't mean anything to him. And what does he have to do with you?"

"What, indeed?" the German said. "I'm beginning to think you are speaking the truth. You know nothing about it."

"Of course I am!" His eyes flicked once more over her body, and impulsively she hugged her chest, covering her breasts with both arms, the gesture causing her to feel both foolish and intimidated. The same protective instinct prodded her into diverting his attention with another question. "How... how long have I been here?"

"You were brought here from San Miguel Sunday night. That was twenty-four hours ago."

She was aghast. "This is *Monday* night?"

"That is correct." The cold blue eyes continued to examine her speculatively, but the hard skepticism was gone. He turned toward the window. "It will soon be morning. Tuesday morning. This man Blanchard... your father-in-law... is already here in Morelia. Does that surprise you?"

"Yes," she said slowly, genuinely surprised.

He turned abruptly to challenge her. "How could he have come here so quickly? How could he know this was where you would be taken?"

"I... I don't know."

"He must have said something to you!"

"No, he didn't. He must have... I don't know, I don't understand anything! Can't you see that?"

For another moment he was silent, staring down at her. At last he nodded, as if to himself, and said, "Perhaps. Strange. There is something here I myself do not understand."

"Why have you done this to us?" she burst out, her emotions on a roller coaster, sliding swiftly from near panic to anger. "We mean nothing to you. I never even heard of you!"

"If that is true, and I am inclined to believe you, it is unfortunate. But it was necessary to have you here.

This man Blanchard was becoming a threat to me. I knew he would search for you, but what I would like to know is how he determined so quickly that you would be brought here to Morelia. But that is enough for now. You are distraught, and you must be hungry." His manner switched suddenly to one of concern, oddly formal and courteous. "We will have breakfast early, and then we will talk again. Think about that, my dear. If there is anything you are hiding from me, it will be better for you to speak the truth. I assure you, that would be much better." The manner remained cool and considerate, but the threat was unmistakable. It struck a chill through her. What kind of man was this? There was a hint of something deeply hostile in him, something irrationally cruel, beyond her experience and understanding.

The German turned toward the door. She wanted him to go, her relief was overwhelming, but she had to ask the terrible question once more, the question he had refused to answer. "You...you haven't told me about Michael. Where is he? What you done with him?"

At the doorway he turned to gaze back at her. "Surely you have guessed the answer by now. Your Michael is dead."

He closed the door on her cry of pain and despair.

6   Morelia

1

Tuesday, she thought. Tuesday, October 2. Red-Letter Day. It ought to be circled in red on every calendar, from this day forward, until death do us part.

Oh, God, she couldn't let him know she was thinking such thoughts. He had enough to worry about.

But it ought to have a name, this day, like Washington's Birthday or Veterans' Day or Thanksgiving. What should she call it? Liberation Day? Victory Day? Seduction Day?

Or just plain Love Day?

Silly. Silly thirty-seven-year-old woman, thinking it's all new, that it never happened before like this not only for you but for anybody, not like this, certain that it is new for him too, not brand-new for the first time but special all the same, a renewal, a coming to life when he thought all this was behind him, over and done with, that all that was left to him was playing out the string, as he had said once, the surprise clear and unmistakable in his tone, during the long afternoon.

Charmian was still a little stunned that it had happened, even though the attraction between them had been growing, intensified somehow by adversity, as if their broken journey from San Miguel to Morelia had enabled them to leap across several hurdles at once instead of taking them one by one along a well-laid track. Push three or four hurdles together and it's as easy to jump them all as to conquer one.

It had started with breakfast. During the night, before she and Kate went to bed, she had been *sure* that Kate Rynders was worried about her husband driving that old car up the mountain in the rain with Jeff, as worried as Charmian was when she saw Bud Rynders' condition. But in the morning Kate had somehow thrown off all her worries, as if she *knew* that the men were all right. She had no way of knowing that at all, but she was cheerful and clear-browed. Without any rational basis—too many women trusted in unreliable intuition, she thought, or in some psychic bond between themselves and those they loved—Charmian herself had begun to feel less anxious, unable to deny Kate's certainty.

In the morning they had walked over to a little corner store on the hill, a family shop crowded with three generations of Mexicans who seemed to be doing nothing but watch while one of the younger men handled the business of selling fresh milk and eggs and a small assortment of canned goods and *pan dulce*, also fresh that morning. They had brought the sweet rolls and *bolillos* and eggs and milk back to the house, and there was the old Mercury sitting in the carport waiting for them, mud-spattered but otherwise none the worse for the night's adventure.

The meeting with Bud and Jeff had been like a reunion, laughter and excitement and everyone talking at once, joy exaggerated by the fears denied. Over a breakfast of eggs and rolls and sugared sticks and coffee Bud Rynders and Jeff Blanchard took turns recounting their story, playing up the imaginary menace of *bandidos* who had not appeared, playing down any real hazards.

Early that morning they had awakened, poured gasoline into the Vega's tank, attached jump cables between the batteries of the two cars, and the wagon had started instantly. They had driven into Morelia without incident and had left the car with Bud's mechanic, a spirited old man named José who had a great barn of a garage and, Bud assured them, was something of a genius with cars old or new. José's preliminary diagnosis had been the guess that something had fouled up the Vega's fuel line and had simply worked its own way loose overnight. He had kept the car to blow out the lines and to check it over thoroughly for any other problems.

Breakfast was relaxed and warm, as if they were all old friends instead of having met the night before. It was only toward the last that the reality outside had begun to intrude, showing in the thoughtfulness in Jeff Blanchard's eyes, the return of worry.

The motels on the hill were still full. Bud Rynders drove them down into the city and deposited them at a hotel called La Soledad. It was a converted *posada* with a huge, open inner courtyard overlooked by the balconies that led to the rooms on each level. The patio was landscaped with flowers and statuary and a fountain. Even the reception desk, a wide and weathered counter, was open to the patio.

There had been a moment near the entrance, tall gates that must once have admitted horse-drawn carriages to the inner courtyard, when it must have happened, when something was decided between Charmian and Jeff without a word being spoken to make the decision awkward or important or questionable. Searching her memory, Charmian could not find the moment.

Jeff Blanchard had gone to the reception desk alone while she lingered in the patio, admiring the openness to the sky—sunny in the aftermath of the storm—and the flowers and the smooth stones of the floor and the handsome Colonial architecture of the old *posada*, which had been beautifully restored. Jeff had returned smiling and picked up his one small suitcase while an elderly bellhop walked ahead of them, bent over her luggage. Jeff had taken her arm and held it, and they had walked that way to the elevator and up to the third floor and together along the open balcony to their room.

Their room. One room. A big, high-ceilinged, delightful room with authentic reproductions of old Colonial furniture that matched the style of the *posada*. There were bright cushions and a woven rug, a colorful handmade spread on the bed, a vase of fresh-cut flowers in the window, a fireplace already laid with wood.

When the bellhop had left them alone, Jeff Blanchard looked at her and grinned. "They don't call it a double bed," he said. "They call it a *matrimonial*."

"Yes..."

"Makes sense, doesn't it?"

"Oh, yes. Yes, it does."

He came over to her and his grin softened into a smile as he pushed the hair back from her face, gently. "I imagine they have other rooms."

"Didn't you ask?"

"Uh-uh."

"That wouldn't have made any sense, would it?"

"That's what I thought."

"Your night on the mountain seems to have done you good," Charmian said, liking the gentle touch of his fingers, the solid strength of his body. And feeling, absurdly, a threatened attack of the jitters.

"Cleared my head, I guess." He glanced toward the bed, his grin returning. "Be a shame not to take advantage of that *matrimonial*."

"A waste," she agreed.

He kissed her then, long and lovingly. They undressed without haste and crawled between the sheets of the cold bed, Charmian's involuntary shivering from the sudden chill soon stilled by the heat of his body, until another, different quivering began. She remembered thinking how glad she was that it had happened this way, without frenzy or shame or awkwardness but with a slow opening of themselves to pleasure and need.

Discovery Day, she thought. Day of Awakening.

And where are you now, Tom Redman? What eager innocent are you charming now, now that the way is clear? She laughed softly within herself, delighted with herself—and with Jeff Blanchard.

They had their midday *comida* at one of Morelia's sidewalk restaurants opposite the beautiful cathedral on Madero, the main street. The city sparkled in the bright sunshine of this October day. The streets were wide and clean, the parks green and lovely, the sidewalks thronged with Mexicans. *Mexicans,* Charmian noted. Not American tourists but Spanish and Indian faces, farmers and laborers and shopgirls and businessmen. And what looked like an invasion of college-age students.

After lunch, walking aimlessly, they discovered St. Nicholas College a few blocks away from their hotel, explaining the throngs of students. Charmian was delighted with the day and the children wanting to shine Jeff's shoes or sell them raffle tickets, with the animated students and the friendly dark faces that watched them along the boulevard and the graceful old Colonial buildings that faced the huge central plaza.

"It's a beautiful city," she exclaimed.

"Yes, it's beautiful."

"We'll have to go see the viaduct. It's almost two hundred years old and still in use."

"All right, but don't ask me to drink the water."

She laughed. "No, just look."

Then, quite suddenly, they weren't looking at the city but at each other, and they made their way back along Madero through the early afternoon crowds and turned onto a side street that led to La Soledad.

"Isn't it almost siesta time?" Blanchard murmured as they paused momentarily in the courtyard, struck by its quiet remoteness from the busy street they had just left.

"I'm sure it is."

And, of course, they *did* have a siesta, afterwards, when they were both spent and a little awed with each other and with themselves. Jeff Blanchard slept before she did, and she thought for the first time that he couldn't have had much rest during the night on the mountain and must be exhausted, even though he hadn't *acted* exhausted until then. Reluctantly she removed her arm from around his waist, not wanting to disturb the rest he needed, and for a moment the harsh reality that had brought them together here in Morelia struck through her joy, bringing shock like pain, and she had to steel herself to keep from thinking about what might lie ahead for either of them, but especially for him. With a spasm of panic she pushed the sudden fear away and held it off. *Mañana*, she thought.

And she concentrated on this day, reliving it moment by moment, savoring it. She was still trying to think of a name for it, only half humorously, when she fell asleep.

2

Jeff Blanchard went out alone in the late afternoon and found that the car was all right—the fuel line had been confirmed as the cause of the previous day's trouble. José had adjusted the timing and the car ran beautifully. Blanchard drove up the hill to find Bud Rynders while Charmian explored a few of the shops along the boulevard.

She returned to their room ahead of him, but he arrived within ten minutes. He came directly to her and kissed her. She saw the quick sobering in his eyes as he drew away.

"I drove past Brugmann's place. It's up close to the village at the top of the hill. It's impressive—looks like a fortress," he added with a scowl. "Those walls are at least ten feet high."

"What about Brugmann's doctor?" Blanchard had told Charmian of his long talk with Rynders during the night on the mountain.

"It's all set up. Bud's arranged it." He broke off. "They're quite a pair, Bud and Kate, aren't they? I think we've forgotten how to make friends that quickly and naturally back home. Or maybe it's just impossible the way we live now. Like the man says, a nation of strangers." He frowned again, his thoughts jerked back to the problem at hand. He hadn't mentioned Mike or Angie, Charmian thought; it was as if he had to force himself to keep emotion at bay. "This friend of Bud's, his name is Carlos Álvarez, is having some sort of birthday fiesta tomorrow. It's not *his* birthday, it's one of his saints' days, so that's the occasion. Rafael Sánchez will be there."

Charmian's pleasure in Jeff Blanchard's success was diluted by a shadow-passage of apprehension, as if she had a premonition of disaster. The danger toward which he was moving was real, a step into a violent world she had never experienced. By God's grace, she thought; that world was always there.

Repressing a shiver, she said, "Did you go to La Cosecha? Were you able to find it?"

"I drove past it. It's in one corner of that motel on the hill, the Vista del Parque, on the uphill side facing the street. We walked right by it in the rain during the blackout last night." His tone hardened. "Bud Rynders checked around for me. Kinney isn't there. He's supposed to be out of town, or so the girl in the shop said."

"Do you think he is?"

Jeff Blanchard shook his head. "He's here. And he knows I'm here. He has to. And tomorrow maybe I'll begin to find out why."

Charmian stared at him for a long moment. Then she said, "But not tonight."

He glanced at her sharply and she thought that he was angry. Then the determined lines of his jaw and mouth softened. "No," he said. "Not tonight."

3

Carlos Álvarez was small and wiry, with an ageless, weathered brown face and the keen, inquiring eyes of a philosopher. He spoke no English, but he was delighted to welcome the stranger from California, the friend of his good friend Rynders, to his birthday fiesta. He and Rynders embraced warmly. They had known each other, it developed, for nearly twenty years. They had fished and hunted in the hot country, explored isolated digs in search of artifacts, got drunk together a hundred times, shared the spartan life of isolated Indian villages few *norteamericanos* had ever visited. When Rynders had finished this account, the old man's onyx eyes glistened with sentimental tears. Grinning, Rynders insisted Carlos hadn't understood a word.

Álvarez had a half-dozen children living, and all were there for the fiesta. The eldest, Juan, who worked in a branch of the Banco de México, had come with his own family; the youngest, a girl of six, stared at Jeff Blanchard in wordless wonder, then giggled and ran off when he smiled back at her.

Young Juan Álvarez poured drinks for his father, Rynders and Blanchard—the best Jamaican rum, Blanchard noticed—and provided a bottle of purified water as a mixer. The party was already in progress. A dozen or so of the old man's friends were crowded around the small, open patio, for the day was sunny and warm. Their wives and older daughters had withdrawn to the kitchen, leaving the men to their drinking and their talk. A *mariachi* group had been hired for the occasion, and they played and sang with genuine enthusiasm. Carlos Álvarez's house was in the city's *barrio*, packed cheek-by-jowl among mud houses without decent water or plumbing or hope. But Álvarez's house was clean, it had a refrigerator in the kitchen and a television set in the living room, good friends gathered around the patio where excellent rum poured freely. It was easy, in that moment, to envy the old man.

Jeff Blanchard wished that he could simply have relaxed and enjoyed the scene. Instead he kept watching Rynders for some signal that Rafael Sánchez had arrived. In the face of Álvarez's cheerful welcome and spontaneous hospitality, his smile was forced. After a while it became strained. One of the old man's daughters was a slim girl of Angie's age. Every time Blanchard saw her at the window or peering out from the doorway, he was reminded of Angie. Angie, who had disappeared from the house in San Miguel forty-eight hours ago, after he had allowed himself to be stupidly decoyed out of the house. Those two days had brought him no closer to finding her.

Rafael Sánchez was a very, very long shot. There was no hard reason to believe he knew anything about Angie or Mike. But he was a link to Brugmann, however tenuous. And Brugmann was involved with Kinney....

But where the hell was Sánchez?

Watching Bud Rynders, who was engaged in a heated, noisy, and obviously friendly debate with several men, Blanchard felt something like resentment. Rynders could enjoy himself. His wife and daughter were safe up on the hill. He was among friends, not a stranger isolated by language and an immense cultural gulf. He had no reason to ask for more than a warm sun, a drink in his hand, lively music and amiable talk. Why should he—

Blanchard broke off the thought, wryly aware of the absurdity of his resentment. Rynders had gone out of his way to help. And anyway, who could judge the depths of another man's happiness or despair

247

from the outside? The truth was that Blanchard envied any man's joy and ease at that moment, be it Rynders or Carlos Álvarez.

He wished that he'd had the good sense to bring Charmian Stewart along, even though Rynders hadn't suggested it. At least she might have enjoyed herself.

But she wouldn't. She watched him too closely, her emotions a touchstone for his. The realization jarred Blanchard, briefly isolating him from the noisy scene on the patio. This wasn't the time to be thinking about her that way. It wasn't a time for anything good to be happening to him. But neither good nor evil chose convenient moments....

Blanchard had been in Carlos Álvarez's patio for about an hour when Rafael Sánchez came. Blanchard was turning away from the rickety table set against a wall of the house to serve as a bar. Glancing across the patio, he saw a man in a white suit standing just inside the low iron gate that served as the street entrance. He was a stocky man, his body soft and swelling, suggesting too little struggle and too many indulgences. His puffy cheeks discouraged the dash of his neatly trimmed mustache and glossy black hair. His suit was rumpled from driving in a warm car, and sweat glistened on his forehead.

Suddenly Bud Rynders was beside Blanchard. "That's him, Jeff. Come along. Rafael!" he boomed as he advanced toward the stocky Mexican. *"Cómo está, amigo!"*

Blanchard stayed close. Through the flurry of greetings he sensed that Rafael Sánchez continued to be aware of him, flicking glances his way, alert and cautious. And disturbed? A glass was thrust into Sánchez's hand, and then—Rynders had succeeded in maneuvering them toward one side of the patio, away from the crowd—the doctor was facing Blanchard.

"Want you to meet one good *amigo* of mine, Rafael. This here's Jeff Blanchard."

The shock was there in the doctor's eyes for only an instant, but Blanchard was certain of it. Then Sánchez's smile denied its existence. His handshake was soft and moist, his nod courteous, his glance already straying, as if there were other interests, old friends waiting to greet him. "You will excuse me, Señor Blanchard? *Por favor?* I must, how do you say, give my respect to my host."

"Hey, wait a minute, Rafael," Rynders protested. "There's something we got to ask you about."

"Un momento," Sánchez murmured, with a generous flash of immaculate white teeth.

He hurried across the patio and into the house, where Carlos Álvarez had disappeared a moment earlier. Blanchard exchanged glances with Rynders. The artist thoughtfully rolled his glass between his hands. "Don't worry, Jeff, we won't let him off the hook. He's—" Rynders frowned. "That son of a bitch!"

Before Blanchard realized what had happened, Rynders was lunging across the patio and through the gate. Blanchard ran after him. Rynders had turned along the dirt side street toward the front of the house and an unevenly cobbled road, where he had parked his car. Blanchard heard his shout. There was the rasp of a small car's engine.

When Blanchard reached the artist's side, a small white car was racing along the street away from Álvarez's house. It bounced through a pothole, righted itself, and skidded into a sharp turn around the nearest corner.

"You saw it?" Rynders demanded. "When he heard your name?"

"He knew who I was."

"Yeah. And he was scared to death!"

4

Blanchard did not return to La Soledad until late that afternoon. After dropping Bud Rynders off, he drove higher into the hills until he came to the old village of Santa María—a few streets of poor, whitewashed mud houses run together, spilling over uneven streets that led away from a large central plaza. There was an old mission church, a family shop or two hardly distinguishable from the houses, a dark cantina, a single craft-and-furniture factory catering to tourists. Blanchard prowled the narrow streets and side roads leading out of the village until he began to think their broken surfaces threatened to dismantle the Vega's undercarriage. Finally he parked the wagon at the east end of the village and explored on foot.

Eventually a path across an open field led him to the vantage point he had been searching for, a promontory of land from which the hillside sloped away steeply, revealing a broad panorama that encompassed the scattered homes and inns in the Santa María hills, and, beyond them, the city of Morelia in the distance far below.

He had little trouble locating Baldur Brugmann's walled estate. It was well below him, but off to the east. Situated at the crest of a low knoll, it offered no easy approach for a closer scrutiny. From lower levels the high, solid walls enclosing the grounds shut off all view of the building and its gardens. Portions of the grounds were visible from this higher vantage, a series of terraces falling away from the house in orderly steps to the perimeter walls. Low stone parapets defined patches of grass and brightly colored flower beds. But the old monastery itself— Brugmann's house—remained inviolate, showing only the angles of its tiled roof, blank white walls, covered terraces. Whatever secrets it held could not be learned from the outside.

Blanchard fought off a spasm of unreasoning anger. He had no proof that Brugmann and Kinney had plotted to kidnap Mike and then Angie. The structure of coincidences and probabilities on which he based the hunch was flimsy and shaky. Logic argued that it was just as likely that Angie, at least, was being held in some remote village far to the north, or even in one of those beautifully restored and very private homes in San Miguel de Allende. Mike too could be anywhere—if he was still alive. But the feeling persisted that Darrell Kinney had wanted the search to bring Blanchard here to Morelia. Rafael Sánchez's disappearance seemed only to reaffirm this conviction.

There was danger here. Blanchard felt that clearly. The game that had claimed Mike and Angie was not one of Kinney's mocking jokes.

But how could the answer possibly lie behind those silent walls where an old German had lived in isolation for more than fifty years? What possible thread joined that old man to him?

He had to find out. Somehow or other, he had to penetrate old Brugmann's sanctuary and confront him. And soon. If Rafael Sánchez's strange conduct meant anything at all, it suggested panic, an urgency of fear that wasn't generated by some remote danger but by something close and immediate. Otherwise, why wouldn't Sánchez have bluffed it out, offering only a blank face as unreadable as any of those Indian faces which had turned toward Blanchard as he drove around the village of Santa María?

Blanchard had no fear over what might happen to him. The anger that periodically shook him like a fever, and the real terror he felt over Mike and Angie, combined to drive out any personal fear. Not even the emotional awakening he had discovered with Charmian could make him afraid for himself and his own future. He wondered bitterly if Mike would ever know or understand how much his father's fate was tied to his.

The reflection seemed self-pitying. Blanchard shook it off angrily. He knew that he was walking a very thin edge. He was close to having used up all of his emotional reserves, drained by these unrelenting days of anguish and frustration and worry. Had Kinney planned that too? Did he remember his old buddy so well? Did Kinney know that he couldn't go on waiting—that he would be driven to act?

When it was dark there would be little trouble in approaching Brugmann's place undetected. For a long time Blanchard studied the terrain—the roads leading up the hill, the nearest houses, the natural areas of concealment—until he was certain that they would remain imprinted on his mind even at night. Then, at last, he turned back to the Vega.

He was not afraid of what might happen to him, but he wasn't so far out of control that he would be foolishly reckless. When he climbed Brugmann's wall, he would not come unarmed. And there was only one way he could get his hands on a weapon quickly. If he was lucky, and Bud Rynders was careless.

Rynders had promised to try to locate Sánchez that afternoon, and he had invited Blanchard and Charmian to come up to his house for supper and what he called "another council of war."

It was still light when they arrived. Blanchard was surprised to find Cal Sedling there. He was dressed with the same casual elegance as he had been the night Blanchard went to his apartment to meet Rynders for the first time. Blanchard tried to conceal his impatience during the first round of drinks, while Sedling inquired about the fate of the Vega and its contents that rainy night on the mountain and flirted with Charmian Stewart in an offhand way, as if he simply wanted to keep in practice. Sedling had a certain indolent charm that seemed to emerge more strongly when he was in the company of a woman. He appeared to be only politely curious about Blanchard and what had brought him to Morelia. Only when he had gone—after about an hour—did Blanchard realize how many questions Sedling had actually asked.

"How much do you know about him?" he asked Rynders.

"Old Cal? Not much. I don't really know how much there is to know, or how much to believe about what he says. To hear him tell it, he's been a prime-time TV writer, if that's the right term you folks use up in Disneyland, and he's living down here on his residuals. He's got some money though. And he doesn't worry about where it's coming from."

"How long has he lived here?"

"A couple months, I guess. We get a lot of people who come and go, like him. My guess is there's some old-line money there, enough to keep him in style in Morelia, but maybe not enough to make it in Acapulco or Cuernavaca, or over in Gringo Gulch in Puerto Vallarta."

"I think he's a liar," Kate Rynders said bluntly, on her way to the kitchen.

"He has a lot of charm," Charmian said.

"That's what he wanted you to think," Blanchard said.

Charmian laughed. She followed Kate to the kitchen. After a moment Blanchard heard the two women talking to Marta, the family cook and maid, over preparations for supper. He wondered if Sedling's unsubtle attentions to Charmian were behind his dislike of the man. Or was it dislike? Was he simply becoming suspicious of every stranger?

Now that they were alone, Bud Rynders told Blanchard about his fruitless search that afternoon for Rafael Sánchez. The doctor had gone under deep cover. The clinic where he worked reported that he was "unavailable." And a call to his home had received a similar polite rebuff. Rynders had made other inquiries, but no one seemed to have any idea where Sánchez might be.

"It won't be easy to dig him out," the artist commented. "When a Mexican wants to shut the door, he's good at it. That's what all those high walls you see in every village are all about. He'll just close you out, and his whole damned family will join up to hold the wall."

"You think it's hopeless?"

"Well, I wouldn't go that far. If Rafael is mixed up in this some way, he can't just disappear into a hole. But it's gonna take time to find him, Jeff."

"Time I don't have."

"Yeah, I know how you feel, but..." Rynders shrugged his heavy shoulders helplessly.

Blanchard was silent. He felt edgy, explosive, as touchy as a jar of nitroglycerine. All he needed was the slightest jolt.

It could work against him, he knew. On the way down from Santa María that afternoon he had stopped at La Cosecha, without much hope of blundering upon Darrell Kinney. The sales clerk, a young and handsome Mexican girl, had been cool to his inquiries about Alan Slater. Protective, Blanchard had thought, and he had spoken angrily. All he had done was increase the girl's hostility. He had learned nothing. Kinney still had the gift of winning friends and influencing people around him—something you could never really learn from a book.

"The real question," said Bud Rynders thoughtfully, "is *why* old Rafael got the wind up."

"He knows something. He's involved in some way, he has to be. Otherwise why—?" Blanchard broke off, feeling the hairs stir at the back of his neck. He turned quickly toward the front window, in time to see a shadow move but too late to glimpse who had made it. He spoke sharply. "Who's that?"

"Where?" Rynders was startled. Then, as the soft strumming of a guitar reached them, he grinned. "Oh, that. Yeah, that's Luis. I guess our little daughter is getting old enough to start serious entertaining. Makes her old man feel his age."

"He was listening," said Blanchard.

Rynders cocked an eyebrow. "You can't figure everyone's in on this, Jeff. Luis Martínez has been coming around here with his guitar for at least a month, ever since Mary got that new miniskirt, is the way I see it. Those two go wandering off around these hills—Mary's got a horse we keep stabled up by Santa María. Hell, Jeff, you can't tie that in with old Brugmann or your pal Kinney, even if Luis has some wild ideas of his own."

Chagrined, Blanchard settled back into his chair near the fire. He stared at the low flames. The evenings were always cool at this altitude, and the fire was welcome. He shook his head, irritated with himself. Rynders was right. He was jumping at every shadow.

"What wild ideas?" he wondered aloud. He was listening for the sound of Charmian's laughter, as if it were the only available prescription for his attack of nerves.

"Oh, Luis is a Communist. Least he thinks he is. There's quite a few of 'em at the college, and they raise some hell for the establishment. Which, as you may have noticed, is why we got all those militia patrolling the streets, trying not to look like *bandidos*. Hell, Jeff, these kids here aren't much different from what we were at that age. Idealists who want to change the world, and find a way of getting back at the people on top who are just as busy making certain they keep everyone else down at the bottom."

"It is not so simple as you make it sound," a voice said from the doorway.

Blanchard turned as a slim young man stepped into the room. Mary Rynders hovered shyly behind him.

"Luis! *Es mi amigo*, Jeff Blanchard. This is Luis Martínez."

The elegant youth regarded Blanchard with a cool

arrogance. The attitude was not exclusively Mexican, Blanchard thought, but it seemed to be emphasized by the *machismo* of Luis Martínez, expressed in its tight pants, black boots, and embroidered silken shirt as much as by his challenging black eyes. Not exactly the dress of the downtrodden masses, Blanchard thought, perhaps unfairly. He was reminded that many of America's young radicals of the sixties had come from well-heeled middle-class families who could afford to send them to college. Like Mike. Blanchard knew that it would have been all too easy for Mike's rebellion to have taken a tougher, more dangerous direction if he had happened to fall into the wrong situation.

Luis Martínez sat on the projecting hearth, cradling his guitar between his legs. Mary Rynders continued to hover near him, as if afraid that he would get too far away. The youth stared at Blanchard with a defiant expression. "You do not like Communists, Señor Blanchard?"

"I don't dislike categories of people. I just don't agree with you. Not if what you want is violent revolution."

"That is because you have already had your revolution."

"Jeff didn't come here to argue politics, Luis," Rynders interjected.

"It's all right," Blanchard said with a faint smile. "Why not?"

"You will not patronize me," Martínez retorted. "I do not need that."

"I didn't mean to sound patronizing, if that's the way it sounded." There was no way to talk to them, he thought. It had been the same with Mike.

After glaring at him for a moment, the young Mexican relented a little, leaning back. "Perhaps I do not always know what it is you are saying, Señor Blanchard. My English is..." He shrugged thin shoulders eloquently.

"You speak English very well."

"For an ignorant peasant, you mean?"

"I didn't say that," Blanchard snapped, nettled in spite of himself.

"No, but that is what you were thinking. How is it that this peasant can talk two languages at all, eh?"

"The trouble with revolutionaries is that they sometimes talk for both sides. That way you can make the other side say exactly what you want them to say."

"No, that is not the trouble with revolutionaries," Luis Martínez retorted. "Our trouble is only that we talk too much and do too little. But that," he added ominously, "will change."

Blanchard wondered if it would really change. Mexico's ruling Institutional Revolutionary Party, itself born out of revolution, had a well-earned reputation for an iron fist coming down quick and hard on dissenters. Kent State had been a shocking event in the United States. It would hardly have made headlines in Mexico.

"You have protest in your country," Martínez said.

"Yes..." Automatically Blanchard's thoughts went from Kent State to Mike and Angie. But they had tried to use the system, he thought defensively, and for that he respected both of them.

"You think it is the same here. It is not so bad, eh? Not so bad that we should make real trouble. Señor Blanchard, you know nothing of Mexico. You see only the pretty señoritas and the happy *mariachis*. You drink your margaritas and buy your... Señor Rynders, what is the word?"

"Souvenirs," Rynders said amiably.

"*Sí*... souvenirs. But the real Mexico is not the Mexico of the *turistas*, Señor. The real Mexico is a country where seventy percent of the children grow up with the malnutrition, did you know that?"

Jolted, Blanchard shook his head.

"Two out of every three children, eh? And in *los Estados Unidos* you have your five percent who cannot find work. In Mexico it is five times as many as that. And for most of them there is not even hope."

"Things must be getting better—they're changing. You have new industry. That means jobs, money—"

"Para quién, Señor? For whom? The rich get richer, just as it is in your country, and the poor get poorer. But here it is more so. Here the poor are very poor, they have nothing, and there are always more of them. And if we protest because we are oppressed, do you know what is our government's answer? It is the same as your government. It is to call out the army! Did you know there are tanks in Mexico today, at this very moment, at the Universidad Nacional?"

"In Mexico City? At the university?" Again Blanchard was startled.

"Sí! They face students with guns and tanks. Here in Morelia you have seen the *granaderos"*—he spat out the word—"but the tanks will come, if *el presidente* decides it."

"Is Echeverría so bad?"

"He is no worse than any other. But how do you think Echeverría became president? Do you know that, Señor Blanchard? By killing students! *Sí!* He was a cabinet minister then, but it was Echeverría who commanded the guns at Tlateloco Plaza four years ago, the summer of our Olympic Games. Hundreds died that time. It made him a favorite with his bosses. He showed that he was a strong man, he was not afraid to kill children, and that is what they want. A strong man to keep the peasants down and the students quiet." Luis Martínez leaned forward, his black eyes hot as lava. "Do you know, Señor, there is a First Military Camp on the outside of Mexico, our capital city, where the army tortures workers and students and teachers? And what does Echeverría do? Nothing! What does Echeverría say? *Nada!* And you say to me that we must not use violence. Tell this to them, Señor!"

"There have to be other ways." Blanchard spoke without conviction, for a part of his mind instantly questioned the words, reminding him of his own

258

plans, his main reason for coming to Bud Rynders' home tonight. What if there seemed to be no other way? What if you saw yourself backed against a wall, as he did—and as Luis Martínez clearly saw himself and his country's hopeless poor? None of us are so far removed from violence, Blanchard thought. All that is necessary is to believe that it's the only way.

"There is no other way." Luis Martínez seemed to echo his thought. "They do not leave us any other way."

"Luis, Jeff is right about one thing," Bud Rynders said, in a tone that suggested there had been enough politics for one night. "You talk too damned much." When Luis turned to face him angrily, Rynders silenced him with a gesture. "I mean, you can get yourself into a hell of a lot of trouble just sounding off like this. I don't mean here, with us. But outside. You'll do yourself and what you believe in a lot more good if you stay out of trouble—and out of jail. Just remember that."

There was a brief silence. Blanchard realized that Charmian and Kate had returned to the room, and he wondered how long they had been listening. Young Mary Rynders watched Luis Martínez with anxious adoration.

Abruptly the young man smiled. "You are right, Señor Rynders. In this way I have talk too much." He rose, the movement fluid and graceful. Lifting his guitar, he stared down at it, then gave a quick, impatient flick of his fingers that struck a dramatic chord. *"Dispénseme, Señor Blanchard. Por favor?"*

Blanchard gave him a troubled nod. There was nothing to forgive.

The opportunity Blanchard had been waiting for came shortly after supper. It was dark then. Charmian and Kate Rynders had stepped outside onto a side patio between the house and Rynders' studio. The two women acted like old school classmates reunited after many years, although from the snatches of talk Blanchard guessed that Kate was inquiring not about school days but about current fashions and news about America, including—there was a note of perplexity in Kate's voice—women's liberation.

"How about a brandy?" Rynders asked. "It's not an offer I make every day, so you'd better take me up on it quick."

"You talked me into it." Blanchard resisted a feeling of guilt over his eagerness to get Rynders out of the room.

A moment later, hearing the artist's voice from the patio as he repeated his offer of an after-dinner drink to the two women, Blanchard went quickly to the rolltop desk at one side of the room. He opened the top right-hand drawer. The gun was there, where he had seen Rynders place it after they returned from their night on the mountain. As he reached for it, he heard footsteps.

Blanchard leaned against the desk, letting his weight ease the drawer shut. He could feel the heat in his face, and he hoped that the shadows at this side of the room, away from the fire and the chairside lamp near it, concealed his flaming guilt.

"A handsome desk," he said. "Where did you find it down here?"

"They turn up now and then. It's a gen-u-wine antique."

"It would cost a small fortune now in the States."

"Not that one. The trouble it took me to restore it, you couldn't pay me enough to let it go. Listen, I spoke too soon about the brandy. The ladies said yes, and the bottle's down to the bottom hole. Can I talk you into some tequila?"

Blanchard managed a laugh. "Ladies first. Tequila will be fine. Or just more coffee."

"No, I got plenty tequila. Real Mexican poison if you drink enough of it."

The artist disappeared once more into the kitchen. Blanchard hated what he was doing. It seemed a lousy return for all the help Rynders had given. But Rynders wouldn't let him have the gun voluntarily, that was certain. He would only try to talk him out of any rash action. There had been enough talk, enough waiting.

Blanchard's heart pounded as he slipped the big Colt from the drawer. When was the last time he had stolen anything, or betrayed a friendship? Quickly he crossed the room and stepped outside. No one was in sight. The Vega was parked out front, and he moved quickly to the car. As he opened the far door, he was watching the windows of the house for any sign of Rynders. He rejected the glove compartment as a hiding place. Charmian might look there for something. Anyway, the compartment was probably too small. Hastily he shoved the Colt under the driver's seat. When he slammed the car door, he saw Rynders in the carport watching him. He knew the blood rushed to his face, and he wondered how much the artist had seen.

"Anything wrong?"

"No, I was...just looking for some cigarettes."

"I didn't know you were addicted."

Blanchard came around the car. He couldn't remember if he had closed the desk drawer after taking the gun. Was Rynders suspicious? He said, "I keep giving them up, but...I guess this is nervous time."

"Kate's got some inside somewhere. I can't get her to quit either."

Back in the house, Rynders handed him a small glass of gold tequila. When the artist went over to the rolltop desk, Blanchard's heartbeat skipped. But Rynders opened a drawer on the left side and, after a moment's rummaging, triumphantly produced a pack of cigarettes. "Hope you can take these chili weeds," he said.

"Anything you've got." Blanchard's relief was so apparent that Rynders grinned at him as he tossed over the pack.

Afterward Blanchard was not sure how he got through the next hour without giving himself away.

Every time Rynders rose, he felt the same anxiety, but the artist never had occasion to go to his desk. Somehow Blanchard managed to talk rationally about the problem of finding Rafael Sánchez or the man who called himself Alan Slater. Rynders promised to make further inquiries in the morning. He knew many of Sánchez's friends in town, and a few of his enemies. Sooner or later, he reasoned, both Sánchez and Slater would have to surface.

No one mentioned Baldur Brugmann again.

Toward the end of that hour, Blanchard began making obvious signals of fatigue. He didn't have to work very hard at it, although the quick sympathy he read in Charmian's eyes gave him an uncomfortable feeling. It was she who suggested they go back down the hill. Neither Bud nor Kate Rynders, perhaps acting out of the same compassion for a harassed father, raised any objection.

The council of war hadn't been very productive, Blanchard thought. But it had given him what he really wanted.

He didn't breathe easily until he was in the car with Charmian, pulling away, glancing back with a guilty wave at Rynders and his wife.

He was driving, and at the corner he had to brake quickly, stopping about halfway into the road as an old car with one headlight careened by without slowing. Made cautious, Blanchard peered up the road. In that moment his plans for the night were completely changed.

For only a brief instant, a light appeared behind the window of La Cosecha.

5

The gates to the *mercado* were locked, the warren of stalls and narrow aisles inside were dark and deserted. But the night was clear for a change, only a blackness over the mountains to the south and west hinting at further rain on the way. There was a nearly full moon, and the broad expanse of paved area surrounding the main market building, where outdoor vendors from the countryside daily displayed their wares on mats or blankets, was awash in a white rain of light.

A policeman in khaki uniform appeared at the nearest intersection, and Luis Martínez shrank deeper into the shadows of one entrance to the *mercado*. He watched the policeman cross the street, pause before the window of the Banco de México, and move on. The voices of some children rose from a side street even at this late hour, and the policeman looked in their direction as he passed. Then he walked on, slowly, a man without a mission.

Martínez felt the tension ease in his ropelike body. He wished that he knew what time it was, but he had no watch. He had sold it a month ago for enough pesos to buy a gun.

The pistol was tucked into his waistband, under his silken shirt.

Soon there would be money to buy many watches, but that was not what it would be used for. Instead it would buy more guns. What he had said to the *gringo*, Señor Rynders' friend, was true. There was no other way. The way of Allende in Chile was no good here; it would not work, for here in Mexico the elections were not truly free. It would not even work for long in Chile, he thought with passionate skepticism. How could the masses triumph when the movement rested on the shoulders of the rich merchants and the fascist soldiers? No, that was only the illusion of victory, too easily snatched away by those who had offered the prize. The only real way to power was to take it from those who had it, who had used it to oppress the people. And it could only be taken truly by force.

But even the movement was corrupted by the system. It also needed money. Money to buy food and silence. Money to buy guns and bullets. Money even to buy paper and ink when the war became a war of words.

It was a vicious circle, Luis Martínez thought. In the end it was not ideas that triumphed. It was always pesos.

An old woman came around the corner and shuffled along the side street. She stopped in the shelter of an alley Martínez was facing. There she lifted her skirts and squatted. He watched her idly. When she had relieved herself she rose, very slowly and painfully, and continued along the street, her crabbed shuffle an obvious evidence of distress. Luis Martínez's reaction was not sympathy but anger. She was one of the poor, the oppressed masses. His response to her plight, her ragged poverty and her pain, was not personalized but general. He was a man of ideas.

Suddenly he drew taut. A small white car had appeared on the Calle Sotero Castaneda. It drove slowly past the *mercado* and turned along the narrow street where the old woman had gone. It passed the niche in which Martínez waited in deep shadow.

After the white car had disappeared along the street, he peered back along Castaneda. No other car was in sight. Sánchez was not being followed.

When the white Renault came again to the corner of the market after circling the block, Luis Martínez raced across the pavement to meet it. The door swung open, he ducked inside. Without coming to a complete stop, the car shot away. At the next corner it swung right again and was soon lost in the shadows of the streets north of the market.

Rafael Sánchez parked the Renault along one of those shadowed streets behind the cathedral and switched off the motor. The silence seemed to vibrate with the engine's busy sound even after it had ceased.

"You saw no one?" the doctor asked after a moment.

"No one follows you." Sánchez was an overly nervous man, Martínez thought. Not one to be trusted beside you if things went bad. But he was not needed for that. "Why should you be suspected of anything?"

"One can't be too careful. You don't know this German, or the man who works for him, the red-haired one."

"El diablo rojo?" Martínez laughed. "He is only one man. And the old one cannot be too dangerous. All that matters is that he is as rich as you say."

"He is rich," Sánchez muttered. "But do not underestimate him."

The younger man eyed him speculatively. "You have said it would be easy. Is it not so?"

Sánchez shifted his compact body in the small seat. Luis Martínez was aware of the smell of his sweat overpowering his cologne in the confines of the little car; the fact intrigued him. Sánchez was not merely nervous. He was frightened. And he was not the one who was taking any risk. Martínez decided that the doctor was right. He should not underestimate the danger.

It was possible, of course, that Sánchez had lied to him, or that he had not told all of the truth.

Martínez had intended to tell the doctor at once about the American in Señor Rynders' house this evening who had spoken Sánchez's name. He had not overheard enough to know why the doctor had been spoken of, and he was not sure that it was important. Now he decided to wait. Sánchez had always been nervous; he had not before been afraid. The fact might be important, and he did not want to make Sánchez any more nervous.

Rafael Sánchez had sought Martínez out about six weeks ago. He had indicated awareness of Martínez's activities with the People's Liberation Army, but in the beginning he had not revealed what was in his mind. Martínez had been wary and suspicious. But it was clear that, if Sánchez knew so much about him already, he could have turned his information over to the police immediately if that was his intention. Since he had not done so, he had a reason... and a reason for pretending to be a friend to Martínez and to the cause of the workers and students.

Finally the night came when Sánchez told him about Baldur Brugmann. The German on the hill, he said, was not the man he pretended to be. Old Brugmann was dead, killed long ago. The man who had taken his place many years ago was a fugitive Nazi, whom Sánchez had treated in small ways over the years as a doctor. The man who called himself Brugmann was also quite old now, as he must be to have been a high German officer in the time of Adolf Hitler. Sánchez, it was soon apparent, hated him.

But it was not until two weeks ago that Rafael Sánchez, at an urgently arranged meeting, had finally revealed what was in his mind. A band of guerrillas had raided a bank in Puebla, escaping with a large sum of money. The story of the robbery was in the Mexico City newspapers, and Sánchez had a copy of *Excelsior* with him that night when he met Martínez. He showed it to the young man and waited for his reaction.

"Yes?" Martínez had said when he put the paper aside. "You are going to help us rob a bank?"

The question had been sarcastic, but Sánchez did not smile. "I will help you do something that is much easier. Those fools in Puebla will soon be caught, and they will be tortured and killed. But what if you were to rob someone who is of no interest to the *federales*? What if you were to rob an old man who is not even known to them, who has a fortune the government does not know exists? Who would hunt you then? Who would care?"

Luis Martínez had known instantly that this was what the doctor had been leading up to from the beginning. He was excited by the proposal, but he was also cautious. He questioned Sánchez carefully. Who else lived with Brugmann behind his high walls? What guards were there? How many? How much money did the German have and where was it hidden? Why did Sánchez believe there was much to be found in the German's house? Why wasn't it in the bank where it would be so much safer, so much harder to steal?

And—most important of all—why had Sánchez come to him with his proposal?

The doctor answered all of his questions carefully, for he seemed to have anticipated each of them. In the end Luis Martínez was convinced. There were only three or four men protecting Brugmann at any time. They would not be expecting an attack, and they would be unprepared. As for the money, the German had escaped with a fortune in gold to Argentina at the end of the war; from there he had come to Mexico. Some of his money was indeed safe in the bank, under another name. But of necessity a man in his position kept large sums with him, for he never left his house and he could not always send someone to the bank when he wished. Moreover, such a man would wisely choose not to have the existence of all of his fortune known, as it most certainly would have been if he had placed it all in banks. There was in his study a small safe, concealed behind a painting. It was old and could easily be blown open if the German could not be compelled to open it. Sánchez could not say how much money would be found there, but it was certain to be a large sum. And the doctor asked only for a fair share of what was taken, which he planned to use to build a clinic for the good of the people. He would trust Martínez to be fair.

Martínez did not immediately agree to the plan, but the more he thought about it, the more it was argued in his cell, of which he was the leader, the more plausible and inviting the idea appeared.

There was only one thing upon which Sánchez insisted. The German and his red-haired assistant must both be killed. About this the doctor was adamant, and his fear of the two men first became visible with this insistence. The provision presented no difficulty. It would be safer for all if the German and his assistant could not talk after the raid.

Besides, the Nazi was a fascist who had preyed upon other peoples and was now a parasite feeding upon Mexico and its people. He did not deserve to live. Nor did those who protected him.

Rafael Sánchez broke into Martínez's reflections. "The time has come."

"When?" the young man asked sharply.

"Mañana."

"Tomorrow? Always it is tomorrow. Why do you—"

"Tomorrow night," Rafael Sánchez said, cutting off Martínez's impatient reaction. "If there is to be any delay, I will tell you. But you are to be ready tomorrow night."

Luis Martínez's thoughts raced ahead, sifting the problems of notifying all those who would participate in the adventure, of gathering their arms, of avoiding the attention of the militia, who were still cruising Morelia's streets. But his excitement was undeniable, and it caused him to forget all about the American in Rynders' house who had mentioned Rafael Sánchez. He said, "We are ready. But now you must tell me everything...."

6

While she waited for Blanchard to return from the garage, Charmian had lit a fire, which had been laid in their absence. She wanted to have the room warm and inviting for him after what had been a frustrating and disappointing day. She undressed quickly and washed away her makeup. Briefly she debated taking a quick shower, but she didn't want him to return while she was in the shower and not there to welcome him. She wanted something other than the room to be warm and inviting. She left her hair loose, slipped into her nightgown, and crawled into the bed between the chilly sheets to wait. Her glance went often to the door.

By now the fire had burned low, and she was frightened. He had been gone too long.

She went back over their last minutes in the car. Blanchard had been pensive during the drive down the hill from the Rynders place, but that had seemed natural. What she had felt then was not fear but a passionate sympathy.

He had surprised her when he let her out in front of La Soledad. The hotel kept an enclosed garage nearby, for it was not always safe to park in the street. The garage had a night attendant. Charmian had looked at Jeff questioningly. "Hop out," he said. "No point in both of us walking."

"Don't be silly. I'll keep you company. Besides, you don't have to park it, they'll do it for us."

"Don't give me an argument, woman," he'd said with gruff humor. She had wanted to do just that, but she had caught the strain of worry and fatigue behind his humor. So she had yielded without another protest.

Had there been something in his manner then she should have perceived, something she hadn't understood?

The clamor of church bells reached her. She glanced quickly at her travel clock without waiting to count the chimes. The towns of Mexico were filled with the din of church bells at night. In some places—San Miguel de Allende was one—they awakened you early in the morning, if they allowed you to sleep at all.

It was midnight.

They had left the Rynderses at close to eleven. Jeff Blanchard had been gone for over an hour since dropping her off at the front of the hotel.

Charmian slipped out of bed and opened the door to the room. From the balcony she looked down at the open courtyard and the fountain three floors below. A caretaker was visible near the main gates, sitting on a chair propped against one wall, his head slumped forward over his chest as if he were asleep. Otherwise the patio was silent, empty.

The last of the church bells tolled the twelfth hour. The night became still. There was a full moon, and it was bright and cold. Standing in the open in her flimsy gown, Charmian felt a sharp chill that seemed to close around her heart.

She should have guessed that Jeff had planned something. But what could it be? What could he hope to find in the sleeping city? What did he mean to do?

Dropping her off had been premeditated, deliberate. Whatever was in his mind was potentially dangerous, and he wanted her out of the way, safe in their room. What else could his disappearance mean?

For the first time she considered seriously the possibility that something had happened to him between the garage and the hotel. That—like Mike and Angie—he had been kidnapped. The back streets of the inner city were dark and empty, narrow corridors the moonlight could not penetrate. He would have been vulnerable, walking alone.

But she didn't believe it. Not only because the idea was too monstrous to be acceptable, though certainly no more impossible or bizarre than Angie's disappearance from San Miguel in broad daylight. It was simply obvious that Jeff Blanchard had chosen some course of action that he had to take alone... or a risk he would not expose her to.

And that meant she could do nothing. Even if the police would be of help under the circumstances, even if they would accept her conviction that Jeff was in some kind of danger, that wasn't what he wanted.

Had he spoken to Rynders? The possibility that the two men might have planned something together brought a flicker of hope. They'd had plenty of time to talk privately tonight. Perhaps it had to do with the missing doctor. She found herself praying that that was it. Rynders seemed cool-headed, competent. He wouldn't have Jeff's emotions clouding his judgment.

She began to shiver. The tremor increased until her whole body vibrated, and she realized she was on the verge of panic. She ran back into her room, slamming the door, and fled to the warmth of the bed.

There she sat huddled with the covers bunched around her, staring at the dying fire and listening to the thudding of her heart, more frightened than she could remember being in her adult life; not for herself but for the man she loved.

What had seemed so awful and destructive just a few short months ago, when she had finally found the courage to walk away from Tom Redman, now seemed childish and trivial. She had needed someone, and Tom had filled a void in her life, a huge emptiness. But the attachment had been shallow, and she realized that it had never engaged her whole heart, any more than it had his.

It was bewildering to discover that, almost overnight, she had come to love another man so completely. Until now she had been preoccupied with the astonishment of it, and the joy. Worry and concern had been there, especially after San Miguel, but now she faced the real terror that was a part of love, the fear of its loss. She contemplated the emptiness of the night ahead, with no sense of being one of an endless procession of women over countless years who had waited and watched, keeping their lonely vigils in empty beds, with dull eyes and an abiding ache of fear.

Jeff Blanchard crouched in the shadows of the narrow downhill street directly across from the Vista del Parque in the Santa María hills, staring at the darkened windows of La Cosecha. He could feel the hard length of Bud Rynders' Colt pressing against his belly. The gun was too big and awkward to carry comfortably without a holster. His right hand kept straying to the smooth wooden gun butt, as if he needed to reassure himself that he could draw it easily from beneath his waistband.

Several times he had asked himself if he could have imagined the light he had seen in the gift shop when he was leaving Rynders' place with Charmian. The question was idle. He had not been mistaken.

At the time he had wondered if Charmian had also seen the light, but she hadn't. She had not mentioned it during the drive into town or when he let her out at the hotel. He hadn't liked lying to her, and he had avoided looking back when he drove away, knowing that she was standing by the open gates staring after him. But there had been no choice. He couldn't involve her any further, he couldn't say anything to her. Like Rynders, she would have tried to stop him. And he might have found it harder to resist her emotional concern than Rynders' arguments.

The light might have meant nothing. For all he knew, the shopgirl might stay there at night. But he didn't think so. The glow behind the window had been there for only an instant. It had winked off almost as soon as he saw it, as if it was not meant to be seen.

There was an iron grille over the windows at the front and side of the shop, and on his afternoon visit he had noted a heavy bar that secured the main entrance. He wondered about the door that led into the shop from the motel's inner court, a convenience for its guests. That entrance might not be barred; security was more essential on the street frontage. He was also curious about the rooms or unit directly over the shop.

The big iron gates to the motel were also closed, with a night watchman posted just inside the entrance. He had looked up when Blanchard walked past the gates a short while ago, after parking the Vega out of sight around a corner farther down the hill. Blanchard decided not to go past the watchman again. No point in arousing his curiosity.

There was no way to cross the moonlit road without being seen from the windows of La Cosecha—if anyone was there. Blanchard started uphill, hugging the buildings along the side of the road to keep in shadow. He ran across the road at the next corner, a full block away. He kept going at a steady trot along the side street, which was unpaved and deeply rutted. He circled the block. A few minutes later he was approaching the motel from the rear.

He wasn't sure what he had hoped to find—a service entrance, perhaps, or a back way through the motel's kitchen, or even an unlocked window that might provide entry into an empty unit. What he discovered quickened his pulse.

The motel was being expanded at the rear. A second-story addition was being constructed over what had been an older, one-level section comprising the west wing of the enclosed square. A temporary skeletal superstructure at the back, fashioned of two-by-fours, gave access for the carpenters to the upper framework being raised. A series of boards had been nailed into place to improvise a ladder.

Blanchard wondered how closely the night watchman guarded the new construction, aware that it was vulnerable to access or simply to keep wood from being stolen.

He shrugged off the worry. He would deal with the watchman if he had to. Nothing would keep him from investigating that light in Darrell Kinney's shop so late at night. Even if he were no longer there, he might have left some evidence of his presence, some proof that he was here in Morelia now.

The temporary structure against the back wall of the motel was rickety, creaking and wobbling when it accepted his weight—but it held. There were enough crosspieces to make climbing easy, and in short order he was easing through the open framework at the new second level.

His luck held. The new unit was butted against the south wing of the building at the corner. Blanchard was able to step directly onto the covered balcony of the older building.

For several minutes he studied the open court below. It provided parking space for about twenty cars in the open, as well as a few closed garages. Off to the left, near the restaurant, was a small swimming pool, its placid surface reflecting the glow of the full moon. But Blanchard hardly saw these details. His gaze remained fixed on the street entrance. The high wrought-iron gates were set between stone walls, the corner unit and the motel office creating an arched passageway that was in shadow. For a while Blanchard could see nothing. Then a match flared. The watchman, just out of sight under the arch, lit a cigarette.

Blanchard turned his attention along the balcony. A half-dozen doors opened from it into as many upstairs units. At the far end of the balcony another door faced him. It opened into the unit directly above La Cosecha.

Blanchard felt no real disappointment. The possibility that La Cosecha might be connected to the rooms overhead had been remote. It seemed more likely that the shop had been converted from the downstairs unit in that corner of the building.

He had to get down the stairs to reach the door to Kinney's shop. There was a flight of steps at each end of the balcony. He chose the one at the far end. It would bring him down close to the shop entrance.

All but one of the units along the balcony were dark. Blanchard heard no sound as he slipped past them, grateful for the shadows of the balcony. Although on many nights the motel's units were filled, the restaurant and bar closed early, and the entrance gates were secured at ten. A late-returning guest could still get in after that hour, but the watchman had to open the gates. Most tourists retired early to their rooms, for the city offered little in the way of night life to attract them. For its real inhabitants, Blanchard suspected, the people in the old city below these hills, life probably didn't cease so early in the night.

The watchman did not appear. No one stirred in the courtyard as Blanchard slipped down the stairs. At the bottom step he paused. The watchman's cigarette glowed, just around the corner some thirty feet away.

Silence dripped around Blanchard like a fine mist. If he made any sound at all, the watchman would hear him.

The courtyard entrance to La Cosecha was a solid door with hand-carved panels. Blanchard placed his ear against the door. How long since he had glimpsed that flicker of light? A half hour, maybe longer. Too long. Kinney might have come and gone quickly. If he was trying to stay hidden, it seemed unlikely that he would stay here. But Blanchard had to find out.

As he had expected, the door was locked. But like most motel locks it was not much of a protection. A security man at the *News* had once shown Blanchard how to open a conventional, spring-latched cylinder lock by simply inserting one of his stiff plastic credit cards into the opening between the door and the frame. As long as there was no deadlatch designed to prevent this kind of attack, the lock would open easily.

He fished a credit card from his wallet. It wasn't as easy as the security guard had made it seem, but after a sweating minute of struggle Blanchard felt the latch release.

He glanced over his shoulder toward the gates. The watchman wasn't watching. Feeling the prickle of tension along his spine and the back of his neck, Blanchard opened the door and stepped into the dark interior of La Cosecha. His hand was on the butt of the Colt at his waist.

The tingling sense of danger sharpened. Suddenly the door slammed shut behind him, and in the same instant something small and hard bored painfully into his spine.

The voice spoke behind him, so close that he could feel warm breath against his neck. "Looking for me, old buddy?"

Darrell Kinney relieved Blanchard of the Colt and directed him into a back room. As they left the shop he clicked on a light. It revealed a windowless storage room. The two men stared at each other in silence. Blanchard felt the jar of recognition, the strange time-slip that wiped away a quarter of a century.

Kinney spoke curtly. "We'll talk upstairs."

At Kinney's direction Blanchard pressed a board in what appeared to be a solid wall of storage shelves. A panel opened, revealing a narrow spiral staircase squeezed into an impossibly small space. "You go first," Kinney said. "But don't try anything, Jeff. You're not up to it."

The staircase led to the motel unit directly over the gift shop, a possibility that Blanchard had considered and discarded as unlikely. He wondered why Kinney had the need for a secret exit, a way of coming and going from his shop without being seen.

Kinney followed him closely up the tight iron spiral, but not close enough to allow himself to be kicked or jumped. Blanchard knew the moment when he might have done anything had passed when Kinney's head and shoulders thrust into view at the top of the staircase, following the barrel of a German Luger.

Kinney pressed a button in a switch panel and Blanchard heard the wall section in the storage room swing closed. "Aren't secret stairways a little out of date?" he said.

"I have enemies," Kinney said enigmatically.

He directed Blanchard toward a chair. The room was part of a conventional motel unit, one large room and bath. This one, however, had a small kitchenette, and it was furnished with handsome Colonial pieces as well as a huge bed and a television set. The air of comfort and elegance suggested that Kinney spent considerable time here.

Kinney dropped into a leather chair. In one hand he balanced the Colt he had commandeered, hefting its weight. The Luger's muzzle did not waver from Blanchard's chest. He didn't mistake Kinney's casual manner for a lack of alertness. Kinney, he thought disgustedly, didn't make careless mistakes.

"Big son of a bitch," Kinney murmured. "You were really going to blow a hole in me, weren't you?"

"If I had to."

Kinney clucked disapprovingly. "That doesn't sound like the old Jeff Blanchard. You didn't used to be so violent."

"You've given me reason. Where's Mike? What have you done to my son?"

The mocking amusement faded from Kinney's eyes. That expression, and the pale, watery look of light-sensitive eyes behind tinted lenses, was disturbingly familiar. "You blame me for that."

"Who the hell else should I blame."

For a moment Kinney was silent. "It's a long story, and I'm not sure you'll believe me."

"Try me." Blanchard was suddenly sick of this cool, polite charade, and his anguish burst out. "Goddamn you, what about Mike? Is he alive?"

Darrell Kinney stared at him. Quietly he said, "Yes, he's alive. And if you'll calm down and hear me out, maybe he can stay that way."

Blanchard sagged back in his chair. He found that his hands were shaking, his stomach churning. Mike was alive! If Kinney wasn't lying, there was still a chance... "How did you know I was coming?"

"You're fairly predictable, Jeff. Don't you know that? I let you see that light when you left Rynders' place."

"You knew I was there?" Blanchard showed his surprise.

"It's a small community up here on the hill, old buddy. And you aren't hard to keep track of. Anyway,

I knew if I let you see that someone was here, you'd come charging back looking for me. I've been waiting for you. And I had to find a way for us to meet without being seen by anyone else."

"You'll have to explain that."

"All in good time, buddy."

"For Christ's sake, stop calling me that."

The mocking smile reappeared. "But that's what we were, Jeff, in the old days. Don't tell me you've forgotten."

"I haven't forgotten anything. But we're not buddies now. I'm not even sure we ever were."

"I don't think you believe that. And if you do, you're wrong."

There was a ring of sincerity in Kinney's words, and in spite of himself Blanchard felt the pull of old memories. They had been friends. They'd been through a lot together, at a special time of youth and the world's turmoil. He had liked and admired the Darrell Kinney he knew during the war. All through the past two weeks he had been aware of an inner conflict, a reluctance to admit that Kinney might be involved in a vicious plot against him and his son.

Kinney had changed surprisingly little in the passage from young manhood into middle age. He was perhaps ten pounds heavier, and he looked more like a man in his early forties than one who had to be over fifty. His hair was still thick and black, except for some distinctive graying at the temples. He still wore it in the same way, brushed straight back. But it was not these physical details that reminded Blanchard so vividly of the younger Kinney. The man's *style* had remained unchanged. The same ready smile. The same sardonic way of talking. The same easy charm and magnetism. If he'd been a politician, the word *charisma* would inevitably have been applied. If he were seen on any street in Los Angeles or New York, wearing a business suit instead of his casual Mexican clothes, he would easily have passed for a successful ad man or a sharp sales executive. Or one of the new breed of politicians, trading on his good looks and his style. Damn it, you don't want him to be guilty, Blanchard thought. But that doesn't matter.

Kinney placed Bud Rynders' Colt on a table. He still held the Luger in a businesslike way. Blanchard wondered if it was a war souvenir.

"If you want me to believe you," he said, "you can start by telling me about Mike."

For a moment longer Kinney studied him. Then he seemed to come to a decision, and he said, "I'm afraid I have to start earlier than that for you to understand. It goes a long way back, all the way back to Germany and the war. I mean the end of it, those last days...."

In silence and with growing incredulity, Blanchard listened as Kinney's strange story unfolded. He told of Carl Creasey being killed in a forced crash-landing of their plane, and of taking refuge in an abandoned castle near the Rhine. There he had stumbled upon a German officer, also hiding out in the castle, and he had learned of a fortune in stolen paintings. "You know me, Jeff," he said wryly. "I was always looking for the big killing, and there it was, handed to me on a platter. I should have killed that Nazi bastard and taken it all for myself, but I thought I needed him. He sold me a bill of goods that he was the only one who could get us to South America, if I could get us to Switzerland. It was a long time before I knew that he was only using me."

Kinney had no regrets over dropping out of the war. For all intents it was over anyway, and he had to look out for himself. In the company of the SS colonel he had escaped to Switzerland with the stolen paintings, and from there they had made their way as planned to South America, where several of the paintings were sold. Eventually, because Israeli agents were trying to trace the source of the paintings, they had fled. More than twenty years ago they had come to Mexico, settling in Morelia.

"My God! That man on the hill—Brugmann!"

"Brugmann's dead. Von Schoenwald killed him and took his place. He's stayed up there all these years, and no one knows who he is except a handful of people close to him."

Stunned, Blanchard saw the dimensions of the danger his son had stumbled into when he recognized Kinney in San Miguel. Harshly he said, "That's why Mike was kidnapped. Because he threatened the two of you!"

"Take it easy, Jeff." The Luger lifted. "You can't jump me. You're not quick enough. And getting yourself killed won't bring Mike back."

"Bring him back? You said he was still alive."

Kinney hesitated, and Blanchard's heart sank. "He was alive the last time I saw him. Hell, Jeff, I had to tell von Schoenwald what happened over there in San Miguel. I didn't want anything to happen to your son, but I couldn't just let him go back home and blow the whole thing wide open. I followed Mike to Guadalajara. I was stalling, trying to figure out how to handle it. That's where Robbins stepped in."

"Who's Robbins?" As he spoke the name, Blanchard remembered. Rynders had spoken of Baldur Brugmann's aide, George Robbins.

"He's a goddamn devil!" Kinney exploded. "He's the one who's been pulling the strings all along, ever since Guadalajara. He's made sure you kept jumping the way he wanted you to jump. That's why he grabbed that girl over in San Miguel."

"Angie... but you were in on that, too."

"Christ, I couldn't do anything else! You think Robbins wouldn't like to see me dead and out of the way? Then he can grab it all, and there won't be anyone alive to say there was anything to grab."

"What about that Nazi—he's giving the orders, isn't he?"

"No! I mean... damn it, Jeff, I don't know! I'm not sure how much von Schoenwald even knows. I can't get close to him. I don't even dare try. Oh, he wanted Mike picked up all right. He had to be silenced."

Seeing Blanchard jerk taut at these words, Kinney spoke quickly. "I didn't want him hurt, Jeff, believe me. I didn't know what to do. Then Robbins moved in and took over. I don't know where he took Mike for sure, but I don't think he's dead. Robbins would have kept him alive in case he could use him in some way. If he'd wanted him dead, he'd have done it there and then, the way he killed that Mex who was in on the kidnapping. I didn't have any part of that—I wasn't even in Guanajuato when it happened."

"This doesn't make sense. Are you saying Robbins is acting on his own? Why would he? Mike didn't threaten him, and neither do I. It's this German who needs to have us silenced—and you."

"Oh, it makes sense," Kinney answered bitterly. "It makes a lot of sense if you think it out." All of a sudden strain was in his face, the strain of a man in his fifties who sees life running out, sees the lost chances and the end of his dreams. "He wants to grab it all. I think von Schoenwald's sick. He's in his sixties, and he's lived all too well these past years. Or else Robbins has just got tired of waiting. I should have seen it a long time ago. He wants everything— he wants what's mine! I gave up my life for my share of what we took out of Europe—my whole life! And all these years that Nazi bastard has kept it for himself, letting me have some crumbs to keep me on the leash. Half of everything was supposed to be mine, but he saw to it that I couldn't touch it. And if I'd ever tried, I'd have been dead a long time ago." A note of self-pity had crept into his tone. "You can be sorry that never happened, old buddy. Then you and your son wouldn't have been dragged into this."

Kinney was visibly shaken, struggling for control. Blanchard had never seen him rattled before. Without seeing and hearing him, he would have found it hard to imagine Kinney bitter and whining ...and afraid. His skepticism worked paradoxically to make Kinney's story more plausible, more convincing.

As Kinney had admitted, he had always been quick to exploit any chance for the quick buck, the easy mark. He was a con man by nature, and like many of his breed he was a ripe target for a cleverer one. Von Schoenwald had exploited his greed and tapped an unexpected gullibility. With the promise and proximity of a fortune, he had kept Kinney captive for half of his lifetime. Kinney could have walked away from the situation at any time, especially in the early years, before the German had acquired a lethal bodyguard to use as a threat. Von Schoenwald could not have followed him. Kinney could have disappeared, taken another name, slipped across the border into the United States and started a new life. But he would have had to write off the dream, to abandon any hope of getting his hands on the fortune in stolen paintings he saw as belonging to him as much as to the Nazi. And now, having thrown away his life, he saw everything slipping away from him, as another predator moved in.

"I still don't understand what Robbins is up to," Blanchard said after a silence. "Why not simply kill Mike and end it there? Why keep me chasing all over Mexico? Why let me get this close to him?"

"I don't have all the answers, but that should be fairly obvious. He wants you here. He means to use you."

"How, for God's sake?"

"To kill von Schoenwald."

Incredulous, Blanchard rose from his chair in spite of the Luger's warning, a black hostile eye that followed his every movement. "He can't make me—"

"He doesn't have to. He'll do the killing himself. But he's set you up for it. Think about it for a minute. He might have trouble with the police if he just knocked von Schoenwald off. He can't do it the way von Schoenwald knocked off old Brugmann, too many people know too much. And he might have trouble getting his hands on all the German's money. But now he's got you to blame. You've been establishing a trail of motive all over this country,

282

not only with the Mexican police but even with the U.S. Consulate. If you're found up there on the hill, with the German dead, no one will believe you didn't do it, even if you're still alive to tell your side of the story. And that isn't in the cards. I can't prove this, Jeff, but I think that's the setup. And I don't think Robbins means to leave me alive to talk either. That's why I've been hiding. That's why I had to get you to find me this way, without anyone knowing. If Robbins knew we were here together—if he even knew about this place over the shop—we'd both be finished."

Blanchard sat down heavily. He tried to sort it all out. There was an insane kind of logic in the pattern Kinney had described. It explained a number of things—the war of nerves in both Guadalajara and Guanajuato, the kidnapping of Angie in San Miguel, all of the steps that had finally brought him to Morelia. It didn't exonerate Kinney for his part in the affair, but it explained him. And it filled Blanchard with contempt for the man who faced him across the room.

"Think what you want about me," Kinney said with acute perception. "But if you want to stay alive, you'd better start thinking more about Robbins."

"You believe he has Mike and Angie up there on the hill? That he's using them to make me come there?"

"It figures."

"Then there's one way you can make me believe all you've been saying. Give me back that Colt, and let me go in there."

"And let you blow a hole in me first?"

"You'll have to take that chance. Unless you want to keep hiding forever."

"You'd be a damned fool to try it. You'd only get yourself killed. That's just what Robbins wants—he'll be waiting for you."

"He'll have to shoot first. And he may not be expecting me so soon."

Kinney stared at him. He wasn't the same man,

after all, Blanchard thought. The resemblances were there, but there was a singular difference it had taken him a while to discern. This Kinney was a beaten man, too frightened to go after what he believed to be his.

"I can do better than that," Kinney said slowly. "We'll have to work it out, and it's too late to try anything tonight. It'll have to be after dark, so that means tomorrow night. But if it's what you want, I can do more than give you your gun and point you up the hill. There's a way into Brugmann's place, a secret tunnel those *padres* built for themselves as an escape hatch a couple centuries ago. I can show you where it is."

Interlude Six: Morelia

1

Ernst von Schoenwald had not slept well. In fact, he had slept badly for some nights, particularly since the night of his sudden and temporary attack of dizziness. It was almost as if he were afraid to close his eyes and give himself up in trust to sleep. As if, deep in his consciousness, there lurked a fear that he would not awaken.

It was a disturbing time for him. He was not accustomed to feeling fear or uncertainty of any kind.

He stepped from his bedroom through a sliding glass door onto the veranda. His room faced east, so that it received the morning sun. He walked slowly to the corner, reaching the main terrace that ran along the north wall of the house, facing the city, paralleled by the long indoor *galería* linking living and bedroom wings. As he reached the corner there was a rush of movement, a warning growl.

"Wulf!" he called sharply.

The dog pulled up a few feet from him. The hairs had bristled over his neck and shoulders. They subsided slowly as the big dog relaxed. He came closer, sniffing von Schoenwald's hand, and received a reassuring scrub of his head and ears. "You are also awake at night, eh? But with you it is necessary."

He stared out beyond the monastery walls toward the valley. There was only a sprinkling of lights to define the mass of the sleeping city, but the entire valley lay in a soft sheen of moonlight. To the German it had always seemed a peaceful place, perhaps because he had remained so aloof from it. Now he sensed a change in his attitude. The city's glowing beauty concealed the ugliness of danger. Enemies hid in its shadows, plotting against him. There was no longer any question of it. Enemies old and new....

He turned quickly at the sound of another door opening. Wulf pricked up his ears alertly, but they dropped as he relaxed again, even before von Schoenwald was able to see who had stepped from the *galería* onto the terrace.

"George?"

"I heard you up. Anything wrong?"

"That is the question, isn't it? I have been waiting for you to give me the answer."

Robbins accepted the rebuke in silence. As he drew nearer, von Schoenwald was able to see the scowl wrinkling his simian features. "We'll find them," Robbins said shortly.

"I am tired of listening to promises, my dear George."

"If you'd let me take care of Blanchard in the beginning..."

"Perhaps. On the other hand, eliminating him might have created other problems. And if, as you insist and I am beginning to believe, our friend Kinney is up to something, are you so certain taking care of Blanchard would have ended it? Besides, we know where Blanchard is. He is at his hotel, making love to a schoolteacher, is that not so? It is Kinney who is hiding from us. And Sánchez."

Robbins' frown deepened. "I don't get that part of it. I don't see where Sánchez fits into this at all."

"Unquestionably we are not meant to see. Find him, George, and we will have our answer. Find both of them." There seemed to be another implied rebuke in the fact that Robbins was not even at this moment down in the city, searching its darkness for the truth.

"Riki is looking for Sánchez now. We're not sitting on our hands. And I'll find Kinney, don't worry about that." The last was spoken with savage venom.

"But I do worry, my dear George," von Schoenwald said. "I do not sleep for worrying. And I don't like that." The complaint was clearer this time, sharper, and again Robbins took it silently. "I don't wish to believe that I can no longer rely on you."

An angry flush crept over Robbins' neck like a dark stain. "You know better than that."

"When will you prove to me that I am wrong? Tomorrow, George? Will I sleep tomorrow night at ease?" The German's face was a mask of winter in his native Alps, the face of a man who knew no pity, accepted no excuses. His eyes, catching the moonlight, glittered like blue ice. "I want them, George! I want them found. I don't care which one you find first, he will tell me what I need to know. I have had experience in teaching men how to talk against their wills, eagerly—I haven't forgotten. Just bring one of them to me."

"What about the girl? Are you so sure she can't tell you anything?"

"She knows nothing! I will take care of her myself, George. She will have very special care. Forget her. Just do what I ask of you." He paused. "And if you are unable to bring me Kinney and Sánchez, then it will have to be this man Blanchard. The girl is ignorant, but I am no longer so sure of him."

"Good," said Robbins with evident relief. "I'm wondering if Blanchard isn't the key to this whole thing. Has it occurred to you that Kinney may already have got to Blanchard? How else did Blanchard get over here to Morelia so quick? There's no way he could have known unless Kinney told him."

"Why would he do that?"

"Kinney means to betray you. He'll do it through Blanchard. Hell, I don't need to tell you—he'd do anything to get his hands on those paintings."

Von Schoenwald studied him speculatively. "An interesting suggestion, George. But he couldn't expose me without exposing himself."

"He might if Blanchard were grateful—and you were dead."

The German's nostrils flared. He didn't like talk of his dying, especially not now. "That would be a strange gratitude toward the man who killed his son."

"Kinney's blamed you for that. You can bet on it."

Von Schoenwald considered this. His mouth was a slash, his nostrils still flared against the thought of death. "Bring me Blanchard then," he said. "Bring me any of them who can tell me where Kinney is. He is the one who matters, George. And he must be found quickly! I am not being capricious in this, or unduly impatient. Whatever Kinney has planned, it must happen soon. There is something else you should know...."

Robbins waited uneasily, not sure where the next blow would fall.

"My investments, as you know, are channeled through Kinney. It has had to be that way. But now I have not had the monthly accounting. It has escaped our attention while we were preoccupied with this other matter. Perhaps we were not supposed to notice. Do you believe that is possible?"

Robbins swore. "That son of a bitch—"

"Find him for me! Find him, and when I am done with him, when he has told me what I have to know, then he will be yours, my dear George. I promise you that. Kinney will be yours."

Von Schoenwald heard the sharp hiss of Robbins' breath, and he knew that he had said enough.

2

From the *galería* a long bank of windows looked out upon the terrace. The two men were plainly visible, talking. The girl had almost been caught by Robbins when he had unexpectedly appeared from his room. Her heart still raced in fright. She was, if anything, more afraid of Robbins than of the German.

But it was the German who had shamed her. Out of despair and humiliation in the kitchen, María Teresa Calderón had learned a new emotion: hatred.

When the men gave no indication of moving from the terrace back into the house, she glanced down at the long kitchen knife in her hand, and her fingers tightened on the rosewood handle.

She crept along the *galería* to the door of the bedroom which had been her room, where the fair-haired *gringa* now slept. She opened the door cautiously. Some light from the window fell across the bed. For a long moment María stood in the doorway, staring at the sleeping woman, a fire of anger in her eyes.

But it was not the *gringa* who had laughed at her.

She turned back along the corridor. When she glanced out at the terrace, her heart gave a great leap. The men were not there! She ran forward quickly, her bare feet soundless on the tile floor. Suddenly she heard their heavier footsteps, their muted voices. She was near the door to the German's study, and she jumped into the shadowed niche as the two men stepped through the doorway from the terrace to the *galería*.

For a few moments longer they stood talking, not twenty feet from her. Then the German turned away, retreating along the wide corridor toward his bedroom. Robbins stood watching him. María seemed unable to breathe. Taut with panic, she waited to be discovered. To reach his room, Robbins had to pass her.

But the red-haired man did not even look her way. Instead, when the German had disappeared, Robbins took a few paces after him, then abruptly turned to the door through which they had come a moment earlier. María watched him move along the terrace outside until she could no longer see him.

For the first time in what seemed like minutes she was able to take a shuddering breath. She knew that she must leave before Robbins returned. But she felt the study door against which she pressed, and the purpose which had brought her to the *galería* in the first place returned strongly. Gripping the long knife tightly, she seized the brass knob of the door and—

Robbins' footsteps sounded close by, returning. Panic drove everything else from her mind. She fled along the corridor, not daring to pause even to look back. Only when she was safely in the kitchen, near the tiny rooms where the servants slept, did she allow herself to hope that she had not been seen. Her heartbeat raced wildly on, long after she had reached her own little room and closed the door.

By then, as her fear ebbed away, a trace of bravado had begun to return.

This time the door to the German's study had been locked. But there would be other nights.

7   Morelia

1

Charmian Stewart breakfasted alone in the narrow, high-ceilinged dining room at La Soledad. Other diners glanced at her curiously. The room was half full of tourists, a French family at one nearby table, the rest Americans. She knew that her sleepless night had left her haggard, with dark circles under her eyes, but was her worry so obvious? She felt like a local tourist attraction. Don't miss the witch schoolteacher in Morelia. Try to catch her in the morning.

The food at the hotel was unexpectedly good, but she could only toy with it. She managed to drink a glass of fresh *naranja*, followed by cups of coffee. Her nervous stomach rebelled at the idea of solid food.

Dawn had found her up and dressed, walking through the deserted streets to the garage. There, to her consternation, she had found the Vega parked.

The attendant, an old man with arthritic hands and a badly stained mustache, had been on duty since midnight. Yes, he remembered the Vega. He also remembered the man who had brought it to the garage some time after he reported for work. The señor had also been driving on another occasion when he had come to the garage in the company of the señora. Was anything wrong?

Charmian didn't know what to make of it. Jeff had returned the car more than an hour after he had dropped her off. Where had he been in the meantime?

And why hadn't he then returned to their room?

In spite of Blanchard's unsatisfactory experiences with the Mexican authorities in Guanajuato and San Miguel, Charmian had been prepared to go to the police that morning. Now she was no longer certain what to do. If Jeff had brought the car back himself, that surely indicated that he was not in trouble. He no longer needed the car, or he didn't want to leave her stranded. But where was he? What had he learned?

Brooding over her coffee, Charmian reluctantly concluded that Jeff wouldn't want her to go to the police. Right or wrong, he was doing what he had to do to find his son and Angie—doing it his own way. Did she have the right to overrule him on her own, without knowing all that he knew? And what could she tell the police? She could see them smiling and nodding, then pointing out what she already knew, that Señor Blanchard had been in no danger when he returned her car. Perhaps he had met another friend in Morelia?

A tall American wearing boots and an overstitched Western suit with leather piping rose from a nearby table and approached. His plump wife and two teen-aged children watched curiously. "'Scuse me, ma'am. Ah couldn't help noticin'. You look like you grabbed onto more trouble than you kin handle. Is there anythin' Ah can do to help?" The stranger's accent was Texan, and that in itself surprised her. Charmian's experience of Texas hospitality ran more to having mechanics rip her off for unneeded repairs to her car than to offers of help. She felt exaggeratedly grateful, and the response nearly brought tears. She shook her head, mumbling almost inaudible thanks, not trusting her voice. Hastily she left money for the check and an overgenerous tip on the table and fled the dining room, leaving the Texans and the other tourists to stare after her.

A half hour later Charmian drove up the hill to the Rynders house. She found Kate at home, preparing for her daily shopping run to the *mercado*. Bud Rynders was in his studio, but he emerged when he heard her talking to Kate.

Charmian saw at once that the artist's expression was grim. Before she could speak, he said, "Where the hell's Jeff?"

"I...I don't know. That's why I'm here. He didn't come back to the hotel last night. He's disappeared! I don't know where he is or what he's trying to do."

"Well, I can make a guess," Rynders said, but the harshness was gone from his tone. "He's getting himself knee-deep in trouble. There was a Colt .45 in the top drawer of that rolltop last night. It's not there now. I saw him putting something in your car earlier on, but I didn't think what it could be. Now I'm damned sure. He took that gun."

"Where..." Charmian faltered. She was appalled by the idea of Blanchard going off alone into the night, armed with a gun, driven by desperation. "Where do you think he'd go?"

"I'm only guessing, but he was sold on the notion that his son and the boy's wife might be up there in old Brugmann's place. I've an idea he means to try to bust in there like a goddamn cowboy with a six-gun! My six-gun," he grumbled.

"I know what's bothering you," Kate Rynders said dryly. "If anyone's going to go around acting like John Wayne, you think it ought to be you."

Rynders scowled at her, but after a moment a mischievous curl touched the corners of his mouth. "Kate, why don't you put those garbage sacks down and fix us some fresh coffee? We've got some talking to do."

"I know," Kate answered as she turned toward the kitchen. "Another council of war."

2

For nearly three hours that afternoon Charmian played the role of a tourist. It was a familiar part, and it should have been easy for her, but this time there was no pleasure in visiting the gift shops in the Santa María hills, dawdling over local curios and artifacts, clay pots and ashtrays, painted trays, leather goods and embroidered blouses. She stayed with it doggedly, emerging often from one shop or another to stare briefly at the shop that was the real purpose for her vigil: La Cosecha.

Bud Rynders had insisted that watching the shop was important, not just a way to keep her busy while he went down into the city to search for Rafael Sánchez. There had been no excitement in the Santa María area the night before, so there was good reason to believe that Jeff Blanchard hadn't charged up the hill with six-gun blazing, trying to break into Brugmann's place. He might show up during the day looking for Darrell Kinney. If not, Kinney himself might appear, and that would be almost as good.

The afternoon dragged on through the siesta hour. By late afternoon, storm clouds were gathering over the mountains. Flashes of lightning, grumblings of thunder, and a westerly wind picked up; the storm was moving toward Morelia.

Charmian's forebodings about the coming night deepened with the approach of the storm. If Jeff Blanchard had failed to act last night, having stolen the gun, would he let another night go by? Rain would offer protective cover, encouraging any reckless plan. But he wasn't a cool-eyed cowboy with his gun, she thought miserably. He was an ordinary man caught up in something he didn't understand, a distraught father pushed close to despair, goaded to violence by something—and someone—incredibly vicious.

At five o'clock, her long vigil having proven unrewarding, Charmian reluctantly returned to her car, which she had parked along the road within sight of the Vista del Parque. Rynders had promised to return by five for another meeting, whether or not he had news. It had been agreed that, if neither of them had any luck, Rynders himself would go to the police. They knew him, he said, and were more likely to listen to him than to a *gringa* unknown to them.

And if that didn't get them anywhere, the artist had promised grimly, he would load up his shotgun and stake out Baldur Brugmann's place himself....

Charmian sat in the Vega, staring toward La Cosecha, remembering her morning trip up to the high-walled estate on its knoll higher in these hills. Rynders had agreed to take her there under protest, and the visit had proved as fruitless as he said it would be. The taciturn Mexican behind the locked gates of Baldur Brugmann's wall knew nothing of a visiting American. Señor Brugmann was receiving no visitors. In fact, no stranger had entered these gates in many years. Brugmann would see no one now. He wished only to be left alone.

Charmian had strained to peer through the gates toward the mystery of the converted monastery. She reached out with all her senses, as if some special perception might tell her if Jeff were there... or Mike and Angie. She had found only blank white walls, a peaceful silence, an old gardener digging in his flower beds, an alert German shepherd watching the activity at the gates. Nothing helpful, nothing suspicious.

She wondered if Rynders was merely humoring her. He had remained skeptical about Brugmann's involvement in any plot, in spite of his promise to camp at the foot of the knoll with his shotgun. That was a friendly gesture, and a generous one. He had said it only to reassure her.

She was reaching for the key in the ignition when she saw the wiry, redheaded man emerge from the doorway of La Cosecha. She hadn't seen him enter—

she must have been in one of the other shops when he appeared. He glanced up and down the road, and Charmian sat rigid when his gaze briefly touched the Vega. Then he turned and strode rapidly up the road to a parked car.

Her heart hammered. This was concrete proof of Jeff's theory—proof that Rynders couldn't deny.

Even before the red-haired man's car pulled away, she was certain of its destination. She waited a moment before starting the Vega and following. She kept at a safe distance, but there was little traffic in the hills and she had no trouble keeping the other car in sight.

At an intersection about a quarter mile below the village of Santa María, she pulled over to the side of the road. A valve ticked steadily in the car's engine, matching the rapid beat of her heart. The redheaded man had turned onto a poorly surfaced side road. It was one she had taken that morning with Rynders. She watched the car until it slowed in front of Baldur Brugmann's place at the top of the knoll and disappeared around the far corner.

The road ended there, she knew. It ended at Brugmann's garage.

She drove slowly back down the hill. Brugmann *was* involved. She had met that wiry little man with the funny orange hairpiece before, at the Motel Campo Bello in Guadalajara.

The same day she met Jeff Blanchard for the first time.

3

"George Robbins," Rynders said. "I'll be damned."

"I must have heard you or Jeff mention his name, but I didn't remember it," Charmian said. "I had no reason to connect it with that funny schoolteacher from Columbus, Ohio. He even had a wife with him.

Her name was... Betty, I think. They seemed so *right*, somehow."

"Wouldn't have been hard to find somebody to play the part with him," Rynders said. He turned to Cal Sedling. "What do you make of it, Cal?"

"I think I'd like to hear the whole story from the beginning," Sedling answered. "If Miss Stewart doesn't mind."

She studied the two men curiously. Sedling's presence at the house when she arrived had surprised her. So far neither man had offered an explanation, and Charmian felt an attack of stubbornness. "Maybe you'll tell me first why you're interested."

"It's more than neighborly curiosity, I can assure you." Sedling had shed his air of indolence, which had served neatly to conceal an alert intelligence and sharply inquisitive brown eyes. Sedling paused as thunder rolled noisily overhead, spilling the pins in a giant bowling alley, and a gust of wind whipped pellets of rain against the windows. "It's a good night for plots and mysteries."

"I don't see anything to laugh about," she said with heat.

"I'm sorry... I didn't mean it to sound that way. Miss Stewart, I work for... an agency of the United States government. Bud here has seen my credentials, if that's good enough for you."

She sought Rynders for confirmation, making no effort to hide her astonishment. Rynders nodded, and she glanced back at Sedling with new interest. At any other time she might have found his quiet statement improbable, suspecting some kind of a joke, but too much had happened in recent days for unexpected disclosures to seem incredible any more. She thought of stories she had heard about clandestine agents of the CIA operating throughout the world on secret and sometimes dubious missions, and she remembered that E. Howard Hunt, Jr., whose name had come up recently in what was beginning to be called the "Watergate affair" in Washington, had once been a station chief of the Central Intelligence Agency in Mexico City. Nothing was improbable anymore. Even Sedling's caution over needlessly displaying his "credentials" seemed somehow quite normal.

Sedling said, "I happened to learn that Bud has been searching for Rafael Sánchez this afternoon. I asked him about it, and one thing led to another. I think it would help, Miss Stewart, if you told me everything you know."

"I still don't understand why you're here—what you're after." She felt a quick anxiety. "Was...was Mike Blanchard involved in anything wrong?"

"Not that we know of. But I'm afraid I can't tell you much more than that. Except this much. We're interested in this man Alan Slater, the one you know as Kinney. I'm even more interested now that Bud has told me his real identity—that's information we didn't have. We're also interested in Slater's relationship with Baldur Brugmann. Along with the Mexican government, we've been curious about some very large sums of money in the Banco Nacional. I can't go beyond that right now, except to tell you this. I don't want to frighten you, but you must realize that the Blanchards have become involved with some people who care very little about human life. I can understand how Blanchard feels, but this is something he can't cope with alone. He'd going to need help, and the sooner we find him the better. I think you'd better tell me whatever you know."

Charmian's concern for Jeff Blanchard heightened as Cal Sedling spoke. "You mentioned the Mexican government. Do they know you're here? Does that mean you can get official help?"

"If necessary. I've already spoken to Mexico City, after Bud filled me in, and they've put me onto the Federal Police here." Sedling regarded her calmly, waiting. It wasn't an emotional thing with him, she thought; it was a job.

She tried to find reassurance in his presence and in his cool, professional manner. For the first time Jeff would have the help he needed to discover what had happened to Mike and Angie. But where was Jeff? Was it already too late?

Thinking of the man who had intruded upon her dinner that night at Lake Patzcuaro, she shivered. Those pale eyes behind their violet-tinted lenses had been examining her with a colder calculation than she could possibly have imagined.

"Start at the beginning," Sedling encouraged her. "When you first met Blanchard and this man Robbins."

Charmian took a deep breath, consciously trying to control her anxiety, and began to talk.

Charmian had finished her story, and Cal Sedling had abruptly left the house for the nearest motel and a phone, when Mary Rynders came in out of the rain. The girl was in tears. With some difficulty Kate pried the reason out of her. She had had a date with Luis Martínez, and he hadn't shown up. Kate soothingly suggested that it was a terrible night for anyone to be out, and any number of things could have kept Luis away.

Charmian stopped listening. A young girl's lovesick turmoil, exaggerating a broken date into heartbreak, hardly seemed important on this night, of all nights....

4

Throughout the day Jeff Blanchard had remained in hiding. Most of the time he had spent in a small back room of the house in Santa María to which Kinney had brought him the night before. The living quarters of the house were behind a shop that sold *petróleo* out of big metal drums. The house was filled with the smells of oil and kerosene. Blanchard wondered at the casual indifference with which those

299

in the house constantly smoked. During the day there were a dozen people around the house, half of them young children who eyed him curiously whenever he appeared or they sidled past his room. No one seemed to speak English, and he didn't try to talk to anyone. "Stay inside," Kinney had warned. "You don't know who might be looking for you. It doesn't have to be Robbins himself."

Kinney was gone most of the day. In the late afternoon it began to rain heavily. Of the ten days Blanchard had been in Mexico—if in fact it was Thursday and he hadn't lost count of the days, which was easy enough when you were away from the settled routine of working days and weekends off—it had rained all but two or three days. He had thought he'd seen enough rain to last him for the rest of the year, but this time he was glad of it. The night would be pitch black. There would be little chance of being spotted once he came out into the open.

Darkness was gathering when Kinney finally returned. Blanchard had been growing edgy, for he was still not sure how far he could really trust Kinney. Not far, certainly. He could only trust the fact that Kinney's fear served his interest. That fear—and Kinney's bitterness toward the German—seemed genuine.

When Blanchard heard Kinney's voice from the *petróleo* shop, recognizable even though he spoke in rapid Spanish, he went to the door of his room and peered along the littered corridor. In his hand was Bud Rynders' Colt.

But Kinney had returned alone. Blanchard relaxed slightly. It might prove nothing...but if Kinney had meant to betray him, he could easily have returned with Robbins and all the other help he needed.

"Hey, don't shoot, it's only me." Kinney threw up both hands in mock horror. He was carrying a brown paper sack in one hand. In the other was a small collection of car tools wrapped in oil-soaked canvas.

300

One of the tools was a lug wrench that could double as a small crowbar.

Blanchard wasn't amused. Take it easy, he warned himself. He asked, "No trouble?"

"No trouble. Robbins is nosing around, though—it's a good thing we didn't try to hole up in that room over the shop. I paid a high price to keep that place a secret, but I wouldn't put it past Robbins to outbid me."

"When do we start?" Blanchard demanded impatiently.

"Hold on, buddy, it's early yet. Did you eat anything?"

"The lady of the house came up with something." That had been around midday, and the something had been a corn tortilla wrapped around what turned out to be fried pork, chopped up and seasoned. Blanchard had eaten it, with misgivings, because he was famished. The *burrito* had been delicious, and he had gratefully accepted another one. He had not, however, taken a chance on drinking either the milk or water offered. Now he said, "I could use something to drink."

Kinney produced a bottle of rum from the paper sack. "I thought of that too."

"That isn't what I meant, but it'll do."

"Let me see if I can rustle up a bottle of *purificada*. Don't trust the stuff you get around here in the big bottles. Sometimes they fill those from the tap. But you can always drink the small capped bottles. Better water than you get in the States."

The comment prompted Blanchard to ask something he had wondered about. "Have you ever gone back?"

"To the States?" Kinney seemed to hesitate. "No, why should I? I've got everything I want right here."

Like a couple of million dollars worth of stolen paintings you can't get your hands on, Blanchard thought.

Kinney found some bottled water and a couple of

glasses. They sat in the small room on the cot, which was the only piece of furniture, not bothering to turn on the bare bulb that offered the only light. Every few minutes lightning flickered, briefly etching their faces in the gloom. The effect was like a neon sign blinking on and off. They spoke little, and Blanchard thought about the way it had been in the days of the war. Then there had been endless talk, born of the closeness of men thrown together in any army far from home.

He did not condemn Kinney for dropping out of the war as he had. It did not even seem surprising. What he could not forget, or forgive, was the knowledge that Kinney's panic over being recognized had led directly to Mike's kidnapping. Whatever had happened after that had still begun with Kinney.

"What's it like outside?"

"Like skating in a barnyard. Watch yourself or you'll be on your ass before you know it."

They had another drink—Blanchard could feel the rum soaking up some of his tension—and he accepted one of the thin black Mexican cigars Kinney smoked. He forced himself to accept the necessity of waiting. He remembered how capricious Kinney could be whenever he felt that he was being pushed. Kinney had good reason not to go near Baldur Brugmann's knoll, and until he had led the way to the tunnel he'd described, Blanchard needed him.

He wondered why Kinney was doing it. The question had recurred throughout the day. For old time's sake? Not likely. Nor as a way to atone for any feelings of guilt. Maybe he simply hoped that somehow or other Robbins would be the one who ended up dead.

It was a sobering thought for a man who had never killed anyone, not even as a soldier. But Blanchard knew that he would use the gun he carried if he had to. He thought of the macabre proof of Mike's capture delivered in Guanajuato, the ring on the headless lizard. The man who had conceived that tactic would not lose anything without a fight. Blanchard had watched Kinney closely when he told that story. Kinney had registered an uneasy surprise that seemed unfeigned. Robbins hadn't told him about the ring. "That's part of his game to keep you jumping the squares the way he wants it," Kinney said. "It sounds like him. I think the bastard's crazy."

The waiting ended. Kinney dropped the butt of his cigar on the floor and carelessly ground it under his heel. "It's as good a time as any." With mocking flippancy he added, "Over the top, eh, Sarge?"

The rain continued heavy. Blanchard was soaked to the skin before he had taken a dozen steps. He had stuffed the Colt under his shirt to keep it dry, and he moved hunched over to protect his middle from the driving rain. Kinney had said they had to travel on foot—he wouldn't risk trying to get close to Brugmann's place in his car. They quickly left the village behind, dark and huddled against the battering of the storm, and moved down a long slope. Both men stumbled and slipped often on muddy ground. Once they were in the open Kinney led the way, and they did not attempt to speak. Kinney wore a black plastic raincoat, which not only kept him dry and warm but also made him practically invisible in the downpour from a few yards away. After a while, however, Blanchard found that he could see quite clearly in the darkness for the short distances necessary to pick his path and to keep Kinney in sight. After a while, too, the rain no longer mattered. There was a point beyond which you couldn't get any wetter. He was bothered far more by the night's cold chill, and by the dramatic flashes of lightning that illuminated the hills and the scattered dwellings, like a scene in a Gothic melodrama.

Blanchard was plodding along in a weary, sodden, sense-deadened stupor when Kinney stopped. Blanchard blundered into him. "Easy!" Kinney hissed. "It's around here somewhere."

Blanchard felt a quick surge of excitement.

Staring upward past the hump of a rise, he saw the fortresslike wall that surrounded Brugmann's grounds. "I was going to climb that wall," he muttered aloud.

"There's a dog inside. He'd have ripped you up before you reached the ground."

"What about the tunnel? Where does it lead to?"

"That's the good thing about it. It comes up right inside the house—takes you into a wine cellar. You don't have to worry about that damned dog."

They spoke in low, hoarse whispers, their faces close together. Kinney wiped his glasses with his fingers, and Blanchard wondered how he had been able to see at all in the rain. Kinney said, "Stick close now."

They crept around the foot of the rise. Moments later they came to a nest of big rocks that formed a natural toe to the slope. The rocks were overgrown by wild brush. Blanchard saw no evidence of a tunnel entrance until they were kneeling next to a thicket of brush and Kinney pressed wet branches aside. Two of the largest rocks leaned against each other to form a wedge-shaped opening. Kinney reached through it to scrape away some mud and debris. He had a small flashlight, and it blinked for an instant. Blanchard saw a weathered wooden door set deep into the rocks. It was secured by a rusty padlock.

He looked questioningly at Kinney, who grinned. "Don't worry, buddy, that's what the tools are for. Maybe we can't bust the lock, but that wood is old."

He wriggled into the cramped space between the rocks. Using the claw end of the lug wrench he had brought, he began to pry at the door hinges. The wood was old and soft and weakened by damp rot. The screws of the top hinge ripped out on the first try. The lower hinge gave way more slowly, but after a moment of grunting effort Kinney managed to wedge the claw of the bar between the hinge and the door. On the next heave the metal burst free.

Kinney pulled back from the opening. "Hell, I

missed my calling," he said, panting.

Movement of the earth around the door had jammed it shut, and the two men had to paw some of the dirt away with their hands before it was possible to drag the door open far enough for Blanchard to squeeze through. Kinney sat back on his haunches. For a moment their eyes met. Then Blanchard moved past him. He wormed through the slot between the rocks and squeezed past the door into a damp, musty darkness. Looking back, he saw Kinney silhouetted against the opening. The stormy sky was surprisingly brighter than the black interior of the tunnel.

"You'll need the flashlight," Kinney said, thrusting it toward him. "But don't use it until you get far enough in."

"Close the door behind me," Blanchard said. There was a moment of silence before he added, "Thanks."

"This is as far as I go, old buddy. I guess you know that."

Blanchard hadn't expected anything else. What was surprising, he supposed, was that Kinney had come this far, taken any risk at all.

"I'm sorry about your kid, and I hope it turns out all right for you. But I won't go in there." Kinney seemed to feel compelled to explain. "Buddies is one thing, I'm not forgetting that, but you're a damned fool, Jeff. I'm not."

Blanchard accepted this without comment. This, too, seemed to be in character for Darrell Kinney. Not only the man facing him at the tunnel opening, but the reckless Kinney of the forties. Blanchard wondered suddenly why he and everyone else who had known him had admired Kinney so much in the days of the war. Why do we always admire the clever con man, the bunco artist, the seller of snake medicine, the slick operator who can get away with something shady? It's as if we were all still children gloating whenever any of us successfully put something over on our parents or teachers, or any authority.

Without another word Blanchard turned away

and entered the blackness of the tunnel. Behind him the wooden door creaked shut, blotting out all light and the almost comforting noise of the storm.

5

Angie Blanchard had kept her eyes fixed on her plate, which she had not touched, refusing stubbornly to look up at the German at the far end of the elegantly set table. It was unreal, she thought. The whole scene was unreal, from the expensive silver and china on the table to the *pollo en mole* and the heaping bowls of fruit. And the company. Michael would—

Grief struck again. It was a wound she could not leave alone. Every time she tried to think of something else, somehow she always touched the open sore. Michael was dead. It was impossible to accept the total nothingness of Michael dead, but she did not doubt the German's pronouncement. Why would he lie? Michael was gone, and there was no one to share anything with, wonder or incredulity or anger or laughter.

Unreal. The German's name, she had learned, was Ernst von Schoenwald. And he was—or had been—a Nazi. A colonel in the SS. How he had come to this remote place was beyond her imagination. The fact that the monstrosity that was Nazi Germany, known to her only in those dreadful film clips of naked bodies being shoveled into pits in German concentration camps, or in melodramatic movies in which the German officers were always portrayed as ridiculous caricatures, could reach out after so many years to claim Michael's life was so appallingly incredible that she could not yet fully credit it.

But von Schoenwald was not a caricature. He was an imposing man in spite of his age, physically handsome and amazingly vital. He was also frightening.

Tonight, she knew, something was very wrong. The German acted strangely. His face had an unhealthy flush. He was icily angry, and when she had refused to come to the table for the evening meal he had had her dragged from her room by the man called Riki. He could not, she thought, force her to eat or to drink his champagne, in spite of the hunger cramps that periodically seized her.

Von Schoenwald was not angry only with her. His mood was savage. He taunted the other man at the table over some failure—she had not always listened to his tirade—and he ridiculed the slender little servant girl, María, when she brought the various courses of the meal. Angie wondered why he took his rage out on a defenseless child. But she had also been startled once when her eyes met the girl's and she saw something unexpected burning there. An emotion directed not at the German but at *her,* as if the girl looked upon her with hatred and resentment.

The night seemed a fitting one for the German's mood, like the background furor in an opera. There had been thunderclaps loud enough to shake the house, lightning that startled the terraced grounds into brilliance, heavy rain beating against the windows of the dining room, as if the heavens themselves had been orchestrated to express von Schoenwald's anger.

Suddenly the lights dimmed, flickered, and went out. Angie heard the man named Robbins swear. Von Schoenwald spoke harshly in the darkness. "Stay where you are." She guessed that he spoke to her, although she had not moved. "The lights will be on in a moment."

As if on signal the lights bloomed slowly. They seemed slightly dimmer than before, but steady. Glancing out the window, Angie saw that the hillside had been plunged into total darkness, although a distant spray of lights from the city was visible through the rain.

"We have an auxiliary generator, you see, Mrs.

Blanchard. This happens quite often, and we are prepared. There is no need to have our meal disturbed." There was heavy irony in the comment as he stared at her untouched plate. "María? Damn it, where is that girl?"

"You sent her for more bread," Robbins pointed out unwisely.

"Did I? And do I need you to tell me what I said a few moments ago, my dear George? Perhaps you find that easier than doing what I send you to do. I might as well have sent María to find Kinney, and you for the bread!"

Robbins flushed, but he did not defend himself. He was afraid of the German, Angie saw, but there was more in his attitude than fear. There was the morose sullenness of a...a rejected lover.

"You are still not hungry, Mrs. Blanchard? Ah, that is better, you have lovely eyes. They should not always be downcast. Doesn't she have beautiful eyes, George?"

He was compelled to reply. "Yes. Very beautiful."

"But look at her closely. See that expression? She despises me, George. Because I am a Nazi, eh? The killer of her beloved Jews. She knows all about Nazi Germany, all the familiar lies."

"They aren't lies," Angie said scornfully, goaded out of her self-imposed silence.

"Ah, she can speak after all. Did you hear, George? Young America speaks. She is going to tell us all about Germany and that terrible man, Adolf Hitler." His tone turned strident, rising in anger. "You Americans...you march and wave signs and shake your fists at your corrupt leaders. That is your idea of protest. And what do you have to complain of? That you are too fat, too soft, too well-fed? That you do not have enough cars and swimming pools? What do you know of hardship and suffering? When I was your age, I starved! All Germany starved! We had nothing! We had been sucked dry by the politicians and the Jews. Yes, you stupid child! Ten million of them—ten million parasites, sucking the blood of our people. They called themselves Germans, but they were not. You have seen it yourself. Where are the ones who called themselves Americans, or English, or French? They are in Israel! Or they are in their banks in America and England and France, counting out the money they have bled from others to send to their beloved Israel. They fed on us, fed on our bodies and our minds. You despise us for what we did to them, but what do you do to parasites? You exterminate them!"

"You're crazy," Angie cried with undisguised loathing.

"Crazy? Ah, how easy it is to answer what you cannot understand! I am mad, as Adolf Hitler was mad. That explains everything." The German suddenly rose, leaning forward over the table. One hand pounded the table so violently that Angie could feel it vibrate. Veins stood out on his red forehead and in his temples. His face was an ugly mask of fury before which Angie cringed inwardly. She saw the little Mexican girl in the doorway, rooted in terror, her dark eyes wide. The German shouted, "What do you know of Hitler? How could you know what he meant to us? You call him evil, sick, insane. But his evil was only that he threw off the yoke your people had placed upon all Germans to keep them crushed! The sickness in him was Germany's sickness, which he took onto himself like a living Christ, which he would have burned out of the sick flesh even if it consumed him. His madness was the madness of all great men—of a Caesar, an Alexander, a Bonaparte!"

"Ernst, please! You are—"

Von Schoenwald silenced Robbins with a glare. "You dare to interrupt me? Why should I listen to you, George? You have news for me? I sent you to find Kinney. Where is he? Where is Sánchez? Now you tell me even Blanchard is missing—you cannot even find him, the man you believe is coming to assassinate me!"

309

There was something wild and terrible in the German's anger, racing out of control, as if some dark fury, long buried deep, was erupting toward the surface, like a black slime gushing from the tapped bowels of the earth. Before it, George Robbins turned white, and Angie felt sick.

María Teresa Calderón, at the entrance to the kitchen, dropped the tray of *bolillos* she had been bringing to the table, turned and fled from the room. "María!" von Schoenwald roared after her. "Come back here! *Regresa! Regresa por aquí!*"

The German kicked back his chair and started around the table. He had taken no more than a couple of steps when a sharp, rasping buzz slashed through the angry tension. Von Schoenwald stopped abruptly. The anger left him as swiftly as it had come.

In a swift motion Robbins leaped from his chair. The two men exchanged quick glances. Robbins ran toward the main hall.

He was gone only a few seconds. When he reappeared, there was an eager excitement in his eyes. "It's the tunnel!" he cried. "There's someone in the tunnel!"

6

The walls of the tunnel had been constructed of mortarless stone, and they were wet to the touch, seeping with moisture from the saturated earth. Near the mouth of the tunnel the floor was a muddy quagmire, but the passageway angled steeply upward as it penetrated the hillside and, as Blanchard climbed, the dirt floor became dry.

The tunnel was rank-smelling. Blanchard had been climbing for several minutes when he heard a quick rustling just ahead, like a stirring of leaves in the wind. He flicked on the flashlight. A huge rat scurried away from him. Farther along the tunnel, several pairs of small red eyes reflected the beam of light, and Blanchard felt his skin crawl. The rats in the tunnel were as large as small cats.

He guessed that they were probably more frightened of him than he was of them, but it cost him an effort of will to move toward them. One rat slipped past him, racing down the tunnel. The others disappeared into the darkness ahead.

The strange isolation of the tunnel threw him back on his thoughts. He was acutely conscious of the heavy revolver in his hand. Would his willingness to use it serve any purpose? Was Mike already dead? Blanchard knew there was little of the killer in him. The two periods in his life when he had been forced to carry a gun had been brought about, as it now seemed, by the same Nazi mentality he despised, the same contempt for human life. The first time he had been a young man. In the current disillusionment over Vietnam, some argued that, like the rest of his generation, he had been sold a similar bill of goods in the forties. Blanchard didn't buy that. Hitler's Germany had not been a Pentagon public-relations story. This time he was middle-aged, overanxious, plodding on legs gone rubbery from the strain of struggling over the rain-soaked hills between Santa María and the tunnel at the base of Brugmann's knoll. It would have been easy to find absurdity in his situation, crawling along a rat-infested hole in a Mexican hillside with a gun in his hand, but there was nothing absurd about defending your own against violence. The choice had not been his. Those who preached and practiced violence, whatever their rationale, made savages of anyone who opposed them. And all too often, Blanchard thought, they then cried out in outrage.

The tunnel seemed airless after a while, and he found himself gasping for breath. Pausing, he turned the flashlight on again.

Its beam fell on a door ten yards ahead.

His excitement was tempered by immediate

dismay. The door was heavy, solid. It would not break down easily, like the door at the end of the tunnel, which had been weakened by long exposure to the elements.

Blanchard ran forward. He played the flashlight's beam over the door. It stopped at a heavy wrought-iron latch. His lips drew back in a mirthless grin, a spasm of relief. The door had no lock. The latch was one of those that could be opened from either side. Ernst von Schoenwald had relied too much on the secrecy of his tunnel.

He pressed down on the latch very slowly, gently. The heavy door, carried on long, rusty iron hinges, creaked faintly as he pulled it toward him, the sound no louder than the squeak of a rat.

For a few seconds Blanchard stood listening at the door. The room beyond was dark, silent. He could feel tension knotting his jaw muscles. He had been gritting his teeth without realizing it. When he drew a long breath his lungs ached.

He jerked the door open and stepped into the room.

It was a small, cramped cellar, lined along both sides with rows of wooden racks displaying bottles lying on their sides. A wine cellar, as Kinney had said, cool and sweet-smelling in contrast to the tunnel. The flashlight picked out a short flight of steps at the far end of the room, leading to another door. A thin bar of light traced the bottom edge of the door.

Blanchard went up the steps cautiously. He paused at the top step, his ear against the door. There was a dim murmur of voices. Self-consciously he cocked the hammer of the revolver. Then, heart pounding, he threw the door open and jumped into a brightly lit kitchen.

The sudden light pressed hard against his eyes, forcing him to squint. He saw a woman standing before a stove, her mouth open as she turned toward him. Another woman stared at him from a nearby sink. Blanchard gestured warningly with his gun. He touched a finger to his lips in silent signal and took another step into the room.

He sensed movement behind the door before he heard a distinct sound. As he swung to meet this danger, someone rushed him from the other side. In his mind he heard the inward groan that never reached his lips, the heart's protest of despair. Something crashed against his shoulder, driving him forward. In the same instant an iron bar lashed wickedly across his right hand. He felt a bone snap in his hand as the gun flew from his fingers. Then the last blow came. It caught the side of his skull as he was falling, and it smashed him onto his face on the tiles of the kitchen floor.

He was never wholly unconscious. Blackness blanketed him as he fell, but there was light around the edges, and there was dazzling pain that caromed from one point to another in his body like the lights on a giant pinball machine—bright explosions of agony in his hand, his shoulder, his head.

He felt himself being lifted roughly and carried through the kitchen, his feet dragging across the tiles. The blackness crept upward around the edges, and he tried to push it back with his will. Ahead of him a pool of softer light appeared, in which the wavering shadows of people moved toward him.

He was thrown onto a chair. As his vision began to clear, he was able to make out a tall man with close-cropped hair looming over him. Behind this man, peering past his shoulder, was Angie.

The fire in his right hand spread up his arm. Talk flew past him, meaningless. There was a moment's silence. He was pulled erect by someone at the side of his chair, his head jerked up by the hair.

The tall man stared down at Blanchard with bright, pitiless blue eyes. The German? The Nazi colonel who had kept Darrell Kinney in greedy bondage for so long? Blanchard saw the answer in those cold eyes.

"So you are Blanchard," the German said. His accent was heavy but he spoke with precision. What was his name? Von something. Von Schoenwald. An aristocrat's name.

"He was alone?" von Schoenwald snapped at the man beside Blanchard's chair.

"Yes. But Jesús is searching the tunnel now, to be sure."

The German grunted. "You are an unlikely Don Quixote, Mr. Blanchard. But you are equally a fool."

Blanchard stared in surprise at the small, wiry man beside him, now holding his gun. He had bright red hair, but the face beneath it was immediately recognizable. The last time Blanchard had seen him he had been bald, driving a black Renault through the hills of San Miguel de Allende, and he had called himself Wilson. But there was no doubt who he really was. This was George Robbins.

Blanchard tried to find Angie again. She was watching him, tears floating in her eyes. A thickly muscled Mexican stood watchfully beside her. In the few short days since he had last seen her, she had thinned out to a startling degree. The tanned and vibrant beauty that had seemed so far-out to Mike Blanchard had altered almost overnight into an elegant boniness, gaunt and pale, and marked by deep circles under her eyes. Blanchard felt the reviving adrenaline-flow of anger. What had they done to her?

Before he could react, Angie spoke. "You shouldn't have come."

"I couldn't leave you here without...without trying."

"Ah, yes, Mr. Blanchard. You had to come. A gallant gesture, surely. But tell me, why did you have to come *here?* How did you know your daughter-in-law was in this house?"

"Kinney told me all about you."

The ice-blue eyes narrowed just enough to show reaction. "Kinney told you! Indeed. But of course...

you were friends in the war. Great friends. But I am surprised you are still so friendly with the man who kidnapped your son."

"I warned you, Ernst," Robbins said.

"Yes, my dear George, you warned me. And you were right. How long have you been in touch with our mutual friend Kinney, Mr. Blanchard?"

The pain in Blanchard's head and shoulder had receded to a dull ache, and his hand was something he told himself he could live with. His head clearing, he was able to speak sharply. "Ask Robbins. He can tell you. From what I hear, he's been masterminding the whole show from the start."

Von Schoenwald smiled condescendingly. "You are much too transparent, Mr. Blanchard. If you are trying to sow confusion—"

"Ask him," Blanchard cut in. "Kinney told me what Robbins has been up to."

The German's glance flicked toward Robbins. In his hesitation was the first hint of doubt, uncertainty. "And what has George been up to?"

"Someone has been making damned sure I found my way here. I don't know all the reasons, but I do know this: Kinney would have been better off if my son had just disappeared in Guadalajara and that was the end of it. He had no reason to lead me right to his door. It doesn't add up at all unless Kinney is telling the truth. He says Robbins is going to kill you and pin the murder on me. He's made sure I have a good public motive—"

Robbins leaped at him. A hand dug into his hair and flung his head back, cracking it against the high back of the chair. The pain from his earlier blow rocketed through his skull. "George!" von Schoenwald commanded.

Robbins released Blanchard and stepped back. He was breathing audibly through his open mouth, and there was a killing fury in his eyes. Watching him, Blanchard was chilled by what he saw—and disturbed. Something was wrong. Accusing Robbins had seemed his only hope, however dangerous it was. But Robbins hadn't acted to silence him. He was simply enraged....

"That is not a very plausible story," von Schoenwald said.

"Why not? He stands to get his hands on a fortune with you out of the way." Blanchard was less sure of his words now, Kinney's words, but he had to carry through. "He wants the same thing Kinney wants—but he's closer to it."

"A reasonable hypothesis, I suppose. But one without evidence. And you forget that I know George very well. He is incapable of disloyalty."

"Is he? Do you really believe that for a minute? About anyone? From what I hear there's a lot at stake. How much is one of those paintings you stole worth today? A million dollars? Two million? Are you so sure he's that loyal?"

Von Schoenwald's thin smile flattened out at mention of the paintings. He stared at Blanchard. The silence lengthened. Then, compulsively, his gaze was pulled toward Robbins.

"Ernst... my God, you don't believe him! Can't you see what Kinney's trying to do?"

"Sending this man to kill me? That hardly seems clever enough for Kinney. He knows that tunnel is alarmed. He knew we'd be warned."

"What?" Blanchard's scalp seemed to lift. He tried to rise. Robbins and one of the bodyguards stepped quickly toward him, and he sank back onto the chair, stunned. "Kinney knew there was an alarm in the tunnel?"

"He arranged for the installation, Mr. Blanchard. That surprises you? Your friend is not what you think—least of all a friend. And we are not as primitive here as you seem to think. The walls are wired, and the gates—no one can break in without giving warning. And in the tunnel there is a seismic intrusion-detector buried under the floor. It is activated when sufficient weight disturbs the surface and the earth movement is communicated to the alarm device. A rat is not heavy enough to trigger the alarm, you see... but a man is. We were warned the moment you walked over the monitored area."

Blanchard shook his head, but the gesture was reflexive, expressing neither denial nor disbelief. His voice was flat. "He knew you'd be waiting for me."

"Precisely. We are not helpless children, Mr. Blanchard. The interesting question is, why did Kinney send you?" The German's face thrust close and his icy calm broke. "Why? I do not believe this innocence!"

Blanchard was silent. Innocence, he thought. Gullibility. He had *thanked* Kinney when he left him at the entrance to the tunnel. When he read the mute sympathy in Angie's eyes, he turned away, unable to accept it, condemning himself.

"An intriguing puzzle." Von Schoenwald was calm again, his tone mocking. "You see, George, it appears that Kinney *wanted* us to catch Blanchard. That does not make it look like a plan to have me assassinated. What would you suggest as an explanation? Could there be this possibility... that Kinney sent him here to warn me? Against you, George?"

"You know that's a lie! Colonel... Ernst, you can't believe—" Robbins broke off, smiling weakly. "You're teasing me. You must be. You know how I feel...." He swung toward Blanchard, his lips drawing back over teeth and gums in a simian snarl. "Kinney put you up to this. Damn you, tell him! Tell him the truth!"

"I don't know the truth," Blanchard said slowly. But he was beginning to see it, part of it. Kinney had tricked him again. Kinney, not Robbins, had been behind all of the devious manipulations that had brought him to Morelia. Kinney had wanted him to confront the German. Kinney had put the gun in his hand, knowing that he would have no chance to use it. All this was clear, but the reason remained hidden. It was like stumbling blindly through fog, finding familiar pieces of a landscape but unable to put them together. *What was behind it all?*

"You know I don't wish to believe what he says, George," von Schoenwald said coldly. "But I require an explanation... a reason to disbelieve. I've told you Kinney is no fool." He broke off, listening, confusion beginning to blur the hostile set of his features. "What was that?"

"I didn't hear—" Robbins also became alert. Thinly, barely audible over the noise of the storm outside, came the snarling of a dog. Then there was a scream that might have been animal or human. An instant later came two sharp cracks of sound, muffled but unmistakable: Gunfire.

"Wulf!" von Schoenwald said hoarsely, pain in the sound. "George—the wall!"

"That's it—that's Kinney's trick!" Robbins cried, almost in elation. "The alarm wasn't reset—that's why Kinney sent him through the tunnel! To trigger the alarm! So there'd be no warning when the real attack came! Don't you see it, Ernst? He had to have someone come through the tunnel!"

Von Schoenwald was shaken, but the old habit of command was instinctive. "Riki—Jesús! Stop them! George, you know what to do."

"Yes. Colonel... into the study, you'll be safe there." He thrust the Colt he had taken from Blanchard into the German's hand. "Kill them, Ernst." His finger stabbed at Blanchard and Angie. "Kill them!"

Jeff Blanchard dragged himself from the chair, thinking only that he might get between the German and Angie. But von Schoenwald seemed not to have heard Robbins' urging. For the first time he was disconcerted, unsure of himself. His lips compressed as more shots rattled in the yard. Shaking himself, he gestured with the revolver. "Both of you—move! You will go ahead of me."

The scattered gunfire seemed to explode into a full-

318

scale war as von Schoenwald herded Blanchard and Angie along the wide *galería*. Blanchard tried to peer through the tall windows overlooking a covered veranda. Puddles of light from the outdoor spotlights ran out quickly in the rainy darkness, revealing little. What was happening out there? Who had come over the wall?

Angie had moved close to him. He took her arm, squeezing it reassuringly. He felt shaky, but his head was clear. His thoughts shifted back to Kinney. Somehow Blanchard couldn't see him climbing over the garden wall in a guerrilla attack. He wouldn't take that kind of a risk. But the attack tied in too neatly with the way he had been used to set off the alarm system to be coincidence. The armed attack had to be part of Kinney's scheme. The object of that attack was also obvious. Robbins and von Schoenwald had to die. What happened to him and Angie might not matter to Kinney, one way or another.

No, Blanchard corrected himself. That was still being naïve. He could talk, he was a danger if left alive. Kinney wouldn't take that risk either.

How long ago had Kinney planned exactly this moment? If there had been any lingering regret in Blanchard's mind over an old friendship, any musty sentiment dragged out of the cellars of memory, the cold-blooded calculation of Kinney's intrigue dispelled it finally.

Von Schoenwald halted before a door halfway along the *galería*. "We will go in—" He stopped in mid-sentence, staring at the paneled door. It stood slightly ajar, and there was light in the room beyond. These facts meant nothing to Blanchard, but he saw von Schoenwald's start of surprise slide swiftly into something stronger, convulsive.

The German reacted. He kicked the door open. Blanchard was ahead of him, and he shoved him through the doorway into a paneled study.

Angie, stumbling into the room after Blanchard, was the first to see the girl. She cried out, "María!"

Then a strangled, choking sound burst from von Schoenwald's throat.

The girl was someone Blanchard didn't recognize, scarcely more than a child. She had jumped away from one wall as they burst through the door. There was a knife in her hand—it looked like a butcher knife—and a defiant terror in her eyes.

Blanchard's gaze went from the girl to the painting on the wall behind her. It had been wantonly slashed. In the same moment he realized that the destruction was part of a pattern. All around the room, paintings had been mutilated, scored, and ripped by the girl's knife.

Von Schoenwald screamed. It was a raw, terrible sound that seemed to be torn from his bowels. The girl attacked him with her long knife, but von Schoenwald lashed out at her with the barrel of the Colt. The blow struck her face, a dull crunch of yielding flesh and bone. It knocked her across the room. She bounced off the wall and crumpled to the floor without a sound, looking like a thin, raggedy doll.

From somewhere in the house—much closer now—came shouts and several shots in rapid succession. A woman screamed, and footsteps raced over polished tile floors. The attackers had broken into the house.

The German seemed not to hear. He stood trembling in the center of the paneled study. His face was bright red, engorged with blood, the veins livid against the swollen flesh. His eyes bulged as he stared at the ruined paintings on the walls. Blanchard looked at them again, and this time he saw something he had not detected in his first startled glance. Where the girl's knife had torn the canvases, the paint itself seemed to have crumbled and flaked away. It was as if only the outer layer of paint had held the pictures together under its fragile bond. Beneath it, the canvases themselves had disintegrated, like the rotten interior of wood eaten away by termites while the visible outer shell seemed undisturbed. The cuts and slashes of the girl's knife had revealed the hidden disease.

Von Schoenwald gave a violent shudder. Froth spluttered over his lips. He staggered and cried out, *"Verdammte Jude!"*

What happened in the next few minutes would always be confused in Jeff Blanchard's mind, but the image of the white-haired Nazi officer remained vivid and ugly, the stuff of nightmares. Afterward, trying to comprehend what had happened, he realized that he had witnessed a lifetime's veneer of self-discipline ripped away in a single moment. The buried rage of the one-time SS terrorist erupted, a massive assault of uncontrolled fury. Somewhere in the German's brain a vessel burst, then another, like an overloaded circuit exploding in a shower of sparks.

In the last moment that rage turned toward Blanchard and Angie, helpless targets. The Colt revolver lifted toward them. Then von Schoenwald fell back. He blundered clumsily into a large oak desk and toppled across it. Blanchard could see that he was trying to move his arms and legs, but they were paralyzed. The man's eyes bulged wildly, alive with the knowledge of what was happening to him, but he could not move.

Blanchard jumped toward him. When he grabbed the gun in von Schoenwald's hand, he found it held in a grip of steel. He had to pry the German's fingers from the gun butt, one by one.

As he jerked the gun free, the door crashed open behind him. Several young men, all wearing the white pajamalike garments of the Mexican peasant, rushed into the room. Their eyes and faces shone with a fierce excitement, as animated as children playing the universal game of cops-and-robbers. But one of them saw the Colt in Blanchard's hand, and his rifle whipped level, pointing toward the danger. Another youth shouted, *"No! No tira!"*

Blanchard didn't understand the command, but the young rebel lowered his rifle. The one who had shouted pushed past him. He too was wearing the white cotton clothes of the *indio,* and Blanchard understood intuitively that it was a kind of rebel uniform, carrying its own message. Astonished, he stared at the youth whose intervention had unquestionably saved his life.

Luis Martínez's dark eyes showed a brief flicker of puzzled recognition. Then he quickly surveyed the room, frowning at the torn paintings, finally staring hard at the man who lay sprawled across the desk. He spoke sharply in English. "That is Señor Brugmann? What has happened to him?"

"He's had...I think it's a stroke."

At Martínez's command two of the rebels ran forward and dragged von Schoenwald from the desk. They propped him in the swivel chair that faced it. As they stepped back, the chair continued to turn, revolving slowly until the German was facing the intruders. He remained rigid in the position in which they had placed him. Only his eyes stirred within their depths, staring out at the room in mute horror.

In a burst of rapid-fire Spanish, Luis Martínez shot questions at the German. When von Schoenwald did not answer, the young rebel leader slapped him across the face.

"That won't do any good," Blanchard said. "Can't you see? He's paralyzed. He can't answer you."

Another flood of angry Spanish vented Martínez's frustration. When the brief torrent ended, he turned abruptly to his waiting followers and gave brisk new commands. Immediately they fanned out through the room and began a hasty search, tearing the mutilated paintings carelessly from the walls, spilling drawers from the desk and from a low chest, sweeping books and artifacts from a set of shelves.

Luis Martínez gave Angie a young Mexican male's swift appraisal. Then he spoke to Blanchard. "I will not ask what you are doing here. I do not care. Just tell me where is the safe. Where does the German keep his money?"

Blanchard shook his head. "I don't know anything about it."

"No hay nada!" one of the searchers cried out angrily. "There is nothing!"

"Hay que estar aquí!" Martínez shouted. "It must be here! I was told—"

He broke off. The others went suddenly still. The wail of sirens rose clearly above the dwindling murmur of the rain. Even as they paused, the piercing sound raced closer.

Another white-clad youth appeared in the doorway. *"Luis! Los federales!"*

Martínez hesitated, casting another quick glance around the study, his eyes perplexed. It was clear that there was no safe behind any of the paintings which had covered the walls, no money in the desk, as he had been led to believe. *Nada.* The sirens screamed louder as they drew near, racing up the hill. The youth swore in anger, but it was the coolness he retained that Jeff Blanchard would remember later. He did not panic or waste time in futile anger.

And when one of the rebels turned his gun toward the German in his chair, Martínez stopped him.

He stared at von Schoenwald for a long moment before he glanced at Blanchard for the last time. "Killing is too good for such a man. Let him live as he is, in his own prison!"

The perception was quick, the judgment pitiless. It was one that Blanchard would never forget. Sometimes he would wonder what it had been like for a man like von Schoenwald to live all those years, even luxuriously, in the monastic seclusion of his walled estate, never free to leave it, never completely safe from the threat of exposure or betrayal, as confined as any prisoner in a cell. But in the end the walls of that prison had shrunk to the dimensions of his own skull. From that ultimate and awful cage the German looked out, his brain still alive in his frozen body, his eyes seeming to telegraph a soundless shriek, as if he begged for the bullet Luis Martínez had spared him.

The rebels fled as the federal militia reached the bottom of the knoll and the leading sirens guttered out. Trying to sort out the swift tumble of events, Blanchard knew that it might be safer to stay where he was, or to retreat to some other shelter in the house and hole up there until the fighting was over. But he couldn't wait—and he would not risk leaving Angie there alone.

When he looked for her, he found her kneeling at one side of the room beside the crumpled figure of the girl von Schoenwald had struck so viciously. Tears splotched Angie's cheeks. "She's dead," she whispered.

Blanchard thrust the Colt under his belt and grabbed Angie's arm. She was trembling, on the edge of hyseria, and she did not resist.

As Blanchard dragged her through the house, there was shooting at the front gates and scattered fire all around the yard. Blanchard found himself hoping that Martínez and his followers could escape over the wall the way they had come, but he knew that some of them would be left behind, victims of the same vicous betrayal that had brought him to this house tonight, pawns in Darrell Kinney's plot.

He saw George Robbins lying on the floor near the front door, where he had apparently been left for dead. But the redheaded man was still alive. As Blanchard led the way past him to the kitchen, he heard Robbins groan, saw him stir. Blanchard didn't stop. Robbins could tell him nothing. In that, as in everything else, Kinney had lied.

A moment later he had reached the cool darkness of the tunnel, pulling Angie with him.

The thick black heart of the storm had passed over the valley, leaving behind a grayer overcast and a thin, intermittent drizzle. On the hill above them, the sounds of fighting had ceased. Jeff Blanchard faced Angie and shook her gently. "Angie! Are you all right now? Can you do what I told you?"

She nodded woodenly.

He pointed toward the motel farther down the road, and the side street just beyond it that led to

Rynders' house. When he had given terse directions, he started her down the road.

She stared back at him. "I don't understand. Where are you going?"

"I'm going to find Mike."

Her head shook loosely, and for the first time since he had found her that night he understood what had happened to her. It was not physical abuse or other torment that had ravaged her face. It was grief. She said, "But it's no use—Michael is dead!"

Blanchard flinched from the pain of the words, so certain and final. He wouldn't accept them. They couldn't stop him. "We don't know that for sure. There's only one man who knows. He's the one I have to stop."

7

From the motel room above La Cosecha, Darrell Kinney had watched the police cars race up the hill under his window, their sirens wailing, followed by open jeeps loaded with squads of rifle-carrying militia. The response was so quick, so soon after the first sounds of gunfire, and apparently so well coordinated between the police and the riot soldiers, that Kinney felt a rising unease. How could the authorities have been alerted so quickly? How could they possibly have been prepared for such a response?

It had to be chance, a bit of bad luck, but... Darrell Kinney left as little as possible to chance, and he was reluctant to believe in it.

He decided it was time to leave. The temptation to remain close to the scene, overseeing the success of his plan, had been too strong to resist, but the decision had been a reckless one. He realized now that the swift action of the authorities was reason enough for prudently going into hiding for a while. But it was not cause for serious worry. There still seemed little likelihood that the soldiers would have arrived at von Schoenwald's house in time to sabotage the plan Kinney had set in motion so painstakingly. The rebels had had the necessity of killing the German and Robbins drilled into them from the start. If they hadn't done it in the first attack, they would certainly kill the two men when they heard the police sirens. Even if they had not been told how essential this was, rage over their failure to locate the promised haul of money would make them kill.

Kinney felt no more compassion for the young revolutionaries than he did for the Blanchards. They were simply pieces in the game, to be moved as he wished. In the case of the rebels, most of them students, Rafael Sánchez had done his work well. He had been the go-between, and the rebels were completely unaware of Kinney's role behind the scenes. No matter what happened on the hill tonight, neither the Mexican authorities nor the rebels would be able to trace the events to Kinney. Sánchez was the only link, a necessary one, but he would not talk if he was sufficiently rewarded. The doctor was a greedy man. And in time that voice could be silenced, that danger removed....

Kinney went down the motel stairs to the courtyard and crossed to the locked garage where he kept his car. He drove it around to the courtyard entrance to La Cosecha. Then he returned to his room over the shop for the suitcase he had packed. At the last moment, after dropping the suitcase into the trunk, he entered the shop and went directly to his office safe. If he was going to be in hiding for any prolonged period—or if something unforeseen had happened on the hill tonight—he dared not leave the money behind.

He had withdrawn a little over $100,000 from von Schoenwald's accounts in Mexico City, where they were kept under Alan Slater's name. Sixty thousand had already been deposited in a bank in San Diego, using Tijuana connections. The balance was in cash, an approximately equal portion of dollars and pesos. All that was left of the promised fortune for which Kinney had murdered Carl Creasey and thrown in his lot with the Nazi officer.

The need to make his move for that money had been the motive for Kinney's plot. He had started to make the withdrawals immediately after the last month's accounting had been given to the German. At that time he had already set in motion the idea of the rebel raid, even though the outcome of such an attack was at best unpredictable. It would have given him time to run, even though it left the strong possibility that he would always be looking over his shoulder for Robbins, if he and the German managed to repulse the attack. But then Kinney had run into the Blanchard kid in San Miguel de Allende, and something had clicked in his mind.

He had followed the youth to Guadalajara. By then he had begun to see the outlines of another, better plan, one incorporating a diversionary tactic that would ensure the success of the rebel raid when it came. If he could kidnap the kid and lure his father to Mexico—perhaps the one man in the world who might plausibly be seen to threaten not only Kinney but von Schoenwald—he could keep the German and Robbins preoccupied long enough to carry out the rest of the scheme.

It had always had to be a flexible plan, but there had been one predictable element in it: Jeff Blanchard. Good old reliable Jeff. He had made the plan work, without ever knowing what he was doing.

Kinney wondered dispassionately if Blanchard was now dead. Had he been killed in the tunnel, or captured and questioned? How bewildered he must have been when he found them waiting for him as he emerged from the tunnel....

Blanchard had not changed. After twenty-eight

years he was still the same fool rushing in blindly, the same true believer. When a man believed in anything that strongly—country, war, religion, a cause or a woman, or even the duties a father owed a son—it was easy to turn that belief against him, in the same way that the blind passion of the young, ardent revolutionaries had been exploited. Blanchard had even believed *him* in the end, in spite of all that had happened. Kinney had actually been concerned over their confrontation and the need to convince Blanchard that he was himself a victim, that von Schoenwald and especially Robbins were the real enemy. He needn't have worried.

Of course the story he had told Blanchard had been convincing because it was very close to the truth. He had only substituted Robbins for his own role.

There remained only one regret in Kinney's mind. Ernst von Schoenwald would have died without ever knowing about the paintings.

Darrell Kinney's determination to steal what was left of the German's money had crystallized the day he discovered what had been done to the stolen masterpieces. That had occurred nearly five years ago, and it had taken him all this time to find the right combination of ingredients for his revenge against the Nazi who had tricked him.

That young Jew had had his revenge, although he had not succeeded in denying von Schoenwald more than a quarter-century of the good life. An artist, the Jew had worked in a chemical plant at the concentration camp where von Schoenwald had found him. An artist with a knowledge of chemistry. In his own way, Kinney supposed, a genius, a discoverer. He had carried out von Schoenwald's instructions to paint over the stolen masterpieces, but he had discovered a way to mix something in his oils—or applied something directly to the originals before painting over it; it was impossible to say which—that would ultimately destroy the paintings. Over a long period of time the chemical he had used had eaten away at the precious substance of the concealed paintings. The damage must already have begun, Kinney realized later, when the first painting was restored and sold in Switzerland, for there had been slight damage even then. More damage had reduced the value of the paintings sold from Argentina, but no one had suspected what was happening to them.

Kinney had made his discovery when, without von Schoenwald's knowledge, he had determined to restore and sell the single small canvas the German had given him in a token act of generosity. Kinney had found the original ruined. The shock had been numbing at the time, soul-destroying, but he had eventually recovered. And from that time he had begun to plan the moment when he could take over what remained of the lost fortune the young Jew had denied to him as well as to von Schoenwald. He had known that the remaining paintings must also have been destroyed, eaten away invisibly under their innocent scenic covers. Ironically, if von Schoenwald had had all of the paintings restored at an early date—if he hadn't been so afraid of bringing in someone expert enough to do the work and trustworthy enough to remain silent about it—most of the originals might have been saved.

At one time Kinney had thought of suggesting to von Schoenwald that Bud Rynders could restore the paintings. Rynders, a hungry young artist then, had been working for Kinney. He had brought La Cosecha into being and made it successful. But Rynders had seen Kinney's painting once and he had shown quick interest in it, puzzled by something in its texture or in the canvas itself. He had wondered, jokingly, if Kinney might have stumbled onto something valuable, a masterpiece painted over. Kinney had decided against using Rynders then. He was too curious, too observant. Kinney had also decided that it was better to have Rynders out of the way. He had managed it in a way calculated to leave

Rynders too angry to remain curious about the painting. He had kicked Rynders out and taken over operation of La Cosecha himself.

But all that was in the past. Now Kinney had pulled off his long-delayed coup. The money he was getting out of it wasn't much compared to the millions that might have been his, but it would free him from the necessity of grubbing for a living in the tourist business. He might set himself up in a luxury hotel in Baja California, which was ready to boom. Or he might even return to the States. He would keep La Cosecha, but someone else could run it for him now. The thought of asking Rynders brought a smile to his lips.

He carried the suitcase with the money to his car, placing it on the seat beside him. For a moment he paused behind the wheel, listening. The rain had thinned out. The night was quiet.

There was no more gunfire from up on the hill. Wondering what had happened, Darrell Kinney felt a return of unease as he reached for the ignition key.

At that moment he had the second great shock of his life, as demoralizing as the discovery of the destruction of his priceless painting.

Jeff Blanchard ran through the open gates of the motel into the courtyard, stopped, and looked straight at him.

For Guillermo Valdez, the raid against the walled estate in the hills near the village of Santa María had been anticlimactic. The charge up the hill had been exciting, and when one of the rebels opened fire before the jeep had come to a stop, Guillermo had been quick to spill out of the vehicle with the others and take cover beside the road. But for him the fight was already over. As it turned out, the rebels had not intended to stay and fight. There was sporadic shooting while the militia organized an attack, but when it came the rebels fought only a holding action to cover their retreat, yielding ground as soon as the fighting became heavy. And Guillermo Valdez was not part of it. Before the rebels had fled into the hills, he had been ordered to a position at the foot of the slope on the east side of the knoll. He didn't see any reason for being there, since the rebels had all retreated in the opposite direction. And now that there was no danger of being shot, he told himself that he had been denied an opportunity to display his courage. What was the use of being trained to fight as a soldier if you were not to be part of the fighting when it came?

Because he felt this way, disappointed and increasingly indignant, Valdez paid little attention to his surroundings. He expected no trouble so far from the house on the knoll, and this judgment was soon confirmed as the intermittent shooting faded away from him to the west, in the direction of the village. He wondered if the rebels had friends in Santa María who would hide them. It might be necessary to search the village, a possibility that did not appeal to him as much as an open battle. There were too many places for the enemy to wait in ambush. Besides, he was one of the people himself, and he did not enjoy their animosity.

Valdez's attention was directed toward the walled *posada* above him. There was still some activity there, but he could see little. The rebels had picked a good, dark night for their attempt to plunder the German's house. Valdez wondered how it was that his troop had been alerted earlier that evening, long before the raid began. Someone in the rebel camp was a traitor, he thought with contempt.

Near the bottom of the knoll was a nest of big rocks, and at one point Valdez was actually leaning against one of them, relaxing. He decided this wasn't a very good idea, in case one of his officers should discover him, so he moved away from the rocks. It did not occur to him to investigate the formation. If he had he would quickly have discovered the door set deeply among the rocks. He had his back in that direction when the door opened and a man dragged himself out of the tunnel.

There were several other sentries positioned around the knoll, but the night was very dark and Valdez could see only one of them clearly. He was twenty yards away, closer to the road.

The man who had emerged from the tunnel saw Valdez the instant he poked his head through the cleft in the rock pile. He drew back quickly. When he looked out again after a moment, he saw that Valdez still had his back turned to him. The man moved with difficulty, dragging one leg, but he was very silent. Valdez felt his presence instinctively at the last second, but he had been too relaxed and inattentive. By the time he started to turn, it was too late. The man struck at his throat with the edge of his hand, an edge as hard as a board. The blow was not a clean one, but it caught the side of Valdez's neck, smashing his windpipe. There was a soft, gurgling sound as the soldier collapsed; that was all. Then the man from the tunnel bent over him and struck again. This time there was no mistake, and Guillermo Valdez died instantly.

The man took the American M-16 rifle from the dead soldier, glanced once toward the nearest sentry, who had neither seen nor heard anything, and limped away into the darkness, dragging his leg. He left a trail of blood behind him in the wet grass, invisible in the darkness. It was not Valdez's blood, but his own.

At that same moment Charmian Stewart stepped alone from the Rynders house into the carport. Kate was in the kitchen preparing cocoa, and Charmian hadn't the heart to tell her she didn't want anything. She stepped to the gate at the edge of street, a muddy track that now resembled a plowed field, the water standing inches deep in the ruts and furrows. She wondered how it was possible to think of such commonplace things. Her mind tricked her, fastening on such small, meaningless details when all she really wanted to think of was Jeff Blanchard—and what was happening at Baldur Brugmann's house.

In spite of the storm she seemed to have spent half of the evening outside, listening apprehensively. There had been some shooting, not quite drowned out by the rattle of the rain on the metal roof of the carport. Every shot had made her flinch, as if she could feel the impact against her own flesh.

Now it was quiet. The rain drifted over the road in a fine mist. It seeped into the carport like fog, chilling her.

She peered past the gate toward the main road. At that instant, lightning opened a jagged crack in the blackness over the east end of the valley. In that brief flash of light she saw someone in the road. A woman.

Charmain pushed through the gate. The figure plodded toward her, stumbling and slipping, yet seemingly oblivious of the ankle-deep water and mud. Charmian stood waiting, almost afraid to call out, not yet willing to believe that what she hoped was true.

When she was only a few steps away, the woman looked up and let out a small cry.

Then Angie Blanchard threw herself into Charmian's arms, sobbing. Charmian held her, not trying to move or speak, unaware of her own tears. One thought pounded in her brain. Only one person would have sent Angie to her this way.

And that meant he was alive, safe, that he too was coming back.

8

When a car in the corner of the courtyard suddenly started up, Jeff Blanchard, his nerves drawn tight, reacted as if the sound were a scream. He didn't recognize the car, a big American coupe, and the driver was only a blurred, anonymous face behind the windshield. But the car was near the entrance to La Cosecha, Kinney's shop—and the driver was in too much of a hurry. In his haste he kept the key turned over after the engine had caught, and the rasp of the flywheel was an unwitting signal. Blanchard had started to jump when the dark headlights leaped toward him.

The car's right front fender scraped the corner pillar, smashing a headlight, missing him by inches. Metal tore as the vehicle careened past him through the open gates. It left behind a sprinkling of broken glass.

Blanchard dragged the revolver from his waistband. The movement with his left hand was awkward and slow. By the time he had the gun clear, the car was skidding sideways into a ditch on the far side of the road. It rocked over hard, righted itself, and shot forward, spitting mud and gravel and spray.

The car was accelerating at top speed when Blanchard ran through the gateway to the road. Before he could take any kind of steady aim with his shaking hand, the car was far down the road, a shrinking target vanishing into the gray mist.

Blanchard wanted to scream obscenities after Kinney. A desperation so strong it made him feel cold shriveled his anger. He tried to think calmly, though his good hand still shook with the weight of the six-gun. If Kinney got away now, he was gone for good. It was all too easy for an American to disappear in Mexico. There were too many anonymous drifters, tourists, retirees...

In that instant of cool, hard clarity, he remembered that the road down the hill had to double back.

He started running. A side lane dipped sharply downhill, passing between the two high-walled inns that catered elegantly to Morelia's more affluent tourists. The road was uneven, rock-strewn, puddled. He slipped and nearly fell several times. The lane came to a dead end overlooking a steep, brush-covered slope. At its foot was the road Kinney had to take.

He could hear the racing car as he reached the edge of the slope. There was a footpath, almost invisible in the darkness. He plunged recklessly down the path. Off to his left a single headlight appeared, filtered by the misty rain. In his excitement he skated on a muddy patch and tumbled out of control. Instinctively he put out his broken hand to cushion his fall, and when he landed he went blind with pain.

When he could see again, kneeling in the mud and brush halfway down the slope, Kinney's car was directly below him.

Blanchard raised the gun and started firing.

The shots were blind, their aim at best reflexive, as if he were shooting from the hip like a movie gunfighter. But as the car sped away from him, the angle of trajectory was good. The sound of smashing glass did not reach him over the roar of the car, but the sudden squeal of tires on the wet pavement did.

He struggled to his feet. The single headlight bobbed wildly, like a flashlight in the hand of a running man. The raw screech of rubber turned into a ripping, tearing dive through the dark-green thicket of brush and trees below the road, where a natural park dropped away to the bottom of the hill. That runaway plunge ended suddenly in a solid, thudding crash.

Blanchard skidded and stumbled down the path to the road. He ran along the edge of the pavement, bent over in pain, holding his right arm and hand against his body in some primitive protective instinct. Though Kinney's car was no longer moving, its engine continued to race at full throttle, guiding him toward it. He could see the single cone of its surviving headlight slashing through the trees at an angle parallel to the sloping hillside.

He tried to remember how many shots he had fired. Three, at least. Maybe four. From the sound of the crash, he might not need another.

He veered off the road along the wide furrow the car had bulldozed through small trees and brush. Miraculously it had threaded among several larger trees until the magic ran out. Then it had slammed sideways against a solid trunk, spun around, and stopped, pointing straight down the hill.

Abruptly the racing engine cut off. The silence that followed was a crushing force. It stopped Blanchard in his tracks.

More cautious now, he approached the car from the rear, gun in hand. He saw a spiderweb spray around a bullet hole in the rear window. Had Kinney been hit, or had he lost control? The windshield had popped out on impact. It lay inverted on the hood, facing skyward like a dish antenna. He couldn't see if it bore another bullet hole.

He had started sweating during his run, and now the sweat was cooling over his body. He began to shiver uncontrollably. Although the rain had thinned out so much that it couldn't penetrate the trees, the night remained damp and cold. He wondered if his hand would still shake if he had to use the gun again.

Then he saw the door on the driver's side hanging open.

Kinney was gone.

He dropped to a crouch in the shadow of the car, his heart thumping. His vision had been affected by the single headlight. He could see nothing but blackness when he turned from the light. All of his senses were acutely alive as he waited. He could smell burning rubber and oil and wet crushed grass. He felt the dampness of his clothes, the heaviness of the humid air. Voices came to him from somewhere down on the main road, off to the left. Other voices, closer—lovers used this park, perhaps even on a rainy night when there was nowhere else to go. He tasted the dryness of his momentary fear, the bitterness of another failure.

Then he heard someone fall near the bottom of the hill, crashing through brush.

Blanchard went after Kinney more carefully now, nursing the strength that was being drained out of him by pain and fear. He felt the weakness of his legs, the sense of dragging a heavy weight as if a harness pulled across his thighs. But Kinney, a man in a hurry, wasn't moving any faster, as if he too were hurt or burdened.

Near the bottom of the hill, at the edge of the wood, Blanchard found some fresh tracks where Kinney had had to cross low-lying ground between the trees and the crown of asphalt. In that depression his tracks had sunk deeply. Crossing the same ground, Blanchard saw that his own tracks did not dig as far into the mud. Kinney was about his own weight. He had to be carrying something.

By the time he reached the road Blanchard felt as if he were moving in slow motion, like a swimmer trying to run in deep water. Kinney was not in sight. Several people were on the road, hurrying toward him, attracted by the crash, long shadows running before them as they passed a street light. To Blanchard's right an old, front-engine bus stood parked. He remembered that this was a waiting station for the buses that ran between Morelia and Santa María during the day. The vehicle blocked his view of the road.

When he moved around the bus, there was still no sign of the fleeing man. He tried to guess where Kinney might run, now that he was on foot. And possibly hurt. As Blanchard stood in the shadow of the bus, indecisive, an almost inaudible squeak of sound drew his attention across the road. At the edge of his vision, near the base of a high, curving concrete wall, a shadow might have shifted slightly as he looked, like a picture jerking out of focus. When he stared hard in that direction, the illusion was gone, the blurred edges of the picture clearly aligned.

But there had been a sound.

The massive concrete structure was the *charro* arena. Nearby was the Casino Charro, a restaurant with a number of cars in the parking lot out front.

Kinney would want a car, especially if he was laboring, and he wasn't above stealing one. But the shadow of movement Blanchard had seen—*if* he had seen it—had been to the left of the restaurant. Near the arena.

Blanchard trotted across the road. After the accident Kinney might be in no condition to show himself in a public restaurant, or even to risk being seen out front. But the empty arena, which resembled a small bull ring, would offer tempting places to hide—underground tunnels and service areas, dark aisles and stairways, a surrounding matrix of stables and exercise rings for the horses when the arena was in use, horse trails and back roads that might lead away from the facility toward the city. A man like Kinney, who had lived for twenty years or more in Morelia, would probably know every corner of the arena, every path across the fields beyond it.

Blanchard wondered what it was that Kinney was carrying, so important that he would allow it to slow him down when he was running for his life, so vital that he couldn't leave it behind. He also wondered if Kinney had been in too much of a hurry to take a gun from the wrecked car. The suspicion grew into conviction. If Kinney had had a gun, he could easily have waited in ambush in the woods near the car.

The arena was a giant curve of whitewashed bricks, supported by cement columns. The first ten feet from the ground were solid; above that the bricks had been set in an open grid, crowned by a tiled suspension roof. Blanchard crept along the solid curve of the wall until he came to an inset entrance. It was barred by a chain-link fence with a gate. The gate was not locked.

He stood very still. That was what he had heard from the other side of the road. The faint creak of the gate.

The interior of the tunnel directly beyond this entrance was black, featureless. If Kinney wanted him, that was a good place.

But if Kinney had retreated into the warren of aisles and stairways away from the entrance, far enough so that he couldn't see it and had to depend on the sound of the gate to warn him, he might become impatient when he didn't hear it...or lulled into thinking he had eluded pursuit.

Going the long way around was a gamble. Blanchard questioned it every step of the way, circling the restaurant and finding his way among the rows of stalls behind it, until eventually he reached the fenced approach that funneled toward the arena. It took him ten minutes. Too long. Instead of fooling Kinney, he might simply have given him an open escape route...and all the time he needed.

But Blanchard had bet on his knowledge of Kinney, just as Kinney had staked everything these past two weeks on his understanding of a gullible wartime friend. Kinney was a devious man. He didn't trust simple solutions. Walking out to safety through an unwatched front gate was too easy; Kinney would have been suspicious of it. He was more likely to have set a trap. And if no one blundered into it, if he became convinced the danger was past, he would find a surreptitious way to leave, a back trail across the fields he had previously noted and remembered. That was the way his mind worked.

Low whitewashed walls boxed in the long equestrian run that led to the arena, which faced Blanchard as he approached, like the open end of a horseshoe. He remembered seeing one of the colorful riding exhibitions given by the *charros* a long time ago, with Elaine. They were almost as popular in many parts of Mexico as bullfights, and a lot less bloody. But there were no happy, noisy crowds now, only shadows and silence and the cold gray mist, the storm's vapor trail. Coming to the edge of the open pit, using the low wall as cover, he studied the semicircle of empty stands. He could make out little detail—rows of bench seats, regularly spaced pillars, the clear white curve of wall enclosing the sandy pit of the arena, the open black mouths of stairwells.

He waited behind a red wooden gate at the edge of the arena. Minutes crawled by. Had he guessed wrong? If so, he had given Kinney at least fifteen minutes start. He—and Mike—would have lost.

Crouching there in the darkness, chilled and battered, Blanchard felt the slow invasion of the fear he had been obstinately holding off, the dread that whatever he did now was already too late.

His thoughts jerked away from pain, but almost immediately he was remembering Angie up there on the hill when he had left her, grief-stricken and despairing, a beautiful child to cherish as if she were his own, if only...

Another wrench, another turning away. But this time his mind threw up an image of Charmian Stewart. He saw her behind the wheel of her little car, driving it with careless expertise, laughing at something he had said. Her head was tilted back, revealing the slender, lovely line of her throat.

Blanchard shook his head, but the tension and the waiting and the fatigue of his body had affected him strangely. He seemed to have lost control of his rambling thoughts. He found himself remembering Mike in a way he hadn't permitted himself during these frantic recent days... the look around his eyes and mouth that was so much like his mother's, the stubbornness that would set into his eyes and his voice when they argued, or even when a subject came up on which he expected disapproval or resistance. It was a look that Blanchard had resented. The acknowledgment was an uncomfortable one. He supposed that he had failed his son in many ways, and it always seemed limp to protest that you had tried to do your best. He had never been able to change what he was for his son. He couldn't change as fast as the world changed, or see life through younger eyes, conditioned by different sights and sounds. In the end he could only let his heart answer for him. That answer had brought him to Mexico, and now, unpredictably, to this silent *charro* arena. But the conviction that that inarticulate message would never reach the one it was meant for was suddenly strong and bitter. It brought the agony of regret that all men know, at some time, in the ageless discovery that there might never be a second chance. He closed his eyes. The body made no distinction: the sting of grief in his eyes was the same as smog.

When he looked up again, blinking, he saw Kinney.

He was standing near the top row of seats, partially concealed by a pillar. He was watching the arena, and Blanchard wondered how long he had been there. The hand gripping his gun shook now in anger; only the distance and the darkness kept him from wasting a shot.

Mist curled around Kinney's feet as he began to descend along an aisle between the benches. For a moment the illusion was created that he was walking on air. Then, near the bottom row, the mist thickened suddenly like smoke. When it blew away, Kinney had vanished.

Blanchard nearly left his cover then. There was a temptation to question not only his eyesight but his mental state. He choked back panic. There was a ramp or stairway near where Kinney had disappeared. He was neither a ghost nor a magician.

But he could be heading for the front entrance.

For another instant Blanchard hesitated. He was in the act of moving when Kinney stepped back into view, and Blanchard dropped quickly back behind the wooden gate.

At the edge of the wall that encircled the arena at the base of the stands, Kinney paused. He glanced around once more. He was carrying what looked like a small suitcase. He dropped it over the wall and quickly vaulted after it to the floor of the arena.

Picking up the suitcase, no longer hesitant or cautious, Kinney started across the arena, heading directly toward the red wooden gate where Blanchard crouched. He was ten yards away when Blanchard's self-control snapped.

When Blanchard's head and shoulders appeared over the gate, Kinney whirled and ran. Blanchard's shot was meant to be wild, but it kicked up sand near Kinney's feet. He stopped so abruptly that he staggered back a step.

Blanchard pushed open the gate and stepped out to face Kinney. He was not surprised to see the familiar, mocking smile appear. "Well, you're a surprise, old buddy," Kinney said. "I didn't think you had it in you."

"If you think I don't have it in me to kill you, you're wrong in that too."

The smile turned off. "Yeah. I wouldn't want to make that mistake. Did you kill Robbins? And von Schoenwald? Or did those junior-league Castros do it for you?"

"Did you use them too?"

"I'd use anybody dumb enough—" Kinney regretted the words even before they were spoken. He tried to cover his uneasiness. "You're hurt, buddy. Hell, you couldn't hit anybody holding that gun like that."

"At this distance," Blanchard said, "yes, I can. Go ahead, start running."

"Now wait a minute. You wouldn't want to do that. Cool it, Jeff! Don't forget your kid!"

"You think I've forgotten? You think I'm so dumb I still don't know you did it all—that it was never Robbins?"

"Okay, okay! But that means you can't shoot."

"Why not?" His voice cracked. He wanted Kinney to run.

"That's obvious, isn't it? If you kill me, you'll never know about Mike. So for God's sake, stop waving that gun at me. Your hand's shaking like a leaf."

"Damn you, if this is another trick—"

"Hell, buddy, you don't think I'd really let your son get killed. You can't believe that."

"Yes, you'd do it—for what's in that suitcase,

whatever it is. And to see that German dead. You'd do anything for that." The tremor in his voice was also in his hand, in the shaking barrel of the Colt. A white line appeared around Kinney's mouth. "And I'll kill you for that."

"Jesus, Jeff, listen to me! Take it easy, for God's sake. Mike isn't dead, I swear it. I can take you to him. You know me, buddy. You don't think I'd play this hand without leaving myself an ace in the hole. That's what Mike is. That's the way it's been all along. I never meant anything to happen to him, you've got to believe that." Kinney was babbling, the words tumbling after each other, but Blanchard still didn't know whether or not to believe him. He had lied too often, and he would certainly lie again to save his life. But the chance that what he said was true couldn't be ignored; the risk couldn't be taken. "Shooting me won't get him back. I'm your only hope, Jeff. Believe me, I'm your only hope."

Then Blanchard couldn't deny the hope any longer. He had to believe. "All right," he said flatly. "Take me to him. Now." As he spoke he relaxed just a little, tipping the muzzle of the Colt slightly away from Kinney's chest because he was afraid that his shaking hand might inadvertently squeeze the trigger. It was only a tiny opening, but Kinney took it. He swung the suitcase.

Trying to duck the blow, Blanchard fired the shot he didn't want to take—and the hammer slammed onto an empty cartridge.

The edge of the suitcase caught his shoulder as he dodged. It caught him off balance, and his body, pushed beyond its capacity, betrayed him. He sprawled onto the wet sand of the arena.

There was a yelp of wild laughter, a bright glitter of triumph in Kinney's eyes as he aimed a kick at Blanchard's head. Rolling, Blanchard caught only a glancing blow. It struck sparks in his skull, and it kept him from grasping immediately the meaning of the sharp crack of sound he heard. He kept moving, trying to scramble to his feet. Only a wheezing burst of air from Kinney's throat brought him around.

Incredulous, he watched Kinney stagger, his legs flopping in a clownish dance. Both hands clutched at his throat, as if he sought to claw away the darkness that swiftly covered his fingers. He fell heavily. With a spreading numbness of feeling, Blanchard knew that he had been shot.

Looking over his shoulder, he saw the patch of bright red that crowned George Robbins' head. A rifle rested on the edge of the arena wall where he had propped it to aim. Even as Blanchard caught sight of him, Robbins slid out of sight. The rifle stayed where it was, balanced on top of the white wall as if it were still ready to fire.

Terror struck Blanchard as he dropped to one knee beside Kinney. The bullet had struck Kinney high in the center of his chest, near the base of his throat. He was dying fast, and the dread of that knowledge was in his eyes. "He's alive," Kinney said in an odd, pleading voice, as if he were afraid he wouldn't be believed when he was making one last claim to be one of the good guys after all. "Mike's alive. I wouldn't kid you now."

Then he died.

Robbins was unconscious when Blanchard reached him. He had been shot in the leg, and one arm had been smashed by another bullet. It was a moment before Blanchard realized there was a third wound, this one in his belly. His face was white, bloodless. Staring down at him, in a state of shock, Jeff Blanchard felt neither gratitude for the shot that had saved his life nor astonishment over the force that had driven Robbins to follow him and Kinney down the hill while he was bleeding to death. He felt only a total emptiness. Darrell Kinney was dead ...and his knowledge of Mike had died with him.

Interlude Seven: Morelia

Charmian Stewart was behind the wheel of the Vega, trying to keep up with the police car that darted nimbly through heavy traffic past the bus terminal, heading toward the north side of the old city on a morning that was achingly bright and sunny, the kind of brilliant day that so enchanted the Spaniards who came to these highlands more than four hundred years ago. Bud Rynders sat in the front bucket seat, swiveling around with one elbow hooked over the seat. He looked at Jeff Blanchard and Angie, who sat together in the back.

"My guess is Sánchez was in on it from the start," Rynders said.

"How much did he know?"

"I don't suppose we'll ever have the answer to that. Not from him, that's for sure. The way things are, he's already in deep, so he's going to try to make himself look as good as he can. How he's telling it is, Kinney suckered him. He didn't know anything about the rebel raid or any of the rest of it." He glanced ahead as Charmian swerved around a truck that rumbled out of a side street in front of her. "If he was the go-between for those kindergarten revolutionaries, nobody can prove it. He'd probably have dealt only with one or two of them, and the leaders got away. The ones who were caught weren't able to identify Sánchez. Rafael is smart that way. He always comes out of the mud with his suit still white and clean." Rynders paused. "I'm glad you kept Luis Martínez's name out of it, Jeff."

Blanchard said, "He kept me from getting killed." Looking past Charmian's shoulder toward the police car, he could see a patch of Sánchez's shoulder, white linen sandwiched between drab uniforms.

"Will Sánchez go to jail?" Charmian asked.

Rynders shrugged. "Maybe so, but I wouldn't bet on it. His family has a lot of clout around here—his wife's family, that is. And like I said, there's nobody to testify against him."

"It doesn't matter," Angie said. It was the first time she had spoken since the ride began from Rynders' house, where she had spent the night after she came weeping to their door. "It doesn't matter. If only Michael is..."

No one answered. In the aftermath of the night's violence, Blanchard found himself agreeing with the girl's words. It didn't matter about Sánchez. Anger had spent itself. Hope was what was left, and last night he hadn't had that. It had been revived a little over an hour ago with the news that the police had routed Sánchez out of hiding. Blanchard wondered if Rynders was correct in his suspicion that a deal had been made between the authorities and Sánchez's powerful family, permitting him to surface. Under the circumstances, he felt surprisingly little bitterness toward the doctor. Perhaps it was true that Sánchez had been duped by Kinney along with everyone else.

"Sedling was responsible for the police getting there so fast last night," Blanchard said. "How did he get onto Kinney in the first place?"

Rynders answered the question. "Seems the CIA and the Food and Drug Administration, or whatever it is, have both been interested in the man we all knew as Alan Slater. He was a curiously active man, is the way Sedling put it. They had some suspicion that he was involved in smuggling drugs into the States, using the cover of his gift shops. He had that legitimate business going, the best cover of all, and a lot of tourists been crossing the border with souvenirs and stuff from La Cosecha for twenty years, nearly. Or they had things shipped to the States. Seems one or more of those packages were opened by Sedling's people. They didn't find heroin or grass, but lots of those other pills, like speed. Sedling figures Kinney had a tie-in with one of the big drug outfits that sell the stuff or make it down here. They couldn't prove how the stuff got in those packages. That's what Sedling was here to find out. Then he and the Mexican government started getting interested in some big transfers of money—Kinney was clearing out Brugmann's accounts in a hurry this past month." He paused reflectively. "Seems like this Kinney wasn't easily satisfied."

"No," Blanchard said. "He wasn't."

They were silent again, and the tension which had been relieved by talk mounted again. It knotted in Jeff Blanchard's stomach. He felt as if he had been on an interminable journey, searching for his missing son. It was hard to believe that less than two weeks had passed since Angie's phone call had jolted his quiet Sunday at home.

Suddenly the police car ahead swung sharply right, turning along a curving driveway. Moments later it pulled up in front of a small, unexpectedly modern hospital. Rynders was opening the door before the Vega had came to a full stop, and the others tumbled out after him.

Sánchez, sweating and visibly agitated, would not meet Blanchard's stare. In the grip of a police lieutenant he was hustled into the lobby of the clinic. He disappeared along a wide, white-tiled corridor. When Blanchard tried to follow, a young policeman stopped him. *"Quédese, Señor."*

"He says to wait here," Rynders translated.

They stayed close together, in the manner of families in hospitals, as if they might find comfort in this closeness to each other. When Blanchard at length spoke to Angie, his voice cracked a little. It sounded loud in the unnatural silence, bouncing off those hard white walls. "He may not be himself, Angie. From what I gather, Sánchez has kept him under drugs, sedated most of the time. He claims Kinney told him a story about Mike being in trouble and needing to be kept on ice for his own good. It doesn't wash, but... the important thing is that he's here. And he's alive."

Angie nodded, reluctant or unable to speak. But there was something in her eyes that had been missing the night before. Hope had made her come alive again, even though she was still afraid to yield to it completely, as if she had learned not to trust promises of happiness too much. Then, as Blanchard watched her, he saw the remote question leave her eyes. Her face awakened to a vivid beauty and joy he had never seen in it before. Even before he turned, he felt the spark of her elation ignite in him.

With Rafael Sánchez walking solicitously at his elbow, Mike Blanchard shuffled along the corridor. He stopped at the edge of the lobby, blinking. He seemed confused, as if he were still half asleep and not sure where he was. Then Angie was running toward him, and Blanchard saw a flicker of recognition cross his face like a ripple across a still pond, awakening it. Angie threw herself at him, knocking him back a step, and then they were embracing each other, the girl rocking back and forth as she hugged him, tears streaming unashamedly down her cheeks.

A long minute passed. Jeff Blanchard felt oddly alone, out of it. Mike hadn't yet seen him. He became aware of Charmian standing beside him. He glanced at her with a wry smile.

"Jealous?" she murmured.

"Maybe a little." His smile slowly broadened into a

grin. "But wait'll he gets a look at you and me. Then it'll be his turn."

He was still staring at her, grinning, when he heard Mike's startled shout.